Silhouette Books
requests the honor of your presence
as
Elizabeth Bannister & Daniel Morgan
and
Caroline Myers & Paul Trevor
and
Christina Tarleton & Marcus di Medici
enter a new life together.

Please share in their joy
as they discover
the wonders and surprises
of marriage.

About the Authors

ANNETTE BROADRICK
lives on the shores of The Lake of the Ozarks in
Missouri, where she spends her time doing what she
loves most—reading and writing romantic fiction.
Since 1984, when her first book was published,
Annette has been delighting readers with her
imaginative and innovative style.

DEBBIE MACOMBER
hails from the state of Washington. As a busy wife
and mother of four, she strives to keep her family
healthy and happy. As the prolific author of dozens
of bestselling romance novels, she strives to keep her
readers happy with each new book she writes.

HEATHER GRAHAM POZZESSERE
considers herself lucky to live in Florida, where she
can indulge her love of swimming and boating year-
round. Her background includes stints as a model,
actress and bartender. She was once actually tied to
the railroad tracks to garner publicity for the dinner
theater where she was acting. Now she's a full-time
wife, mother of five and bestselling writer.

SOLUTION:

Marriage

Annette Broadrick
Debbie Macomber
Heather Graham Pozzessere

Silhouette Books

Published by Silhouette Books New York

SILHOUETTE BOOKS
300 East 42nd St., New York, N.Y. 10017

by Request
Solution: Marriage

Copyright © 1993 by Harlequin Enterprises B. V.

STRANGE ENCHANTMENT
Copyright © 1987 by Annette Broadrick
MAIL-ORDER BRIDE
Copyright © 1987 by Debbie Macomber
THE DI MEDICI BRIDE
Copyright © 1986 by Heather Graham Pozzessere

ISBN: 0-373-20096-X

CONTENTS

A Note from Annette Broadrick

The idea for *Strange Enchantment* haunted me for a long time before I actually attempted to write it.

The marriage of convenience is a well-established, time-honored plot line and an unexpected pregnancy can be a strong motivating force to move the story along. However, *Strange Enchantment* was written for the Silhouette Romance line and the guidelines are firm. There is to be no premarital sex in a Romance.

What to do, what to do.

But the characters insisted that I tell their story, so when I gave in and began to write, I attempted to skip over the hows and whys of the pregnancy by opening the story after the event had occurred. First I wrote from his viewpoint with the meeting as a flashback. Didn't work. Then I tried a flashback in her viewpoint. Still didn't work. Eventually, I had to face the fact that the story would have to be told as it took place.

The end of the first chapter finds Elizabeth in Dan's apartment in a heated embrace. The beginning of the second chapter finds her waking up hours later, still in his apartment.

I finally came to the conclusion that neither the author, the editors nor the publisher has any control over what the characters do between chapters.

Thank you for requesting Dan and Elizabeth's story once more.

Annette Broadrick

STRANGE ENCHANTMENT

Annette Broadrick

This book is dedicated to Judy Talley,
whose daily encouragement kept me writing—
with my gratitude...

Chapter One

Your biggest problem, Elizabeth, is that you don't live here with the rest of us. You're off with your romantic English poets who have been dead for years, hiding away from today's world and all that's going on around you, refusing to face reality.''

"That isn't true, Philip, I—"

"Of course it's true. We've known each other for seven years. Seven years, Elizabeth! It took me five years to convince you to marry me, and for the past two years you've refused to set a date. Yet you aren't honest enough to admit you don't love me so I can get on with my life.''

"I do love you, Philip. It's only that—"

"That you're afraid of life, and of feelings and of being human. I know. I've tried to understand you, because I love you. How many couples have been together this long without ever making love? If I didn't love you, and continue to hope that you'd overcome your hesitancies, I would have walked away years ago. But I'm sick and tired of waiting, Elizabeth. Tired of pushing you, tired of watching for some sign that you're ready for me, willing to take an active part *in our relationship. You don't seem to need or want me in your life and I no longer have the energy or desire to force a place for myself."*

"I can't seem to help it, Philip. It has nothing to do with the feelings I have for you. I really do love you."

"I don't believe you're capable of love, Elizabeth. You don't even understand what you've put me through. I can't take any more of this. I came over tonight to tell you that I'm ending our engagement. I want out."

"Oh, Philip, please don't feel this way. We can set a date. My classes will be over in six weeks. Maybe we can—"

"No. We can't. There is no more we, Elizabeth. As much as I love you, I can't take any more. Goodbye, Elizabeth."

A misty fog swirled and eddied between them as he turned away. He disappeared from view and she cried out. The scene shifted, and suddenly there was noise and confusion, lights flashing, flames licking twisted metal.

A faceless voice explained in a kind voice. "No, it wasn't his fault. Some idiot suddenly swerved into his lane. He must have jerked the wheel to avoid the collision and lost control. Yes, he's still alive, but just barely. Yes, you can see him now."

"Philip, can you hear me? Philip, please don't die. I love you so. Please give me another chance. Oh, Philip, please don't die."

"PHILIP!"

The echoes of her scream filled the bedroom and Elizabeth Bannister jerked upright in her bed. Tears streamed down her face and her tumbled hair fell across her forehead, dotted with perspiration. She pushed her hair back with a shaking hand and began to take slow, deep breaths in an effort to calm her racing heart.

Would her nightmares never end? Philip had died over six months ago, but her dreams kept replaying their last conversation over and over, never deviating, never offering her an opportunity to change anything.

She had sat by Philip's bed for three days, waiting for him to regain consciousness, waiting to tell him he was wrong—

he had to be wrong. She loved him and she truly wanted to marry him.

He'd never regained consciousness.

Elizabeth forced herself to get out of bed and go to the bathroom for a drink of water. She wondered when she would ever get a good night's sleep again.

All her friends had been so sympathetic and understanding about her grief. If they had only known how much she blamed herself. Maybe if he hadn't been upset with her, maybe if she could have explained—

Explained what? That she was merely a cardboard figure of a woman? That she didn't know how to reach out and involve another person in her life? That although she wanted to, she was afraid to get close to someone?

Philip had been right. He'd been extremely understanding and compassionate. But he had reached his limits.

No one knew he had ended their engagement the night of the accident. She hadn't needed to make any explanations. Her grief was certainly understandable.

She glanced into the mirror over the sink. Her cheekbones stood out too prominently in her face and her skin was too pale. She had never regained the weight she'd lost after Philip's death.

The alarm sitting next to her bed went off, cheerfully announcing it was time to begin her day. Elizabeth taught English literature at a small college in Westfield, New York. Her classes had been the only thing that had helped her keep her sanity.

Or had she kept it?

Sometimes she wondered. She knew Janine was worried about her. They had known each other since they'd been roommates in college. Janine had become the closest person in her life. She understood Elizabeth's background and her fear of attachment. Elizabeth remembered their telephone conversation from the previous weekend.

"Why don't you come on down here next weekend? It will do you good. You haven't been to Manhattan in over a year.

I'll get tickets for a play. We'll go out for dinner. You need to make an effort to get out and see people again.''

Of course Janine was right, but Elizabeth had turned her down, out of habit more than anything else.

She had to break out of the endless whirling cage she seemed to occupy. She felt as though she were a small animal forever racing in circles, looking for a way out of the circular spin she was in. But how?

A sudden line of poetry sprang to her mind: *Had we but world enough, and time.* There was no more time for her to change things between Philip and her. His only legacy to her was tied up in his last words to her.

Had he been right? Was she incapable of loving anyone? She had seen so little love while growing up, how could she possibly recognize it? All Elizabeth knew was that with Philip she had felt warm and safe and comfortable. But there had never been a desire to become closer to him.

The grave's a fine and private place,
But none, I think, do there embrace.

Why did Marvell's poem keep coming back to her, with its wry message of how fleeting a lifetime can be?

With Philip in her life, Elizabeth had felt no need to explore her feelings. She had been content with her life and her career. Losing him had been one of the most traumatic things that had happened to her. It ranked right up there with the knowledge she'd slowly assimilated over the years that no one had ever really wanted her or loved her, not from the time she was born. No until Philip.

And she had failed him. Learning to draw close to another person—to trust and rely on someone beside herself—was something that seemed foreign to Elizabeth. She had learned early in life to rely solely on herself. She was all she had. Even as a small child she had known that she must not ask anything of others. It was as though she had built an invisible force field around herself, and she remained inviolate and safe from the emotions of other people. Unfortunately her emotions had also been stopped from growing, as well.

The question now was, what did she intend to do about her life? She could continue the same way, refusing to let life touch her on any level, or she could reach out and begin to take part in the process of life again. The decision was hers to make, no one else's. Did she have the courage to take that first step into the unknown world of emotions and personal relationships?

She could try.

Elizabeth looked at the clock with a new determination. Was it too early to call Janine? She would take the chance. Picking up the phone by the bed, she punched in the numbers and waited as the phone rang repeatedly on the other end. Finally she heard a mumbled response.

"H'lo?"

"I was hoping you'd be awake by now," Elizabeth began.

"Oh, hi, Beth." Janine was the only person who had ever shortened Elizabeth's name. "Normally I would be, but we all worked late last night and I decided to sleep a little longer this morning. What's happening with you?"

"I was wondering if I could change my mind about your invitation for this weekend?"

"Of course you can! I'd be delighted to have you. How soon can you get here?"

"My classes are over at noon. Could you meet me at the station around four o'clock?"

"Certainly. And bring something festive and sexy to wear. I'm invited to a party tonight."

"Oh, don't let me ruin a date for you."

"It's not a date in that sense. I didn't want a date to this one. The host is Ryan Davidson, someone I met several months ago, who I definitely want to cultivate. He said I could bring a guest. You'll be perfect. Ryan throws the greatest parties because he knows the most fantastic people. It will give you a chance to greet the world."

Elizabeth smiled at her friend's enthusiasm. "I'm not at all sure I'm ready to greet the world just yet. But I've decided to at least open the door to it."

"That's a start, anyway. I'll see you at four. And I'll see what I can do about getting tickets for a show tomorrow night. We might as well make a grand celebration out of your visit."

Elizabeth felt her tension slip away. Janine would be good for her. Her uncomplicated view of life was just what Elizabeth needed at the moment.

"Would you stop fussing with that neckline, Beth? You look absolutely gorgeous. Just relax."

They waited at the bank of elevators in the lobby of Ryan Davidson's luxurious condominium building, watching the lights of the elevators signal the floor they passed.

"I shouldn't have let you convince me to wear something of yours, Janine. I don't feel at all like myself in this outfit."

"You look smashing. With your black hair and that flame-colored dress, you're going to be the hit of the evening."

"That's what I'm afraid of. What am I going to say when someone asks how much I charge?"

"Just because I refused to let you wear the dress you bought for your faculty soirees, that doesn't mean you now look like a professional call girl. Believe it or not, that dress is very conservative by New York standards."

"Why, because my navel is covered?"

Janine laughed and stepped into the elevator.

"Stop worrying. The only reason you keep tugging at the neckline is because the dress suggests you actually have a bosom to reveal. Let the unendowed eat their hearts out."

The party was well under way from the sounds of it when the door opened. Elizabeth had a sudden intense desire to turn around and run, but it was already too late. Janine had coaxed her into the foyer and was introducing her to a tall, smiling man with warm brown eyes and a mop of mahogany curls.

"Ryan, I would like you to meet my very good friend, Elizabeth Bannister. Beth, Ryan Davidson does something marvelously mysterious in international banking."

Ryan laughed. "Hardly mysterious, I'm afraid. Do you live here in New York, Elizabeth?"

"I live upstate. I'm visiting for the weekend."

"So glad you could come. Let me get the two of you a drink."

He turned and motioned for them to precede him across the open foyer and down the two steps into his massive living area. The room formed a circle. The outer wall was made of glass, except for a functional fireplace that added the rough texture of fieldstone to the elegance of glass and plush carpeting.

Elizabeth felt overwhelmed by the number of people, the bursts of conversation and laughter and the music that seemed to be competing with the voices. She would never become accustomed to this type of entertainment, but it certainly forced her out of her protective rut into modern-day life.

Her sweeping gaze paused momentarily and her eyes darted back to the fireplace and the man who stood in front of it. He looked relaxed and comfortable as he sipped from his drink and listened intently to the voluble conversation coming from a man several years his senior.

Why did she feel that she recognized him, when she was certain she'd never seen him before in her life? It wasn't so much his looks—because it was possible she'd seen a picture of him—but the essence of the man that seemed to reach out and draw her attention to him.

Ryan paused and introduced Janine and Elizabeth to a group of people and Elizabeth unobtrusively studied the man in front of the fireplace.

He wasn't particularly tall, but seemed beautifully proportioned. He had a classic, clean line that reminded her of another time, and she shook her head, feeling confused.

Perhaps she had spent too much of her life reading poetry. She studied the way his hair, a mixture of brown gilded with blond highlights, framed his face. She couldn't tell the color of his eyes. A heavy fringe of dark lashes surrounded them. There were probably women who would kill for those long lashes, she thought with inner amusement.

His hands fascinated her; their slender length looked so capable, yet sensitive. He held his glass with unconscious grace while he gestured with the other one.

He must have felt her scrutiny, because he paused in what he was saying and glanced around, their gazes meeting with sudden impact. Elizabeth could feel the color flood her cheeks at being caught staring, and she tried to drop the gaze, but found herself unable to look away.

His eyes were gray—the soft gray of early morning before the new dawn has cleared away the mist. A magical feeling of inevitability washed over her. Elizabeth smiled.

Without taking his eyes off of her, the man slowly moved toward her, walking away from his companion as though he no longer existed.

What am I doing? she thought with sudden alarm. For a moment Elizabeth had forgotten. She was not in her small town any longer. This was not the place to smile at strangers. What had she been thinking of?

She forced her glance away and looked to Janine for assistance, but Janine was gone. She and Ryan had continued across the room, while she, stupidly, had stood there and stared at the stranger, who was inevitably coming closer.

"So there you are" were his first words when he paused in front of her. "I've been waiting for you."

His voice was low and it caused a rippling effect to spread through her. As he looked down at her, she was enveloped by his warmth.

"You have?" she heard herself respond, feeling at a loss.

"Yes. For years." He held out his hand to her and she glanced down helplessly. He was holding it toward her, not in the form of a handshake, but as a joining of the two of them. Feeling almost mesmerized, Elizabeth slowly placed her hand in his.

He smiled and his smile brought a flash of inherent beauty to his face, so that he seemed to glow with it. Suddenly Elizabeth felt as though she had been waiting for him to appear in her life for years and she recognized his greeting to be an acknowledgment of the strong sense of familiarity that seemed to create a bond between them. Deftly he guided her over to the fireplace and to the man with whom he'd been speaking.

"I'm sorry to have deserted you so suddenly, Henry. I didn't want to take the chance of losing her in this crowd," he explained with apparent sincerity. "Henry is a writer," he offered.

"I'm Beth," she heard herself say to her own surprise, since she thought of herself as Elizabeth. This man was having a very strange effect on her. "I'm an inveterate reader," she said to Henry with a smile. "Have I read any of your work, by any chance?"

Henry glanced at the two younger people standing before him and smiled in delighted surprise. They seemed so suited. He couldn't quite put his finger on what it was. There were no visible characteristics that were similar, but there was a sense of family—as though they had grown up together, were in tune with each other—that he found rather intriguing under the circumstances.

"I write philosophy under the guise of science fiction, which I have found to be fulfilling as well as enjoyable."

"Not to mention highly lucrative," his companion added. He looked down at Elizabeth. "I'm very pleased you made it tonight, Beth. I'm Dan, and I'm in advertising." He continued to hold her hand, strengthening the nonverbal bond forming between them.

"Don't let him kid you, Beth," Henry chided gently. "Daniel Morgan is 'in' advertising the way Iacocca is 'in' automobiles. Dan has one of the most successful agencies on Madison Avenue. I've enjoyed watching his climb."

"Henry used to be one of my professors in college," Dan explained with a smile. "He tried his best to drum some sense into Ryan and me. The three of us used to sit around until all hours of the night in deep discussions about the meaning of life."

Henry nodded. "I think we all learned something from the experience. I quit teaching and started devoting myself to my writing full-time."

"Did you miss it?" Elizabeth asked with sudden interest. "The teaching, I mean?"

"At first. I missed the social interaction. Writing is a very lonely business. But I realized that writing was what I needed to be doing." He lifted his glass in a slight toast. "If you two will excuse me, I see someone over there I've been trying to talk to for some time." He knew they would barely notice his departure.

Dan and Elizabeth stood there in silence for a few moments and she searched for something to say. Bemused, she looked down at their clasped hands.

"What do you do when you aren't reading, Beth?"

She suddenly heard Philip's voice saying, "You live in another time with our English poets, refusing to face life," and for some reason she didn't want Dan to know who and what she was. For this one evening, she could be anything and anyone she wished and it wouldn't matter.

"If you promise not to mention it, I'll tell you. I spend most of my time visiting planets in this galaxy. Tonight was my turn to visit the planet Earth."

Her straight-faced explanation seemed to startle him, and she smiled. She could never remember having been so whimsical before. Everything in her life had always been governed by rules and regulations. There had never been time for fantasy and imagination.

His eyes seemed to dance with amusement. "Does Ryan know?"

She shook her head. "No one knows."

He moved closer to her and whispered. "Then your secret is safe with me."

They laughed and Elizabeth felt herself relaxing. This was going to be fun.

Daniel Morgan couldn't believe what his senses were telling him. This delightful young woman seemed to have bewitched him.

His first glimpse of her had shaken him more than he wanted to admit. She was like someone out of a dream he'd once had and had forgotten, until he glanced up and saw her watching him, waiting for him.

She was small, with satiny skin that looked like porcelain, warm but very pale. Her midnight-dark hair framed her face, accentuating the purity of her profile. But it was her eyes that fascinated him. They were so darkly blue they appeared almost black. Their almond shape gave her an exotic look that suggested she was not of this world.

He shook his head at his imaginings, unconsciously trying to clear it. The dress she wore made a brilliant contrast to her pale skin and dark hair, its vibrant red charmingly hugging her delicate curves, highlighting her small waist and curving breasts. Dan had a sudden urge to gather her in his arms to make certain she didn't suddenly disappear.

"May I get you a drink?"

She enjoyed the sound of his voice. Its deep quality seemed to wrap around her, hugging her with its warmth.

"Yes, please," she said, nodding.

"What would you like?"

She had no idea. Elizabeth rarely drank. "You choose."

When Dan returned, he handed her a fruit-punch drink that seemed innocuous enough and she gratefully sipped it, unaware of its potent content.

Dan found a small unoccupied sofa and motioned for her to sit down. "Are interplanetary travelers allowed to discuss their travels?" he inquired politely.

She took a quick sip of her drink to hide her smile. Demurely she explained, "Not really. We're here to study life on the planet. Would you mind telling me about yourself?" she asked politely. Pointing to her left ear and the small earring there, she added, "If you will speak directly into the microphone I won't have to bother taking notes."

Dan surprised himself by following her instructions. Casually he began to talk about himself, something he rarely did with anyone. Her obvious interest kept him talking, her questions spurring him on. A couple of times he refilled their drinks, unaware that she was not used to drinking.

The room glowed with a mystic light—or so it seemed to Elizabeth. She felt as though she had come to a costume party where no one had any idea who she was. She could do as she pleased, say the most outrageous things, and it was all right. Nothing seemed real.

"Why don't we go somewhere to eat? Would you like that?" Dan finally asked.

Elizabeth glanced around. If anything, the party had grown noisier and more crowded. She thought his suggestion was excellent.

"Let me tell Janine I'm leaving. I'll be right back."

Janine nodded absently when Elizabeth explained that she and Dan were going out for something to eat. "Okay. Glad you met someone nice. Ryan said Dan is a fantastic guy. I already checked him out for you. He's been married once, been divorced for years, doesn't date much, and Ryan was delighted to see him so engrossed in you." Janine kissed Elizabeth on the cheek. "Go and have fun. You've got a key. I'll see you back at the apartment."

Elizabeth floated through dinner and a couple of dances, but when she complained about the loud music Dan readily admitted the noise didn't help much with conversation.

She never remembered later how they ended up going back to his apartment, rather than his taking her to Janine's, but it seemed a very logical progression of events at the time.

"You live alone?" she asked, standing in the middle of a comfortably cluttered living area.

He grinned. "Can't you tell? I have someone who comes in once a week to straighten up the worst of it. Actually, I'm not here all that much."

"You work long hours, I can tell."

He motioned for her to sit down and then joined her on the couch. "Yes. But how can you tell?"

"Because you lead a lonely life."

Her comment startled him. Either she was astute at reading people or she was psychic. Either way, she was intriguing.

"I suppose I am, in a way. The agency has become my family. The wife I don't have, the children, the companion. I've enjoyed the struggle, but I guess I've never taken the time to do anything about widening my interests."

"Every life needs balance," she pointed out sagely.

"And is yours balanced?"

Of course not. I live a very one-dimensional life. I have no close friends, no family. I recognize your loneliness because it reflects mine.

"Of course mine is balanced," she replied. "All interplanetary beings lead balanced existences. Otherwise we would spin out of control instead of floating where we need to go."

He laughed, as she had meant him to. When he stopped laughing he kissed her.

Elizabeth wasn't prepared for his kiss. She had been around so few men in her life. Philip was the only man she had gotten to know well enough to allow his touch, and because he had recognized how untutored she was, his patient approaches had been very limited, she now acknowledged to herself.

She should not have enjoyed Dan's kiss. She should have pushed him away, explained that she had a problem, that she was afraid of people, of getting close, of physical intimacy.

But she didn't.

Elizabeth Bannister seemed to have retreated for a little while. Beth, the all-wise, all-knowing interplanetary being had taken her place. Beth relaxed and waited to experience the next few minutes with wonder.

As soon as Dan touched her he realized an astounding paradox. The beautiful, alluring, sensuous woman in his arms seemed to have very little experience. Her lips remained firmly closed, her hands rested in her lap. He felt no resistance coming from her, but very little response, either. He paused, pulling away slightly, and looked down at her. Her head rested on his shoulder and her eyes were closed. A slight smile hovered at the corners of her delectable mouth.

She seemed to be relaxed and enjoying their closeness, but she was making no effort to encourage him. Was it possible that she didn't know how? He began to wonder if her amusing story might have some merit, after all. Where else but outer space would he find a woman with so many loving attributes so seemingly untouched?

She opened her eyes slowly and stared up at him. When her gaze met his, she smiled, a slow, enticing smile that caused a tightening deep within him. He had never seen eyes like hers. They fascinated him, mesmerized him, made him forget who he was, who she was, and that he had only met her hours before.

"I want to make love to you," he said in a husky voice.

"Do you?" she replied in a sleepy-sounding tone.

"I know it's too soon."

"Of course," she wisely agreed.

"I guess I'd better get you home."

"Yes."

He continued to look at her curled up in the shelter of his arm. One more kiss wouldn't hurt. Then they would leave.

This time when he kissed her, he coaxed her to open her mouth. The kiss deepened and they both lost all sense of time, perspective, propriety and preservation.

Elizabeth felt as though she were truly a creature of the universe, floating in space, lost in the feelings that Dan evoked within her. She felt like a new person, full of freedom to explore and investigate these strange new sensations that Dan seemed to know were buried deep inside of her, waiting to be released.

Why did it feel as though she had always been a part of his life? Why did being in his arms seem so natural to her?

Their kiss became a prelude, a tentative joining of themselves to a new whole, a new being who had never before existed.

What was happening between them seemed natural and inevitable, as though they had been together many times before. Elizabeth felt totally at one with him.

Dan felt her tentative response to his kiss and his arms slowly tightened around her. He felt as though he were witnessing a cocoon as its occupant began to unfold and unfurl to become a living, quivering butterfly. Elizabeth's light touches on his face and shoulders seemed to loosen the restraints he'd placed on himself.

He was caught up in causing and watching her tentatively loving responses as he kissed her repeatedly, returning time and again to the soft sweetness of her mouth, as though drinking from the fountain of life.

She didn't stiffen when her dress slid from her shoulders and fell in a rich flow of color around her waist. His mouth and tongue began to love her with delicate touches, his hands softly caressing her. Instead she began to imitate his movements, removing his shirt and the clothing that seemed to prohibit her from enjoying the feel of his body against hers.

Later Elizabeth would wonder at what point she should have called a halt to what was happening. She would try to understand what had happened to her lifelong fears of inadequacy and her natural inhibitions.

But all she could even remember was the indescribable feeling of his gentle, tender kisses.

Chapter Two

Elizabeth woke up suddenly, her heart beating wildly, and for a moment she thought her recurrent nightmare had awoken her once more.

But this was worse. This wasn't a nightmare. It was reality.

The warm, hard body of the man who held her close caused her to remember what she had done. Her head swam, but she forced herself to try to think.

She was in Dan's apartment on Dan's couch with Dan's arms wrapped securely around her!

She had finally totally and completely lost her sanity.

Elizabeth lay there, trying to still her racing heart and her breathing, deathly afraid she would wake him up. What could she say to him? How could she possibly explain something she didn't understand herself?

She listened to his breathing, reassured by its strong, even rhythm. Could she get up without awakening him? She could only try.

By the time she was downstairs, thankfully crawling into a taxi, Elizabeth was shaking so badly she could scarcely stand. By New York standards it wasn't all that late. Probably Janine wouldn't think a thing about her coming home at this time. She might not even notice that Dan had not accompanied her.

What was she going to tell Janine? And how could she live with what she had done?

Only time would give her those answers.

"Did you have fun last night?" Janine asked over coffee the next morning.

Elizabeth refused to meet her eyes. "I suppose."

"You don't sound too enthusiastic. I'm surprised—the two of you seemed to find enough to talk about."

Elizabeth sipped carefully from her cup. "I know. At times I almost felt as though we were old friends, catching up on the years we'd missed in each other's lives." She set the cup down and forced herself to meet Janine's gaze calmly. "It was very strange."

"Is he going to call you again?"

"I doubt it."

"How can you be so sure? Did you argue or something?"

Or something. How can I explain what happened? I don't understand it myself.

"I think he was being polite, that's all." Besides which, he hadn't bothered to get her phone number.

Janine sighed, shaking her head. "What would you like to do today? We don't have to leave for the theater until seven."

Elizabeth forced herself to smile. "Something energetic that will get us out in the air."

"Just what I needed. A fresh-air fiend for a friend." She stood and placed her cup in the sink. "Well, don't just sit there. Let's get moving."

For the next two days Elizabeth forced herself to get into the spirit of the frivolous weekend, to push all her thoughts of either Philip or Dan out of her head. At least being with Dan had proved one thing. She wasn't frigid. She had enjoyed his touch. She'd felt safe and secure and had relaxed with him.

Perhaps now she would be able to let Philip rest in peace. She wasn't what he had needed in his life—she could better understand what he had tried to explain to her. What she had felt those few hours spent with Dan made a mockery of her relationship with Philip. She had failed him.

Facing that, and actually coming to terms with it, she could get on with her life, putting away her memories, of Dan as well as Philip.

The very thought of seeing Dan again made her shudder with embarrassment. At least she'd had enough sense not to tell him much about herself. There was no reason to think they would ever meet again.

Elizabeth made up her mind to treat the evening with Dan as a learning experience. It had certainly been that! She had come away from his apartment with the knowledge that she would never be the same again. Her entire perspective of herself and her life had made a sudden shift during those few short hours.

Although she recognized that she and Dan had shared something very special, Elizabeth knew she wasn't ready for a relationship with anyone. She needed to get in touch with herself, first.

Dan would never know the impact he'd made on her life. Unfortunately she was too embarrassed ever to risk contacting him to tell him.

She doubted very much if he'd care.

The hell of it was, he didn't even know her name.

Dan Morgan impatiently shoved his executive chair away from his desk and stood up. Sitting there thinking about her wasn't getting any work done.

So what else was new? Three months had passed since he'd met her. Three months since he'd spent an enchanted evening with a woman he'd never seen before. Or since.

Why couldn't he forget her?

Thrusting his hands into the pants pockets of his handsomely tailored suit, he wandered over to the window of his office and looked out at the traffic on Madison Avenue. He didn't see the traffic. Instead, smiling blue eyes stared back at him, their blue so clear he felt as though he could see down into the very center of her being. For three months that steady gaze had haunted him. Her eyes would suddenly appear to him as he fell asleep at night, or sometimes just as he began to wake in the morning. On a few occasions they had appeared in the middle of an advertising presentation to a client and he would be temporarily distracted, having to hastily remember where he was and force himself to continue.

Who was she? And why had she had such a profound effect on him?

He'd known many women in his thirty-seven years, but he'd never missed any of them as deeply as he now missed Beth. His marriage to Carol had ended almost eight years ago by mutual agreement. They had recognized that whatever had caused them to decide to face the world together got lost somewhere along the way to professional success. Their interests had diverged widely once they had launched their careers.

So why did he have such a sense of loss now, after spending one evening, a few short hours, with a woman he knew absolutely nothing about?

He had everything he wanted in life, didn't he? It was true that he had no family, but, then, he and Carol had congratulated themselves on having the wisdom not to bring a child or children into their busy world to be divided between single parents.

Had anyone asked him a few years ago if a family was an important element to him he would have shrugged the question off. Since meeting Beth, however, his thoughts had kept returning to a home and children, as though by her very arrival in his life, certain sparks of yearning for permanency had been ignited.

By any measuring stick, he'd be considered successful—
but at the moment, none of his past triumphs seemed to
matter.

He wandered back to his desk and sat down once again.
For the past three months he'd become aware that something vital was missing in his life. Meeting Beth had brought
the message home to him.

The question was—what was he going to do about it?

He knew he had rushed the relationship. He'd had three
months to lament the fact that, given another chance, he
would have handled the evening in a much different manner. But something important had happened between them.
He was certain he hadn't imagined it. Why else would she
have made love with him?

He still remembered his shock at discovering that she had
never been with a man before, but by the time he'd become
aware of the fact it had been too late to draw back, to
apologize, or to question.

Dan Morgan wasn't in the habit of making love to a
woman he'd just met, either, but she had no way of knowing that. He had thought he would explain later. At the time
all he could do was dedicate himself to making her first experience as pleasurable and as satisfying as he knew how.

She had responded—he was certain of that. Her response had been hesitant, her inexperience obvious, but Dan
had felt certain that she had wanted him, too.

Now he was no longer sure about anything.

When they had fallen asleep on his sofa, Dan would have
sworn there was no way she could have moved without
awakening him instantly. Yet she had disappeared from his
life without a trace.

Dan leaned back in his office chair, disgusted with himself.

How had he managed to spend an evening with her and
not find out her full name, where she lived, where she
worked and how he could contact her again?

Was it possible he had dreamed their evening together?

He glanced at his wristwatch and decided to try once again to track her down by the only source he had. He picked up the phone and punched out a number.

"Ryan Davidson, please." He waited a moment, and when he heard his friend's voice on the phone he voiced his relief and frustration at finally making contact. "Damn it, Ryan, you have to be the hardest person to get in touch with I've ever known."

"Well, hello, Dan, it's great to hear from you, too," Ryan responded in a dry voice. "I take it you've missed me."

"Where have you been? I've been trying to reach you for three months."

"Earning my living. International banking does call for a certain amount of traveling," he drawled. "What's made me so popular with you these days?"

"I need to know a name."

"I had a feeling it wasn't my wit and charm that made you persist in your long search for me."

"I met someone at your party."

"Congratulations. Glad you decided to join the human race again. Who is she?"

"That's what I want you to tell me."

"Do we have a bad connection? You aren't making much sense."

"Her name is Beth and that's all I know."

"I don't remember any Beth at the party."

"Well, she was there—please take my word for it. She came with an attractive blonde that you seemed to know. Beth is a brunette...she wore a flame-red dress...looked like—"

"Oh, sure, I remember now. She came with Janine Shepard. I recall admiring your taste, now that you mention it."

"Fine. What's her name?"

"I don't remember. You know how it is when you're introduced to someone. I seem to remember the two of you sitting over in a corner, talking most of the evening." Ryan chuckled. "Are you telling me you forgot her name?"

"I never knew it. She introduced herself as 'Beth.' That's as far as we got with introductions."

"Well, I'm afraid I can't help you. Dan. I don't know any more than you do."

"What about Janine?"

"What about her?"

"Maybe she would give me her number, name, or something?"

"It wouldn't hurt to try. Of course Janine spends half her time on the West Coast, but maybe you can find her if you're that determined."

Dan's language turned the air blue, which only seemed to amuse his friend.

"I can't remember ever hearing you so overwrought about a woman, Dan," Ryan offered. "She must have really gotten to you."

"Something like that."

"Well, I'll give you Janine's office number. Maybe someone there can help you locate her. Good luck, fella."

With a mixture of reluctance and relief, Elizabeth watched the students in her course on English Romantics file out of the room. The reluctance came because she no longer had anything scheduled for the rest of that Friday and she had an entire weekend free to try to come to grips with her life, something she didn't relish but could no longer postpone.

The relief came from knowing that despite everything that had happened to her recently, she had managed to remain professional enough not to display her turmoil to anyone around her.

She had managed to interest her students with the work of poets she had long admired: Blake, Wordsworth, Byron, Shelley and Keats. For the time span of the class, Beth brought life into writings of different historical periods so that they tugged at the imagination of those who read them. In little more than six weeks of class, she had most of her students hooked, eagerly asking for more.

After locking the door to her classroom, Elizabeth left the English building, where she had taught for the past five years. The crisp October weather had changed the color of the leaves and lent a sharpness to the air.

She paused on the steps, breathing deeply, encouraged by the steady cycle of nature. Things changed yet ultimately stayed the same. She could count on the cycle of seasons to keep their time-proven progression—autumn, followed by winter, followed by spring.

Spring.

No matter where her thoughts might begin, they always ended up at the same place. There was no turning away, not pretending any more. She had to face herself, what she had done and how she was going to cope with the future.

Elizabeth tucked her chin into the upturned collar of her tweed coat and started across the grounds of the college. By following her normal routine in the small college town, she tried to instill in herself the courage to accept change without allowing it to completely destroy her peace of mind.

She needed to stop at the grocery store for Misty's cat food. There was also cleaning to pick up and a book newly released to buy at the bookstore.

Elizabeth had been alone most of her life. Sharing it with someone new would take some getting used to.

A slight stirring of excitement caught her unaware. No matter how often a sense of fear swept over her, a certain amount of anticipation continued to build.

Elizabeth Bannister crawled into her economy car, oblivious to the small smile on her face.

The morning sunlight brought Elizabeth a sense of well-being that had been missing in her life recently. She had been tired by seven o'clock the night before and had gone to bed early. She got tired much more easily these days, she realized.

There were a lot of changes going on inside her, she decided ruefully when she was unable to fasten the button on her jeans. *And it's going to get worse before it gets better,* she reminded herself.

So what if she seemed to have contracted a touch of pregnancy? She tried to be whimsical about a very serious situation. It wasn't as though she would be branded with a scarlet A on her forehead. She had always kept her private life to herself. When her condition became too obvious to ignore, she would come up with some reason why she had never told anyone about her marriage and eventual separation.

It was no one's business but her own.

What she had discovered in the deep soul-searching of the night before was that she very much wanted a child. In a matter of weeks the baby had become very real to her—someone to care about as well as care for.

Her own childhood had been so barren—placed in various foster homes, afraid to get attached to anyone because she knew they would never be permanent in her life. She had never felt she belonged anywhere.

Her baby would never have that feeling, she decided fiercely. He would know he was loved and wanted.

She stood in the kitchen, looking out the window at the back lawn, while she absently stroked Misty, a lilac-point Siamese who'd been entertaining her as well as keeping her company for almost two years. Together they watched the birds eating and the squirrels gathering nuts. No doubt Misty would love to run outside and make it clear they were there only because of her tolerance of their presence.

Elizabeth tried to picture a small child playing in the yard, and smiled. The cottage would make a good home for a child. They would have a comfortable life together; she knew they would.

The doorbell rang and she frowned slightly. She couldn't imagine who would be visiting her on a Saturday morning. She had no close neighbors and didn't know any of them very well, anyway. Janine was out of town and she always called first to make sure Elizabeth had nothing planned.

The bell rang again impatiently and she started for the door. More than likely it was a would-be magazine salesman who was eager to make as many calls as possible.

Elizabeth glanced into the hall mirror and grimaced. She had hastily put her hair up in a haphazard knot that already threatened to tumble down and her face was bare of makeup. Maybe it was close enough to Halloween to convince her visitor that she was a witch and to leave her alone.

She was smiling at the thought when she opened the door. Elizabeth froze. The sudden shock of seeing Dan Morgan on her doorstep took her breath away.

Dan had imagined several different reactions to his visit, but never had he pictured the expression of shock on Beth's face. For a moment he thought she was going to faint, but then she seemed to draw herself up to her full height, so that he could almost see the stiffening of her spine.

Here goes nothing, he thought with a mental shrug. "No one told me where interplanetary creatures rested on weekends, so I've had a bit of a problem tracking you down." He smiled, a tentative, almost vulnerable smile that seemed to spread warmth throughout Elizabeth's entire body. "So how have you been?"

He looked even better than she remembered him. The bulky hand-knit sweater he wore emphasized his tan and the light gray—almost silver—of his eyes. His smile caused the blood in her veins to rapidly heat.

When she first opened the door and saw him, Elizabeth thought she was going to faint. He was the last person she ever expected to see. Then the events that took place the last time they were together flashed in her mind and she could feel the color suddenly flooding her face. How could she possibly face this man again?

"Hello? Are you tuned into Earth language this morning?" he inquired politely. "May I come in?"

His quiet questions brought her out of her temporary paralysis and she nodded abruptly. "Of course. I'm sorry, you startled me." She stepped back, motioning him into the hall. As her gaze dropped, she realized with horror that she still wore the jeans that refused to button. The sweater she had grabbed hurriedly that morning had shrunk when she'd washed it. Her body was carefully outlined.

"Coffee is on the counter in the kitchen, if you'd like to go on back. Let me get into some presentable clothes," she said breathlessly.

His smile was gentle. "Don't change on my account. You look just fine." He took her hand and drew her down the hallway with him, pausing in the doorway of her sunny kitchen.

"It's like living outside, isn't it?" he asked. "You can almost hear the squirrels chattering and the bird-song is beautiful." He paused and looked down at her. "You're very fortunate."

"Yes. I've enjoyed living here."

"Have you been here long?" He seemed to be totally relaxed and at ease, as though they had only parted the day before.

"Uh, two years. I bought it two years ago." She poured the coffee and asked tentatively, "Have you eaten?"

He shook his head. "No. I left home early and didn't stop for anything but gas."

"You *drove* up here?"

"I enjoyed it. Autumn is my favorite time of the year."

"Why?"

"I'm not sure. It could be the way the air smells, the colors—"

"No, I mean why did you drive? Why are you here?"

His steady gaze met hers with calm deliberation. "To see you, of course."

To give herself a moment to come to grips with this unexpected arrival, Elizabeth began to search her refrigerator, pulling out the ingredients for an omelet. She tried to think of something to say, but her mind was blank.

"Janine said to be sure to tell you hello."

She glanced around at him. He had taken a seat in one of her captain's chairs, his long, muscled legs stretched out before him, his feet crossed at the ankles. He looked so natural sitting there, as though he were at home.

"When did you talk to Janine?"

"Yesterday. She's been out of town and I only managed to catch up with her yesterday afternoon." There was a certain amount of satisfaction in his tone that she didn't quite understand.

"I thought she was in Los Angeles."

"She is."

"And you called her out there?"

"Yes."

Once again Elizabeth was at a loss for words.

Dan decided he'd said enough for a while, so he sipped his coffee and enjoyed the peacefulness of Elizabeth's cheerful kitchen. Whenever he thought he could get away with it he would look at her, trying to drink in his fill of her like a man who had been in the desert for days without water. He was starved for the sight of her.

How strange, when he'd only been around her once. And yet he could have described how her face looked, how her skin felt, the shape of her eyebrows, the silkiness of her hair. It was almost as if she were a part of him.

She placed two plates of food on the table, poured more coffee, then sat down across from him and forced herself to eat. Elizabeth tried not to think about who he was and why he might be there. He had made a long trip and she had no reason to assume that his reason for looking her up was anything more than a sudden whim.

"Why did you disappear like that?" he asked finally, after paying her the compliment of eating everything on his plate. Either he had enjoyed her cooking or he hadn't eaten in a few days.

What could she say? "Does it really matter? That was several months ago."

"You don't have to tell me how long it's been—I know. And yes, it matters very much to me."

When she met his silver gaze she knew she owed him the dignity of the truth.

"I was embarrassed."

"About what?"

"About what had happened."

"You mean, because we made love?"

Why was it necessary to spell it out? She nodded her head. "Yes."

He reached over and touched her hand. "There was no reason to be embarrassed."

"I'm not used to going to parties and leaving with someone and . . ."

"I know. I was very much aware of that, believe me."

She could feel the color fill her face.

"You're still embarrassed," he said, a hint of disbelief in his voice.

"Yes."

With sudden decision he stood up and brought her to her feet. Circling his arms around her, he pulled her close to his body. "Nothing about our first meeting was normal, Beth— we both know that—but that doesn't mean you need to be embarrassed. We're way past that in our relationship."

She refused to meet his gaze. Instead she stared over his shoulder and watched a bluebird land on a branch near the window. "We don't have a relationship," she finally muttered.

Her attitude bewildered him, even though her friend had warned him. She was so different from the vivacious, smiling woman he had met in New York. What was wrong?

"Did I misread the situation?"

"What do you mean?"

"I thought what we shared that night was something very special. Was I wrong?"

"I didn't expect to ever see you again," she managed to hedge.

"Yes, I'll admit you did a very good job of being mysterious that night. But I thought that by the end of the evening you had begun to trust me. But I guess your disappearing act wasn't accidental. You had no intention of seeing me again."

She remained silent.

"Beth?"

Slowly her gaze left the window and she forced herself to look up at him. Was it possible she saw pain in his eyes?

"Yes?"

"I want to see you again. I'm not trying to create a complication in your life. I just want to be a part of it, whatever part you're willing to share." His hand slipped under her chin and his thumb rubbed across her cheek in a motion that Elizabeth felt was almost hypnotic. "Is that asking so much?"

"I don't date."

He waited, but she didn't elaborate.

"That's it?" he finally asked. "That's your explanation? Don't you ever make exceptions?"

"I have a full schedule of classes that keeps me busy and I—"

"So you're going to dismiss what happened between us, just like that? As though none of it matters?"

"I don't see any future in our trying to see each other, do you?"

"Yes, as a matter of fact, I do. I see as much of a future as either one of us cares to make of it."

She could feel the warmth of his body radiating through the sweater and tailored pants he wore. Unobtrusively she tried to step back from him, but he merely tightened the hold he had on her, bringing her even closer to him than before. Her breasts, slightly swollen and tender, pressed against his chest, and she could feel the bare stretch of her middle touching him where the sweater didn't quite meet to cover her unbuttoned jeans.

"It wouldn't work, Dan. There's no place in our lives for each other. We live too far apart to try to see each other except on the most casual basis."

His hands began to massage along the length of her spine. She felt so good to him and it had been so long since he'd held her in his arms. He had never wanted a woman as much as he wanted her. "I have never felt casual about you, not since the first time I saw you."

His lips sought the soft place on her neck where he particularly enjoyed touching, just under her ear, and he kissed her, keeping her close to him. Then he eased away from her slightly.

"So the answer is no," he finally said when she remained silent.

"I suppose, although I never heard a question."

"The question has to do with us, with our seeing more of each other, with deepening the relationship that we started a few months ago."

"Then the answer is definitely no."

He tightened his arms around her again and kissed her—a hard, punishing kiss. How could she say no to what they obviously shared? How could she pretend not to notice how well they went together, how well she fit him, how well her body—

He jerked back from her and glanced down. Her sweater had ridden up a little more, baring the slight beginning of a swell that disappeared behind the zipper of jeans that she was unable to fasten.

Dan could feel his heart begin to race at the thought of what such evidence could mean. Beth was slender, obviously not overweight, and yet—

Was it possible? But of course it was. Like some callow youth he had done nothing to protect her, and she—it had been her first time, of course she wouldn't have been prepared for what had happened.

He pulled away from her, searching her face for confirmation. Her cheeks were flushed and her eyes overly bright as she watched his expressive face register what he was thinking.

Dan dropped his hold on her and walked away, trying to come to grips with what he suspected and what it meant, if it were true.

She wasn't going to tell him. She was going to let him walk out of there without knowing. He felt a slow burning anger begin to build within him. If he hadn't spent the past several months playing detective he never would have found her, never would have learned about the consequences of their evening together.

Slowly he turned around and faced her from across the room. She stood there watching him warily, her arms protectively folded across her waist, effectively hiding the evidence.

With a deliberately level tone, Dan asked, "When is our baby due, Beth?"

Chapter Three

Hearing it spoken aloud made it seem so much more real, and Beth felt her heart leap at his question. She tried to think of something to say, but her mind was curiously blank.

"Don't try to deny it, because I won't believe you. You're at least three months pregnant and I know for a fact there wasn't anyone else before me."

"I'm not denying it," she said in a quiet voice.

"But you weren't going to let me in on your little secret, were you?"

His anger surprised her. "I don't intend to ask you for anything, if that's what you think."

"Am I supposed to feel grateful for that? Did it ever occur to you that I might want to know if I'm about to become a father?"

As a matter of fact, it hadn't occurred to her. From the moment she had learned for certain that she was pregnant, it had never entered her mind to try to contact him. How could she? His name was fairly common, and although she had been at his apartment, she knew she'd never be able to find it again if she tried.

She had never considered trying. It was as though the baby were a gift to her, to fill the loveless void in her life. Other women raised children on their own. It never occurred to her to think she couldn't. It didn't occur to her now.

"Are you saying you want to see my baby once it arrives?"

He walked over to her and stood there, watching her. "I'm saying that I want to do more than see it. I want to be part of its life, share in its care and feeding. I want to be a full-time father."

"But that's impossible. I mean, we don't even know each other. We live hundreds of miles apart. We—"

"We are going to become parents, Beth. All other considerations have to be set aside for the moment. We have shared in one of the greatest miracles life has to offer—we have created a life together. Neither one of us could have done it without the other. I believe I have just as much right as you do to be a part of our baby's life once it gets here."

Beth felt as though her knees were going to give way. Shakily she reached behind her and felt for the chair. She lowered herself slowly.

"I see," she finally managed to say.

"I doubt it. I'm not too impressed with your ability to see anything but your own wants and desires."

She glanced up at him, facing his anger. "There's no reason to be insulting."

"Beth, I haven't even begun to be insulting. I'm trying to make you look at this from a viewpoint other than your own. Do you think you're being fair to the baby, insisting on a single-parent relationship?"

"I never thought there was a choice."

"Well, think again. I am here to tell you that I insist on being dealt into this hand."

He walked over and poured what was left of the coffee into his cup.

After several moments of silence, Elizabeth asked, "What do you suggest we do?"

He forced himself not to show his relief that she had finally admitted he might have a say in the matter. She sounded uncertain, a feeling he could certainly identify with.

He moved over and sat down in the chair beside her and took her hand. "We'll work out something—you can depend on it."

"Have you ever wanted children?" For some reason she couldn't picture him with a family.

He laughed, a dry sound that echoed with irony. "I never felt I had a choice. All the women I know are too wrapped up in their careers to consider taking time out for a family."

"I understand their feelings. I've always been wrapped up in my career, too. That's one reason Philip—" With shock she realized what she had been about to say and she stopped abruptly.

Dan sat forward in his chair. "Who's Philip?"

"He was my fiancé," she said quietly.

"Was?"

"He was killed in an automobile accident last winter."

"Had you been engaged long?"

"Two years."

"And he had never made love to you?" he asked, his voice full of disbelief.

She bit her lower lip and shook her head.

"What sort of relationship was that?"

"A loving relationship. Philip loved me. And I loved him. We just weren't in a hurry and I—I needed time to—"

She couldn't say anything more.

After a few moments Dan sighed. "I'm sorry. I shouldn't have expected you to defend your decision. It just surprised me, that's all. You're such a warm and loving person that I—"

She shook her head, determined to stop him. "But that's the whole point. I'm not a warm and loving person. I never was. I've never let anyone get close to me, not even Philip.

I kept postponing the marriage, kept insisting we wait, until—" her voice broke slightly "—it was too late."

Dan ran his hand through his hair, feeling her pain and
wishing there were something he could say.

"I suppose your pregnancy came as quite a shock."

She attempted a smile. "You could say that."

"Life really has some strange twists, doesn't it?" He
stood up and walked over to the counter, glancing with surprise at the cup of cooling coffee he had poured and forgotten. Looking at her, he said, "Why don't you put on
something a little warmer and take a ride with me? We'll
drive through the countryside, enjoy some fresh air, talk
about what we can do about all this." He leaned on the
counter. "It's not the sort of thing that can be ignored in
hopes it will go away."

Maybe he was right. Nothing would be resolved by
dwelling on the past. She nodded. "I'll be back in a few
minutes."

Dan allowed himself a quick sigh of relief. He felt as
though the building blocks of his life had been dumped out
in front of him, all the pieces he'd put together so carefully
lying in a pile, waiting to be sorted through and dealt with.

What still perplexed him was that he felt closer to Beth
than to anyone he'd ever known, including his parents, Ryan
or even Carol. He felt as though he could feel her pain, her
uncertainty, her embarrassment, as though he were a part of
her.

How could that be? They were strangers.

No. Never strangers. Not anymore.

He suddenly envisioned what it would be like to wake up
every morning and find Beth beside him. Somehow he
would have to convince her that their being together was a
viable solution to their situation.

It would be the greatest campaign he'd ever launched, and
the most important.

"You picked a beautiful day for a ride in the country,"
Elizabeth offered several hours later.

They had been driving in silence, each caught up in rather serious thoughts. She hoped to lighten the atmosphere somewhat.

Dan had been watching her unobtrusively as she quietly sat next to him in his small foreign car, trying to discover what it was about her that intrigued him so. She had a quiet stillness about her that he found very peaceful. Her serene expression touched him and he could almost see her sitting there holding a child. Their child. His heart lunged suddenly in his chest at the thought.

By what series of circumstances had they been brought together at that particular time in their lives? He certainly wasn't in the habit of picking up women and taking them home with him. In fact, he'd never done it before. That just wasn't his style. But it had seemed natural to share with Beth his retreat from the rest of the world.

And it had certainly been evident that she wasn't accustomed to such behavior. Suddenly he wanted to know more about her and Philip, and wondered how to ask.

"I'm glad you agreed to come with me," he finally replied. "I find the scenery much more pleasurable when I share it, don't you?"

She smiled. "That's hard to say. I rarely share anything in my life."

Hoping he sounded casual enough, Dan asked, "Did you and Philip enjoy getting out, enjoying the scenery?"

"Whenever he could get away. He had a law practice in Boston that took most of his time and energy."

So far, so good. She had answered the question as casually as he had asked. "How did you two meet, anyway?"

She smiled. "At college. He was the most persistent person I ever met. Eventually Janine, who was my roommate, felt sorry for him and joined him in insisting I spend some of my time on social activities."

"Why did you keep turning him down?"

"Oh, I don't know exactly. I was at school on a scholarship and I felt I needed to account for every minute of my time, just to prove myself worthy."

"What were your parents like?"

He felt her stiffen, and could have bitten his tongue for bringing up an uncomfortable subject.

"I don't know. I never knew them. I was raised in foster homes."

"So you don't have any relatives?"

"No."

"Do you stay in touch with any of the people you knew?"

"There was one—I called her Auntie Em—I wrote to once I left her home. She had fallen and broken her hip, so she couldn't look after me anymore, but she insisted we stay in touch. I think she was very proud of me. At least, I hope so." She glanced out the window. "She died my senior year of college."

They drove for a while in silence while Dan digested the information he'd been given. What it added up to was a person who had retreated inside herself, never allowing anyone to get close to her. For both their sakes, and for the sake of the baby, she needed to overcome her fear of relationships.

He hoped he could come up with the answer.

"Are you hungry?" he asked lightly.

"A little."

"Do you find yourself wanting to eat more these days?" he asked with a grin.

"Not really."

"Have you been to a doctor yet?"

"Yes."

"Why do I feel like I'm interviewing a reluctant guest on a talk show?"

"I'm not sure what you want me to say."

"Well, for starters, I'd like to know what the doctor said, if he thinks you're healthy, what suggestions he made for your diet and exercise. That's nothing major, I'm sure, but it's interesting to me, since I'm only going to be allowed to sit on the sidelines during this production."

"Oh. Well . . . he said I was healthy, a little thin for my height. He gave me some vitamins, told me to take care of myself and to come see him again in a month."

"Is that anything like take two aspirins and call me in the morning?"

"Similar. He forgot to warn me that if I didn't eat a large breakfast before taking the vitamins, they'd make me sick. But it didn't take long for me to figure that out."

"What about morning sickness?"

"I don't have anything like that."

"Then you're very fortunate. My sister was convinced she was going to die before she got past that stage."

"I didn't know you had a sister."

"You didn't? That's odd. I felt sure I told you every single, solitary thing about me the night we met. I must have talked for hours."

"I enjoyed it. You're so different from the other people I know."

"In what way?"

"Oh, more open somehow. More willing to share your thoughts and feelings. You aren't quite as regimented in your thinking as some of my fellow faculty members. I found you refreshing."

"Not to mention forward."

She wasn't sure how to respond to his last remark. "Not forward exactly. It was just that I had never been in a situation like that before. Everything that happened seemed to be so natural that I never really knew when to call a halt to what was taking place."

"I realized that later. I should have been in better control and normally I am, but that night seemed so different somehow. I can't really explain it."

"I know. Neither can I. I didn't feel like me that night. I was someone else, someone witty and charming . . . alluring."

"You still are, you know. Witty, charming and alluring."

"Actually, I'm rather shy."

They glanced at each other, holding the eye contact for a brief moment, and began to laugh.

Elizabeth recognized the absurdity of her situation. She experienced a tremendous relief to be able to share her feelings with someone else. Besides her doctor, no one else was aware of her pregnancy, even though she knew that sooner or later she would have to acknowledge it. Now that she felt herself relaxing, she discovered how much control she had kept over her feelings. She no longer felt a need to hide behind a facade of professionalism.

Dan stopped at a rustic inn for dinner. Elizabeth had not been out for dinner with anyone since Philip's death and she realized how much she had been punishing herself for what had happened to him, even though she knew she had had no control over the circumstances.

"Candlelight becomes you," Dan said with a smile.

Elizabeth self-consciously touched her forehead where curling wisps of satiny black hair fell from her topknot.

"I'm not really dressed for a place like this."

"Of course you are. You look beautiful."

He grinned as he watched her cheeks flush with soft color.

She couldn't help but think how much the soft lighting enhanced his finely chiseled features, the light reflecting in the silver-gray of his eyes. She wondered if her baby would have eyes like his and blinked in bewilderment at the unusual thought. There was every possibility that her child would look very much like the man seated across from her.

The dinner was leisurely and Dan kept the topics of conversation light because he knew what he had to say to Beth later might very well upset her. So he postponed that particular discussion until he took her home.

"Would you like some coffee?" she asked politely after inviting him inside.

"I don't think so. However, I would like to talk with you a few minutes before I start back."

She turned around from hanging up his jacket in surprise. "You're going back tonight?"

"Yes."

"That really isn't necessary, you know. I have a spare bedroom if you'd like to wait until morning."

"No. I have a presentation I need to work on tomorrow. I only need a few hours' sleep and I'd rather get on the road tonight."

"Oh." She noticed that he seemed a little restless, and silently motioned him to her sofa. "Sit down."

He sat, watching her as she gracefully sank into the chair across from him. "I've been doing a lot of thinking today," he began.

Her eyes caught his attention once again, their serious expression causing him to pause and search for just the right way to say what he was thinking.

"I came here looking for someone who has haunted me for over three months."

Elizabeth didn't know what to say. She continued to watch him, a little wary of his next words, wondering why the relaxed companion of the day suddenly appeared so grim.

"You are already very special to me, Beth, or I wouldn't have taken the time and trouble to track you down. And I want... Oh, God, how do I say this? I want to have the right to be with you through the next few months, help with whatever I can. Do you understand that?"

"I appreciate your offer, but it isn't necessary."

He knew he wasn't getting across what he needed to say, but he had never been faced with such a situation before.

"I want to marry you, Beth," he finally blurted out.

He saw her flinch at his words and his heart sank.

"Marry me?" she repeated with disbelief.

"Well, it isn't all that strange, is it? Under the circumstances, I mean."

"But you don't even know me!"

"Is that what you're going to tell our child someday? 'Sorry, dear, but I couldn't marry your father. I didn't know him.'"

"Of course not. It's just that there's no need for us to marry."

"I believe that there is. And because I do, I think my wishes should count just as much as yours. I take it you don't want to marry me."

Elizabeth heard the hurt in his voice and she didn't know what to say or do to help minimize what he was feeling.

"Please don't take it personally."

"There's no other way to take it. It's a very personal matter. You happen to be carrying my child. How much more personal can we get?"

She shook her head, confused and upset. "I don't think I'm capable of marrying anyone," she finally admitted.

"There's nothing to it, actually. We can go before a justice of the peace, say a few words, sign a paper, and it's over."

"That's not what I mean. It isn't the ceremony—it's the living together afterward."

Dan allowed a sigh of relief to escape him. "Oh, is that all? Well, we can deal with that. I certainly am not going to insist on any husbandly rights, if that's your concern. Besides, you'll need to stay here and finish out whatever classes you have scheduled before the baby arrives. I'll have to stay in Manhattan...that's where I make my living, after all."

"Then what's the point of getting married?"

"So that our child will know that we are both willing to accept the responsibility of becoming parents. It's not as though we won't see each other. I can come up here. You can visit me over the holidays. I'm hoping you'll consider coming to New York to have the baby, so I can be with you."

He watched the expressions on her face, trying to will her to see how important their marriage was.

"Would it have to be permanent?" she asked thoughtfully, and once again his heart sank. She wasn't even going to consider making it a true marriage.

Dan had never thought so quickly in his life before. Nothing that had happened to him had been this important and he didn't want to blow the whole thing by some hasty remark.

"I will leave that decision up to you, Beth. Why don't you see how you feel after the baby comes? If you find marriage too restrictive and want your freedom, I won't fight you."

"What about the baby?"

"I think we both care enough about the baby to decide, when the time comes, to do the best thing for all three of us. Don't you?"

How could she know that? How could anyone know how another person might behave? As far as she knew, the minute she said her vows he could become some raving maniac, forcing her to his will.

She almost giggled at the absurd thought. Dan Morgan was the least likely person she knew to become a maniac.

"All right."

That was it? All right? he thought. He had just managed to convince her to marry him and she was sitting there quietly, watching him, as though they had agreed on the next political candidate to run for governor.

"Fine." He stood up, determined to leave before he said something that might blow the whole situation. He went over to the hall closet and retrieved his jacket. "I'll give you a call sometime next week so we can make the final arrangements as to when and where, if that's okay."

She nodded. "Okay." She had stood when he did and walked over to him.

Carefully he slipped his arms around her waist. "Thank you, Beth. I promise that you won't be sorry you trusted me. I won't abuse that trust."

Her smile was a little wobbly, but her gaze was steady as it met his. Elizabeth had already discovered that Dan enjoyed physical contact. She recognized that he wasn't even aware of how often he ran his finger along her cheek, took her hand in his, or as now, placed his hands around her waist.

He didn't mean anything by it, she knew. She would just have to get used to it. Actually, Elizabeth had discovered earlier that day that she rather enjoyed being close to him, which was strange. She'd always resented other people who made a habit of trying to touch her.

Dan Morgan was different somehow.

Forcing himself not to pull her into an embrace, Dan leaned over and contented himself with a soft kiss. Her mouth relaxed under his, surprising him. Their one night together seemed to have taught her something about how to share a kiss.

Almost imperceptibly, he drew her closer, savoring the lack of resistance as she allowed him access to her warm mouth. Ever mindful of not frightening her, he deepened the kiss, delicately touching her with his tongue, exploring softly as though reacquainting himself with her once more.

Elizabeth recognized the melting sensation within her that had caused her to lose all her inhibitions the first time she'd met him, and slowly stiffened.

Dan immediately slackened his hold, although there was no way he could disguise the effect she had on him.

His harsh breathing sounded loud against her ear as he held her to him, stroking her back with a trembling hand.

"I'm sorry. I didn't mean to come on so strong."

She smiled into his shoulder. "That's all right. All this is just a little confusing to me right now."

"I know, and I don't want to add to the confusion." He dropped his hands and stepped back. Giving her a crooked smile, he said, "Besides, I need to get moving." He reached behind him and opened the door. "I'll call you in a few days."

"Do you have my number?"

He grinned. "Yes. Janine was very thorough."

"Why didn't you call before you drove up?"

He didn't want to admit how afraid he'd been that she would refuse to see him. He hadn't wanted to give her a choice.

"Oh, I needed to get away for a while. Even if you hadn't been home I would have enjoyed the trip."

"Take care driving back."

"You can count on it. I'm not going to take any chances that I won't be around." His grin was contagious and she responded with a smile that caused a lump to form in his throat.

"Bye, Beth."

"Bye, Dan." She had never corrected him about her name. Actually, she rather liked his calling her by that name. It brought him closer somehow.

Dan strode over to his car and got in, determined to get away from there before he allowed her to see what he was really feeling.

She had agreed to marry him. He had to keep that thought in mind and not let the stunning revelation he'd experienced when he'd held her in his arms to disrupt his thinking. He would need to make plans, discuss options and try to treat the coming marriage as though it were no more than a business merger.

Under no circumstances must he allow Beth to realize that he had fallen in love with her. If he did, he knew he'd never have a chance of winning her on a permanent basis.

And win her he was determined to do.

Chapter Four

November 2 was a cold, blustery day in New York City. Dan met Elizabeth's train and she felt a moment of wonder that the man standing there, so attractive and radiating a quiet self-confidence, would be her husband in a few short hours.

She was aware of the moment he first spotted her—his face lit up in a smile that almost took her breath away. If he had any doubts about what they were about to do, he certainly hid them well. He was beside her in a few strides, picking her up and swinging her around with an exuberance that caught her unaware.

"I didn't think you were ever going to get here!"

She glanced at her watch in surprise.

"Oh, the train was on time. It's just that I've been counting the hours."

He draped his arm across her shoulder and hurried her to the exit of the station. "Are you hungry?"

She started laughing.

"What's wrong?" he demanded.

"Nothing's wrong. I just feel as though I've been whisked off the train by a whirlwind and I'm not sure what I'm supposed to do or say."

He grinned sheepishly. "Sorry." He pulled her closer to him. "Is it all right to be excited on my wedding day?"

Since she had been unable to sleep at all the night before and her heart had been indulging in aerobic exercises all morning, Elizabeth didn't feel she had any room to criticize. She smiled up at him. "I'd much prefer you to be excited than upset by it," she admitted shyly.

"I hope it's all right with you...I asked Ryan and Janine to stand up with us."

Elizabeth stopped walking abruptly. "You told them about us?" she asked, her eyes wide with apprehension.

Oops, you really blew it this time, Dan admitted to himself. He guided her into a waiting taxi before answering.

"I didn't realize you intended our marriage to be a secret."

"I didn't. I mean, I don't. But I suppose I thought we'd just go do it and not mention it to anyone."

"Why?"

"Because of all the questions and everything."

"Beth," he explained in a carefully neutral tone, "there were no questions other than why we didn't let anyone know sooner. As far as people are concerned, what we're doing isn't unusual."

"Janine knows better."

She knew her friend very well, Dan decided. He'd spent a rough few minutes on the phone when he called and told Janine of his plans. Somehow his sincerity must have come across, because she eventually believed he knew what he was doing. She wasn't as sure about Elizabeth.

"She sounded very pleased for us," he said cautiously, leaving out ninety percent of their conversation regarding the marriage.

"You told her about the baby," she stated in a flat tone.

"No."

"You didn't? Then what reason did you give for our getting married?"

"The oldest reason in the world. We fell in love and wanted to spend the rest of our lives together."

"Oh, Janine would never believe that."

"She did." *Eventually,* he added silently.

"I should have called her. Was she upset that I hadn't told her?"

"More surprised than upset, I'd guess. I explained that you had asked me to notify her and she accepted that. Frankly, it never occurred to me that you wouldn't want her to know. She was pleased her schedule permitted her to be with us today."

Elizabeth heard the bewilderment in his voice and realized that her attitude was ridiculous. Unaware that she did so, she impulsively reached over and took his hand, squeezing it lightly. "I'm glad she's going to be there. The news just caught me by surprise. Thank you for thinking of her."

Dan stared down at her hand, at the delicate shape of it, resting so trustingly in his. He felt as though that same hand had squeezed his heart, and for a moment he couldn't think of anything but the fact that for whatever the reason, this woman had agreed to marry him. He was more aware of the trust implied in that gesture than ever before, since Janine had explained more of Beth's background to him, as well as her relationship with Philip.

Poor Philip. He must have really loved her and she had seen him as a brother, although Beth didn't seem to realize that. Philip had wanted more from her than she had been willing to give. Was he, Dan, making the same mistake by hoping that with time and patience their marriage could become a complete sharing of themselves with each other? Only time would tell, and Dan had more than enough time to spare.

Janine and Ryan were waiting for them at the civil office where the ceremony was performed.

Later Elizabeth could barely remember what had taken place, it had happened so fast. All she knew was that after a very short period of time they were all leaving and she was wearing a golden band decorated with several diamonds worked into an intricate design.

"I didn't get you a ring," she said quietly while Janine was listening to something Ryan was saying.

"You still can, you know," he said with a smile.

"Would you want to wear one?"

"If you chose it for me, yes, I would," he admitted.

"I would like to propose a toast," Ryan said later over dinner. "To Dan and Beth, a pair who seem to belong together. May your forevers continue in peace and joy."

They all laughed and sipped the champagne that Ryan had ordered for them.

"You know, that's true," Janine admitted. "I noticed the first night they met how suited they seemed to each other."

Dan glanced down at Elizabeth, who wrinkled her nose at him. He laughed, recognizing her self-consciousness.

"Well, as you can see, it didn't take me long to make sure Beth was convinced we belonged together." He reached under the table and gently squeezed her hand.

They were all going on as though the marriage were perfectly normal, and Elizabeth wondered what Ryan and Janine were going to say when they discovered she was going to have a baby in a little more than five months' time. Would they feel as though they'd been tricked into believing the marriage was a love match?

She had no idea and she wasn't ready to face their reactions just now. She silently blessed Dan for his instinctive understanding of her feelings.

Elizabeth knew that Dan would never intentionally cause her distress. It was a warm, comfortable feeling and she felt a surge of freedom at the thought. He might not love her, but he respected her and was willing to give her the space she needed.

Dan Morgan was a very unusual man and she was beginning to realize how fortunate she was . . . in many ways.

"There's one thing I haven't mentioned," Dan began as he let her into his apartment later that evening.

He sounded so worried she felt an immediate need to soothe him. Instead she waited for him to continue.

"I only have one bedroom here and I was hoping you wouldn't feel it too restrictive if we shared it whenever you were in town."

Step number two was just about to be launched. If the first step was getting her to agree to marriage, the next step was to get her accustomed to the casual intimacy of marriage.

"I have an oversize bed, so I'm sure you won't feel crowded. Actually, three or four people could rest comfortably in it." He led her across the living room and flipped on the light in the bedroom to show her what he meant. The room was decorated in shades of warm browns and tans. A very masculine room. And the bed was indeed large.

Elizabeth tried her best to overcome the faint panic she felt at sharing a bedroom with him. Of course she knew he wouldn't attack her. He'd made it very clear that she had nothing to fear from him in that regard. So what was wrong with sharing the room with him?

She already knew him well enough to know that he wouldn't allow her to sleep on the sofa and she felt it unfair to expect him to give up his bed for her.

Walking over and glancing into the bathroom, she kept her face turned away from him when she said, "I'm sure there will be room enough for both of us." Then she turned around. "I doubt that I will be here all that much, really."

Oh, yes you will, if I have my way, he silently disputed.

"Great. You're welcome to the bathroom first, if you'd like."

She really was tired. The busy day—combined with no sleep the night before and the champagne at dinner—had almost caused her to fall asleep on the way to Dan's apartment.

"Thank you. If you don't mind, I think I will get ready for bed. I'm a little tired."

He walked over and cupped her face in his hands. "You may be tired, but you look radiant. You made a beautiful bride, Mrs. Morgan."

She could feel that melting sensation once again, and this time he hadn't even kissed her. Elizabeth couldn't understand the effect he had on her. She went up on tiptoe and kissed him lightly on the lips.

"Thank you for today. You made it very special."

He could have cheered at her totally natural response to his touch. Instead he kept his tone matter-of-fact. "I wanted it to be special for you because you're very special to me."

He immediately saw the flash of apprehension in her eyes and hastened to find a suitable explanation for his remark. "You're the mother of my unborn child and deserve the best I have to offer."

He could feel her relax and realized how close he'd come to undoing everything he had managed to accomplish so far.

"I almost forgot about the baby today, what with all the excitement. I suppose we should have told Janine and Ryan," she suggested reluctantly.

"We'll tell them soon enough. Chances are we won't be seeing very much of them, not with their travel schedules. It's a wonder they ever manage to be in town at the same time."

"Do you realize that your college roommate and my college roommate introduced us to each other?" she asked, her eyes dancing with amusement.

"Which just goes to prove that higher education is never wasted. Do you suppose they're going to demand a commission or something?"

She laughed, and he realized how often he tried to amuse her so he could hear her clear, tinkling laughter.

"Did you tell your students you were getting married?"

"No. I've never given details of my personal life to my students. As far as any of them know, I've been married for years."

Dan had a glimpse into the lonely life Beth had built for herself and vowed that he was going to do everything in his power to show her the rewards of sharing with others.

He patted her familiarly on her bottom and said, "Go get your shower, woman. I'm about ready for bed myself."

Startled by the intimate gesture, Elizabeth glanced up and saw the watching amusement in his eyes. *I refuse to get rattled by our new relationship. But it isn't fair. He's already accustomed to being married. This is all very new to me.*

She disappeared into the bathroom, while Dan walked over and turned back the covers of the brand new bed he'd had delivered the day before.

Elizabeth had hoped she would be asleep by the time Dan came out of the bathroom. No such luck. When he opened the bathroom door she almost leaped straight up.

Stop being ridiculous. You're a grown woman, for heaven's sake. Your attitude is absurd. Dan Morgan knows you better than any other man. There is nothing to be afraid of.

Her little pep talk helped immensely and Elizabeth managed to relax somewhat, until she felt his weight on the bed and realized he was now lying somewhere nearby. She could feel herself tensing and deliberately began some deep-breathing exercises she had learned in an effort to relax several months ago.

"Good night, Beth," he said from the darkness.

"Good night."

"Are you warm enough?"

She felt that her racing blood had warmed her body to the point where she was probably feverish. "Yes. I'm fine."

She waited, but he didn't say anything more. She felt the bed move and decided he must have turned over. Great idea. She gingerly shifted to her side so that her back was to him.

Turning over was the last thing she remembered.

Sometime during the night the warmth of two bodies must have proved to be irresistible. That was the only explanation Dan could think of when he awakened sometime in the early dawn to find Beth curled up in his arms.

Her head was on his shoulder, her hand rested on his chest and her knee was nestled rather intimately between his thighs.

His body had already reacted to her provocative position and he gingerly began to move away, hoping she wouldn't wake up and think he had coaxed her into that position.

Nothing could have been farther from the truth. Dan had lain awake for hours, all too aware of their proximity and knowing he had no intention of doing anything about it.

He still couldn't believe he'd managed to convince her to sleep with him their first night together. He was not going to ruin that strategic gain by letting her discover how much he wanted to make love to her. And if she woke up now, there was no way she would not know.

She sighed when he tried to remove his arm from under her head and he froze. When she didn't stir, he began once again to move his arm, slowly, ever so slowly, until it was free. Next was her hand and knee.

Inching away from her, he finally managed to free himself, and crawled over to the edge of the bed, when what he wanted to do most in the world was pull her closer and enjoy all the marvelous ways two people could enjoy each other. The need to reexperience what they had once shared had tortured him for months, but he reminded himself to be patient. Time was on his side, if he managed the situation correctly.

She was definitely worth the wait.

Elizabeth dreamed once again, but this time it wasn't Philip who stood there telling her he wanted out of their relationship. It was Dan's voice that told her he was tired of waiting, tired of trying to make love to a two-dimensional person who had no feelings or emotions.

She called his name, but he didn't answer. He walked away disappearing into the mist, and she awoke with a sudden jerk.

Faint daylight lit the room. Her heart was pounding and she couldn't remember where she was. Then the events of the day before fell into place and she realized she was at Dan's apartment.

He was practically hanging on to the edge of the bed because she was sprawled across the middle. How embarrassing. Hastily wriggling back to her own side, she tried to come to grips with her dream.

She had never seen Dan as he had appeared in her dream and Elizabeth faced the fact that she would never want to. She had to acknowledge that she cared too much for him to want to see that look of contempt that her dream state had transposed from Philip's face to Dan's.

She could never blame Philip. She hadn't shown him affection. Her love for him had been too internalized, but now she had a chance to show Dan that she appreciated him. The question was how.

He had never given her any reason to believe that he wanted more from the relationship than what they had originally agreed upon. She would have to be careful not to disgust him with open displays of affection.

She didn't know much about giving affection, but there was no time like the present to begin to learn. With that resolve, she relaxed and fell asleep once more.

Elizabeth awakened sometime later to an empty room, filled with sunshine. She had just thrown the covers back and stood up, when Dan appeared in the doorway.

"Good morning."

Dan hadn't meant to startle her, but he didn't want her to think she was married to a Peeping Tom, either, so he had spoken as soon as he realized she was awake.

Elizabeth glanced over her shoulder and hastily grabbed the robe she'd left out the night before.

"Good morning."

"Coffee's made and breakfast is started."

She smiled. "What service."

"You provided the same for me when I was visiting you."

"That's true."

"Anyway, I'm used to getting up early and saw no reason to disturb you." He wondered if she was aware of their cuddling position the night before. "Did you sleep all right?"

She flushed, remembering how much room she'd taken up. "Oh, yes, thank you. How about you?"

Other than facing a cold shower at six in the morning, he'd done very well. "I was fine," he managed to say. He walked over to her. "I enjoyed waking up and finding you in my bed."

She tried to laugh, but it sounded a little shaky. "That sounds a little different than it really was."

"I'm still very pleased to have you here. I hope you'll be comfortable."

"Oh, yes. I'm sure I will be." Remembering her early-morning resolve, she shyly slid her hands around his waist and hugged him. "You're a very genial host."

Dan felt as though someone had suddenly knocked the breath out of him. Her move had caught him totally off guard.

He didn't know what to do with his hands. Left to their own devices, he was certain they would naturally fall and cup her delectable derriere. Concentrating on keeping them above her waist, he placed his hands lightly on her back.

When she lifted her face and trustingly closed her eyes he almost groaned. Obviously his willpower was going to be tested in the coming months. The question was, could he deal with the temptation without succumbing?

Dan attempted a light kiss on her rosy mouth only to discover that she was prepared to participate in a long, leisurely kiss that effectively wiped out all his plans for a safe distance between them.

Elizabeth enjoyed Dan's touch. She tightened her hold, running her hands along his strong muscular back, enjoying the feel of his bare skin against the sensitive pads of her fingers. Although he wore a sweater, she had quickly run her hands beneath it in order to touch him.

The thin gown and matching robe she wore proved to be no protection from Dan's restless hands. The kiss deepened and he felt her breasts pressing against his chest.

She felt so good in his arms. For a moment he forgot his plan. Instead all he remembered was that he held his wife in his arms and that he loved her very much.

He had picked her up and placed her on the bed before he realized what he was doing. Forcing himself to loosen his hold, he sat down beside her, releasing her gently.

"You go to my head, did you know that?" he whispered on a ragged breath.

"You seem to affect me the same way," she admitted, embarrassed to meet his gaze.

"I think maybe we should go have some coffee and consider getting some fresh air, don't you?"

She wondered why she felt so disappointed, when she had never had any intention of having an intimate relationship with him. She wasn't ready for that. Or was she?

Elizabeth couldn't understand what was happening to her. How could she have changed so much from the person who had been engaged to Philip? How could she have felt so strongly for Dan, a complete stranger, the first time she met him? Why did she feel that she wanted more than anything else to experience his lovemaking again?

She sat up, pushing her tumbled hair away from her face. "I think maybe you're right."

He grinned, rubbing her cheek lightly with his thumb. "I was afraid you'd see it my way."

She laughed, suddenly free from her embarrassment and chagrin at the unfamiliar sensations he provoked whenever he touched her.

Elizabeth had never known anyone like Daniel Morgan. She was almost convinced he was one of a kind.

She discovered that she wanted to be the kind of person he deserved—a warm, loving woman who could give back to him as much as he gave.

She would have to give that some thought. Sharing yourself with someone else was never taught in school. Elizabeth wasn't sure how she could study up on it.

But she knew she was determined to learn.

Chapter Five

The day before Thanksgiving arrived with blowing snow and traveler's advisories not to travel. A sudden gust of wind caused the limb of a tree to brush against the window, and Elizabeth woke up with a start.

She sat up in her bed and stared out the window in consternation. The snow that had started the evening before continued to fall. With a feeling of dismay, Elizabeth reluctantly settled back into bed again.

He would never be able to make it up there today. Glancing at the clock on the bedside table, she decided she might as well get up. The alarm would go off in another half-hour, anyway.

She shoved off her covers and felt around for her fuzzy house slippers, feeling the draft of cool air on her ankles.

Tugging on her warm, old housecoat, Elizabeth padded over to the bathroom, trying to fight her disappointment.

She hadn't seen him since their wedding three weeks earlier and had been counting the days until Thanksgiving. When Dan called last night, his plans were to leave Manhattan no later than three o'clock, which meant he'd arrive at her house that evening.

Neither of them had expected the snow to hang around and become a full-fledged winter storm.

Changes had taken place during the past three weeks. Physically her body had taken on a spurt of growth that had forced her to go shopping earlier than she'd planned to find some comfortable clothes. It was as though the baby had suddenly decided to get serious about the idea of growing and becoming part of the world.

She methodically soaped her body and glanced down at her stomach with a slight smile. No one looking at her could possibly make a mistake about her condition now.

Not that she had any trouble seeing her toes, but given the fact that she seemed to have doubled in size in the past few weeks, she had a sneaky hunch her toes might disappear from view any day now.

She wondered what Dan would think when he saw her. If he saw her, she mentally corrected herself.

There had been some emotional changes, as well. His nightly phone calls had made a considerable difference in her life.

Elizabeth absently reached for the water control and turned it off, then stepped out of the shower.

Only her daily routine had stayed the same. She still taught her classes, came home and graded papers, prepared for classes and in her spare time read and watched a little television.

Dan's phone calls had become a focal point in her life. They usually came between nine and ten o'clock each night.

She smiled at some of the nonsensical conversations they'd had.

"Good evening," Dan had said one night last week, "I'm trying to get in touch with an interplanetary traveler and was told she could be reached at this number."

He'd sounded very professional and serious.

"Perhaps I could help you," she replied, trying to hide her amusement.

"Oh, I sincerely hope so," came his relieved reply. "I understand that traveling between planets can become quite an ordeal, particularly when it comes to finding your favorite foods. Have you noticed any problem in that area?"

"Not really. You'd be surprised how innovative McDonald's and Burger King have been in expanding their franchises."

"Why, I had no idea! I'm sure you find it a relief. But does a Whopper really taste the same on Venus?"

"Close enough. Their mustard has a strange consistency, though. But that's just one of the hazards of traveling we learn to accept."

"I've been meaning to ask—have you noticed a tendency lately to crave certain unusual foods?"

"Well, yes, now that you mention it," she admitted thoughtfully.

"I knew it. I had a strong hunch that you were feeling deprived stuck up there with nothing but students and faculty to look after your needs."

Elizabeth could almost see his eyes sparkling with amusement when he paused.

"What are you craving?"

"Pretzels."

"Pretzels! Those aren't rare and exotic."

"I never said they were."

"But I expected you to want something that was hard to find, like strawberries, or maybe watermelon."

"Sorry. I just like to munch on pretzels. It's probably the salt or something."

"I don't suppose you have any trouble finding them at the local market, huh."

"Not at all. In fact, I'm enjoying some now. Care to join me?"

"Very much. But not to help you eat pretzels." His voice dropped slightly. "I miss you, Mrs. Morgan."

And she missed him, too, which seemed very strange to her. She didn't even know him, and had only been around him a few times. Perhaps it was her pregnancy that was affecting her usually sensible attitudes.

"Is this where I'm supposed to recommend two aspirin, et cetera?" she asked with interest.

He laughed. "I'm afraid that won't cure what ails me. So how have you been?"

"Since last night when I talked to you?" she asked, her amusement obvious. "Fine."

"Are you making fun of me?"

"Not in the least. The phone company must love you."

His voice sounded serious. "Would you prefer that I not call so often?"

"I enjoy hearing from you, Dan." She was surprised to discover how true that was.

"I think about you often, you know. I seem to have developed the habit and can't seem to break it."

"How did your presentation go today?"

"Extremely well. I seemed to be in rare form. Got the account, which means I'm going to have to hire some more help. I seem to be expanding faster than I dreamed possible."

"I'm happy for you."

"How about you? Are you expanding on schedule?"

"Yes, as a matter of fact, I am."

"When do you go to the doctor again?"

"The day after Thanksgiving."

"Great. I'll be there to go with you."

"Are you sure you want to?"

"Absolutely."

"If you weren't planning to come up here, how would you be spending your holidays?"

"Oh, I don't know. I might have gone out of town, visited some friends in Virginia. Or I might have stayed here and worked up some ideas for an upcoming campaign. Why?"

"I just wondered. You seem to have adjusted very well to not having a family."

"My sister and I are still close, if that's what you mean, but she's busy with her family in California."

"I was thinking about your parents."

"They've been gone a long time, Beth, as I explained the night we met."

"I remember. You seemed so well adjusted about it all."

"That's because I don't believe in living in the past. They had a happy life together, and Mom didn't outlive Dad by more than a few months. They gave us their love and expected us to pass it on to our families."

"You were very lucky."

"Yes, because now I have a family to share all of that love with."

"I wish I had known my parents." She had finally put a secret wish into words for him.

"Once you get involved with our baby you'll probably discover that your parents gave you what was most important—your life and your ability to make whatever you want out of it."

"I suppose. At least, I'm working on that attitude these days."

"Glad to hear it. There's nothing more futile than looking back and wondering 'what if,' since there's not much we can do about our past."

"As a matter of fact," she said thoughtfully, "my daily life seems to be picking up considerably."

"How's that?"

"Oh, my students are becoming inquisitive. Someone noticed the wedding band, another noticed my new style of clothes, and they've actually come up and casually questioned me."

"And how did you handle their questions?"

"Differently than I had imagined I would. They seemed truly interested in me the person, rather than as their professor. It surprised me. I explained that we had what was considered, I suppose, a modern marriage, and that we commuted to be together."

"And what was their response?"

"Even more interest, since many of them are trying to reconcile career possibilities with strong ties they are currently forming. I was amused that they treated me as though I were an expert in those areas."

"Did you enjoy yourself?"

"Yes, I really did. I ended up having coffee with a couple of the women—one who had been married a couple of years, the other still contemplating what would be the right choice for her. I rather enjoyed being part of the group, sharing my thoughts and feelings about society and the way it functions."

"So there's a good possibility I might call some evening and find that you're not at home," he suggested.

Elizabeth heard the pleasure in his voice and wondered about it. "Oh, I doubt it, at least not during the week. I still need my sleep."

"Which reminds me. It's past your bedtime. Take care of yourself... I'll call you tomorrow night."

"You take care, too. Thank you for calling."

She'd hung up smiling. It was fun to have someone to share her day with. And it gave her something to look forward to, waiting to hear from him again.

Elizabeth had also begun to count the days until he arrived.

Now she dressed and went into the kitchen. Snow lay in soft piles on the lawn and trees. It was really beautiful, if a person didn't have to go out in it. The forecast called for more snow. Of course Dan wouldn't bother coming up. He would be foolish to risk the trip.

"It looks like we'll spend Thanksgiving with each other again this year," she said to Misty, who was curled up near the floor heat vent. "It won't be the first time, will it?" Misty glanced up at her and twitched an ear, then stretched and yawned. "Yes, I can see you're as excited about the prospect as I am."

Pouring water into the coffee maker, Elizabeth began making her breakfast.

She thought of all the baking and preparations she had done, looking forward to having Dan there.

Up until now, her holidays had been little more than extended weekends. She rarely went anywhere, content to stay at home. It was only after meeting Dan that Elizabeth had discovered a restlessness stirring within her, as though something were missing in her daily routine.

She didn't want to get attached to him. There was no reason to think the marriage would continue after the baby was born. Of course, once the baby had arrived, she would have a child to occupy her time and thoughts. She already knew herself well enough to know that someone like Dan Morgan would not be interested in her as a person. He saw her as the mother of his child and she realized that in that respect she was very important to him.

He really wanted this baby. She rubbed her abdomen and smiled. This was one child who would be greeted with two loving parents. Not like her, handed over at birth before any details could be discovered about her natural parents. Even the name her natural mother had given at the hospital was phony, as well as the address.

Nothing like that would ever happen to her baby, she knew that with a certainty. Carrying her breakfast dishes to the sink, she decided to buy some baby patterns and try her hand at sewing. She might even try to make an afghan. That was as good a way to occupy her long weekend as anything she could think of.

Elizabeth drove to work very carefully, thankful that her street had been cleared and that she wasn't far from the campus. She tried very hard not to think about her disappointment with the weather.

Of course Dan wouldn't come up, no matter what he had said the night before.

As soon as she arrived home after class that afternoon Elizabeth decided to call Dan. There was no reason to sit and wonder if he was coming.

She was unable to reach him. His secretary explained that he was meeting with a client and wasn't expected back to the office that afternoon.

She pictured Dan sitting with an attractive woman, going over ad layouts, and almost laughed at her imagination. What if he was? She certainly had no ties on him, regardless of their legal situation. Their understanding was clear. He was there for her if she needed him with regard to the pregnancy. But that was all.

He had never acted as though he minded giving up his social life because of their marriage. Perhaps because he hadn't actually given it up. Granted, he called each evening. But there was no reason to suppose he stayed at home once he hung up the phone.

Stop it! She was behaving like a possessive, jealous wife, which was certainly not the case. She had no reason to feel possessive or jealous. And she had no idea how it felt to be a wife. A real wife. A wife who was loved and cared for, held in esteem.

When Elizabeth finally went to bed that night she was resigned to spending the rest of the week alone. The snow had never stopped falling, and the traveler's advisories were suggesting that people stay home unless it was an emergency.

She wasn't sure what woke her up later. According to the clock, it was a little past eleven. There was no sound on the street. Elizabeth lay there for a moment, listening. As she turned over restlessly, trying to fall asleep once again, she heard a noise.

She felt around the bottom of the bed and discovered that Misty was no longer in bed with her. No doubt she had found something to play with and was batting it around in the other room, but Elizabeth knew she wouldn't get any more sleep until she investigated.

When she came out of her bedroom she saw the kitchen light was on. Misty had never bothered with light switches and no self-respecting burglar would be so bold. So it must be—

"Hello, Beth. I was afraid I'd wake you up." Dan stood there in his stocking feet, his heavy boots lying beside the chair. Never had his smile been more beguiling.

She realized she was standing there in her bare feet, in an old flannel gown that was warm but far from glamorous. She was so happy to see him she couldn't think of anything to say.

A cold draft of air seemed to circulate around the room and she shivered slightly. "How did you manage to get here?"

"Followed a snowplow. Sorry it took so long."

She couldn't believe he was actually there. Elizabeth forced herself to sound relaxed and offhand. "I didn't expect you to come."

He had picked up his boots and started carrying them over toward the back door, where a rubber mat lay, when she spoke. He stopped and glanced back at her.

"I told you I'd be here."

"That's before the storm blew in."

He dropped his boots and went over to the coffeepot. Quickly measuring coffee and water, he said, without looking up, "It isn't unusual to have snowstorms at this time of year, you know."

She fought the urge to throw herself into his arms and hold him, just to make sure he was real. "I thought you would change your mind about coming," she offered in a noncommittal tone of voice.

His steady gaze met hers for a moment in silence. "Is that what you hoped?"

She felt the tension building between them. Of course that wasn't what she had hoped, but she didn't want to embarrass him with her eagerness to see him.

"No, of course not." She smiled. "I'm just surprised you managed to get here, that's all."

She looked like a young girl to Dan, in her long flannel gown and her hair done in a single braid. Bare toes peeped out at him, and he realized she hadn't stopped to put on her slippers.

"Don't you think you should get some shoes on? That is, if you intend to stay up for a while."

She glanced down at her feet. Now that he was here she was wide-awake. Without a word she disappeared down the hallway.

Dan glanced over at Misty, who had met him at the door when he arrived.

"I sincerely hope you've been taking your duties as official watch cat seriously. Has she been eating all right? Getting enough sleep? What do you think?"

Misty stared back at him without blinking, and he smiled. "If you know, you certainly aren't going to tell, are you?"

When Elizabeth returned the coffee was ready, and he poured out the brew, placing the cups on the table.

"I tried to call you today," she mentioned, trying to sound casual, "but your secretary said you weren't there and she didn't expect you back."

"Did you tell her who you were?"

"No. I didn't think it mattered."

"Of course it mattered. She has standing instructions to give you my exact whereabouts and a phone number if you should ever call."

She could feel a warm glow begin to swell within her at his words and tone. "Well, it wasn't important, really. I was just going to tell you about the storm and suggest that you might not want to drive up until it cleared."

"Then I'm glad you didn't reach me, since I would have ignored your advice, anyway."

"I'm glad you're here," she murmured.

He had been studying his coffee, and glanced up at her when she spoke. Her cheeks were flushed, either from sleep or from his presence. He wasn't sure what he hoped might have caused the tension he sensed within her. He didn't want to upset her, but he also wasn't going to let her talk him out of their spending time together.

"So am I." He leaned back in his chair and stretched his arms high over his head. "It's been a long day."

"When did you leave?" She tried to ignore the way his sweater tightened across his chest, and forced herself to meet his gaze. She was surprised to discover him watching her intently.

"Sometime around six. My meeting ran over and traffic held me up. I thought about calling to let you know, but by the time I remembered I hadn't called I was already on my way."

She smiled at the frustration she heard in his tone.

"You should sleep warm enough," she offered. "There's an electric blanket on your bed."

He lifted his brow slightly. "*My* bed?"

She flushed. "Well, uh, yes. I aired the guest room for you."

He studied her for a moment in silence. "I see."

"I'm afraid my bed isn't as large as yours and I've been a little restless lately. I wouldn't want to keep you awake."

"Heaven forbid," he responded dryly.

"I'm being silly, aren't I?" she finally asked.

"Not really. You just have a habit of surprising me every so often, that's all. I will be more than willing to sleep wherever you want me." He shoved his chair back and stood up. "As a matter of fact, I could almost fall asleep here at the table." He walked over and placed his cup in the sink, then reached over and unplugged the coffee maker. "I think it's past time for both of us to be in bed."

As though he had always lived there, Dan checked all the doors to see that they were securely locked, then waited in the hallway until she went into her room.

"See you in the morning," he said gently.

"Yes." Elizabeth absently noted that Misty did not follow her into her room. No doubt she had already decided Dan would make a better bed partner.

As she crawled under the covers, Elizabeth wondered what it would be like to sleep with him on a regular basis. He had already been up when she'd awoken both mornings the time she'd stayed with him in New York. She had been concerned that she might crowd him in her small bed as she had in his large one. He might have found himself on the floor, in that event.

The sound of the shower in the main bathroom drifted into her room and she sighed. She wished she better understood proper etiquette in a situation such as theirs. She certainly wasn't much of a hostess, but she supposed he was used to looking after himself.

We're spending Thanksgiving together. He's really here! A sense of anticipation swept over her—a feeling she hadn't experienced since she had lived with Auntie Em. Elizabeth knew better than to expect too much, of course. He was doing the correct thing, spending the holidays with his wife. It was up to her to see that he wasn't bored.

Dan stood under the shower, feeling somewhat defeated. What had he expected? He had to continually remind himself that she was merely tolerating him in her life because he hadn't given her much choice. Just because she had sounded more warm and friendly on the phone than she appeared to be in person had been no reason for him to get his hopes up.

Besides, they had only been married three weeks. He knew it would take longer than that for them to start building ties of friendship.

If only she didn't affect him so strongly whenever he saw her. Her eyes continued to fascinate him, and his body remembered quite well the intimacy they had shared. If it weren't for the fact that he knew she was pregnant, he would almost swear she was still innocent. She had such an untouched air about her, as though she had been locked away from life.

Well, he had knocked down all the walls by his careless action and it was up to him to protect her now.

If she would let him.

Chapter Six

The smell of freshly brewed coffee and frying bacon wafted into Elizabeth's consciousness the next morning, adding to the sense of well-being that her dreams had left with her.

Now that she was awake she could no longer remember the dream, but she had felt safe, secure and very loved. She stretched, rolled over and found a cup of hot coffee sitting beside the bed.

Glancing over at the door, she saw Dan leaning against the doorjamb with his hands in his pockets, watching her.

"Good morning," he said with a half smile.

"You're up early," she managed to mumble.

"I know. It's too nice a day to stay in bed. I thought we might go for a walk after breakfast and enjoy the day," he said, looking out the window.

Bright sunshine caused the snow to sparkle, and the trees glistened with an icy brilliance that almost hurt her eyes.

"Looks like the storm decided not to hang around," he said when she didn't say anything.

Elizabeth wasn't used to waking up and finding someone in her room. It was very disconcerting. She forced herself to act with a semblance of nonchalance and reached for the coffee.

"Thank you for room service."

"My pleasure."

"Have you been up long?"

"About an hour. Misty has kept me company."

"I should have warned you to shut your door. She feels as though she can sleep wherever she pleases."

"She won't get an argument from me. Breakfast should be ready in about ten minutes. Is that okay?"

"Certainly. I'll be right here." He nodded and walked out of the room.

When he'd brought the coffee to her, he was once again mesmerized by the sweet innocence of her face. She had been curled up on her side, her hand under her cheek, her long lashes sweeping over softly tinted cheeks. A slight smile curved her mouth and it had been all he could do to refrain from kissing her.

Easy does it, fellow, he reminded himself. *One wrong move and she won't even accept your phone calls.*

He supposed this weekend was as good a time as any to practice patience. *Think of all the character you're building,* he decided, amused at the thought.

As tired as he'd been, Dan had found himself lying awake for hours the night before, trying to decide the best tack to take with Beth.

By the time he fell asleep, he'd decided to behave as though their marriage were perfectly normal, with one notable exception—they didn't share a bedroom.

His smile was warm and welcoming when Elizabeth joined him in the kitchen.

"Blue is a very becoming color for you," he offered casually, placing her plate of food in front of her.

Elizabeth glanced down at the sweater she had on. Janine had given it to her for Christmas the year before and she seldom wore it, the royal blue was so bright.

"It matches your eyes," he added with a grin.

"Thank you." All his clothes looked fantastic on him. She had a hunch he already knew that.

They made plans over breakfast, and because of Dan's relaxed manner Elizabeth found herself relaxing in turn. He continued to treat their situation as though it were normal, which helped.

During the next four days they enjoyed each other's company. Dan accompanied her to see the doctor and asked interested, discerning questions. After the initial awkwardness of introductions, Elizabeth had little to do but listen to the men discuss her pregnancy.

Dan took her to dinner Saturday, teasing her about eating leftover turkey for the remainder of the year. He treated her with an unobtrusive protectiveness that she found rather endearing.

And when he got ready to leave on Sunday evening, Elizabeth discovered she had to fight a tendency to burst into tears. No doubt her emotional behavior had something to do with her pregnancy.

"How would you like to spend Christmas with me?" he asked just before he left.

"How long would you want me to stay?"

"As long as you wished."

"What about Misty?"

"Can't you bring her?"

"I suppose, if you don't mind."

"Since she's part of the family, I don't see an alternative, do you?" he asked with a smile.

Part of the family. Elizabeth felt a slight tingle at his words. She'd never been part of a family, but had always been the one looking on. She grinned.

"I've never had her away from home before. There's no predicting how she'll behave."

"We can practice teaching her manners, then."

For the first time since he'd arrived Dan walked over to Elizabeth and carefully slid his arms around her. "Are you going to be okay between now and then?"

She tried to ignore her reaction to his being close, but it was difficult. The scent of his after-shave and the touch of his warm hands on her back affected her strongly. She forced herself to concentrate on his question. "Of course."

"Will you call me if you need anything?"

"I'm sure I won't need to."

He tightened his arms around her for a moment, then relaxed slightly and began to massage her stiff spine. "Call if you just want to chat, okay? I've been the one calling all the time. It would be nice to hear from you, too."

"I hate to bother you. I know how busy you are."

"Never too busy for you. And the next time you call, you make sure my secretary knows who you are, understand?"

She nodded.

He could feel her slowly begin to relax, her body resting against his. Dan felt that his patience over the past few days definitely needed a reward. Surely she wouldn't think he wanted more from her if he indulged in a kiss now that he was leaving.

She had placed her hands on his chest as though prepared to push him away, but now her hands had slipped up to his shoulders, where she absently stroked the hair round his neck and ears.

"Will you kiss me goodbye, Beth? I always seem to be the one kissing you." His voice was low and she quivered slightly at its husky tone.

Going up on tiptoe, she carefully placed her lips on his. They felt firm and yet they easily molded themselves to hers. Elizabeth discovered she enjoyed kissing Dan. She soon became absorbed in the pleasurable activity.

He could feel her breasts pressing against him and it was all he could do not to reach down and touch them. How many times had he lain in bed thinking about her—how beautiful she looked, how warm and inviting—but he forced himself to allow his hands full play on her back only.

Elizabeth felt as though she were drowning in sensation. His exploring tongue gave her a sense of being possessed and she tightened her hold around his neck. She became aware of his hard body closely molded to hers and the effect their kiss was having on him.

For the first time in her life, Elizabeth enjoyed the knowledge that someone wanted her, even if it was only an elemental need.

Pausing to catch her breath, she buried her face in his sweater for a moment.

Attempting a lightness he was far from feeling, Dan managed to say, "Now why couldn't I have gotten a reception like that? Are you so pleased that I'm leaving that you want to give me a rousing send-off?"

She laughed a little raggedly. "I just wanted you to know I enjoyed your being here."

"Well, believe me, I'm not complaining." He kissed her ear, along her jawline and softly touched her lips with his once more. "I enjoyed being with you, too. You're a very special person."

She opened her eyes and stared at him in surprise. "Oh, no. I'm perfectly ordinary, you know."

"Whatever you are, I'm glad I found you."

"We certainly started our relationship off in a rather unorthodox manner," she pointed out.

His eyes sparkled. "So we did. Whoever said a courtship had a set of rules that had to be followed?"

"Is this a courtship?" She had begun to tremble at his words.

"I'm doing my best, Mrs. Morgan, although admittedly I'm out of practice."

She slid her hands down from his neck and absently stroked the muscled surface of his chest. "It isn't really necessary, you know. I understand how you must feel about everything that has happened."

"I doubt that very much. But eventually you may discover that particular piece of information. However, I'm going to insist that you find out on your own, with little to no assistance from me." He carefully set her back from him. "And if I don't get moving, I'll be driving most of the night."

He leaned over for his coat and slipped it on, the collar framing his neck. She reached up and carefully smoothed the collar down, enjoying the softness of the cashmere.

"Somehow I feel as though we've been playing house this weekend. None of it seems real," she admitted a little shyly.

"There's nothing wrong with that occasionally. We both have needed time to adjust to each other and the situation. Don't worry about it."

"You don't feel as though you're being cheated?"

His wicked grin made her wish she had kept her thoughts to herself. "Honey, you just hold that thought and we'll discuss it over Christmas, okay?" He kissed her lightly on the nose, picked up his bag and opened the door. "Don't forget to call."

Elizabeth stood there long after the door had closed and the sound of Dan's car leaving had died away. Why had she suddenly felt the need to clutch him to her?

Misty meowed softly as she brushed against Elizabeth's ankle. She looked down at her. "You're going to miss him, too, aren't you?"

Misty's blue eyed gaze met hers in an unblinking stare.

Elizabeth turned back and walked into her cozy living room. All at once the room, the entire house, seemed empty. How could one person's presence make such a difference?

For the next few weeks Elizabeth kept herself busy, preparing end of the quarter exams and reading the papers handed in. Being alone was something she had always taken for granted. Even when Philip had been a part of her life, she'd grown used to not hearing from him often. They had both been so busy and she had been caught up with her need to gain recognition at the college.

Philip had been comfortable in the background of her life and she had tended to take him for granted. She couldn't imagine ever taking Dan Morgan for granted.

No wonder Philip had wanted out of the relationship. He had been right. She hadn't offered him very much.

Of course she had nothing much to offer Dan, either. Through a quirk of fate she had become the instrument that would give him a child. She couldn't help but wonder if he ever thought of her as anything more than a person who was going to present him with his link to posterity.

As Christmas grew closer she became more and more nervous about her visit. Why hadn't it occurred to her when he suggested it that if she were to visit him they would be sharing the same room and bed? He could have come up there, but would have only been able to stay four days. She wouldn't need to return to school until after the first of the year.

Elizabeth wanted to spend more time with him. That was the reason she had chosen to meet him in Manhattan. She found him fascinating.

Nothing seemed to bother him. He had come to terms with his life and his role in it. Even the thought of having a child and finding himself married to a stranger hadn't seemed to throw him. She wished she could better understand how he managed to be so accepting of their situation.

Her life had suddenly changed direction during the past six months. All her ideas regarding herself and her goals were shifting rapidly. Dan seemed to be the only constant in her life at the moment. She smiled. If she didn't know better, she'd think she had a schoolgirl crush on the man.

Dan Morgan wearily opened the door to his empty apartment. He'd been pushing himself for the past two weeks, trying to get as much done as possible so that he could spend most of Beth's Manhattan visit with her.

Every night he had to fight the impulse to call and check on her, something he had sworn not to do. He had recognized during his visit upstate that he needed to give her more space. Although she had always sounded pleased to hear from him, he couldn't help but feel that she felt he was pursuing her for some reason.

He *was* pursuing her, but he hoped that he could be subtle enough not to let her become aware of it. Her shocked expression when he'd mentioned courting her had led him to believe she hadn't thought of him in such a guise. So maybe it was better he had backed off.

From now on, he would take his lead from her. Once the baby was born maybe she'd be more receptive to him. Perhaps even learn to trust him.

After a long, relaxing shower Dan crawled into his king-size bed and stretched out with a sigh. She'd be there tomorrow. In his bed.

He smiled, remembering her flannel gown. Not exactly the fantasy garb most men might dream about. He drifted off to sleep, knowing he only had hours to wait.

He doesn't want me to come. That's why he hasn't called since he left in November, Elizabeth decided on the train going south. Of course she could have called him, she reminded herself tartly. But what reason would she have given?

One evening she had tried calling his apartment, but there had been no answer and she refused to try again. She felt better not knowing for sure if he was home.

She'd know by the way he greeted her if he was glad to see her. But, then, he'd always been polite. Did she dare mention how much she had missed his phone calls? Would he think she was making demands on him? He'd already done so much.

Elizabeth was no longer sure what she wanted from him, but she felt such a yearning to see him again. They'd been married a little over seven weeks and he already seemed so much a part of her life. He'd taken over her thoughts, and some of her dreams had made her blush to remember them.

Why hadn't he called her?

He doesn't want me to come.

Her thoughts traveled in circles during the entire train ride from Westfield to Grand Central Station.

The station was crowded when she got there and she had a fleeting thought that he might have forgotten she was coming in that day.

Not that it mattered. She had his address and was certainly capable of finding a cab.

The man in front of her stepped aside, so that she had a better view of the crowd. When she spotted Dan he was shouldering his way through the crowd purposefully, his eyes on her.

Her legs almost collapsed in relief. Of course he was there. He'd said he would be. He pulled her into his arms and hugged her tightly.

"Don't squeeze too hard," she managed to say breathlessly. "He doesn't like to be pushed."

He laughed, a happy, relieved sound that warmed her heart. "So it's a he. When did you discover that?"

She grinned a little sheepishly. "Oh, I didn't find out by any scientific means. He's just been moving around so vigorously I decided referring to him as 'it' seemed to be insulting. He's already got such a personality, I can't think of him as just a being any longer."

He draped his arm around her, protectively guiding her toward the exit. "Can you believe this mob? Everybody is trying to get somewhere else on the Friday before Christmas. I'm sure interplanetary travel isn't half so crowded."

Would he ever let her forget that nonsense?

Dan took Misty's carrying case and pulled Elizabeth close to his side. When they made it outside he looked down at her and said, "You look wonderful." He kissed her on the cheek before helping her into the waiting cab.

"I look fat," she corrected ruefully.

"No way. Your cheeks bloom with health, your eyes sparkle—"

"And I'm gaining too much weight."

"Says who?" he said a little belligerently.

"Me," she responded in a small voice.

He pulled her close in his arms and gave the cabbie an address. "You're just a nice armful." He tilted her chin up and kissed her softly. "I hope you're hungry. I made reservations for dinner a little early so we can get home at a halfway decent hour. We'll swing by my place and I'll let

Misty do some exploring while we're gone. It will give her a chance to get acquainted on her own.''

"Sounds like a good idea." She couldn't get over how great he looked with his hair windblown and his scarf looped around his neck. He radiated health and vitality and she had never been so glad to see anyone before.

"I'm looking forward to playing house again for a week or so," he said in a low voice.

"Me, too. I've missed you."

"That's news to me. Why didn't you call?"

"I didn't want to bother you. Why didn't you call me?"

"I didn't want to bother you."

They looked at each other for a moment, then began to laugh.

He took her gloved hand in his and tucked it into his coat pocket. "What did the doctor say this time?"

"That I'm healthy and the baby is progressing nicely."

"Has he given you a due date?"

"March 15."

Dan wasn't sure how to phrase his next question. The more he had thought about it, the more he wanted her to stay with him and have the baby in Manhattan, but would she want to change doctors?

Otherwise he knew he would gradually go out of his mind, knowing she was alone. What if she slipped and fell, or needed help and couldn't reach anyone? It didn't bear thinking about.

Somehow during the next couple of weeks he'd have to find a way to broach the subject.

When they arrived at his apartment later that evening Elizabeth felt ready to drop she was so relaxed. The strain of wondering what would happen during this visit and wondering if he still wanted her to come had long since disappeared in a haze of contentment.

Dan had kept her entertained all evening with stories about the advertising agency and some of their clients, and what it was like to work with some colossal egos.

However, on the way home he had become silent and she had sleepily rested her head against his shoulder. She refused to think about the next two weeks. Instead she would enjoy each day as it arrived.

Her eyes opened in surprise when he ushered her into the apartment. Christmas decorations gave a festive air to the room.

"How beautiful! When did you do all of this?"

"Last weekend. I've never bothered with decorations before, since I generally spend my Christmases in California. I decided we needed to get into the spirit of things here."

"Did you tell your sister why you didn't come out this year?"

"Naturally. I said my pregnant wife wasn't up to traveling these days."

Elizabeth tried to decide if he was serious. His crooked smile gave no hint of his thoughts.

"So she knows you're married."

"I saw no reason not to tell her."

"Of course not. Uh, what did she think about the pregnancy?"

"She thought it was way overdue."

"Overdue! That's hardly the case."

"About ten years was her estimate."

"Oh."

"So she's really very pleased with me and said I couldn't have given her a better Christmas present, even if I wasn't going to be there in person. She'd just about given up hope of ever being an aunt."

Elizabeth hadn't given the idea of her child's extended family much thought. Of course her baby would have an aunt, and cousins, even if he didn't have grandparents.

Dan came up behind her and began to knead her shoulders.

"Oh, that feels good," she admitted.

"If you'd like, I'll massage your back tonight."

"Oh, you don't need to bother."

"Believe me, it's no bother. I'd enjoy feeling like I could help. I noticed a couple of times this evening you seemed a little uncomfortable."

"Either you're very observant or I haven't developed a good poker face yet. But I swear he's bowling in there and putting a lot of body English on the ball!"

"Go take a shower and I'll get some lotion."

By the time she was out of the shower, Elizabeth had begun to have second thoughts. If he needed lotion, then he needed a bare body, and she wasn't at all sure she could strip down in front of him, husband or no husband.

She needn't have worried. One small light barely lit the room, and when she gingerly crawled onto her side of the bed, he motioned for her to turn her back to him.

"Relax, try to get the two of you comfortable, and I'll do the rest."

He slid the long length of her gown slowly up until her back, hips and legs were exposed and gently began to massage her muscles.

She forgot to be embarrassed, because his hands felt so good on her tired muscles. No one had ever touched her like that before. In fact, rarely had anyone ever touched her, except for an occasional hug. Even Philip had kept his distance.

Elizabeth drifted off to sleep in a pleasurable haze of sensuous satisfaction, the rhythm of his hands lulling her.

Dan had spent many a night thinking about, and later dreaming about, touching Elizabeth. The present situation was both a pleasure and a torment.

He was delighted to discover that she no longer tensed whenever he touched her. But he wondered if it was just as bad to have her drift off to sleep as though his touch didn't disturb her in the least.

Her satiny skin glowed in the soft light, the gentle curve of her hips accentuating the indentation at her waist. The baby was a small ball in front, leaving her looking very unpregnant from her backside.

Dan had to remind himself that she was indeed very pregnant and that it would do him well to remember that.

Eventually he capped the lotion bottle and turned off the light. Her breathing was steady and quiet. He slipped her gown back down and cautiously curled up to her back. She didn't move.

He let out a sigh of contentment as his hand rested on her stomach. The baby gave a sudden kick and he stroked it gently, wanting to murmur that he meant no harm at all; he just wanted to love both of them.

Dan fell asleep with Beth in his arms. Now that she had arrived, he had everything he could possibly want for Christmas.

Chapter Seven

Elizabeth woke up sometime during the night and discovered that once again she had managed to crowd Dan, although he seemed unaware of it at the moment. Somehow she had managed to place her head on his bare chest. Her leg was thrown over both of his.

The position felt very natural to her. She shifted slightly and discovered that his arm held her firmly to his side.

She felt warm and very content and drowsy. If he was uncomfortable, surely he would complain. Until he did, she decided to enjoy being so close to him.

Elizabeth drifted off to sleep again without moving.

Dan shifted restlessly in his sleep, the evocative scent of Beth's perfume haunting him. His dream had her holding him, loving him. He responded to his dream by drawing her even closer, his mouth searching blindly for hers.

The kiss seemed to last forever. They shared a tenderness, a mutual giving, that seemed to answer the questions, solve the mysteries, explain and summarize their relationship. At last he could touch her as he had wanted to for so long.

His hands found her soft breasts and he lightly touched them, aware of their sensitivity, enjoying their fullness.

A sudden thump vibrated between them and Dan's eyes flew open.

The room was dark except for the lighter square of the window behind his draperies. For a moment he was disoriented, until he realized that the dream wasn't a dream. He held Beth in his arms and his hands had found the warmth of her body.

Their baby had objected to the tight embrace they shared.

"Beth?" he whispered.

"Hmmm?" she mumbled.

He smiled, realizing she was still asleep. She certainly responded well in her sleep. Her sleeping position seemed to have become a habit with her, only this time he refused to move away from her. Wasn't this what he wanted, for her to become accustomed to him?

He gently rubbed her rounded stomach. He wanted her right where she was, in his arms. From the looks of it, at least unconsciously, that's where Beth wanted to be, as well.

"Good morning." Elizabeth heard his whisper in her ear before she was fully awake. She started to stretch, only to discover that she was locked closely against his side with no way to escape.

Her eyes flew open.

The room was flooded with sunlight and Elizabeth turned her head slightly on her firm, muscled pillow.

Dan shifted, pushing up on one elbow, so that her head slipped off his shoulder. She glanced up at him and saw a very wicked grin and sparkling eyes.

"You once mentioned that I might want something more from this marriage," he reminded her.

Her heart seemed to be pounding so hard she was certain he could hear it.

She forced herself to continue to meet his gaze. "Do you?"

"What do you think?"

From their entwined position Elizabeth had no doubt how he was affected. The hard, muscled length of his body pressed against her from shoulder to toe.

"I think I could be in trouble," she admitted with the hint of a smile.

"You could say that."

He leaned down and kissed her lightly. "However, I would never want it to be said that I took advantage of my position."

"You're certainly operating from a very strategic location, I have to admit."

Since she couldn't move without his compliance, they both understood what she meant.

"Would I be presuming too much, do you suppose, if I decided you wouldn't mind our relationship becoming a little closer?"

She glanced down. "A *little* closer? I don't think we could get much closer than this."

"Oh, I don't know. It might be fun to explore the possibilities."

Elizabeth felt as though she could scarcely catch her breath. None of her thoughts seemed to be connected. They appeared to fly about her head with no semblance of order.

Dan's hands had not been still while he talked. Her gown had somehow become unbuttoned, leaving her rather unprotected from the waist up. His long, sensitive fingers were taking full advantage of that fact.

The baby gave a sudden lurch, effectively breaking the tension that seemed to be mounting between them.

"Good morning to you, too," he said, patting her stomach.

Elizabeth couldn't face what was happening. She felt so misshapen and unattractive. She didn't want Dan to see her like this and yet she didn't want to tell him to stop, either. What a bewildering array of emotions were sweeping through her.

Dan wondered if Beth knew how expressive her face was. Gently he pulled away from her and sat up, trying to ignore his body's protest. "What would you like to do today?" he asked, trying to overcome his shortness of breath.

She wished she knew! Her body and mind seemed to be having a constant war whenever she was around him.

Elizabeth found her gaze following Dan as he slipped out of bed and stood up. A pair of bikini briefs hugged his taut hips and she watched with fascination the way the muscles of his back rippled when he stretched.

He turned around and caught her watching him. She didn't appear to be repulsed by the sight of him, which gave him hope. He sat down on top of the covers, making sure she was warmly tucked beneath them. "Would you like to check out some of the city Christmas decorations, or would the crowds be too much for you?"

She reached out and stroked his face with her fingertips. "I don't think I'd mind a little sight-seeing. It sounds like fun."

Good, he thought with relief. *If we have to spend much time alone here at the apartment, I won't be responsible for losing my grip on my precarious control.*

Elizabeth had never enjoyed a day with so much whole-hearted abandonment before in her life. Dan teased her about everything, and they laughed and joked like a couple of kids. More than one person smiled as they passed the two of them, their arms wrapped around each other's waist.

Her fears were forgotten; the uncertain future was pushed away, and Elizabeth delighted in the happiness of the present.

More than one feminine eye noticed Dan as they wandered through the stores and eventually stopped for lunch, Elizabeth noted. He never seemed aware of the attention he received.

Refusing to keep her out so that she got overtired, Dan eventually whisked her back to the apartment and insisted she rest because he had tickets for *The Nutcracker Suite* that evening.

Feeling like a small child, Elizabeth obediently stretched out, knowing she was too keyed up to do more than rest, only to fall into a deep, reviving sleep for more than two hours.

Dan had dinner ready when she woke up so that all she had to do was eat and get ready for the evening. Elizabeth had never felt so pampered in her life.

She tried to put her feelings into words that night. Elizabeth was already in bed when Dan came out of the bathroom, once again wearing only a pair of briefs that left very little to the imagination. He crawled in beside her as though used to finding her in his bed, and then he surprised her by pulling her over to him and resting her head on his shoulder.

"Thank you for today," he said, while he ran his fingers through the silky softness of her hair.

"Oh, Dan. I'm the one who owes you...so many things. You've managed to make Christmas a magical time for me. I'll never forget today...never."

He chuckled and she could feel the rumble where her ear pressed against his chest. "You reminded me of a little girl, your eyes were so wide taking in everything."

"I guess I never realized what this time of the year could really mean to people. It's a time of sharing and giving."

"I know. It's a yearly reminder of love and the wondrous things that love brings to people's lives, if they'll accept it."

She snuggled closer to him, smoothing her hand across his chest, enjoying the tactile sensation. "In recent years I've managed to treat the holidays as a vacation from school and tried not to think about how other people spent them."

He lifted her chin and pressed his lips gently against hers. "Now we can start some family traditions of our own, can't we?"

Her heart leaped at his gesture and his words. His suggestion had such a sense of permanency and it touched her deeply.

"That's true. We can," she managed to respond.

They lay there together in contented silence. Elizabeth had almost drifted off to sleep, when Dan spoke again.

"Are you sorry you married me?"

His question surprised her. "Of course not. Why do you ask?"

"Because I didn't give you much choice, as I recall."

"I'll admit the idea took some getting used to. And I'm not at all sure I really feel married. Not with our present living arrangements."

She couldn't have given him a better opening.

"Why don't you stay here, then? They're going to have to replace you this spring, anyway. Then we'd have some time together before the baby gets here."

Elizabeth couldn't think of anything she'd enjoy more. "Are you sure I wouldn't be in the way?"

He laughed, a relieved, relaxed sound that made her smile. "Do you look like you're in the way?" He allowed his hands to rest lightly on her back and side, as though enjoying having her in his arms. "We could find a larger place, if you'd like."

She looked around the darkened room. "I like this place."

"So do I, for now. But the baby will need a room of his own eventually."

Once again Elizabeth heard the intention of permanency in what he was saying. Would it be possible to build a marriage on the unusual basis with which this one had started? At that moment, she felt as though anything were possible if a person could only believe in it.

Dan shifted, turning to her, and Elizabeth could feel the tension in his body. "I want to make love to you so much." His husky voice emphasized his need.

He kissed her. It was a kiss of claiming and possession, of longing and intensity. Nothing else mattered at the moment.

For a second, Elizabeth felt a panicky feeling of inadequacy. She knew so little about expressing herself. She wanted Dan to know how much he meant to her and that she was willing to deepen the relationship. Could she show him?

He slipped her gown off carefully, then began to explore her softness with a gentleness that told her more than anything he could have said in words that he would never rush her or take advantage of their relationship.

Dan felt her response to him and it was as though a weight had been lifted from him. As private a person as Beth was, he knew she wouldn't be willing to share herself without trusting him.

She appeared to be with him during each successive step toward intimacy. He refused to rush her. Instead he luxuriated in her touch as she hesitantly imitated him as he explored her.

Then he felt her stiffen and he paused. His mouth had found her breast and he immediately pulled back, afraid he'd hurt her.

"I'm sorry. I didn't mean to hurt you."

"You didn't. I mean—I'm not sure what it is, but—"

Her voice sounded frightened and he could feel an inner alarm going off. It wasn't a fear of lovemaking that caused the panicky tone in her voice.

"What is it, Beth?"

"I think it's the baby," she whispered.

"What about the baby?"

"I had a pain in my abdomen. A sharp pain."

Dan tried not to panic. It wasn't time for the baby. It was much too soon.

He sat up and turned on the light. Elizabeth looked pale, her eyes wide in her face. He tried to sound calm. "Why don't I take you over to the hospital emergency and let them check you, all right?"

"It's probably nothing. They'll think we're being silly."

"I don't particularly care what they think. I'd be pleased to discover it's nothing, believe me. But I don't want you getting upset."

While he talked Dan began to throw on his clothes. Then he reached into his closet and found one of her maternity dresses. He laid it on the bed. "Do you feel up to getting dressed?"

Gingerly she crawled out of bed and reached for her clothes.

Dan called the lobby of his building and asked them to have a cab waiting, then he helped her finish dressing. He hoped it was nothing. *Please let it be a gas pain or too much excitement. Don't let anything be wrong with the baby.*

The hospital staff immediately took over in a quiet, efficient manner as soon as Dan and Elizabeth arrived. The doctor in charge had her change into a gown for an examination, while Dan waited out in the hallway.

"The waiting room is just down the corridor, sir," one of the nurses pointed out.

"No. I want to be here, in case she calls for me."

The nurse smiled. "I'm sure she's going to be all right."

"Does that come in the form of a written guarantee?"

She shook her head. "Is this your first baby?"

"Yes."

"Don't worry. These unexplained pains come without any rhyme or reason. They don't necessarily mean anything."

When the doctor came out of the examining room Dan was still waiting in the hall. The doctor nodded and said, "The baby seems to be all right, Mr. Morgan. However, I have told Mrs. Morgan that she should make plans to spend as much time off of her feet as possible between now and her delivery date."

"What's wrong?"

"Just a precaution. There's no reason to alarm either of you. I'm just saying that sensible precautions will ensure that nothing goes wrong."

Dan thought about how close they had come to making love and it scared him. They didn't dare take any risks. "May I take her home now?"

"I don't see why not. She'd much prefer to spend Christmas at home, I'm sure."

By the time they got back to the apartment, Elizabeth was laughing. "Dan, you don't have to treat me as though I'm going to break, you know. The doctor said I probably did too much today. I'm not used to so much activity."

"Beth, will you call the school and explain to them that you're going to stay here with me? There's no way I'm going to let you out of my sight until that baby arrives safely."

"Who are you going to hire to run the agency while you sit and watch me?"

"Now you're making fun of me."

"Not at all. If you like, I'll teach you to crochet. We can sit here together and make baby clothes and watch daytime television."

She began to laugh even harder at the look on his face. "Yes, I'll call the school, Dan. I have already decided I'd like to stay before everything started to happen."

When they returned to bed, Dan deliberately shifted to his own side. He was not going to take any chances. "Good night, Beth."

Elizabeth turned on her side, trying to find a comfortable position. "Good night, Dan. I'll try not to keep you awake."

"No problem. If you have any more pains, tell me."

"Okay."

"Beth?"

"Hmmm?"

"Take care of yourself, please."

"I have been."

"I know. I just don't want anything to happen to you or the baby."

The warm tenderness in his voice brought tears to her eyes.

"Nothing will happen. But since I'm supposed to take it easy, and tomorrow is Christmas Eve, maybe we should cancel our plans to go out."

"Absolutely. It will be nice to have a quiet evening at home." *If I can remember to keep my hands off of you,* he thought with a pang.

Elizabeth lay awake long after Dan's even breathing convinced her he was asleep. They had so nearly made love tonight and she had wanted it to happen. Perhaps it was just as well something had prevented it.

While lying in the examining room, waiting for the doctor, Elizabeth had come face to face with the fact that she was in love with Dan. The thought scared her. She didn't want to love him. She was afraid to become that attached to anyone, but love hadn't given her a choice.

She would have to come to terms with how to handle her feelings and wait to see how he felt for her. Just because he wanted to make love with her didn't mean he loved her. She understood that. Wouldn't it be wonderful, though, if he could fall in love with her, too? She drifted off to sleep trying to imagine what their life together could be.

Chapter Eight

Within a few weeks, Elizabeth felt comfortable with her new routine. The college had understood her concern for her pregnancy and arranged for her to have the necessary time off.

For the first time in her life, Elizabeth discovered that she could enjoy playing the role of housewife, at least on a temporary basis.

She had breakfast prepared each morning by the time Dan had showered and dressed. At first he protested, insisting she needed her rest and that he was used to preparing his own meals. Elizabeth explained that she had nothing else to do but rest after he left, and she enjoyed spending those few minutes each morning with him. The warm look he gave her made her pulse race and he agreeably sat down and ate the meal she prepared that first morning, and, after that, never said another word about her getting up when he did.

After he left each day, she straightened the apartment. He absolutely refused to let her do the heavy cleaning after explaining she had no business stooping and bending when she was alone and couldn't get help if she needed it.

So Elizabeth stopped feeling guilty about spending so much time reading and making clothes for the baby.

She had been in Manhattan almost three weeks when she called Janine at work.

"Well, hello, stranger," Janine said after Elizabeth identified herself. "You're a hard person to catch at home. I've tried calling you several times, but could never get an answer."

Elizabeth had told Janine the day of her wedding that she would continue to teach, so it was natural that Janine had assumed she was still in Westfield. There was so much to explain to her friend.

"Actually, that's why I called. I'm here in Manhattan and wondered if you would like to meet me for lunch."

"Let me check my calendar real quick here," Janine replied. Elizabeth could hear pages flipping. "I just got back to town yesterday. You should see my desk! Oh, good, I don't have anything down until two-thirty. Why don't we meet at the little place across from my office at one? It will be great to see you again!"

Elizabeth dressed with special care. There was no way to hide her condition, but she wanted to look as attractive as possible.

She made certain that she arrived first and found a table so that she could watch for Janine. When she came sailing through the door a few minutes later, Elizabeth waved, then watched her friend weave her way through the crowded restaurant.

"God, you look ravishing," were Janine's first words when she sank into the chair across the table from Elizabeth. "Marriage obviously agrees with you."

Elizabeth laughed. "I believe you're right. I've never felt better in my life."

Janine busied herself removing her gloves and coat, then picked up the menu. "I wonder what the special is today? I'm starved."

As usual Janine looked slender and elegant, every inch the successful businesswoman. Elizabeth hadn't realized how much she had missed talking with her.

Janine glanced up. "What are you planning to have? You never have to worry about your weight...." Her words faded away as she took a closer look at the dress Elizabeth wore. "Beth?" Her eyes widened. "Aren't you wearing—I mean, isn't that a— Are you—?"

At that moment the waitress arrived to take their order. The interruption gave Elizabeth some time in which to respond. She had never seen her former roommate at a loss for words and was more amused than discomfited now that the time to tell her had come. "The word is pregnant, Janine," she said, once the waitress departed. "And yes, I am going to have a baby," she added gently, enjoying the shocked expression on her friend's face.

"But that's awful! I mean, you haven't been married long. And your job? What are you doing about your job? And Dan. How does he feel about it? Oh, Beth—" she reached over and took her friend's hand and clasped it between hers "—I'm so sorry," she murmured in a bereaved tone.

Elizabeth burst out laughing. She couldn't help it. Janine was so obviously stricken. To Janine and her life-style, a pregnancy would no doubt represent catastrophe. Elizabeth could understand and empathize with her reaction, but she also had to let Janine know her own feelings about the matter.

"I'm delighted with my pregnancy," Elizabeth replied. "Dan seems to be taking it in stride. I'm living here in Manhattan now, as a matter of fact. He didn't like the idea of my living alone in Westfield."

Janine studied her friend for a moment. "Well, I must admit you're certainly glowing. I've never seen you more beautiful."

Elizabeth flushed slightly. "Thank you."

"So when is this blessed event to take place?"

Elizabeth had hoped she wouldn't be asked a direct question. She also knew she would not lie. There was no point. Sooner or later Janine would know the truth.

"Mid-March."

"March! But Beth—"

Janine's words were cut off so quickly it seemed as though an invisible hand had clamped across her mouth. She sat there for a moment, and from her expression Elizabeth could tell that Janine was rapidly putting all the pieces together. She had always known that Janine had a quick mind. She was once again reminded of that fact.

"How did Dan know?" were her first words.

"What do you mean?"

"How did he know to search for you? When I talked to him the first time he said you hadn't told him your name, where you lived or what you did for a living."

"That's true."

"Then how did he know you were pregnant?"

"He didn't."

The waitress appeared with their meals, placing the dishes silently in front of the two women. Janine studied Elizabeth in silence for a moment, then sighed. She looked tired and somehow defeated.

"What's wrong?" Elizabeth asked, after sampling a bite of food.

"Nothing, really. It's just that every time I think I've broken through the barriers and that we've become close friends, I find another barrier I never knew existed."

"Janine, you're the closest friend I've got. You know me better than anyone."

"That's what disheartens me so. You never mentioned a thing to me about that night, what happened or what followed later, when you discovered you were pregnant. That must have been a very traumatic time for you, when you could have used some support. That's what friends are for, honey. And you never said a word."

"I didn't mean to hurt your feelings."

"I know you didn't. You're just used to facing the world alone. You've never depended on anyone else in you life."

"That's because there was never anyone to depend on."

"Maybe not, when you were a child. But once you were older, I was there, then Philip and now—"

"And now there's Dan," Elizabeth finished for her.

"Yes," Janine said thoughtfully. "There's Dan. He didn't strike me as the type to come on so strong the first time you met. He struck me as the type my mother used to describe as a perfect gentleman."

Elizabeth could feel her face burning. "He is. And he was." She forced herself to meet her friend's amused gaze. "Truly, he was."

"Well, honey, I don't think a true gentleman gets a girl pregnant on their first date."

"Janine!" Elizabeth glanced around them, desperately hoping that none of the other people in the busy restaurant had heard her.

"Sorry. I didn't mean to shock you," Janine teased. "All I'm saying is that I'm surprised at both of you."

"So was I. That's why I didn't tell you the next day. I was too embarrassed."

Janine laughed. "Oh, Beth, I adore you—you're so refreshing. Embarrassed, of all things."

"Well, how did you think I would feel about it? All the time I was with Philip and he never ... We didn't— Then I meet Dan and—" She waved her hand helplessly.

"Did Dan know you were a virgin?"

Elizabeth glanced around hurriedly, then leaned across the table. "Would you mind lowering your voice? There's no reason to make an announcement to everyone in the room!"

Janine's eyes sparkled at the reprimand. In a whisper she said, "Well, did he?"

"We never discussed it. Neither one of us intended for it to go that far. It just happened. I really can't explain it."

"Is that why you married him?"

"I thought so. Now, I'm not so sure."

"What do you mean?"

"He made a very convincing argument that he deserved to help raise his child and marriage made a logical step toward being able to do that, but— Oh, I don't know. I can't see myself marrying anyone I didn't care for. I look back even now and I'm amazed at what happened the night we met. It seemed so unreal—like a fantasy or something enchanted."

"Some enchanted evening, huh? I believe it's already been done in song," Janine quipped.

"Well, whatever it was, Dan has a powerful effect on me. I agreed to marry him, and until the baby is born, I agreed to quit work and live here with him."

"Sounds like love to me," Janine said with a grin.

"I know," Elizabeth replied softly.

"It couldn't happen to a nicer person, you know. You deserve a little happiness and I'm pleased as punch for you."

Elizabeth grinned. "So am I. Sometimes I can't believe it's me. We seem to be so relaxed with each other, and I enjoy his wry sense of humor. He doesn't seem to get uptight about anything."

"With the luscious Beth in bed with him every night, I'm sure he manages to work out all of his tensions."

Elizabeth seemed to find the contents of her glass all engrossing. She didn't raise her eyes when she replied. "Actually, we haven't made love since that first night." When Janine didn't say anything Elizabeth finally glanced up. Her friend's astonished expression caused her to chuckle.

"I've never heard a stranger tale in my life," Janine finally managed to say.

"That was the arrangement when we first decided to marry, you see, and...well..."

"And he's never made any overtures toward you that he might want the arrangement changed?"

Elizabeth wished she could discuss the situation without blushing. After all, this was Janine, who had shared with Elizabeth the details of every romance she'd ever had. So why should Elizabeth be so shy with her now?

"Well, Dan is a very affectionate person, so he holds me and kisses me frequently."

"Good for Dan," Janine commented dryly. "For a moment there you really had me worried. Does Dan seem to mind that there's so little to your, uh, sex life?"

"Not that I can tell, but what do I know about men? He's very patient with me, loving and kind—"

"Trustworthy and loyal. Dear Lord, Beth, you make him sound like a Boy Scout."

Elizabeth grinned. "He probably was at one time, now that you mention it."

"No doubt." Janine leaned back in her chair. "Well, whatever he's doing seems to be working. You're obviously happy."

Elizabeth nodded. "I am."

"So what's going to happen when the baby arrives? Will you go back to teaching? Live here in Manhattan? What?"

"I intend to resume teaching this fall. I'm not sure how that will work out as far as Dan is concerned. He says to take one step at a time, that we will work something out. Who knows? He may prefer a long-distance relationship once the reality of a demanding baby hits him."

"Somehow I doubt that," Janine said slowly. "Something tells me that Dan Morgan understands his priorities and I have a strong hunch you and that baby are at the top of his list."

Elizabeth's expression grew dreamy. "I hope so."

Dan came home early that afternoon and found Elizabeth asleep. For a moment his heart seemed to stop. Was she not feeling well? He walked over to the bed and leaned over.

Elizabeth opened her eyes and saw him. Her spontaneous smile encouraged him greatly. Glancing at the clock, she sat up and put her arms around his neck. "You're home early," she said, kissing him.

He sat down beside her and pulled her into his lap, his mouth never leaving hers. When they finally paused for breath, both of them were a little shaken.

"Maybe I'd better come home early more often, if I'm going to get that sort of welcome."

"I always kiss you hello."

"I know. But there's something about you all warm and cuddly from sleep that I find particularly arousing." He looked at her closely. "Are you feeling all right?"

"Oh, I'm fine. I just ate too much for lunch and it made me sleepy, so I came home and decided to take a nap."

"Did you go shopping?"

"Oh, no. I met Janine for lunch. It's the first time I've seen her since we got married."

Dan looked at her with a speculative gleam in his eye. "No doubt she noticed your new shape."

"Indeed she did."

"And?"

"And what?"

"Aren't you going to tell me her reaction?"

"Oh, about what you'd expect. Surprised, pleased for me."

She sounded very relaxed and casual, and Dan decided that she had come a long way in her attitude in the weeks since they married. He still held her to him, enjoying the closeness, pleased to see how naturally she accepted his embrace. His campaign was definitely showing progress.

He helped her with dinner, a simple meal that didn't take long to prepare. Dan told her about his day while they ate, making the story amusing so he could enjoy watching her whenever she laughed.

Having her in his life had changed his perspective about everything—his business, his goals and his enjoyment of life. He found himself eager to come home, to be with Beth, to watch her laugh, see her smile, and to hold her close to him in the still, quiet darkness of the night.

"Did Janine mention Ryan today?" he asked.

"No. Most of our conversation was about the baby."

"I wonder if they're seeing each other?" he mused.

"When would they have time, with Janine on the West Coast so much? And didn't someone mention that Ryan travels a great deal as well?"

"Yes, he does. Too bad they don't coordinate their schedules so they might end up in the same city at the same time occasionally."

They smiled at each other. "We sound like a typical pair of matchmakers, don't we?" Elizabeth commented.

Dan stood up and stretched. "That we do. Neither one of them would appreciate our efforts, if they knew." He rubbed his neck wearily.

"Does your neck hurt?"

"It's just a little stiff."

"Why don't you go stand under a hot shower and see if that helps? If not, I'll massage it for you." She stood up and started to clean off the table.

"You don't have to do that."

She smiled at him. "I know. But I also know how good a massage feels."

Later, when he came out of the shower he found her waiting for him. She was in her voluminous nightgown that made her look about ten years old.

She crawled into bed and patted the place next to her. He didn't need to be coaxed. After pouring a small amount of lotion on her hands, she briskly rubbed them together to warm the liquid. Then she began to apply it to his neck and shoulders in long, smooth strokes.

Dan groaned his appreciation.

Elizabeth had never been given the opportunity to touch him so freely. Although she had never given him a massage before, she had learned a little of the technique from the ones he gave to her.

As she kneaded the muscles in his neck, she felt him relax. Elizabeth smiled to herself. She knew how good that must feel. She was enjoying it, as well. The muscled plane of his shoulders sloped into the slim line of his spine. Her hands followed the contours of his body, from his broad shoulders down to his narrow waist.

Elizabeth had never realized how much enjoyment could be derived from touching someone. Was that why Dan seemed to find so many reasons to touch her?

Living with Dan was quite an education for her. She wondered how he felt about their arrangement. He never said and she didn't want to make an issue of it.

She noticed that he was asleep. Reaching over she turned off the light and settled down on the pillow next to him. He turned over, pulling her into the curl of his body and placed his hand over the baby. The baby thumped an acknowledgment.

"Good night, you two," he murmured into her ear.

"Good night," she whispered, feeling at peace in the circle of his arms.

Chapter Nine

By mid-February Elizabeth felt as though she had spent her entire life pregnant and ugly. Not being able to teach had begun to make the days drag by. She was tired of reading and bored with sewing. Trying to be cheerful and good company to Dan when he was home had brought out a hitherto unsuspected acting ability that had surprised her.

She had vowed to herself that Dan would not be made to suffer for what, after all, was her problem. For some reason her body hadn't adapted well to the pregnancy. The doctor she'd found in Manhattan had been optimistic that she could carry the baby full term with plenty of rest and care. She was basically healthy. A little narrow in the pelvic area, perhaps, but he had assured her that complications could be kept to a minimum with her cooperation.

She cooperated with a grim determination. Part of her determination was to convince Dan that everything was all right in her little world.

Whenever he was home she never had to pretend. The more she was around him the more she grew to love him.

If only she could have the baby and return to being slender and supple once again. Elizabeth wanted to show him how she felt toward him and how much she appreciated him, but the opportunity never seemed to present itself.

And for the past several weeks he had begun to treat her like a favorite elderly aunt, although he seemed to enjoy her company, keeping her entertained with humorous anecdotes about the business world. In addition, he suggested short outings to keep her from going completely out of her mind.

But he was notably unloverlike.

Elizabeth discovered that she missed his affectionate hugs and kisses. She missed his touch. As she had grown heavier he had gotten into a routine of massaging her back each evening before she went to sleep, but his touch was impersonal.

What could she expect? He was probably appalled at her size and shape. And no wonder. He couldn't be held responsible for not loving her, she could understand that. Elizabeth's daytime fantasies seemed to center around the time when she would look attractive enough to make him aware of her as a woman.

At times she was convinced that would never happen. She would be the only woman in history to spend the rest of her allotted years pregnant.

Dan glanced at his desk calendar. Today was February 20. The baby was due in less than one month. He ran his hand through his hair, creating a ruffled effect, and sighed.

Another month. He reminded himself that he had successfully completed two months during which he'd been with Beth every day—and night—and had managed to keep his hands off of her. For some reason he had thought it would become easier with practice. That certainly hadn't been the case.

She became more delectable with time. He had never seen a pregnant woman move so gracefully—even lightly—before. And her skin glowed with a translucence as though a light were turned on inside her.

He had also noticed a definite softening and tenderness in her eyes whenever she looked at him—which had almost been his undoing on more than one occasion. There were times when he had a definite feeling that she was his just for the taking. Except he couldn't take her, not until after the baby arrived safely.

The back rubs were a nightly form of torture he'd managed to devise for himself during the past several weeks. Never before had he realized the masochistic tendencies in him that must have lain dormant for years. He had actually been the one to suggest them.

They seemed to help her and that was the important thing. And he had gotten used to staying awake most of the night, trying not to think how soft and warm she felt.

At one point during the dark hours he decided that this was his punishment for his behavior the night they met. Because he indulged himself he was now forced to live with her, sleep with her and not make love to her again.

He felt the punishment overly harsh. Then it occurred to him that the worst punishment would have been not to have found her at all, but to have spent his life looking for her.

He'd paused in his furious thoughts and listened to her soft breathing nearby, and smiled. No. It was easier to wait for her and be beside her during the wait.

Cold showers had become a way of life for him.

The phone rang, effectively erasing his frustrated thought. "Hello?"

"Hi, Dan. You probably don't remember me, but we met last year when you were in California. My name is Selena Stanford."

Not remember Selena Stanford? She must be kidding.

"Of course I remember you, Selena. How is Adam?"

"Couldn't be better. Would there be a chance that we could see you sometime this week? We're flying into New York tomorrow and we're hoping to discuss an advertising campaign several of us here on the West Coast would like to launch. Are you interested?''

"I never turn down an offer like that. How long are you going to be here?''

"Until the weekend. We're not bringing the children, and I don't like to be away from them too long.''

"Why don't you plan to have dinner with me tomorrow evening and we can chat and go from there? Besides, I'm eager to introduce you to my wife.''

"Your wife! Congratulations, Dan. I hadn't heard you had gotten married. I think dinner sounds fine. I'll call you as soon as we get to the hotel, if that's all right.''

"Sounds good to me. See you tomorrow. Oh, and Selena?''

"Yes?''

"Thanks for thinking of me.''

"Who are you kidding? When it comes to advertising, yours is the first name on the list. Bye for now.''

Dan hung up the receiver with a smile. Selena Stanford. A big name in show business. He wondered what sort of advertising she had in mind. She had her own agent, so it couldn't be personal. Shrugging, he decided to wait and see.

If nothing else, living with Beth had certainly taught him patience.

"Are you sure you wouldn't prefer a larger apartment?'' Dan asked Elizabeth that night over dinner. "You must feel very cooped up here. It was never meant for more than one person and I knew I wouldn't be spending much time here, anyway.''

"Positive. As much as I enjoy Manhattan, I don't want to raise the baby here. The apartment is fine for your needs.''

"You don't intend to stay here once the baby arrives, I take it,'' he said in a careful tone, trying not to sound as though the thought of her leaving panicked him.

She looked at him in surprise. "How can I? It's a little far to commute from here to college.''

"And you intend to teach after the baby comes," he commented, making a statement more than asking a question.

"Not immediately afterward of course, but, yes, by next fall I expect to have found a housekeeper."

"And what about us?"

She hadn't heard that cold tone since he'd first discovered she was pregnant and hadn't intended to tell him. "Does having an 'us,' as you put it, preclude my continuing with my career?"

The candlelight that Beth had added to the table hadn't helped Dan to stay objective about his wife's beauty. The soft glow made her eyes sparkle, and when she looked at him with that level gaze he had an intense desire to grab her and love her until she admitted she didn't want to leave him.

He tamped down those prehistoric man tendencies and tried to be reasonable.

"Of course not. I don't mind commuting. We might look for a home somewhere between here and Westfield, so that getting to and from work wouldn't be too difficult for either one of us."

She smiled at him, that magical smile that seemed to reach deep down inside of him and tug. "You must have given the matter some thought."

He took a sip of his wine and nodded. "I want to give this relationship every possible chance to work. At the very least we need to live together. It's important to me to have daily contact with the baby." *And you,* he added silently.

The baby. Don't forget the purpose of the relationship, Elizabeth reminded herself.

"We'll have time to look before school starts," she said agreeably, and Dan felt like cheering. She hadn't said no. He felt like jotting down the date and marking another victory in his campaign to build a permanent—and loving—relationship with the beautiful woman seated across from him.

After that, Dan kept the conversation on lighter subjects and the rest of the evening passed quietly.

"What would I do without you?" Elizabeth murmured a few hours later while Dan massaged her back and shoulders. "You've been so good to me."

"That works both ways, you know. You've been very good to me."

She twisted her head slightly so she could see him. "How is that?"

"You've given me something to look forward to in my life, a reason to be putting in the long hours I do. I look forward to coming home to you each evening." His hand slowly rubbed across her lower back. He was glad she was unaware of his pulse rate at the moment. "You're doing a great job of hiding how restrictive you find the pregnancy, and I know how hard that has been for you to accept."

"You weren't supposed to notice."

"Oh, I notice lots of things."

"Even that sounds ominous."

"Are you aware of how little you complain?"

"Misty would argue with you on that point."

"Therefore I have cooked up a little reward for you."

She rolled onto her back so that she could see him. His bland expression gave nothing away. "Oh, really? What's that?"

"I checked with your doctor and he said that if you spent most of tomorrow off your feet I had his permission to take you to dinner tomorrow night. So we have reservations at Maxwell's Plum."

"Oh, Dan, that sounds delightful." She leaned up on one elbow and slid her hand around his neck. "Thank you," she murmured, pulling him toward her until their lips met.

She was breaking Dan's unwritten rule of physical contact, but how could he resist such a warm and loving thanks?

When she drew back a few moments later, they were both a little breathless.

"We'll also have someone with us."

"Ryan and Janine?"

"No. I tried to reach them, but they're both out of town. But there's someone special I want you to meet. She'll be in town for the next few days and agreed to have dinner with us tomorrow night.''

"She?" Elizabeth felt a definite sinking sensation settle over her.

"I've only met her once before, when I was out on the West Coast, but I was very impressed with her. She's never let her success in two different careers stop her from being a very warm and caring person. I know you're going to love her."

With a buildup like that, how can any self-respecting wife do anything but hate the woman on sight, Elizabeth decided wryly. When was the last time she'd heard that tone of warm affection in Dan's voice? *Not since you became pregnant.*

"Who is she?"

"Selena Stanford."

"The movie star? The writer? Oh, Dan, I can't possibly meet her looking like this." She saw the expression of startled surprise on his face and realized how that had sounded. "I mean, I look so fat and awkward and—"

"Selena will certainly understand what you're going through. She has twins, from what I understand."

Elizabeth remembered Selena from a television series she'd co-starred in a few years back. She'd been on a very successful show, then she disappeared for a while. Last spring she was nominated for an Academy Award for a screenplay she'd written. All that talent and looks, too. Elizabeth groaned.

Ordinarily she would be delighted to meet her. But not now. "I can't, Dan. Really."

"I'm having one of the department stores send you over a selection of dresses to choose from so you'll have something different to wear. I thought you'd enjoy getting out, and your doctor felt it might be good for you."

She could hear the tone of concern in his voice and pulled herself up sharply. What was she doing? He wanted to do something for her and here she was acting like a spoiled child. It could have been worse, she supposed. What if he'd wanted her to meet Queen Elizabeth? *Try to keep things in perspective,* she silently reminded herself.

"Of course I'll go, Dan. I'm just being silly. Blame it on the pregnancy. What time should I be ready?"

He was just as concerned over the sudden switch. Now she was being bright and cheerful. Too bright and cheerful. He could see the strain around her eyes and he wished he knew what he could do to help her.

"We should leave here by seven. We'll be meeting them there."

"Them?"

"Selena and Adam, her husband."

"Oh." She gave him a serene smile. "That sounds like fun." With a determined tilt to her chin, she added for good measure, "I can hardly wait."

Dan's first sight of Beth the next evening took his breath away. Her dress was a deep blue that emphasized eyes that didn't need anything to make them memorable. The style of the dress drew attention to her creamy shoulders and drew his eyes to her cleavage, which the pregnancy had enhanced more than his heart would be able to stand, he was certain.

She'd done something exotic with her hair, pulling it up and away from her face, leaving the clean, patrician features glowing beneath expert touches of color.

"You look like a princess," he said, as though unaware he had spoken aloud.

She gave him a modified curtsy. "Thank you, kind sir."

He couldn't take his eyes off of her. She began to smile, and he realized he was staring. "You're like no other woman I've ever known."

Her smile faltered somewhat at the intensity evident in his voice. He shook his head slightly, as though coming out of a daze. "Let me get my shower. I should be ready in twenty minutes or so."

"There's no rush. I just thought I'd be out of your way when you got home."

Out of his way. That was a laugh. He walked into the bathroom and smelled her scent, felt the moist heat that had been generated by her shower and knew that tonight was going to be a subtle form of torture.

Elizabeth had seen Dan in his business clothes and dressed casually, but she had never seen him looking so striking before. The black suit he wore brought out the blond highlights of his hair and made his eyes gleam with a silver glow. He looked like someone who had stepped out of an advertisement for Caribbean Sea cruises—sensually magnetic.

"Wow!" was her only form of expression to his presence when he walked back into the room.

"Wow?" he questioned. "From an English professor?"

"Literature," she corrected.

"Close enough."

"You're right. Give me a while and I'll try to write an ode to how you look tonight."

He laughed. "I can hardly wait. Are you ready?"

Was she ready to share him with some glamorous and stunning movie star? He must be out of his mind.

"Of course." Her acting abilities continued to astound her.

Smiling, they left the apartment and hailed a cab. Upon arrival at the restaurant they were immediately ushered to their table. Dan ordered them each a glass of wine to enjoy while they waited.

"I've never been here before," Elizabeth commented, taking in the decor and the number of people there.

"As you can tell, it's a popular place. And the food is magnificent." He idly noted that the man two tables over couldn't seem to keep his eyes off of Beth's neckline and he had a strong urge to discuss the matter with him. Selena couldn't have made a more timely arrival, he decided, when he spotted her at the door.

He stood and waited for them to reach the table. "Good to see you again, Selena," he said with a smile. He offered his hand to Adam. "You, too, Adam." The tall man smiled as he took the chair next to his blond and beautiful wife.

"This is my wife, Beth . . . Selena and Adam Conroy," Dan said, finishing the introductions, and sat down.

"I was delighted to hear you had married, Dan," Selena said with a mischievous grin. She turned to Elizabeth. "I certainly admire your taste."

"Behave yourself," Adam said to his wife. "She may not understand your sense of humor."

Selena's eyes danced. "I'm sure she will. Just as she knows that wasn't a joke. I'm very sincere," she added with a wink.

Elizabeth couldn't help but like the irrepressible Selena, who managed during the course of dinner to draw her out, little by little. Before Elizabeth could quite decide how it had happened, she and Selena were chatting as though old friends—about husbands, babies and being a celebrity.

"There are times that being a celebrity has its compensations," Selena admitted to the other three as they drank their coffee after dinner. "And that's when I want to get an important message to people. At least they stop and listen, and that's the first step." She set down her cup and looked at Dan. "That's where you come in, Dan. I need your help to know how to get their attention and I knew you'd have some suggestions."

"What's your message?"

"I want to get people involved in the hunger project."

"We've certainly become more aware of the world hunger in the past few years," Dan admitted.

"We need to educate the people to face the fact that each of us is responsible for the situation and that none of us can turn our back."

"But it's always been there, Selena," Dan pointed out.

"I know. But the time to change their thinking is now, Dan. We need to stop world hunger. It's an idea whose time has come. As soon as a person becomes aware that he makes a difference, whole avenues open up to allow changes— necessary, miraculous changes. There are no limitations to what people can do when they realize their own potential."

"And that's what you want to point out?"

"Yes, in a way that will grab their interest, cause them to find out more about what is being done and how they can help."

"I'd enjoy working with you on some ideas, Selena. I cleared tomorrow's calendar so that we could spend some time together. You can fill me in."

She laughed. "Adam's the one who has all the facts and figures. I knew that photographic mind of his would be invaluable." She glanced at Elizabeth. "In the meantime, if you will excuse me, Beth and I will visit the ladies' room."

As soon as they reached the lounge Selena explained. "I can remember those last few weeks of pregnancy when you seemed to spend more time in the bathroom than anywhere else. Thought you might enjoy a visit."

Elizabeth laughed. "I appreciate your thoughtfulness." When she returned to where Selena was combing her hair, she asked, "How old are your children?"

"Almost four. Adam is already dropping little hints that he thinks we should have more."

"How do you feel about that?"

"It's not a bad idea at all." She grinned. "I've never found any of Adam's suggestions unreasonable." Her reflection in the mirror doubled the softly dreaming expression she wore. Her gaze met Elizabeth's. "How about you? Do you want more children?"

Elizabeth wasn't sure what to say. "We, uh, we've never discussed it. This pregnancy wasn't exactly planned."

"Very few of them are, you know. But Dan is so obviously proud he's going to be a father. He's adorable . . . and very much in love."

"Why do you say that?"

"Oh, no reason, other than the fact that he can't keep his eyes off you and he's so proud of you. He could hardly wait for us to meet you. I'd say the man is really a goner." She tilted her head slightly, meeting Elizabeth's gaze in the mirror. "You mean you didn't know?" she asked with amused disbelief.

"He's never said," Elizabeth admitted with a slight shrug. "That's the problem with unplanned pregnancies, some-times—"

"Oho. So for some reason you've decided that Dan did the gentlemanly thing and offered himself to save your honor?"

"Something like that," Elizabeth said, her face flushed.

"Oh, honey, are you ever reading Dan wrong. He's not some naive farm boy, you know. I'm sure he would have worked out some alternative solution if he hadn't wanted to marry you. He's too straightforward to waste time with game playing. I haven't known him long, maybe a year, but I found out some fundamental things about the guy, and you'll never convince me he married you for any other reason than that he loves you."

Hearing it put into words made Elizabeth realize how much she hoped Selena was right. Perhaps Dan wasn't try-ing to make the best out of an awkward situation.

"I don't know much about men," Elizabeth admitted, hoping Selena understood what she meant.

She must have. "You only need to understand one man—the one you love. And sometimes that takes all kinds of pa-tience and giving him enough space so he doesn't feel hemmed in. Adam and I didn't exactly have the most or-thodox of courtships ourselves. Fortunately I didn't get pregnant before he had come to terms with our relation-ship, so I wasn't faced with decisions regarding a family at that point, but I do understand what you're going through." She opened the door and waited for Elizabeth to join her. "Believe me, it will be worth the wait. Sooner or later Dan will admit to you how he feels. You just watch."

The women were laughing when they returned to the ta-ble and Dan was relieved to see they were enjoying each other's company. They made a study in contrasts. Selena was tall and blond; Beth was diminutive and a brunette. But they were both stunning, and several appreciative glances had followed their sojourn back to the table.

He reached for Beth's hand once she was seated and stroked it. "Are you feeling tired?" he asked in a quiet voice.

"Not really."

Selena spoke up. "If you'd like some advice, I'd suggest you call it an evening. Believe it or not, being pregnant takes more stamina than most people realize."

Dan agreed quickly and before she knew it, Elizabeth had been bundled up and whisked home. But not before Selena had hugged her and insisted on being notified as soon as the baby arrived.

Later, as Dan went through the exquisitely painful yet addictive back rub, Elizabeth drowsily commented on the evening. "I was really surprised to find Selena Stanford so friendly."

"I told you she was really special."

"And I agree. Of course, knowing that she thinks you walk on water probably influences your opinion of her somewhat."

"You mean because she admires your taste?" he asked with a grin.

"I wonder what she'd think if she knew what a terrific back rub you give?" she asked in a muffled voice, her head buried in her arms.

"Promote me for the presidency?"

"Without a doubt."

Dan thought she was almost asleep and he knew he was in for another restless night when she finally said, "I admire my taste, too."

His hands paused in their movement. "Do you?" he whispered.

She nodded, refusing to look at him.

He pulled the covers up to her shoulders and patted them. "That's a start, anyway."

Chapter Ten

March 3 seemed to be a harbinger of spring. Blue skies and temperate breezes hinted at the warmer weather coming.

Elizabeth woke up with all kinds of energy. She busied herself with the apartment, which took about half an hour because she kept it spotless. Afterward she felt too restless to sit and do handwork.

She decided to strip and rewax the kitchen floor. She needed to feel a sense of accomplishment. Spring housekeeping must be an instinctive feeling buried in all of us, she decided later as she knelt on her hands and knees to scrub.

The exercise felt good. In fact, everything felt good to her. She caught herself humming, experiencing a deep happiness. Everything in her life seemed to be working: her doctor said she was progressing nicely—whatever that meant; she had a handsome, attentive husband and was owned by a cat who tolerated her with amused affection.

What more could anyone ask?

It was only when she stretched out on the bed for her nap later that afternoon that Elizabeth decided she might have overdone her day a little.

She had an ache in her lower back that wouldn't go away. In fact, it seemed to be getting worse. The baby wasn't due for another two weeks at best. The doctor had already commented that the baby was a little smaller than he had expected so near the due date and that she might not deliver for three to four more weeks. She groaned at the thought, then forced herself to relax and get some rest.

Sometime later she woke up, knowing that something was wrong. Her water had broken. She called the doctor immediately and reported what had happened. No, she hadn't noticed contractions as such. Yes, she had some lower back pain, but that seemed to be chronic. Yes, she could get to the hospital within the hour.

So this was it. March 3. Elizabeth recognized the adrenaline flowing through her. She was scared. She was excited. Now was the time to faced what had to be done.

But first she had to call Dan.

His secretary put her through to him without delay. Now that the woman recognized her voice, Elizabeth always reached him immediately.

When he answered, she could tell he was distracted, and she wished she had the courage to lie to him. But he'd never forgive her.

"Dan Morgan," he said into the phone.

"Hi, Dan," she began, trying to find a way to soften her news.

"What's wrong?" he demanded. She rarely called him at work, not unless he specifically asked her to call. And that tentative tone of voice was not natural for her.

So much for trying to break the news gently. "My water broke."

"Oh, my God."

"It's nothing to be alarmed about. The doctor wants me at the hospital, so I thought I'd call and—"

"Stay right there. I'll be there in ten minutes."

"Dan, there's no reason for you to leave work. I haven't even started contractions. This being a first baby means I'll probably be there for hours before—"

"Don't move. Don't do anything until I get there."

The phone slammed down and she flinched.

"Oh, dear. He's going to be one of those fathers everybody makes fun of," she informed Misty wryly.

Her bag had been packed for a couple of weeks, so all Elizabeth had to do was to change into something to wear to the hospital and wait for Dan to arrive.

He burst into the apartment a short time later and came to an abrupt stop when he found her waiting patiently for him in the overstuffed chair by the sofa.

"You okay?"

"I'm fine. You made good time."

"I took a cab. It was faster than getting the car out."

She stood up and he immediately wrapped his arm around her. "My legs are still in good working order. Are you ready to go?"

"The cab's waiting."

"Would you mind getting my suitcase? It's in the closet."

He disappeared into the bedroom and returned in less than a minute with her bag. Keeping a close hold on her, Dan escorted Elizabeth out of the apartment, made sure the door was locked, then took her down the elevator to the waiting cab.

"Are you sure you're okay?" he asked again while the cab took them across town.

"I'm fine."

"Are you in any pain?"

Not the kind of pain she had expected. Her lower back felt as though it were going to snap in two, but she saw no point in mentioning it.

Once again the hospital employees seemed to know exactly what needed to be done with the minimum amount of fuss. Dr. Fitzgerald was there by the time she was undressed and in bed.

When he was through with his examination he sat down beside her on the bed and took her hand. "I noticed your husband referred to you as Beth. Would you mind if I call you that?"

His voice sounded very gentle and soothing, but the serious expression in his eyes worried her. "Of course not."

He sat there for a moment, studying her in silence.

"There's something wrong, isn't there?" she finally asked.

"We don't know why these things happen, Beth. There never seems to be an understandable reason, and it seldom helps to analyze deeply."

"I'm going to lose the baby."

"Not if I can help it. But I can't make any guarantees. I'm going to do the best I can and I'm counting on you to do the same."

All Beth could think about at the moment was Dan. He wanted the baby. He married her for the baby. And now they might lose it.

"I need your permission to do a cesarean section. At the moment that seems to be the safest thing for both you and the baby."

"Whatever you want to do."

"Fine. I'll have the nurse in here in a few moments and give you a shot to relax you before surgery." He squeezed her hand and stood up.

"Are you going to tell Dan?"

"Of course. And we'll hope for the best. But sometimes, Beth, it's better to be prepared for the worst."

She lay there after the door closed, listening for voices, but all she heard were muffled sounds.

The pain seemed to be surrounding her, crowding down on her so that she could scarcely breathe. Tears trickled down her cheeks. Her baby. Her beautiful, longed-for baby.

The door opened and the nurse came in. Before the door slowly swung shut again she heard Dan's voice.

"Don't let anything happen to Beth, Doctor. I know you're doing your best, but if there's a choice and you can only save one of the, don't allow Beth to die, do you hear me? We can have other children. No one can replace her."

She heard the doctor answer in a soothing voice. "We're going to do our damnedest to save them both, but I understand how you feel, Dan. Believe me, you aren't alone. She's your wife, and you love her.''

"Of course I love her. I waited for years to find her, and then when I did, I managed to get her pregnant and jeopardize her life!"

"You didn't get her pregnant without some assistance from her, you know. Don't blame yourself, okay?''

Beth could no longer hear them, but she would never forget Dan's words.

I've waited for years to find her. I love her. I've waited for years to find her. I love her.

He was waiting in the hallway when they wheeled her into surgery. The shot had made her very drowsy and she sleepily smiled at him.

She was too pale, Dan decided. Her black hair framed her face, her dark, delicate brows her only color. He took her hand and walked beside her. When he had to let go he kissed her palm and gently laid her hand down again.

Beth's dreams were strange and disjointed. Voices and singing kept weaving in and out of her consciousness. She felt different—lighter, full of energy, filled with joy.

Dan loves me. He loves me . . . loves me . . . loves . . .

"Beth?"

Her eyes opened slowly and she fought to focus on the shadowy figure beside her. Her back no longer hurt, but she felt a heaviness on her stomach that hadn't been there earlier.

The baby must have gained so much weight that—

The baby?

"The baby . . ." she whispered through dry lips. She managed to focus on Dan and notice that strain had drawn lines down his face she'd never seen before.

"I don't know. They're still working with him."

"Him?"

He smiled slightly. "You were right. It's a little boy."

"Have you talked with the doctor?"

"He's turned him over to the pediatrics people. The baby is small, Beth, and they had trouble getting him to breathe."

She could feel the tears running down her cheeks once again. "I'm sorry," she whispered.

"Oh, God, love, so am I. So sorry that I've put you through so much pain. I'm sorry about so many things."

She saw the moisture in his eyes. "I'm sorry our son is having a rough time. But we don't have to give up hope."

He nodded. "I don't intend to, believe me. You said yourself he's a scrapper. He'll hang in there if at all possible—I'm sure of it." He leaned over and kissed her on the forehead. "Get some sleep. I'll see you in the morning."

"Dan?"

"Yes, love."

"Thank you for being with me. I'll never forget how much you've done for me."

Fear gripped him at her remark. She sounded as though she were saying goodbye. The doctor had warned him that she would be weak. She'd lost a lot of blood. Neither she nor the baby were out of the woods yet. Not by a long shot.

"Get some rest," he repeated. "I'll see you in the morning."

Dan stepped out into the hallway and sighed. The past few hours had been some of the worst he had ever spent. He wasn't sure at the moment if he was ready to face what the future might bring.

The apartment seemed empty when he got back. Misty greeted him at the door, looking behind him as though wondering what he'd done with Beth.

"She's at the hospital," he explained, no longer feeling ridiculous to be talking to an animal. Misty seemed to understand everything that was said to her. She immediately left the door and went over and sat by her empty bowl.

"I know. It's time to eat. Thanks for reminding me. We both need to keep up our strength."

The doctor had convinced him to go home and get some rest. He was right. He'd be no good to anybody if he didn't take care of himself.

After feeding Misty, Dan stared into the refrigerator blankly. Beth had left a salad and roast. Forcing himself, he ate, cleaned up his dishes and went to bed.

He never noticed the brightly shining, newly waxed floor.

"Your wife is running a fever this morning, Mr. Morgan," the day nurse informed him. "The baby is holding his own. We're keeping him in an incubator, which is standard procedure for a child that small."

"Has the doctor been in this morning?"

"Oh, yes. He was in quite early. He's prescribed medication for Mrs. Morgan to clear up the infection."

"May I see her?"

"Certainly. She may be asleep, though. The pain medication that's standard after surgery has kept her drowsy, which is just as well. Her body needs time to heal."

Dan opened the door and peered into the shadowed room. The blinds and drapes were closed.

She lay there so still. He couldn't shake off the feeling of desolation that swept over him when he saw her.

He sat down in the chair by the bed and her eyes opened.

"Hello," he offered.

"I thought I was dreaming."

"About what?"

"You. I thought I dreamed you were here."

"I just walked in."

She smiled. "Maybe my dream brought you here."

"Sounds possible to me."

He stood up and moved closer, taking her hand. "How do you feel?"

"Like I'm floating several inches off the bed. Whatever those shots are they're giving me, they're powerful." She studied his sober expression. "Have you seen the baby?"

"Not since last night."

"What does he look like?"

Dan thought a moment. "It's hard to tell. He looked so damned small!"

"Could you tell the color of his hair?"

"It looked dark, like yours."

"And eyes?"

"No. He never opened them."

"Have you decided on a name yet?"

"Have you?"

"Would you mind if we named him after you? We could call him Danny."

"If that's what you want."

"Yes." Her eyes closed briefly and he could see the struggle she had opening them.

"Don't fight it, love. Let the medication have it's effect."

"You've been calling me that since you brought me in."

"Calling you what?"

"'Love.'"

He didn't think he could talk around the lump in his throat. "I've always thought of you as my love," he admitted.

"But you never told me."

"No."

"Why not?"

"Because I didn't think you'd want to hear it."

She smiled. "Well, what do you know. The great Dan Morgan is finally wrong about something."

She sounded slightly inebriated and he almost laughed. "I take that to mean you wanted to hear it."

"It would have been nice all that time when I felt so fat and ugly."

"You were never fat and ugly. You have always been a beautiful woman, and I love you to distraction."

"I'm so glad." She sighed with contentment. "I love you, too."

For a moment he thought he'd imagined the words. She said them so casually. His eyes met hers and he saw the tender light in them that he had noticed more than once.

"Do you, Beth? Do you, really?"

"Of course. How could I help but love you? You're one of the most wonderful men in the world."

"Hold that thought, love, until you get out of here. I have a hunch I'd like to pursue this conversation when you've recovered a little more." He could feel the blood rushing through his body.

"Does that mean you want to make love to me?" she asked with drowsy interest.

Dan caught himself looking over his shoulder to make sure one of the nurses hadn't walked into the room. "The thought has crossed my mind on more than one occasion since I first met you."

"You hid it well, then. You never seemed to show that much interest in me."

"That's all you know. I've had a rough time keeping my hands off you for months."

The smile she gave him was dazzling. "I'm delighted to hear it." He smiled back and they looked at each other in silence for a few moments.

Then he squeezed her hand. "Go back to sleep. You probably won't remember a single word of this conversation later."

"Don't count on it. I've gotten the distinct impression you intend to lose some of that restraint you've been practicing. I'll do all I can to help you toss it out the window when I get home."

"I can hardly wait."

He watched as her eyes closed again and he continued to hold her hand until her even breathing convinced him she was sound asleep once more.

Then he tiptoed out of the room. He wanted to go visit Danny and give his son a pep talk about fighting and holding on.

When the phone rang the first time Dan groggily thought it was the alarm and reached over to the nightstand for the switch to turn it off. By the second ring he was wide-awake, aware that when the phone rang at four in the morning, it was rarely good news.

"This is Riverside General Hospital, Mr. Morgan," a feminine voice said. "The doctor thought you'd want to know that your son is having some difficulties breathing and that you might want to be here."

"I'm on my way," Dan said. He was dressed and going out the door within minutes.

When he arrived on the floor, the nurse assured him that everything possible was being done. They had not disturbed Beth, so Dan stayed out in the hallway, waiting for word, praying that the tiny baby made it.

He didn't know how much time passed before the young pediatrician in charge joined him.

"He's doing much better now. I'm sorry to have awakened you this morning."

"I'm glad you did."

"He's tenacious—I'll give him that. Let's hope he doesn't give us another scare like that one."

"Amen," Dan agreed. "Have you told my wife?"

"Not yet."

"I don't see any need to alarm her at this point, do you? Particularly if he's through the crisis."

"I'll leave that to your judgment, Mr. Morgan."

The men shook hands briefly and Dan walked down to Beth's room.

Weak sunlight filtered through the window. Her color was much better and she seemed to be resting. He stood watching her for a moment before he had to go back home to clean up.

Her eyes opened and she saw him. "You're here early, aren't you?"

He smiled. "I missed you."

She held out her hand, and he stepped closer to the bed and took it. Studying him in the early-morning light, she frowned slightly. "You haven't shaved."

"It's the new look, didn't you know?" He leaned over and kissed her.

She placed her hand on his cheek and rubbed it lightly. "Whatever you say," she responded doubtfully.

"Has the doctor said when you'll be able to go home?"

"Not until I quit running this stupid fever."

"How about Danny?"

"That depends on how fast he gains his weight. They told me last night he's eating well. In fact, I'm supposed to be able to feed him this morning."

He hoped that nothing had changed in that respect.

"I called a realtor yesterday to start looking for a place upstate. But I'd rather wait until you're up to looking with me."

"Are you sure that's what you want?"

"More than anything else." He leaned over and kissed her again. "I'll be back tonight. Get well in a hurry, love. I want you home."

She watched him leave the room with a slight frown on her face. Something was bothering him, but she supposed she'd have to wait until he was ready to tell her.

Her husband could be stubborn on occasion, she'd discovered during the past months. She smiled. Otherwise he would never have found her last fall. Beth shifted, trying to get comfortable. There were worse traits, she supposed, than stubbornness.

Chapter Eleven

Elizabeth felt as though she'd been away from the apartment for a month, rather than ten days. She feasted on the familiar color scheme of the bedroom and enjoyed the feeling of being home.

Danny slept peacefully in his crib in an alcove of the bedroom.

The hospital staff was amazed at the progress he'd made. After a wobbly first few days, he started gaining strength as well as weight. Earlier the doctor had warned her that Danny might need to stay at the hospital when she was discharged, but by the time they had her temperature back to normal, both of them were pronounced ready to greet the world.

Dan came out of the bathroom and crawled into bed with her. "At last," he muttered, holding her close. "I've got you where I want you."

She turned a little gingerly, still aware of her incision, and hugged him. "No wonder you're such a success. You have marvelous ideas."

"Is Danny all right?"

"Fine. Ate like a little pig and went off to sleep."

"I think he's going to have your eyes."

"All newborns' eyes are blue."

"Maybe they won't change."

"He's got your features."

"A nice mix."

He kissed her lightly, felt the warmth and softness of her mouth and groaned. Deepening the kiss, Dan held her closer, enjoying having her in his arms once more.

Dan's touch seemed to set off tiny explosions deep within Elizabeth, like depth charges, causing a chain reaction of heat to race through her.

Eventually he drew away, drawing a deep breath. "I seem to have lost all that restraint I've been hanging on to." He edged away from her slightly. "You go to my head."

Elizabeth fit her body to his in the sleeping position that had become natural to her. "It's good to be home."

Dan agreed, but he had forgotten how strongly she affected him, being there in bed with him.

He forced himself to think of other things, until he finally fell asleep with Beth curled up beside him, his son resting nearby.

"Beth?" Dan called.

"I'm in here," she replied, carrying Danny out of the bedroom. "What are you doing home?"

"Just as I suspected," he said without expression. "While I'm off slaving all day, trying to support your extravagant tastes, you're spending time with another man."

He lifted Danny from her shoulder and cuddled him under his chin.

"I wouldn't exactly consider him a man, but he's certainly growing," Elizabeth admitted. "So why are you home?"

"You aren't pleased to see me?" he asked.

She grinned. He knew better. During the past two months she had made it clear that she enjoyed being with him, sharing his home and the care of his son. In short, there was no doubt that he was aware of her feelings for him.

"I am delighted to see you, Mr. Morgan. Absolutely delighted. To what do I owe this unexpected treat?"

"How about taking a ride with me? I think the realtor may have found something."

Elizabeth hadn't realized he'd been actively looking for a home for them. After being up with a baby all hours of the night, Dan could easily have changed his mind about a wife and child. She knew better, of course. He'd had too many opportunities to shy away from the situation if he'd wished.

For a man who'd been a bachelor a short year before, Dan had taken to fatherhood with amazing speed.

"Let me get some of Danny's things together."

They were on their way north within the hour.

"I know this is going to sound strange," Dan said quietly after they got away from the heavier traffic, "but I dreamed about a house last night. Don't ask me why. But I could practically draw the house plans the dream was so clear. The house sat back from a winding street, up on a hill, with several trees that looked as if they'd always been there." He seemed to be remembering more as he talked. "The walkway to the front door was made of bricks laid in an intricate pattern, and a large bay window was by the front door, so that you could see inside to a comfortable room with a fireplace. The furniture reminded me of the kind we had when I was growing up—sturdy, almost childproof."

He glanced at Beth. "Now that I think of it, you were in the dream."

"Oh? Doing what?"

"You were just there, as I recall. There were children around. I remember that."

She looked down at the baby in her arms, placidly sleeping. Children, not just one. Glancing up at Dan once more, she couldn't help but remember—

"I guess the weird thing about it is that I rarely remember dreams. Do you?"

She thought of her recurring dream about Philip. "Not lately. I used to dream all the time, though."

"Good dreams?"

"Not particularly."

The realtor had given them directions to the house they were to view, agreeing to meet them there.

Elizabeth felt as though what was happening wasn't real. She'd gone through the previous months, waiting for the baby's arrival, deliberately pushing the future away. Suddenly the future had arrived and she wasn't at all sure she was ready for it.

Following the directions, they turned onto a narrow street that began to wind upward around a hill.

"Eight-seventeen. There it is," Dan began, then fell silent.

The house was set back from the winding street on a hillside. A large bay window was located by the front door. When they pulled into the driveway behind the realtor's car, they saw him waiting for them on the brick walkway that led to the front door—a brick walkway with an intricate design.

"I don't believe this," Dan muttered.

He helped Elizabeth out of the car. He knew before they reached the front door what he would see through the bay window. A large fireplace with bookshelves on either side dominated one wall. He was relieved to find the room empty of furniture. At least something was different from his dream.

They wandered through the house in silence. Elizabeth couldn't get over how familiar it seemed to her. There were no secrets. She knew which doors led to the basement, to the pantry, the linen closet, the master bedroom. She gazed out of one of the windows that faced the back. A sloping lawn covered with large trees ended at a high wooden fence. A safe place for children to play.

Children. She looked down at Danny once more. Was it possible he was going to have someone to play with?

The realtor did his work well. He pointed out specifics, but made no effort to coerce. Perhaps he realized he didn't need to push. When Elizabeth went back downstairs Dan was waiting in the hallway. He looked a little pale.

"What do you think?" he asked in a slow voice.

"It's a dream house, wouldn't you say?"

If anything, his color faded even more.

"It's not funny, Beth. The last time I felt this way I—"

She waited, but he seemed to be at a loss for words.

"You what, Dan?"

"I was remembering the night I met you at Ryan's and how I felt when I first saw you. You seemed so familiar, as though I'd known you for years but had lost touch with you." He shook his head a little, as though bewildered. "And now this house. I don't understand."

"Neither do I."

"Do you feel it?"

"I feel a sense of familiarity. Is that what you mean?"

"Yes. I suppose that's as good a description as any. We're going to buy it, aren't we?" he asked thoughtfully.

"If you feel that we can afford it."

"That's the irony of it. This house has been vacant for over a year, according to the realtor. The people who own it moved to the West Coast and they've had trouble selling it because of its size." He looked up the curving staircase. "This house is too big for three of us. The realtor had already mentioned that to me, but it was a good location and the price is excellent, so he thought it worth mentioning."

"Maybe we'll have to produce a family to fill it," she suggested with a slight smile.

Dan remembered the problems of her last pregnancy. "No. It's too dangerous."

"We'll see." She turned away and started for the front door, where the realtor had discreetly disappeared earlier. Pausing, she glanced over her shoulder. "What do you think? Shall we make an offer?"

"For some reason, I don't feel as though we have a choice. It looks as though we're home, love."

* * *

By the time they returned to the apartment they were both excited, laughing at how easily everything had fallen into place. Closing could be scheduled in a few short weeks. It would take them that long to decide what furniture they wanted to keep and move and what needed to be purchased for the new home.

"Don't you think you should keep the apartment in Manhattan, in case you need to stay in town occasionally?"

"If I have to stay in town, I'll get a room at a hotel and insist that my wife join me. No. I don't intend to keep the apartment."

They talked through dinner, through Danny's feeding, and when Elizabeth went in to take her shower Dan followed her in to make a suggestion, only to stop when he realized what he had done.

She had reached into the shower to adjust the water temperature, when she heard his voice and looked over her shoulder.

He hadn't meant to invade her privacy. He'd been following her around the apartment all evening while she took care of things, and out of habit had continued to do so.

She stood there, slender once again, without anything hiding her from him. Except for their first evening together, he'd never seen her completely unclothed. That had been almost a year ago.

For a brief moment the events of that year flashed through his mind: the months of trying to forget her, then searching to find out who she was; finding her and discovering she was pregnant with his baby; convincing her to marry him; visiting in her home; having her move in with him; seeing her in pain at the time of delivery; fearing that he was going to lose her.

In a few short months she had become an integral part of his life and yet he'd been unable to express his love for her physically.

Elizabeth could feel a warm flush cover her body as Dan stood there, staring at her. She didn't know why she should be embarrassed. He was her husband, after all. He'd been very considerate, never pushing for physical intimacy after Danny's birth.

Slowly she turned toward him. "I'm sorry. I didn't hear what you said."

"I've forgotten," he mumbled, stepping into the room and closing the door. He touched a wisp of hair that curled before her ear. "You are so beautiful," he whispered, "and I love you more than I thought it possible to love anyone."

She began to unbutton his shirt. "The shower's big enough for two. Think we should do our part to help conserve water?"

He slid his hands on either side of her neck, his thumbs tilting her chin until he could touch her mouth with his.

She'd become addicted to his kisses. He was always so gentle. Tonight he was even more so, as though waiting for her to pull away. Elizabeth had no intention of pulling away.

The past year had taught her a great deal—about herself, her perception of the world and the people with whom she came into contact. She wasn't the same person who had gone to Ryan Davidson's party to pretend for a few hours that she was someone else. Elizabeth had gotten in touch with who she was and begun to remove the barriers she'd erected so many years before—just in time for Dan Morgan to come striding into her life.

She wanted him in every way a woman could want a man—as her companion, as her partner, as her lover, as the father of her children.

His shirt hung open and she tugged at the shoulders, trying to remove it. Dan reluctantly let go of her long enough to shrug out of his shirt. With economical movements he removed the rest of his clothing and stood there before her, a question in his eyes.

"I love you, Dan," she said quietly.

He felt his knees quiver slightly. How long had he waited to see that look of love and trust in her eyes? He reached behind her and opened the shower door. "After you, milady."

There wasn't much room, but the cramped quarters didn't seem to bother them. Dan took his time carefully covering Beth with soap, turning her away from him to lovingly stroke her back.

"I've missed getting to massage your back," he offered once she had rinsed and started to cover his broad shoulders with suds.

"I can't imagine why. I'm sure you found it quite tedious."

"Hardly. It was the only time I could trust myself to touch you."

She tugged at him slightly to turn. Once he was facing her she knew how affected he was by their closeness. "Can you trust yourself to touch me now?"

"Not if I have to walk away once we're through with our shower."

"You don't ever have to walk away from me, Dan."

"You know that I love you, don't you?"

"Yes. You taught me what love is all about. It isn't a taking—it's giving . . . and sharing . . . and trusting."

"And you trust me?"

"Yes."

"Despite what happened our first evening together?"

"Aren't you ever going to forgive yourself for that? I was a willing participant."

He pulled her close to him. "Hmmmmm, so you were." He began to plant small kisses along her jaw, up her cheek, until he found her mouth.

His kiss was no longer gentle. A surge of possessiveness swept over him. He'd campaigned long and hard to win her. Dan couldn't believe the waiting was over.

They took their time drying each other, stopping to kiss and caress each other. Then Dan picked her up and carried her into the bedroom, placing her on the bed. The night-light glowed nearby, but Dan couldn't see her expression as he stretched out beside her.

She placed her hand on his chest, rubbing it across the muscled surface. Elizabeth could feel the heat emanating from his body.

Any fears she might have had were gone. She loved this man and wanted to be a part of him.

Soft touches became trembling caresses. Whispered phrases joined breathless pleas and muffled moans of pleasure. Even in the midst of their loving passion, they were aware of the baby close by, the baby who had brought them together in what had become a strange enchantment.

Epilogue

"Do you intend to teach next year?" Janine asked, watching Beth efficiently preparing dinner in her large country kitchen.

Beth glanced down at her as yet flat abdomen and smiled. "Good question. We haven't discussed it."

"It seems to me there're several things you haven't discussed," Janine offered tartly. "Such as overpopulation."

Beth laughed. "I don't think our family is going to create world-wide famine, do you?"

"But you had such a tough time the first time. How can you forget?"

"I've never forgotten. But I didn't have any trouble with the other two, remember?"

"But four children, Beth," she chided. "Nobody has that many children in today's world. It just isn't done."

"It is in our family."

The back door flew open and a dark-haired, blue-eyed boy of eight years or so paused in the doorway. "When are we eating, Mom?"

Beth glanced around at him, casually inspecting the dirt on his jeans and the stain on his shirt. "It will be another hour, Danny. You'll have time to get bathed and cleaned up."

"Oh, Mom, do I have to?"

She nodded toward Janine. "We have company tonight."

Janine looked over at the boy and winked. He reluctantly grinned in response.

"Where are Amy and Melissa?" Beth asked.

"They're outside pestering Mark." In his most adult voice he said, "He isn't used to girls, Mom. I wish you'd make them behave."

"What are they doing?"

"Amy keeps wanting to put bandages on him. She says she's going to be a doctor. And Melissa keeps trying to read to him."

Janine raised a brow slightly. "Melissa can read?"

"Well, she thinks she can." Danny shrugged. "She's pretty good at talking about the pictures for a three-year-old," he admitted from his advanced years.

"Why don't you have the girls come in and get cleaned up, too? Maybe then they'll leave your friend Mark alone."

"I can try," he said with a resigned expression, disappearing from view once again.

"How long has Amy been planning to be a doctor?" Janine asked with a grin.

"Since the time we had to rush Danny in for stitches after he fell. She was very impressed with all the goings-on."

"But she's only seven. She could always change her mind."

"Of course."

Janine continued to watch her friend, taking in the changes in her. She was still slender—having children didn't seem to affect Beth's weight. Her hair was much shorter now. It was cut in a cap of curls around her head, making her look almost as young as her son, whose mop of black hair always seemed to need a brush.

"What does Dan think?"

"About what?"

"Your pregnancy, Beth. That was what we were discussing before Danny the whirlwind arrived."

"Oh. Well, you know Dan—"

"Not the way you do. Obviously."

They laughed, enjoying the camaraderie.

"He seems to revel in the family. He's hired some good management people, so he doesn't spend as much time in Manhattan as he did. He insists he'd just as soon be here with the kids while I teach, since I only have classes two days a week. He didn't like having a live-in housekeeper." Her face flushed a little at the memory. "He said she cramped his style."

"I can imagine."

"Of course I have plenty of help. Gladys comes in each morning and does the heavy cleaning." She placed a casserole in the oven. "There, that should do it. Want to join the men in the other room?"

Janine glanced at the door into the hallway. "In a moment. I uh, there's something I wanted to talk to you about."

"Sure."

Beth pulled up another bar stool and sat down beside Janine.

"Ryan has asked me to marry him."

"You're kidding me!"

"I know. I can't believe it, either. And the problem is, I don't know what to say to him."

"You've been in love with him for years. What's there to think about?"

"You . . . and Dan . . . and your family. I'm not at all sure I could handle all of this. I'm damned good at what I do, but it has nothing to do with domesticity."

"Come on, Janine. Ryan has known you long enough to understand that."

"But he may expect me to change. You changed."

Beth glanced out the window to make sure the children were getting ready to come inside. Amy was mothering Melissa as usual and Melissa was doing a better job of tolerating her than usual. Perhaps it was going to be a quiet evening after all.

"I changed because this is what I want, Janine. Not because Dan asked me to."

"But didn't you feel the pressure?"

"No. I'm not sure I know how to explain this, but I'll try. Dan and I belong together . . . in this house . . . with a large family. We've known that from the beginning."

"You mean like fate, or something?"

"It was just a feeling we had. I had let my early life warp me a little and the relationship with Philip didn't help. But meeting Dan brought my life into a sharper focus and I realized what I was doing to myself by constantly clinging to the hurts of the past. Once I let go, I was free to enjoy life and all it offered."

"And you feel being a wife and mother is the end-all and be-all of existence?"

"Of course not. I still teach, which I love, but my horizons have broadened to include Dan and the children. Everyone is different, Janine. Don't try to fit yourself into a mold. Be honest with Ryan. Tell him of your concerns. You might be surprised to discover he's not interested in a family, either. You have a good relationship now. Marriage will only give you an opportunity to improve on it."

"Aren't you two ever going to join us?" Dan slid his arms around Beth from behind and hugged her around the middle. "Ryan and I are totally bored with each other's company."

"Now that I'll never believe," Beth said, resting her head for a moment against his shoulder.

"What if I said I missed you?" he whispered.

"I might be persuaded to believe that."

"What would it take to convince you?"

"I swear you two act like a couple of newlyweds," Janine complained good-naturedly.

Dan laughed, a relaxed, happy sound that danced around the room.

"What's so funny?" Ryan asked, leaning against the doorjamb, his hands in his pockets.

"Never mind," Beth responded, sitting up and looking around at Ryan. "Would you guys like something else to drink? Dinner should be ready in thirty minutes or so."

"Not me," Dan responded. "Unless you have some lemonade made." He grinned at Ryan. "I can't handle the hard stuff anymore. Must be out of the habit."

"I know what you mean. When I developed that ulcer I learned not to drink anything stronger than milk." He looked over at Beth. "I understand congratulations are in order."

Her gaze met Dan's and she formed the words. "Loudmouth." He just grinned, totally unabashed.

"That's right."

"You seem to be trying to rebuild the economy singlehandedly. Glad it's you and not me. I couldn't handle being tied down. Guess I'm too used to traveling without having to worry about anything more than how soon I need to get to the airport."

Beth exchanged a significant glance with Janine.

"That doesn't mean I don't intend to spoil your kids rotten, though," Ryan continued. "I think I'll go see what they're up to out there."

He sauntered over to the back door and stepped outside. Janine nodded slightly at Beth and said, "Think I'll join you, Ryan, love. There's something I wanted to tell you."

"Ah, alone at last," Dan whispered, gathering Beth into his arms once more. She giggled at the lecherous tone of voice.

"For all of two minutes, max."

"Hmmm. In that case, I'll just stand here and nibble a little before dinner." He kissed her under her ear, then took little nips along her neck.

"Dan?"

"Hmmm?"

"Are you sorry about the baby?"

He jerked away as though she had struck him. "Sorry? Are you kidding? Danny and I have to see about evening up the numbers around here." He leaned back, keeping his arms around her so that he could see her face. "Are you?"

"Of course not."

"One more should fill the remaining bedroom upstairs."

"Yes," she agreed with a smile.

"I've enjoyed living here with you, Mrs. Morgan."

"Time seems to have flown by, hasn't it?"

"I suppose, in one sense. In another way, I feel that I've always been with you and that I always will be with you. Kinda strange, I know."

"I feel the same way. I'm glad we found each other when we did."

"Me, too. It was getting a little lonely, waiting around. Especially when I didn't even realize what I was waiting for."

"Until Ryan's party."

"Yeah. Until the night of Ryan's party."

They walked to the back door, arms around each other, and watched their family entertaining their guests.

* * * * *

A Note from Debbie Macomber

I'm very pleased Silhouette has decided to reprint *Mail-Order Bride*. I love Caroline's two maiden aunts and their age-old cure for a broken heart. Their methods were rather drastic, but in the end it all worked out. I know you'll enjoy this story with its twists and turns, and the celebration of Caroline and Paul's love.

My family's been doing a bit of celebrating this year, too. Last September, my husband, Wayne, and I commemorated our silver wedding anniversary. That's twenty-five years of living, loving, crying, laughing and praying. The laughing and praying were what got us through raising our four offspring. Now our children are at the age when they're marrying. What a special time this is for Wayne and me.

Now that our daughter, Jenny, is married and our son, Ted, is engaged, I've given a good deal of thought to what marriage is really all about. I wish I could say I've got it down pat, but I don't. If asked to define it, I'd say marriage is the bonding of two hearts, a blending of two distinct personalities into one homogenous relationship. It's living one day at a time, helping each other, listening, loving, crying and laughing together. It's sharing dreams and encouraging each other to be the best we can be. It's opening our hearts and our lives to one another.

I hope you enjoy Caroline and Paul's story.

Debbie Macomber

MAIL-ORDER BRIDE

Debbie Macomber

Prologue

"I'm so dreadfully worried about dear Caroline," Ethel Myers murmured thoughtfully, sipping her tea from the dainty porcelain cup. Her fingers clutched a delicate lace-trimmed handkerchief and when a tiny droplet of moisture formed in the corner of her eye, she dabbed it gently. "Sister, I do believe the brew is much stronger today."

"Yes," Mabel admitted gingerly. "But remember what Father said about the brew enhancing one's ability to solve problems."

"And we must do something to help Caroline."

Mabel sighed and sadly shook her head. "Perhaps if you and I had married suitable gentlemen all those years ago."

"Oh yes, if we'd married then maybe we'd know how to help that sweet, sweet child." Ethel's faded blue eyes brightened momentarily. "You do remember that George Guettermann once asked for my hand."

"As I recall, Mother was quite impressed with him."

The slender shoulders sagged slightly. "But Father was suspicious from the first."

Mabel sighed heavily. "Mr. Guettermann did cut such a dashing figure."

A wistful look marked Ethel's fragile features. "If only he hadn't already been married."

"The scoundrel!"

"We must learn to forgive him, Sister."

Mabel nodded and lifted the steaming pot of brew. "I was thinking of Caroline's young man. Another cup, Sister?"

"Oh dear, should we?" Ethel's fingers flew to her mouth to smother a loud hiccup, and she had the good grace to look embarrassed.

"We must find a way to help her."

"Poor, poor Caroline." Ethel agreed as Mabel filled the cup to the bright gold rim.

"There was something in his eyes."

"George?"

"No, Sister. Caroline's young man."

"I do agree, there was indeed something about his eyes." Ethel took another sip of tea and lightly patted her breast at the strength of their father's special recipe. "Sister, the brew . . ."

"We must think!"

"Oh yes, I do agree. Think. We must help dear, dear Caroline."

"If only her mother were alive."

"Or grandmother."

"Grandmother?"

"Great-great-grandmother, perhaps. She would know what to do to help Caroline. You know how her great-great-grandmother frowned on the courting; she said it simply wasn't necessary."

"Grandmother would. Asa Mercer brought her to Seattle with the other mail-order brides and she and Grandfather knew each other less than twenty-four hours before they married."

"A courtship wasn't necessary and they were so very happy."

"Very happy indeed and very compatible."

"With twelve children they must have agreed quite nicely," Ethel said, and giggled delightedly.

"It's such a shame marriages aren't arranged these days," Mabel said thoughtfully, taking another long sip of the tea.

"If only we could find Caroline a husband."

"But, Sister..." Mabel was doubtful. For over fifty years they'd been unable to locate husbands of their own. It was unreasonable to expect to come up with one for their beloved niece.

Ethel's hand shook as she lowered the fragile cup to the saucer. "Sister, Sister. I do believe I have the solution," her voice wavered with excitement as she reached for the morning paper.

"Yes?"

"Our own Caroline will be a mail-order bride."

Mabel looked doubtful. "But things aren't done like that in this day and age."

Ethel fumbled with the printed pages until she located the classified section. She folded back the unwieldy page and pointed to the personal column. "Here, read this."

Mabel read the ad aloud, her voice trembling. "Wanted— Wife for thirty-two-year-old Alaskan male. Send picture. Transportation provided." The advertisement listed the name of Paul Trevor and a box number.

"But, Sister, do we dare?"

"We must. Caroline is so desperately unhappy."

"And she did have the opportunity to select a husband of her own."

"And the beast left her standing at the altar."

"The scoundrel!"

"We mustn't tell her, of course."

"Oh no, we can't let her know. Our Caroline would object most strenuously."

"Sister, I do believe the brew helped."

"Indeed! Another cup?"

Ethel lifted her cup and her older sister automatically re-filled it. A small smile of satisfaction lifted the edges of her soft mouth. "Father's recipe was most beneficial."

"It always is, Sister."

"Oh yes, indeed."

Chapter One

The roaring sound of the jet sliced through the air as the Boeing 767 prepared to land at the Seattle-Tacoma International Airport. Caroline Myers watched the thick tires bounce over the runway with the realization that she would soon depart Seattle for unknown adventures in Alaska.

"Do you have everything, dear?" Mabel asked her niece for the third time in as many minutes.

"Aunt Ethel, Aunt Mabel, please—I cannot allow you to do this."

"Nonsense," Ethel said with an imperceptible cluck. "This vacation is our gift to you."

"But Alaska in October?"

"It's lovely, dear heart. I promise."

"Yes, lovely," Ethel agreed, doing her best to hide a soft smile. "And we have the nicest surprise waiting for you."

Caroline stared suspiciously at her two maiden aunts. Mischief danced in their sparkling blue eyes. At sixty-nine and seventy, they were her only living relatives in Seattle, and she loved them dearly.

"But this trip is too much."

"Nonsense."

"Hurry, dear, or you'll miss your plane."

"One question?"

Ethel and Mabel exchanged fleeting glances. "Yes?"

"Why the blood tests? I didn't know anything like that was necessary for travel within the United States."

Mabel paused to clear her throat, wildly casting her eyes about the terminal. "It's something new."

"A gubernatorial decision, I . . . I believe," Ethel stammered.

"Now take this," Mabel instructed, handing her niece a neatly packed wicker basket. "We filled a thermos with Father's special tea in case you need it."

"I just may," Caroline said, doing her utmost to swallow a chuckle. She'd been eighteen when she'd first discovered the potency of her great-grandfather's special recipe.

"And do write."

"Of course. I'll send a postcard every day." Caroline kissed both aunts on the cheek and hugged them gently. Ethel sniffled and Mabel cast her a look of sisterly displeasure. Again Caroline grinned. Her two great-aunts had been a constant delight for all of her life. They were charming, loving and thoroughly enchanting. The two had done everything they could to cheer her after Larry's defection. The sudden memory of the man she had loved with such intensity produced a fresh wave of pain that threatened to wash away the pleasure of this moment.

Ethel sniffled again. "We shall miss you dreadfully," she announced, glaring at her sister.

Caroline threw back her head and laughed aloud. Her long blond hair fell like a cascading river down the middle of her back. "I'm only going to be gone a week." Again Ethel's and Mabel's eyes avoided hers and Caroline wondered what little game they were playing.

"But a week seems so very long."

"You have your ticket?" Mabel asked hurriedly.

"Right here." Caroline patted the side of her purse.

"Remember, a nice young man will be meeting you in Fairbanks."

"Right," Caroline said, eyes twinkling. Her aunts had gone over the details of this vacation a minimum of fifty times. "And he's taking me to..."

"Atta," the great-aunts chimed, bobbing their heads in unison.

"From there, I'll be met by..."

"Paul Trevor." Ethel and Mabel shared a silly grin.

"Right, Paul Trevor." Caroline studied her aunts surreptitiously. If she didn't know better, she'd think they had something up their sleeves. For days, the two of them had been acting like giddy teenagers, whispering and giggling behind her back. Caroline had objected to this vacation from the first. Alaska in early October wouldn't have been her first choice; she wouldn't have argued nearly as strenuously had they suggested Hawaii, but her two aunts had been so insistent that Alaska was the best place for her that Caroline had finally agreed. This was their unselfish gift to her in an effort to heal a broken heart, and she wasn't about to ruin it by being stubborn. She couldn't bear to inform them that it would take a whole lot more than a trip north for her heart to mend.

The flight attendant announced that the plane was now boarding and called off the number of Caroline's row. Caroline hugged her aunts and secured her purse strap over her shoulder.

"Do be happy, dear," Ethel said, pressing her frilly lace handkerchief under her nose. Her eyes misted with emotion.

Mabel's voice seemed strained as she echoed her sister's words and clenched Caroline's free hand. "Happiness, child. Much, much happiness."

Shaking her head at the strange behavior of the two, Caroline entered the long, narrow jetway that led to the belly of the Boeing 767. The flight attendant directed her to the first-class section, and, again, Caroline had cause to consider how her aunts could possibly afford this trip. She clipped the seat belt into place and pressed the recliner button, leaning as far back in the wide seat as possible.

From inside the airport, Ethel and Mabel stood looking at the sleek body of the aircraft that would carry away their beloved niece.

"It's fate, Sister," Mabel said softly.

"Oh, indeed. Paul Trevor chose her over all those other women."

"He sounds like such a good man."

"And so handsome."

"Only he wrote that he has a beard now. Does Caroline like men with beards?"

Ethel gently shook her head. "I really couldn't say."

"She'll grow to love him."

"Oh yes. Given time, she'll be very happy with Paul."

"Perhaps she'll be as compatible with him as Grandmother was with Grandfather."

"Twelve children. Oh, Sister, what a delightful thought." Ethel pressed her gloved hands to her rosy cheeks and smiled through the misting tears.

Doubts vanished and the two shared a brilliant smile before turning away.

"We did our best for her," Mabel stated happily. "Her mother would have been proud."

"Her great-great-grandmother, too," Ethel said, and the two giggled with pure delight, causing several curious glances to be cast in their direction.

Caroline slept for most of the night flight to Fairbanks. She was exhausted from a hectic week at the office. As a private nurse for Dr. Kenneth James, an internist, she often put in long days and odd hours. Dr. James gave her the week off without a complaint and then, on Friday morning, shook her hand and wished her much happiness. Now that she thought about it, Caroline found his words puzzling. One didn't find happiness on a vacation. Happiness was the result of a satisfactory relationship. Like hers and Larry's... His name drifted with such ease into her mind that Caroline shook her head in an effort to free her thoughts.

Straightening in her seat, she noted that the cabin lights were dimmed. The only other passenger in the first-class section was sleeping, and the two attendants were drinking coffee in the front cabin. When one of them noticed that Caroline was awake, the attractive woman approached her.

"You missed the meal. Would you care to eat something now?"

Caroline shook her head. "No, thanks."

The tall brunette responded with a slight nod and returned to her coffee. Caroline viewed the trim body as she walked away. The flight attendant was more the type of woman Larry should marry, she mused, unable to keep her thoughts from wandering to her former fiancé. She'd known from the beginning how completely dissimilar Larry's and her tastes ran. Larry liked late, late nights and breakfast in bed while she was a morning person, eager for each new day. Caroline enjoyed the outdoor life: hiking, camping, boating. Larry's idea of roughing it was doing without valet service. She liked cornflakes with chocolate syrup poured over the top, milk mixed with Pepsi, and spaghetti for breakfast. Larry much preferred formal dinners with nothing more exotic than meat and potatoes. But they'd loved each other enough to believe they could overcome their differences and learn to compromise. *She* had loved *him*, Caroline corrected herself. At the last minute, Larry had buckled under to his doubts and had sent his witless brother to contact her an hour before the wedding ceremony. Humiliation engulfed her, threatening to smother her.

For the first week, Caroline hid from the world. Her two beloved aunts had hovered over her constantly, insisting that she eat and sleep, taking her temperature in case she'd worked herself into a case of the ague. Caroline assumed that the ague must be something dreadful and allowed them to fret over her. At the time, it would have taken more energy to assure them she was doing fine than to submit to their tender ministrations.

A month passed and Caroline gradually worked her way out of the heavy depression that had hung over her head like a constant thundercloud, threatening a fierce squall at any time. She smiled and laughed, but strongly suspected that her two maiden aunts were unconvinced. Every time she was with them, they stuck a thermometer under her tongue and shook their shiny gray heads with worried frowns.

Larry contacted her only once to stammer his regret and to apologize repeatedly. If she hadn't been so much in love with him, she might have been able to accept that he'd probably done them both a favor. Now there were whole hours when she didn't think about him, or hunger for information about him, or long to be held in his arms. Still, the thought of him with another woman was almost more than Caroline could tolerate, but given time she would learn to accept that as well.

This disaster with Larry had taught her that she possessed a far stronger constitution than she'd ever believed. She had been able to smile and hold her head high, and return to work a week after the aborted wedding. It hadn't been easy, but she'd done it with a calm maturity that surprised her. She was going to come out of this a much wiser, more discerning woman. Someday there would be a man who loved her enough to appreciate her sometimes wacky ways. When they fell in love and the time was right, she'd think about marriage again. But not for a long time, Caroline decided—not for a very long time.

As the plane approached the runway, Caroline gathered her things, preparing to disembark. Just as her aunts had promised, there was a man waiting for her in Fairbanks. She had no sooner walked off the plane than the middle-aged man with bushy eyebrows and a walrus mustache held up a piece of cardboard with her name printed across it in bold letters.

"Hello, I'm Caroline Myers," she told him, shifting the wicker basket from one hand to the other.

"Welcome to Alaska," he told her with a wide grin and offered his hand. "The name's John Morrison."

Caroline took it for a brisk shake. She liked him immediately. "Thank you, John."

The man continued to stare at her and rubbed the side of his square jaw. Slowly, he shook his head, and a sly grin courted the edges of his mouth. "Paul did all right for himself."

"Pardon?"

"Ah, nothing," John responded, shaking his head again. "I'm just surprised is all. I didn't expect him to come up with anyone half as attractive as you. I don't suppose you have a friend or two?"

Caroline hadn't the faintest idea what this burly bush pilot was getting at, or why he would be curious about her friends. Surely he'd flown more than one woman into the Alaskan interior. She was like any other tourist visiting Alaska for a one-week stay. She planned on getting plenty of rest and relaxation on the direct orders of her two maiden aunts. In addition, she hoped to sleep until noon every day, take invigorating walks and explore the magic of the tundra. Her aunts had mentioned Paul Trevor's name on several occasions and Caroline believed that they must have hired him as her guide. She wouldn't mind having someone show her the countryside. There was so much to see and do, and Caroline was ready for it all.

Once John had collected her suitcase, he directed her to the single-engine Cessna and helped her climb aboard.

"It won't be long now," he said, placing the earphones over his head and flipping several switches. He zipped up his fur-lined coat and glanced in her direction with a thick frown. Then the control tower issued instructions and John turned his attention to the radio. Once on the runway, the plane accelerated forward and was soon aiming for the clear, blue sky in a burst of power that had Caroline clenching her fingers together as if that alone would help to keep them airborne. She was accustomed to flying, but never in anything quite this small. In comparison to the wide-bodied jet, this Cessna seemed delicate and fragile.

"You might want to check some of those boxes back there." He jerked his head toward the large pile of sacks and cardboard boxes resting next to her suitcase at the rear of the plane.

"What should I be looking for?"

"A coat. It's going to get damn cold up here."

"All right." Caroline unhooked the seat belt and turned around to bend over the back of the padded cushion. She sorted through the sacks and found a variety of long underwear and flannel shirts.

"Paul's right about you needing this equipment. I hope the boots fit. I got the best available—fur-lined, naturally."

"Boots?"

"Lady, trust me. You're going to need them."

"I imagine they were expensive." She had a few traveler's checks with her, but if Paul Trevor expected her to pick up the tab on a complete winter wardrobe then he had another thought coming.

Caroline located the thick coat, but it was so bulky that she placed it over her knees and slipped her arms into a cozy flannel shirt.

"What did you bring with you?" John asked, eyeing the wicker basket at Caroline's feet.

"My two aunts sent along something to eat. They don't trust meals served on a commercial flight."

John's chuckle had a musical sound to it. "Smart women."

Now that he'd mentioned the basket, Caroline discovered she was hungry. It'd been hours since she had last eaten, and her stomach growled as she lifted the wicker lid to discover one side loaded with thick sandwiches and the promised thermos. The second half of the basket contained a brightly wrapped gift. Somewhat surprised, Caroline lifted the package and tore off the bright paper and ribbon. The paper-thin, sheer negligee with the fur-trimmed sleeves and hemline baffled her further.

John saw her blink in wonder and gave a loud laugh. "I see they included something to keep your neckline warm."

Caroline found his humor less than amusing and stuffed the gown back inside the basket. She'd never thought of her aunts as senile, but their recent behavior gave her cause to wonder.

She shared a thick turkey sandwich with John and listened while he spoke at length about Alaska. His love for this last frontier was apparent with every sentence. His running dialogue included a vivid description of the rolling tundra and varied wildlife.

"I have a feeling you're going to love it here."

"I like what little I've seen," Caroline agreed. She'd expected the land to be barren and harsh. It was that, but mingled in with the terrain was a subtle beauty, an elegance that instantly captured Caroline's heart.

"That's Denali over there," John told her. "She's the highest peak in North America."

"I thought McKinley was."

"Folks around here prefer to call her Denali."

"What's that?" Caroline pointed to the thin ribbon that stretched and wound its way aimlessly across the rugged countryside below.

"The Yukon River. She flows over two thousand miles from northwest Canada to the Bering Sea."

"I'm impressed."

"Is there anything you'd like to know about Paul?"

"Paul Trevor? Not really. Is there anything I should know?" Like her two aunts, John seemed to mention the other man's name at every opportunity.

He gave another merry chuckle. "Guess you'll be finding out everything about him soon enough."

"Right." She eyed him curiously. The way things were going, she'd be anxious to get a look at this man who insisted she have all this costly gear.

"He's a quiet man, but you'll grow accustomed to that."

"I usually chatter enough for two. I think we'll get along fine. Besides, I don't plan on being here that long."

John frowned. "I doubt that you'll ever get Paul to leave Alaska."

Caroline was offended by the brisk tone. "I don't have any intention of trying."

The amusement faded from John's rugged face as he checked the instruments on the front panel. "You aren't afraid of flying, are you?"

She hadn't thought about it much until he mentioned it. "Afraid? Why should I be afraid?"

"It looks like we may be headed into a bit of a storm. Nothing to worry about, mind you, if you aren't accustomed to a few jerks now and again. This could be a real roller coaster for a while."

"I'm fine." The sudden chill in the cabin caused Caroline to reach for the thermos. "My aunts make a mean cup of tea. Interested?"

"No, thanks." He focused his attention on the gauges and slipped his seat belt into place. Caroline mimicked his actions, her fingers trembling.

The first cup of the spiked tea brought a rush of warmth to her chilled arms, and when the plane pitched and heaved, Caroline refilled the plastic cup and gulped down a second. "Hey, this is fun," she said with a tiny laugh twenty minutes later. If the truth be known, she was frightened half out of her wits, but she put on a brave front and held on to the cup with both hands. Her aunts' tea was courage in a thermos.

By the time John announced they were within a half hour of Atta, Caroline's cheeks were a bright rosy hue and she was as warm as toast. As they made their descent, she peeked out the window at the uneven row of houses. A thick blanket of snow covered the ground and curling rings of smoke rose from a dozen chimneys.

"It's not much of a town, is it?"

"Around three hundred. Mostly Athabascans—they're Indians who were once nomadic, following caribou and other game. Once the white settlers arrived, they established permanent villages. Nowadays, they mostly hunt and fish. Once we get a bit closer you'll see a string of caribou hides drying in the sun."

"How interesting." Caroline knew that sounded trite, but she didn't know how else to comment.

"Paul's the only white man there."

"Oh."

"Naturally you'll be there now."

"What does Paul do?"

John gave her a curious stare. "I thought you would know. He keeps tabs on the pump station for the pipeline."

She brushed aside the soft, blond curl that fell over her face. "I thought he was a guide of some sort."

As the Cessna circled the village, Caroline saw what appeared to be tiny ants scurrying out of the houses. Several raised their arms high above their heads and waved. "They see us."

"They've probably spent days preparing for your arrival."

"How thoughtful." The village must only entertain a handful of tourists a year, she thought, and residents obviously went to a great deal of trouble to make sure that those who did arrive felt welcome. Caroline rubbed her eyes. It seemed the whole world was pitching and weaving. The people and the houses blurred together and she shook her head, hoping to gain some of her bearings. The thermos was empty; Caroline was more than a little intoxicated.

A glance at the darkening clouds produced a loud grumble from John. "It doesn't look like I'm going to be able to stick around for the reception."

"I'm sorry." John was probably a local hero. This welcoming party was likely to be as much in his honor as her own. By now it appeared that the entire village was outside pointing toward the sky and waving enthusiastically. "I don't see any runway."

"There isn't one."

"But..."

"There's enough of a clearing to make a decent landing. I've come down in a lot worse conditions."

Caroline's long nails cut into her palm. She didn't find his words all that reassuring. Why her aunts would choose such a remote village was beyond her. This whole trip was turning into much more of an adventure than she'd ever dreamed.

As the plane descended, she closed her eyes until she felt the landing wheels bounce over the uneven ground. She was jostled, jolted and jarred, but was otherwise unscathed. Once they came to a complete stop, Caroline breathed again.

The single engine continued to purr as John unhooked his seat belt. "Go ahead and climb out. I'll hand you the gear."

Using her shoulder to pry open the airplane door, Caroline nearly fell to the snow in an effort to climb down gracefully. A gust of wind sobered her instantly. "Lordy, it's cold."

"Right, but Paul will warm you," John shouted enthusiastically over the engine's noise. He tossed out her suitcase and a large variety of boxes and sacks. "Good luck to you. I have a feeling you're the best thing to happen to Paul in a long while."

"Thanks." She stood in the middle of the supplies and blinked twice. "Aren't you coming with me?"

"No time. I've got to get out of here before this storm hits." He waved, shut the door and a minute later was taxiing away.

With a sense of disbelief, Caroline watched him leave. Already she could see a team of dogs pulling a large sled racing toward her. She waved on the off chance they couldn't see her. Again the earth seemed to shift beneath her feet, and she rubbed her eyes in an effort to maintain her balance. Good grief, just how much of that tea had she drunk? Apparently enough!

By the time the first dogsled arrived, she'd produced a synthetic smile. "Hello," she greeted and raised her hand, praying no one would guess that she was more than a little tipsy.

"Welcome."

The man who must be Paul Trevor walked toward her and handed her a small bouquet of flowers. He was tall and dark, and from what she could see of his bearded face, reasonably attractive. Untamed curls grew with rakish disregard across a wide, intelligent brow. His eyes were as blue as her own, and were deep and thoughtful. She had taken to John Morrison immediately, but Caroline wasn't sure that she would like this man. John had spoken of him with respect, and it was obvious that he was considered a leader among the villagers. But his intensity unnerved her. His eyes held the determination of a mule. Caroline wasn't about to let him intimidate her; however, now wasn't the time to say much of anything. Not when her tongue refused to cooperate with her brain.

"Thank you." Caroline smelled the flowers, expecting to savor the sweet scent of spring, only to have her nose tickled by the prickly needles. Startled, her eyes popped open.

"They've been dried."

"Oh." She felt like a fool. There weren't flowers in Atta this time of year. "Of course—they must be."

"Everything's ready if you are."

"Sure." Caroline assumed he was speaking of the welcoming reception.

The large group of natives quickly loaded her suitcase and the other boxes onto the sleds. Caroline took a step toward Paul and nearly stumbled. Again the ground pitched and heaved under her feet. She recognized it as the potency of the tea and not an earthquake, but for a moment she was confused. "I'm sorry," she murmured and shook her head. "I seem to be a bit unsteady."

Paul guided her to the dogsled. "It might be better if you sat." He pulled back the thick hide and helped her into the sled. The huge husky turned his head around to examine her and Caroline grinned sheepishly at the dog. "I don't weigh much," she told him, and giggled. Good grief, she was beginning to sound like her aunts.

The short trip into Atta took only a matter of minutes. Paul helped her out of the sled and led her into the long narrow building in the center of the village. Candles flickered all around the room. Tables filled with a wide variety of meats and other dishes lined the walls. A priest, Russian

Orthodox, Caroline guessed, was dressed in a long gold robe. He smiled at her warmly and stepped forward to greet her, taking her hand in his.

"Welcome to Atta. I'm Father Nabokov."

"I'm pleased to meet you, Father." Caroline prayed that he didn't smell her aunts' brew on her breath.

"Are you hungry?" Paul had shed his thick coat and took hers. The force of his personality was defined in his stance. On meeting him, Caroline understood why both John and her two aunts had found occasion to mention Paul. His personality was forceful, but there was a gentleness to him as well, a tenderness he preferred to disguise.

"Hungry? No... not really," she replied tentatively, realizing that she was staring at him. Paul didn't seem to mind. For that matter, he appeared to be sizing her up as well, and from the lazy, sensual smile that spread from his mouth to his eyes, he appeared to like what he saw.

If Caroline could only have cleared her mind, she felt she might have been able to start up a witty conversation, but her thoughts were preoccupied with the noisy murmuring around her. It looked as though the entire village was crammed inside the meeting hall. Someone was playing music, but it wasn't on an instrument that Caroline recognized. A fiddle player joined the first man and the festive mood spread until everyone was laughing and singing. Several helped themselves to plates and heaped large amounts of food from the serving dishes.

"Perhaps it would be best if we started things now," Father Nabokov suggested. "It doesn't look like we'll be able to hold things up much longer."

"Do you mind?" Paul glanced toward Caroline.

"Not in the least. Why wait?" Nearly everyone was eating and drinking as it was, and she could see no reason to delay the party. Someone brought her a glass of champagne and Caroline drank it down in one big swallow. The room was warm and she was so thirsty. The worst part was keeping her eyes open; the lids felt exceptionally heavy and without much effort she could have crawled into bed and slept for a month.

The music stopped and Paul made an announcement that brought instant silence. The villagers shuffled forward and formed a large circle around Paul, Caroline and the priest.

Caroline smiled and momentarily closed her eyes, awaiting the announcement that appeared to be forthcoming. She felt so warm and relaxed. These wonderful, wonderful people were holding some kind of ceremony to welcome her. If only she could stay awake.

Father Nabokov began speaking in what Caroline assumed was Russian, his voice soft and reverent. The smell of incense filled the air. She made an honest effort to listen, but the priest's words were low and monotonous. The others in the room seemed to give heed to his message and Caroline glanced around, smiling now and again.

"Caroline?" Paul's strong voice cut into her musings.

"Hmm." She realized the meeting hall was quiet, each serious brown face regarding her expectantly as though they were waiting for some kind of announcement from her. Paul slipped an arm around her waist, pulling her closer to his side.

"Would you like him to repeat the question?" Paul questioned softly, regarding her with a thoughtful frown.

"Yes, please," Caroline said quietly. If she knew what these people expected of her, then maybe she'd understand. "What's he saying?"

"It's in Russian. He's asking you if you'll cherish and obey me."

without turning until she could have swived into Dougald's
arms? I wouldn't

The music stopped and Paul made an announcement. She
brought herself silence. The Buildings startled forward and
formed a large circle around Paul, Caroline and the priest.

Caroline smiled and murmured, as she drew near, as the
line shuffled forward that she wanted to be forthcoming. She
felt ... warm and excited. Everywhere ... she would of those
... were calmer. So a ... kind of fondness was welcome but, in
truth, she could stay awake.

Father Nabokov began speaking to Paul. Caroline
noticed new Nana saw the voice grit and reverent. The swell
of the ... filled the air. She made an inward effort to resist
but the patterns were there too and they were too late. Too late
... already. The ... it over a ... and ... suddenly ... pieces ... and
everyone ... seemed so reverent ... the ... and the life ...
around ... Paul ... his ... eyes peace her into her ... message ...
forlorn. She realized she ... knowing that it was a piece ...

Chapter Two

"Cherish and obey?" Caroline repeated, stunned. This
welcoming reception was more than she could understand.
How she wished she hadn't had quite so much of her aunts'
brew. Obviously this little get-together in her honor was
some kind of elaborate charade—one in which Caroline had
no intention of participating.

The circle of round faces continued to stare anxiously at
her, each growing more and more distressed with the
amount of time it took for her to respond to the simple
question.

"Caroline?" Even Paul's gruff voice revealed his uneasiness.

Caroline opened her mouth to announce that if they were
going to play silly tricks on her, she didn't want to have
anything to do with this party. She looked at Paul and
blinked. "I thought you were going to be my guide." Apparently folks took the guiding business seriously in these
parts.

Father Nabokov smiled gently. "He will guide you all
through your life, child."

A clatter rose from the crowd as several started arguing loudly. Father Nabokov raised his arms above his head and waved in an effort to bring order to the party. "Miss Myers." He paused to wipe his brow with a clean kerchief that magically appeared from inside his huge sleeve. "This is an important decision. Would you like me to repeat the question?"

Paul's intense blue eyes cleared as his gaze pinned hers, demanding that she answer the priest.

An older man, an Athabascan Indian who was apparently a good friend of Paul's, interceded. "You can't back down now—you agreed earlier."

"I did?" What had her aunts gotten her into now? Everyone continued to glare at her and Caroline grew unsettled at the resentment that flared briefly in the brown-eyed stares. "Could I have something cold to drink?"

"It's a bit unusual," Father Nabokov said, clearly discomposed. For a second time, he reached for the kerchief and rubbed it over his brow and one eye.

"Walter," Paul called to the older man who immediately stepped forward.

A minute later, the white-haired Athabascan approached the three with a tall glass of champagne. Paul handed it to Caroline, who hurriedly emptied the contents and sighed audibly as the bubbly liquid tickled the back of her throat. She returned it to the man Paul called Walter and smiled her thanks. "This is excellent champagne."

Walter nodded abruptly and glanced briefly in Paul's direction. "Paul wanted the best for you."

Caroline noted the censure in the old Indian's voice and again felt a growing sense of unease. "What was it you wanted me to say again?"

Paul's posture stiffened and he expelled an impatient sigh. "Yes would suffice."

"All right then," she agreed in an attempt to be as amicable as possible. Everyone had gone through so much trouble on her behalf, cooking and planning this reception for her arrival. She hated to disappoint them, although she briefly wondered if all tourists were subjected to this type of party—the priest, the incense, the two altar boys robed in white, not to mention the entire village. Her lovely, adorable aunts had sent her to the one place in the world where she would feel welcomed and secure.

"You do?" Father Nabokov looked greatly relieved.

"Sure," she concurred brightly and shrugged her shoulders expressively. "Why not?"

"Indeed." The priest grinned, then grew serious and turned his attention to Paul. The priest's eyes glowed as he gazed upon them both. Caroline felt Paul slide his arm around her once again, but she didn't object. She attempted to give the man of God her full attention, but the room was so warm and everything was so pleasant. She fanned her face with both hands and with some difficulty kept a stiff smile on her lips.

Paul took her right hand and slipped a simple gold band on her ring finger. It looked like a friendship ring and Caroline thought it a fitting gesture. These people did seem friendly.

"I now pronounce you man and wife," Father Nabokov proclaimed solemnly and raised his right hand, moving it in the sign of the cross as he granted them a spiritual blessing. "You may now kiss the bride."

Wife! Kiss the bride! Caroline was completely stunned. She tried to smile, but none would come. She turned to Paul, her eyes filled with questions.

"That's not right, is it?"

Paul didn't answer her. Instead, he turned her in his arms and his gaze narrowed longingly on her face. Before she had the opportunity to voice her uncertainties, Paul lowered his head toward hers. Caroline's heart thundered nervously and she laid her hands on his chest and gazed up at his bearded face. Surely he could tell that she was stunned. A wedding ceremony! She must be dreaming. That was it—this was all part of a dream. Paul's cobalt-blue eyes softened. Gradually, as though in slow motion, his mouth settled warmly over hers. His touch was firm and experienced, moist and gentle—ever so gentle. *Nice dream,* Caroline mused, *very nice, very real.* She hadn't expected a man of his size and vocation to be so infinitely tender.

Enjoy it, girl, Caroline thought, kissing him back with all the eagerness she could muster. Dreams were over far too quickly. The world spun off kilter, so she slipped her arms around Paul's neck to help maintain her balance. Bringing her body closer to his was all the encouragement he needed. His hands slid over her hips, pressing her ripe body invitingly against his own. His grip tightened and molded her torso to his so that her breasts were flattened against his hard chest. Willingly, Caroline surrendered to the sensual upheaval. From the moment Larry had left her at the altar, she'd been dying to be held in a man's arms and kissed as though there was no moment but this one, priceless space in time.

Father Nabokov cleared his throat, but Caroline paid no mind to the priest's appeal. She may have had her doubts about Paul, but she willingly admitted he was one great kisser. Breathless, they broke apart, but continued to stare at each other, lost in the wonder of the overwhelming response.

Paul draped his wrists over Caroline's shoulder. A hint of a cynical smile touched his mouth. "For a minute there I didn't think you were going to go through with it."

"Is this a dream?" Caroline asked.

Paul gave her a funny look. "No."

She laughed. "Of course you'd say that."

His eyes were as blue as anything Caroline had ever seen and she felt lost in the fathomless depths. The tremulous smile she gave him was by a mouth still on fire from his kiss. Involuntarily, she moistened her lips and watched as his gaze darkened.

"Let's get out of here," he growled. Briefly his eyes left hers. Without another word, he hauled Caroline into his arms in one movement and stalked toward the door.

Caroline gasped at the unexpectedness of the action, but the villagers went crazy, resuming the dancing and singing. "Where . . . where are we going?"

"The cabin."

"Oh."

Already his lengthy strides had carried him halfway across the floor. The Athabascans cleared a path and Walter stood ready, grinning almost boyishly as he opened the large wooden doors. Walter chuckled as Paul moved past him. "Don't be so impatient. You've waited this long."

Paul growled something under his breath that Caroline couldn't understand and continued walking.

"How far is the cabin?" she asked dreamily.

"Too far," Paul said with a throaty chuckle. Her ready response to his kiss had been a jolting shock. He'd thought he should progress to their lovemaking with far less urgency—court her, let her become acquainted with him first. Yet the moment her mouth had opened to his, he'd recognized that there wasn't any reason to wait.

Leaning back in his arms, Caroline sighed wistfully. "Why is it dark?"

"It's October, love."

"Love?" she repeated, and sudden tears misted her eyes. She hadn't expected to be anyone's love—not after Larry—not for a very long time.

Paul went still. He could deal with anything but her tears. "What's wrong?"

"Nothing," she murmured, and sniffled. She should know not to drink champagne. Tears had always been a by-product of Dom Perignon.

"I want to know." He smoothed the hair from her temple and softly kissed her there. His words revealed a stark truth: he cared. He was the kind of man who would do all he could to make her world right.

If he hadn't been so tender, so gentle, Caroline could have fought against the unwelcome emotion. But he was all that and so much more. She felt hot tears sear a path down her

"Perhaps that would be best. I have lots of questions for you, but I'm too sleepy now. We'll talk in the morning. Okay?" She took a step toward the doorway and her peripheral vision picked up the sight of the silky fur-hemmed nightgown that had been a gift from her two aunts. It was spread across the top of the large brass bed, and resembled a lifeless ghost.

"I'll give you some time alone then," Paul said, heading for the front door.

It closed after him and Caroline stood in the middle of the cabin, wondering at the puzzling events of the day. She'd traveled thousands of miles, participated in some strange Alaskan ceremony, thought she was in a dream, kissed a man whose name she barely knew and then wept in his arms. Alaska was some kind of state!

Moving into the single bedroom, undressing as she went, Caroline paused to admire the thick, brightly colored handmade quilt. The small lamp on the table illuminated the room and Caroline recognized her clothes hanging beside those belonging to a man. Probably Paul. He was a gentleman. She didn't know what the craziness was all about; she'd settle that in the morning. She might even be married. A giggle escaped her as she sat on the edge of the mattress. Married! Wouldn't Larry love that. Paul would understand that there'd been a mistake. Her initial impression of him had been wrong; he'd intimidated her at first, but he was actually gentle and caring. She'd witnessed that quality in him a multitude of times in just the past hour.

Her clothes fell onto the floor as she stripped. With complete disregard, she kicked them under the bed. In the morning, she'd remember to pick them up.

The sheer gown slid over her outstretched arms and down her torso. The fur tickled her calves and Caroline smiled, recalling John's comment about the fur keeping her neck warm. It appeared that Alaskan men had a sense of humor, although she hadn't been overly amused at the time. Married! This simply had to be a dream.... When she woke, they'd straighten everything out.

The bed was soft and warm, and Caroline crawled between the sheets, stifling a wide yawn. Her head was cushioned by a thick feather pillow and her last thought before she flipped off the lamp was of the mountain she'd seen from the plane—Denali. Somehow its magnificence comforted her and lured her into a gentle sleep.

Outside, Paul paced the area in front of the cabin, glancing at his watch every twenty seconds. He was cold and impatient now. With the music from the reception echoing around him, he refused to return to the meeting hall. Caroline had wanted some time to prepare herself and he had reluctantly granted her that, but he wasn't pleased. In time she'd learn to be less shy; there wouldn't be room for modesty when winter arrived.

Once he was certain that she'd had as much time as any woman would possibly require, Paul returned to the cabin. The bedroom light was out and he could see the outline of her figure in the bed. His bed. Waiting for him. He recalled the way her soft, lush body had felt against his. With vivid clarity he remembered the way her big blue eyes had looked at him when she had suggested going to bed. Then she'd asked him if she was dreaming. The woman was drunk—drunk on her wedding night. From the time he'd received her letter, Paul had decided to wait for the rewards of marriage until she was ready. But oh Lord, that kiss. For a moment he'd thought she had been as eager as he. He wanted their lovemaking to be slow and easy, but hadn't anticipated her effect on him to be this powerful. The restraint required not to rush to her side weakened him. The taste of her lips lingered on his own and the sample left him craving more. He yearned to hold her breasts and feel their scrumptious weight in his palms. He hungered to taste the sweetness of her mouth again. Pausing to chase away a vision of her, he took a deep breath and leaned against the counter.

In an effort to gain perspective, Paul took down the bottle of Jack Daniel's from the cupboard and poured a stiff drink. He had to think things through. He was convinced she didn't believe their marriage was real, yet she had to know that he had brought her all this way for exactly that purpose. During the wedding she'd looked so confused and unsure. As her husband, he fully expected to claim his marital rights, only he preferred to wait until she was a tad more sober. He wanted a wife and had made that evident in his letter. This was to be a real marriage in every way, and she had come to him on his terms without question. Yet he felt as nervous as a callow youth.

He sat at the table and downed the drink, waiting for its numbing effect. If anything, sitting there and thinking about Caroline in his bed, dressed in that see-through silk gown, had the opposite effect upon him. He'd hoped to cool his passion with sound reasoning and good whiskey, but had ended up fanning the flames.

Standing, Paul delivered the empty glass to the sink and noted that his hands were trembling. He felt like a coiled spring, tense, ready. Oh yes, he was ready.

He moved into the bedroom and undressed in the dark, taking time to fold each piece of clothing and set it on top of the dresser. For a moment he toyed with the idea of sleeping elsewhere, but quickly rejected the thought. He'd be the laughingstock of the entire community if he spent the night anyplace but beside Caroline.

She was asleep, he realized from the evenness of her breathing. Silently he thanked God for that. Five minutes earlier and he would have come to her like a wild beast. As it was he was barely able to restrain himself.

The mattress dipped as he carefully slid in beside her. She sighed once and automatically rolled into his arms, nestling her head against his chest. Paul's eyes widened with the force of his resolve.

Without pause, Caroline stroked her fingertips over his lean ribs. He swallowed convulsively against the sweet torture of her touch and strengthened his self-possession by gently removing her hands from his torso. If only she could appreciate what he was giving up.

"Love," he whispered in her ear, brushing back the thick curtain of blond hair. "Roll onto your side, okay?"

"Hmm?" Caroline was having the sweetest dream. Not for a moment did she believe the man beside her was real. He was part and parcel of the warm, exciting fantasy that had begun earlier.

"I know you would prefer to wait." Paul couldn't believe he was telling her this; she'd come so willingly into his arms.

"Wait?"

"Never mind," he whispered. "Just go back to sleep." Unable to resist, he kissed her gently on the brow and shifted his weight away from her.

Unexpectedly, the comforting, irresistible warmth beside her moved and Caroline edged closer to it. With a sigh of longing, she buried her face in the hollow of his neck.

"Caroline, please, this is difficult enough," he whispered, inhaling harshly. She flattened her hand against his tight abdomen and slowly brushed her lips over his.

With every muscle, Paul struggled for control. Any second and he'd be irrevocably and completely lost. He feasted on her mouth with the intense hunger of a greedy, starving man. Caroline's mouth opened to his as their tongues met, warred, dueled and surrendered. Paul was the one to break the contact, twisting so that he lay on his back. His control was slipping fast; another minute and he wouldn't have been able to stop. Her mouth—oh what a mouth she had, soft and more luscious than any honey he'd ever tasted.

Caroline felt unbearably hot. She loved the secure surroundings; if only she didn't feel like she was sitting on top of a fireplace. The thought was so illogical that she bolted upright, giggled and tossed the blankets aside. She fell back onto the pillow and raised her hands above her head, intertwining her fingers. The ceiling was spinning around and around. In an effort to block out the dizzying sight, she closed her eyes and sought anew the security of the dream resting at her side.

Again Paul tried to move away from her and again had little success. Caroline wanted him close. She couldn't understand why he kept leaving her. If he was part and parcel of her dream, the least he could do was stick around for the fun part. She reached for him again, locking her arms around his neck, kissing him.

"Caroline, for God's sake, stop it."

"Why?"

"Because you're drunk," he hissed.

She giggled. "I know." Her fingers roamed over his sleek shoulders. "Please kiss me again. Has anyone ever told you that you're a great kisser?"

"I can't kiss you." *And remain sane,* he added silently.

"But I want you to." She sounded like a whiny child and the sound shocked her. "Oh, never mind, I wouldn't kiss me either." With that she let out a noisy yawn and pressed her cheek against his hard chest. "You have nice skin," she murmured before closing her eyes.

"You do too," he whispered, and ran his hand down the length of her spine. "Very nice."

"Are you sure you don't want to kiss me?"

Paul groaned. His nobility had some restrictions and he wasn't going to be able to hold off much longer with her wanting him to hold and kiss her every ten seconds.

A soft, purring sound came from deep within her throat as she sighed. He felt like velvet—warm, smooth, and so inviting. Caroline purred again and closed her eyes. It wasn't until later that she realized that the prickly feeling over her soft breasts was caused by his chest hairs. Her hands reveled in his strength as they roamed down the corded muscles of his shoulders.

"Good night, love," he whispered, kissing the crown of her head. He continued to hold her close, almost savoring the sweet torture.

Caroline smiled, content. Just before she gave into the irrepressible urge to sleep, she felt his kiss, and prayed that all her dreams would be this real and this delicious.

* * *

Snuggling closer to the warmth at her side, Caroline woke slowly. Her first conscious thought was that her head ached. It more than ached; it throbbed with each pulse and with every sluggish heartbeat as her memory returned, muddled and confused. She rolled onto her back, holding the sides of her head between her hands, and groaned aloud. She was in bed with a man she barely knew. Unfortunately, he appeared to be well acquainted with everything there was to know about her. Extremely well acquainted. Her first inclination was to kick him out of the bed. He'd taken advantage of her inebriated state, and she bit back bitter words as a flush of hot embarrassment brightened her cheeks.

Opening her eyes and looking at him were impossible tasks. She couldn't face the man.

"Good morning," the deep male voice purred.

"It...wasn't a dream, was it?" she asked in a tone that was faint and apprehensive.

Paul chuckled. "You mean you honestly don't remember anything?"

"Some." She kept her eyes pinched shut, too mortified to face him.

"Do you remember the part about us getting married?"

Caroline blinked. "I'm not sure."

"In case you don't, I suppose I should introduce myself. I'm Paul Trevor, your husband."

Chapter Three

"**T**hen it was real!" Still holding her head, Caroline struggled to a sitting position. Gradually her eyes opened and she glared down at the bearded man beside her.

Paul was lying on his side, watching her with an amused grin. He leaned on his elbow and slowly shook his head. "I can hardly believe that you didn't expect to be married."

The heat in her face was enough to keep the cabin warm for the entire winter. "I knew at the time you...you weren't all dream." She was honest even at the expense of her stubborn pride.

"We're married, love."

"Stop calling me your love. I am not your or any other man's love, and we've certainly got to do something about annulling this marriage." She winced at the flash of pain that shot through her head.

"If you'd rather I didn't call you love, I won't."

"Call me Caroline or Miss Myers, anything but your love."

"I am your husband."

"Will you stop saying that?"

"I have the paperwork to prove it."

Caroline tucked the blankets under her arms and scowled at him with all the fury she could muster. "Then I challenge you to produce them."

"As you wish." He tossed aside the blankets and climbed out of the bed, standing only partially clothed before her.

Caroline gasped and looked away. "I would really appreciate it if you'd put something on."

"Why?" He tossed a questioning glance over his shoulder.

The red flush seeped into her ears and she swallowed convulsively. "Just do it.... Please."

Chuckling, Paul withdrew the slip of paper from his shirt pocket. "Here," he said, handing it to her.

Caroline grabbed it from his fingers and quickly unfolded it. Disregarding the effort it took to read, her gaze quickly scanned the contents. The document looked official enough and her name was signed at the bottom, although she barely recognized the signature as her own. Vaguely she remembered Paul having her sign some papers when they had entered the meeting hall. At the time, Caroline had been so bemused she'd thought it was something to do with registering a guest.

"I signed first," Paul explained, "and gave you the pen."

"Yes, I remember... but at the time I assumed it was something all tourists did." It sounded so ridiculous now that she wanted to weep at her own stupidity. "The party yesterday was our wedding reception, wasn't it?"

"Yes."

Caroline shook her head in utter bewilderment. "I... I thought Atta received so few tourists that they greeted everyone like that."

"Caroline, you're not making any sense."

"I'm not!" she shouted, and winced. "You should look at it from my point of view."

"But you agreed to marry me weeks ago."

"I most certainly did not!"

"I have the letter."

"Now that's something I'd like to see. I may not have been in full control of my wits yesterday, but I know for a fact I'd never heard of you until..." The words died on her lips. "My aunts—my romantic, idealistic, scheming aunts...they couldn't have. They wouldn't..."

Paul regarded her suspiciously. "Whose aunts?"

"Mine. Just get the letter and p-please..." she stammered, "please put something on. This is all extremely embarrassing."

Grumbling under his breath, Paul reached for his pants and slipped them over long legs, snapping them at the waist. Next he unfolded his shirt and slipped his arms inside the long sleeves, but he left it unbuttoned. "There. Are you satisfied?"

"Somewhat." Speaking of clothes reminded Caroline of her own state of skimpy dress. When Paul's back was turned, she scooted to the very edge of the mattress in a frantic search for her cords and sweater. She remembered undressing, but she couldn't recall where she'd placed her things.

Stretching as far as possible while in a crouched position, Caroline flung her hand down and made a wide sweep under the bed and managed to retrieve her sweater. Fearing Paul would return at any minute, she slipped her arms into the bulky sleeves and yanked it over her head. Shaking her hair free of the confining collar, Caroline came eye to eye with Paul.

He stood over her, his grin slightly off center. "Just give me that letter," Caroline demanded.

"Would you like me to read it to you?"

"No." She grabbed for it. "I don't appreciate these sophomoric games, Paul Trevor."

"Go ahead and read it for yourself while I fix us something to eat."

"I'm not hungry," she announced sharply, jerking the envelope from his hand. Food was the last thing on her mind at the moment.

Humming as though he hadn't a care in the world, Paul left the bedroom while Caroline's eyes narrowed on his back. The audacity of the man to appear unruffled at this unexpected turn of events was too much for her usually bright sense of humor.

The instant Paul was out of sight, Caroline tore into the letter. The creases were well worn and with a mild attack of guilt she realized that he'd read the neatly typed page repeatedly.

Dear Paul,
My name is Caroline Myers and I'm responding to your advertisement in the Seattle *Post-Intelligencer*. I am seeking a husband to love. My picture is enclosed, but I'm actually more attractive in person. That isn't to say I'm the least bit vain. I enjoy fishing and hiking and Scrabble and other games of skill. Since I am the last of the Ezra Myers family left in the Northwest, I look forward to having children. I'm a nurse currently employed by Dr. Kenneth James, but can leave my employment on two weeks' notice. I look forward to hearing from you.

                                        Most sincerely,

The evenly shaped letters of her name were penned at the bottom of the page in what Caroline recognized as her Aunt Mabel's handwriting.

With sober thoughts, Caroline dressed and joined Paul in the kitchen. He pulled out a chair for her and handed her a cup of coffee.

She laid the letter on the table. "I didn't write this."

"I thought that might have been the case." He wasn't sure of what was happening, but he knew one thing—they were married and he'd waited too long to give her up now.

Her face flushed, she wondered just what *had* happened after the ceremony. Oh Lord, she should remember something as important as that. "I have these two maiden aunts...." Caroline hedged, not knowing where to start an explanation.

"So I gathered." He pulled out the chair across from her and set his elbows on the table. "They answered my advertisement?"

"Advertisement? Apparently so."

"How'd they convince you to marry me?"

"That's just it.... They didn't." Caroline dumped a tablespoon of sugar into the coffee and stirred it several times.

"Then why did you go through with it?"

"I...wasn't myself yesterday. I...I didn't fully realize what was happening." She recognized how utterly ridiculous that sounded, and hurried to explain. "You see, Aunt Mabel and Aunt Ethel—they're actually my great-aunts, but I've always just called them Aunt—anyway, they told me they were giving me a trip to Alaska."

"Why?"

She wasn't sure of how much she wanted to reveal. She understood the reason her two scheming aunts had answered Paul's personal ad. They'd been worried about her after the breakup with Larry. The question was how was she going to untangle herself from this unfortunate set of circumstances. "The purpose for my agreeing to come to Alaska isn't important."

"Few people choose to visit Alaska on the brink of winter."

She wished he would stop arguing with her. Keeping her cool under these conditions was difficult enough.

"Was it because of Larry?"

Caroline felt her blood run cold, then rise to her face. "They told you about Larry?"

"No, you did."

"I did!" Her blue eyes clashed with his and then quickly lowered. "Oh Lord, is there anything I didn't tell you?"

"I imagine there's quite a bit." He paused to drink his coffee. "Please go on. I'm curious about how you got yourself into this predicament."

"Well, Aunt Mabel and Aunt Ethel insisted I take this trip. I'd never been to Alaska and they kept telling me how wonderful the fishing and hiking is. I didn't know how they could afford it, but..."

"They didn't."

"What do you mean?" She wrapped her fingers around the hot mug. This was getting more complicated by the minute.

"I paid for it."

"Terrific," she groaned. She'd need to repay him for that and God only knew what else.

"Then John Morrison met me in Fairbanks and the ride to Atta got a bit rugged and in order not to show him how frightened I really was, I drank the thermos of tea my aunts sent along."

"Tea?"

"Not regular tea," Caroline corrected. "My aunts have a special brew—their father passed the recipe on to them."

"I see." One corner of his lip curved upward in a futile effort to contain his smile.

Caroline wasn't fooled. "Damn it, would you stop looking amused? We're in one hell of a mess here."

"We are?" He cocked one eyebrow expressively. "We're married, Caroline, and the ceremony is as legal as it gets. We stood before God and man with the whole village as witness."

"But you don't honestly expect me to honor those vows.... You can't be that unreasonable."

"We're married."

"It was a mistake!"

"Not as far as I'm concerned."

"I'll have it annulled," she threatened.

His grin was wide and cynical. "After last night?"

Her cheeks flamed even hotter. So something had happened. "All right," she said tightly, "we'll get a divorce."

"There will be no divorce."

"You can't be serious! I have no intention of staying married to you. Good heavens, I don't even know you."

"You'll have plenty of time for that later."

"Later? Are you nuts? I'm not staying here a second longer than necessary. There's been a terrible mistake and I want out before something more happens."

"And I say we make the best of the situation."

He was being completely unreasonable. "Just how do you propose we do that?"

"Stay married."

"You're crazy." She stood up so abruptly that the ladder-back chair went crashing to the floor. "Let's talk this out in a logical fashion."

"The deed is done." As far as Paul was concerned, there was nothing to discuss; she was here in his home and they were legally married. He wasn't going to let her leave him now.

"Deed," Caroline echoed, feeling slightly sick to her stomach. "Then we...I mean last night, you and I...we...?" Her eyes implored him to tell her what had happened.

Paul yearned to assure her that they had shared only a few kisses, but the instant he explained that nothing—well, almost nothing—had happened, she'd bolt. "Caroline, listen to me. It's too late for argument."

"Not from my point of view." Her arms were wrapped around her stomach as she paced the floor. "I want out of here and I want out now."

Paul's mouth thinned with irritation. "That's unfortunate because you're staying."

"You can't force me."

His frustration was quickly mounting. "Would you give us a chance? I'll admit we're getting off to a shaky start, but things will work out."

"Work out!" she cried. "I'm married to a man whose face I can't even see."

Paul ran his hand over the neatly trimmed beard. "It's winter and my beard is part of nature's protection. I won't shave until spring."

"I...I don't know you."

Despite himself, he chuckled. "I wouldn't say that."

"Will you stop bringing up the subject of last night?"

Caroline was surprised by Paul's low chuckle. "Now what's so damn funny?" she demanded.

"You're a passionate woman, Caroline Trevor. If it's this good between us in the beginning, can you imagine how fantastic it will be when we know each other better?"

"Stop it!" Furious, she stalked across the room and stood in front of the small window. A thin layer of snow covered the ground and in the distance Caroline made out the form of a small plane against the blue sky. Her heart rate soared as she contemplated her means of escape. If the plane landed in Atta, she could sneak out before Paul discovered she was missing. Hope sprang eternal.

"Caroline?"

She turned back to him and pressed her hand to her breast. "Were you so desperate for a wife that you had to advertise? That doesn't say a whole lot about your sterling character."

"There are few opportunities in Alaska, love. I don't often get into Fairbanks."

"I already asked you not to call me that."

"I apologize."

He didn't look the least bit contrite and his attitude infuriated her further. "Why did you choose me? You must have received more than one response."

"I received several." *Hundreds, if the truth be known.* "I chose you because I liked your eyes."

"Wonderful!" She tossed her hands in the air.

"But your aunts were right—you are more attractive in person."

Caroline couldn't believe what she was hearing. Paul Trevor honestly expected her to honor her vows and live here on this godforsaken chunk of ice. She was frantic now and growing more desperate by the minute. "I . . . have disgusting habits. Within a week you'll be ready to toss me to the wolves."

"There isn't anything we won't be able to work out."

"Paul, please, look at it from my point of view." Her eyes pleaded with him.

Paul struggled with the effect her baby blues had on him. Refusing her anything was going to be damn difficult, but the matter of their marriage was something on which there was no compromise. "We'll discuss it later," he told her stiffly, and turned away from her. "I've got to get out to the station."

"What station?"

"The pump station by the pipeline."

"John told me something about it." Already her mind was scheming. She'd let him go and pray that the plane circling overhead would land. If it did, then she could convince the pilot to get her out of Atta before Paul even knew she was gone.

"I won't be more than an hour or two."

"All right." She slowly rubbed the palms of her hands together. "And when you get back, I'm certain we'll reach some agreement. It could be that I'll be willing to stay."

Paul eyed her suspiciously, not trusting this sudden change of heart. While he shrugged his arms into his coat, he spoke. "I want your word, Caroline, that you'll remain here in the cabin."

"Here? In this cabin?"

"Your word of honor."

Caroline swallowed uncomfortably; she didn't want to lie. Normally she spoke the truth even to her own detriment. "All right," she muttered, childishly crossing her fingers behind her back. "I'll stay here."

"I have your word?"

"Yes." Without flinching, her eyes met his.

"I won't be long." His hand was on the doorknob.

"Take your time." Already, the plane was landing; she could hear it in the distance. "While you're gone, I'll find my way around the kitchen," she said brightly. "By the time you return, I'll have lunch ready."

Again Paul eyed her doubtfully. She sounded much too eager to have him leave, but he didn't have the time to worry now. Giving her a few hours alone to think matters through was best. She'd given him her word and he was forced into trusting her. Already he was an hour late; Walter had said he would stand in for him, but Paul had refused. The station was his responsibility.

The second the door closed after Paul, Caroline dashed into the bedroom and jerked her clothes off the hangers, stuffing them back inside her suitcase. With a sense of guilt, she left the winter gear that Paul had purchased on her behalf. He'd gone to a great deal of trouble and expense for her, but she couldn't be blamed for that.

A quick check at the door revealed that Paul was nowhere within sight. She breathed a bit easier and cautiously walked out. Although the day was clear, the cold cut straight through her thin jacket.

A couple of Athabascan women passed Caroline and smiled shyly, their eyes bright and curious. She returned their silent greeting and experienced a twinge of remorse at this regrettable subterfuge. If he'd been more reasonable, then she wouldn't have been forced into doing something this drastic.

The plane was taxiing to a stop at the airstrip where she had been delivered less then twenty-four hours before.

Caroline watched from the center of town as the pilot handed down several plywood crates. A few minutes later, he arrived with the dogsleds.

"Hi." She stepped forward, forcing a calm smile.

The tall burly man looked surprised to see her. "Hello."

"I'm Caroline Myers." She extended her hand for him to shake and prayed he didn't detect her nervousness.

"Burt Manners. What can I do for you?"

"I need a ride to Fairbanks," she said quickly. "Is there any way you could fly me there?"

"Sorry, lady, I'm headed in the opposite direction."

"Where?" She'd go anyplace as long as it was away from Atta and Paul.

"Near Circle Hot Springs."

"That's fine. I'll go there first, just so it's understood that you can fly me to Fairbanks afterward."

"Lady, I've already got a full load. Besides, you don't want to travel to Circle Hot Springs. It's no place for a lady this time of year."

"I don't care. Honest."

"There isn't any room." He started to turn away from her.

"There must be some space available; you just unloaded those crates. Please." Caroline hated the way her voice whined, but she was desperate. The sooner she got away, the better.

"Is that the warmest coat you've got?"

He was looking for excuses and Caroline knew it. "No. I've got another coat. Can I come?"

"I don't know...." Still, he hesitated.

"I'll pay you double your normal fee," Caroline entreated, and placed her hand on his forearm. "I'm desperate to get to Fairbanks."

"All right. All right." Burt rubbed the back of his neck and shook his head. "Why do I feel like I'm going to regret this?"

Caroline barely heard him as she made a sharp turn and scurried across the snow toward the cabin. "I'll be right back. Don't leave without me."

She arrived back at the cabin breathless with excitement and relief, and hurried into the bedroom. Taking the coat Paul had purchased for her went against everything she'd ever known, but she would repay him later, she rationalized, once she was safely back in Seattle. To ease her conscience, she quickly scribbled out an IOU note and propped it on top of the kitchen table where he was sure to find it along with a quick apology for the lie. Her suitcase remained just inside the doorway. She reached for it with one hand and her purse with the other.

The dogsleds and the men were waiting for her when she returned and she climbed aboard, feeling jubilant. Getting away from Paul had been so much easier than she'd anticipated. Of course he could follow her, but that was doubtful unless he had a plane, and she didn't see a hangar anywhere.

As Burt had explained, the seating was cramped.

He talked little on the short trip, which suited Caroline just fine. There wasn't a whole lot she had to say herself.

The landing strip at Circle Hot Springs looked even more unreliable than the one at Atta. Caroline felt her stomach pitch wildly when the Cessna's wheels slammed against the frozen ground, but she managed to conceal her alarm.

They were met by a group of four hunters who quickly unloaded the plane, delivering the gear into a huge hunting lodge. When they'd finished, one of the men brought out a bottle of whiskey and passed it around. The largest hunter, the one called Sam, offered the bottle to Caroline.

"No thanks," she said shaking her head. "I prefer to drink mine from a glass." Burt had said that Circle Hot Springs wasn't any place for a lady, but she'd assumed he'd been concerned about the climate.

"Hey guys, we've got a classy dame with us." Sam laughed gruffly and handed her the bottle. "Take a drink," he ordered.

Fear sent chills racing up and down her spine as Caroline frantically looked to Burt. "I said no, thank you."

"Lay off, you guys," Burt called. "She doesn't have to drink if she doesn't want to."

An hour later, Caroline was convinced she'd made a horrible error. The men sat around drinking and telling dirty jokes that were followed with smutty songs and laughter. Their conversation, or at least what she could hear of the coarse language, was filled with innuendos directed toward her. The more she ignored them, the more they seemed to desire her attention.

While the men took a break, Caroline crept close to Burt's side, doing everything possible to remove attention from herself.

"You okay?" Burt asked.

"Fine," she lied. "When do we leave for Fairbanks?"

He gave her an odd look. "Not until tomorrow morning."

"Tomorrow morning? That long?" She gulped. Oh good God, what had she gotten herself into now?

"Hey, lady, you asked for this."

"Right." She'd progressed from the frying pan and had landed directly into the hot coals of the fire. "I'll be ready first thing in the morning." Although it was the middle of the afternoon, the skies were already beginning to darken.

The hunting lodge had a large living room with a mammoth fireplace. The proprietor/guide introduced himself and brought out another bottle of whiskey to welcome his latest tenants. Caroline refused a drink and inquired politely about renting a room for the night.

"Sorry, honey, we're all filled up."

His eyes were twinkling and Caroline didn't believe him.

"You can stay with me," Sam offered.

"No, thanks."

"Such a polite little thing, ain't you?" Sam placed his arm around her shoulders and squeezed hard. The smell of alcohol on his breath nearly bowled her over. "The boys and me came here for some fun and excitement and are real glad you decided to join us."

"I'm just passing through on my way to Fairbanks," she explained lamely, and cast a pleading glance at Burt, but he was talking to another one of the men and didn't notice her. She groaned inwardly when she noted the glass of amber liquid in his hand.

"We came into Circle Hot Springs for a little fun. You knew that when you insisted on flying here, I'll bet." Again he gave her shoulders a rough squeeze.

Caroline thought her vocal cords had frozen with fear. As the evening progressed matters turned from bad to worse. After the men had eaten, they grew louder, and even more boisterous. Burt had started drinking and from the looks he was giving her, Caroline wondered just how much protection he'd be if worst came to worst. From the way he was staring at her, Caroline realized he'd be little help against the burly men.

Sam polished off his glass of whiskey and rubbed the back of his hand across his mouth. "I don't know about the rest of you yahoos," he shouted, attracting the attention of the small party, "but I'm game for a little entertainment."

"What do you have in mind?"

"Burt brought it for us. Ain't that right, little lady?"

Caroline's eyes pleaded with Burt, but he ignored her silent petition. "I...I didn't say anything like that, but...but I think you should know, I'm not much of a singer."

The men broke into boisterous laughter.

"I can dance a little," she offered, desperate to delay any arguments and discover a means of escape. Her heart felt as though it were refusing to cooperate with her lungs. She'd never been so scared in her life.

"Let her dance."

The whiskey bottle was passed from one member of the party to the next while Caroline stood and edged her way toward the front door. If she could break free, she might be able to locate another cabin to spend the night. Someplace warm and safe.

"I'll...need some music." She realized her mistake when two of the men broke into a melody associated with stripteasers.

"Dance," Sam called, clapping his hands.

"Sure." Caroline was close to tears of anger and frustration. Swinging her hands at her sides, she did a shuffle she'd learned in tap dance class in the fifth grade.

The men booed her efforts.

She offered them a feeble smile and stopped. "I guess I'm not much of a dancer, either."

"Try harder," someone shouted, and they all laughed again.

The log door swung open and a cold north wind caused the roaring fire in the mammoth fireplace to flicker. The man's head was covered with a large fur-lined hood. He flipped it back and stared at Caroline, his eyes cutting straight through her.

"Paul!" She'd never been so glad to see anyone in her life. She wanted to weep with relief.

"What's going on here?" he questioned gruffly.

"We're just having a little fun," Burt said, coming to a stand. "Do you know the lady?"

Paul looked directly at Caroline and slowly shook his head. "Nope. I've never seen her before in my life."

Chapter Four

Caroline stared with utter astonishment as Paul took a seat with the other men, removing his parka and idly setting it aside. Someone handed him a drink, which he quickly downed. Not once did he glance in her direction.

"Well," he said after a short moment, "what's stopping you? Dance."

"Dance?" Caroline echoed.

"Dance," all the men shouted simultaneously.

"And no more little girl stuff, either."

Caroline's anger simmered just below the surface. Couldn't Paul see that she was up to her neck in trouble? The least he could do was rescue her. All morning he'd kept insisting he was her husband and nothing she could do would change that. Well, good grief, if she ever needed a husband it was now. Instead, he appeared to find her predicament highly amusing. Well, she'd show him!

Heaving a deep sigh, she resumed her soft-shoe shuffle, swinging her arms at her sides. She really did need the music and if the men weren't going to provide it, she'd make her own. "On the good ship Lollipop..." she bellowed out.

The only one she seemed to amuse was Paul, but his laugh would be better described as a snicker. Although Caroline avoided looking at him, she could feel the heat of his anger. All right, so she'd lied. And so she'd taken the coat. She did intend to pay him for it, plus what he'd spent on the airplane ticket.

The men were booing her efforts again.

"I told you, none of that Shirley Temple stuff," Sam shouted, his voice slurred. "You're supposed to entertain us."

As much as she hated to reveal her fright, Caroline stopped and her gaze silently pleaded with Paul. Again he ignored her.

"Take your clothes off," Sam insisted. "That's what we want."

"Paul?" she whispered, and her voice trembled. "Please." When she saw him clench his fists, she knew she'd won.

"All right, guys," he said, agilely rising to his feet. "The game's over. I'd like you to meet my wife."

"Your wife!" In a rush, Burt Manners jumped from his sitting position. "Hey, buddy, I swear I didn't know."

"Don't worry about it."

"She came to me begging to leave Atta. I told her Circle Hot Springs was no place this time of year for a lady, but she insisted."

Paul's mouth thinned. "I know."

"You need me to fly you back to Atta?" Burt offered eagerly.

"No, thanks, I've got someone waiting."

"You do?" Caroline was so relieved, she felt faint. Another minute of this horrible tension would have been unbearable. The men were looking at her as though she were some terrible cheat who had swindled them out of an evening's fun and games. And from the way Paul kept avoiding eye contact, she wondered what he would do to her once they were alone. She'd gone from the frying pan into the fire and then back to the frying pan again.

Burt stepped outside the hunting lodge with them to unload Caroline's suitcase from his plane. With every step, he continued to apologize to Paul until Caroline wanted to scream. Paul already knew that she'd practically begged the other man to take her away from Atta. He didn't need to hear it over and over again.

"Fact is," Burt said, standing beside his Cessna, looking uneasy, "I didn't know you were married. If I'd had any idea she was your wife, I never would have taken the little lady."

Paul offered no excuse for her behavior. He was so silent and so furious that Caroline expected him to explode any minute. Without a word, he escorted her to the waiting plane and helped her inside. Every movement was that of a perfect gentleman. She didn't need him to shout at her to realize he was enraged, his calm screamed at her far louder than an angry tirade.

Once aboard the plane, Caroline smiled weakly at the pilot and climbed into her seat. No sooner had she buckled her safety belt than the engines roared to life and the Cessna taxied away.

Paul remained rigid for the entire flight. By the time they circled Atta, Caroline was weak with dread. For the last forty minutes, all she had been able to think about was what Paul was going to do to her once they landed. He'd been so gentle the day before, and now . . . now he looked as though it wouldn't take much for him to strangle her. She'd lied to him, stolen from him and embarrassed him in front of his friends. Maybe he'd be so glad to be rid of her that he'd give her the divorce. Maybe this whole fiasco could be annulled. Oh heavens, why wouldn't he tell her what had happened last night? She rubbed her temples, trying to remember the events following her arrival. She remembered him kissing her and how good it felt, but beyond that her memory was a foggy blur.

When the plane approached the runway, Caroline closed her eyes, preferring not to watch the frozen tundra rising to meet the small aircraft. The Cessna jerked hard once, then again, and for a moment Caroline was certain they were going to crash. A fitting end to her day, she thought gloomily: death. She swallowed down a cry of alarm and looked frantically to Paul, who was seated beside her. His face was void of expression, as though such a bumpy landing was nothing out of the ordinary. When they eased to a stop, Caroline sagged against the back of the seat, weak with relief.

The older Athabascan, Walter, was standing with a team of huskies to meet Paul and Caroline. His ageless eyes hardened when he caught a glimpse of Caroline, and his angry glare could have split a rock.

"See that Bill has a hot meal and place to spend the night," Paul instructed his friend, apparently referring to the pilot.

"Right away."

Once inside the cabin, Caroline turned her back to the potbellied stove and waited. Paul walked past her and carried her suitcase into the bedroom.

Silently, Caroline removed her parka and hung it beside Paul's. The cabin was warm and cozy, dinner was simmering on top of the stove and the enticing smell was enough to make Caroline feel limp. She hadn't eaten all day.

Still, Paul didn't speak and she waited a minute before she broached a conversation.

"Okay, I'm ready," she said when she couldn't stand it any longer. She stood at attention, her fingers clenched together.

"Ready for what?"

"For whatever it is you're going to do to me."

"I'm not going to do anything."

"Nothing?" Caroline uttered in stunned disbelief.

Paul crossed the tiny kitchen and took down two bowls from the highest cupboard.

"But I lied to you."

His eyes narrowed. "I know."

"And I stole the coat."

He nodded.

"And..." Her voice trembled. "I made a fool out of us both."

Paul lifted the lid to the cast iron kettle, filled each bowl to the top with stew and carried them to the table.

Caroline's fingers gripped the back of the kitchen chair. "You must be furious with me."

"I am."

"Then don't you think you should divorce me? I mean— it's obvious that I'm a terrible person. If I were you, I'd be willing to admit I made a bad choice and go on from there." She eyed him hopefully.

He sat down, neatly unfolded the napkin and laid it across his lap. "There will be no divorce."

"But I don't want to be married, I..."

"The deed is done."

"What deed?" she screamed. If she'd had a wedding night, a *real* wedding night, surely she'd remember it.

"We're married," he stated calmly, reaching for his spoon. "Now sit down and eat."

"No." Stubbornly, she crossed her arms over her chest.

"Fine. Then don't eat."

Caroline eyed the steaming bowl of stew. Her mouth began to water and she angrily jerked out the chair. "All right, I'll eat," she murmured hotly, "but I'm doing it under protest." Eagerly, she dipped her spoon into the thick gravy mixture.

"I can tell," Paul said.

When they'd finished, it was Paul who cleared the table and washed the dishes. Wordlessly, Caroline found a dish towel and dried them, replacing the bowls in the overhead cupboard. Her mind was spinning with possible topics of conversation, all of which led to one central issue: their marriage. She earnestly prayed to find a way of getting him to listen to reason.

An hour after dinner, Paul turned off the lights in the living room and moved into the bedroom. Caroline could either follow him or be left standing alone in the dark.

The instant her gaze fell on the bed, Caroline knew she could delay no longer. "Paul, listen to me—there's been a terrible mistake."

"There was no mistake," he countered, starting to unbutton his shirt.

Briefly, Caroline recalled running her fingers through the tufts of dark chest hair. She felt the blood drain from her face and turned away in an effort not to look at him. If there was anything else to remember, she didn't want to do it now. "The mistake wasn't yours, I'll admit to that. But you must understand that I didn't know anything about the wedding."

"We've already been through this and no amount of talk is going to change what happened. We're married, and that's how we're going to stay, so you'd best accept it."

"But I don't want to be married."

Paul heaved a disgusted sigh. "Would it make any difference if I were your beloved Larry?"

"Yes," she cried, then quickly changed her mind. "No, it wouldn't. Oh hell, I don't know."

"The subject is closed," Paul said forcefully. "We won't discuss it again."

"But we have to."

From behind her, Caroline heard Paul throw back the covers and climb into bed. Slowly, she turned, feeling more unhappy and depressed than at any other time in her life.

"Surely you don't believe I'm going to sleep with you?"

"You're my wife, Caroline."

"But . . ."

"Why do you insist upon arguing? We're married; you are my wife and you'll sleep in my bed."

"I won't."

"Fine," he grumbled. "Sleep on the floor. When you get cold enough you'll come to bed." With that, he rolled onto his side and turned out the light, leaving Caroline standing in the dark. She remained where she was for a full minute, indecisive, exhausted, bewildered.

"Paul?"

"Hmm."

"If I . . . If I come to bed, will you promise not to touch me?"

A long moment passed. "After the stunt you pulled today, I doubt that I could."

Caroline supposed she should have been relieved, but she wasn't. Slowly, she undressed and climbed between the clean, crisp sheets. She shivered once and cuddled into a tight ball. As weary as she was, she had expected to fall directly into a deep sleep, but she didn't. In fact, a half hour later, she lay warm, cozy and wide awake.

"Paul?" she whispered.

"What?"

She bit into her bottom lip to hold back the tears. "I'm sorry about today."

"I know."

"Under normal conditions, I would never have done anything so stupid."

"I know that, too."

"Do you know everything?" she flared.

"No."

"I'm glad to hear it."

Another five minutes passed. "Paul?"

"What is it now?"

"Good night."

"Good night, love." She could hear the relief in his voice and her eyes drifted closed.

The next thing Caroline knew, Paul was leaning over her, gently shaking her awake.

"Caroline, it's morning."

Her eyes flew open in alarm and she brushed the thick blond hair from her face. "What time is it?"

"Five o'clock. You'll need to get up and get dressed. There's coffee on the dresser for you."

Maybe he'd relented and had accepted the impossibility of their circumstances. She struggled into a sitting position, her eyes finding his. "Up and dressed? Why?" she asked, hoping he had decided to send her back to Seattle.

"You're coming with me."

"Where?"

"To the pump station."

Her spirits sagged. "But, why? I don't know anything about that...."

"I won't trust you alone again. I don't have any other choice but to bring you with me."

"I'm not going to run away again. I promise."

"You promised before. Now get up and get dressed."

"But, Paul, I won't..."

"I don't have time to argue with you. Either you do as I say or I'll drag you out of bed and take you with me dressed as you are."

Caroline didn't doubt him for a second. "Aye, aye, commander," she said in a crisp, militarylike voice and gave him a mocking salute. Furious, she threw back the sheets and reached for her cords.

Caroline never spent a more boring morning in her life. Paul sat her down in a chair and left her to twiddle her thumbs for what seemed like endless hours. After the first thirty minutes, she toyed with the idea of walking back to the cabin, which she found preferable to sitting in a chair, a punishment more befitting a misbehaving child. However, she quickly discarded that idea. All she needed was to have Paul return to find her gone. If he was furious with her after yesterday, it would be nothing compared to his anger if she pulled the same trick twice. So, although she was bored senseless, Caroline stayed exactly where she was.

Paul returned and she brightened, pleased to have some human contact. But to her dismay, he walked directly past her to another desk and took out a huge ledger, proceeding to record data.

"Paul?"

"Shh."

She pressed her lips together so hard her gums hurt.

He lifted his head when he'd finished and glanced at her expectantly. "You wanted something?"

"I want to go back to the cabin."

"No."

"After what happened yesterday, you can't believe I'll try to get away again." He returned to his work and refused to look at her, ostensibly studying his ledger. Caroline's blood was close to the boiling point. "What are you going to do? Keep me with you twenty-four hours a day?"

"You gave me no option."

"You can't be serious. I'm not going to run away." She pointed to the front door. "There are crazy people out there."

He didn't respond.

"Paul, please, I'll go nuts sitting here with nothing to do."

"Get a book and read." His response was as uncaring as the arctic wind that howled outside the door.

"Oh, I get it," she said in a high-pitched, emotional voice. "So this is to be my punishment. Not only are you going to keep me as your prisoner, but I'm to suffer your company as well. How long?"

"How long what?" With deliberate care, he set his pen aside.

"How long before you learn to trust me? A week? Ten days? A month?"

"I can't answer that. It depends on you."

She flew to her feet, her fists knotted. "Well, you'd be wise to never leave me alone again, because the minute I get the chance, I'm high-tailing it out of here. Somehow, some way, I'll find a way to escape. You can't keep a person against his will. This is the United States of America and slavery was outlawed a hundred years ago."

"A hundred and twenty."

"Furthermore, you're the worst possible husband a woman could ever have. I refuse to be your wife no matter what some piece of paper says." She waited for him to argue with her and when he didn't, she continued her tirade. "Not only that . . . You've got to be the most stubborn man

I've ever met. Stubborn and unreasonable and...and... chauvinistic to boot!''

Paul nodded. "I know. But given time, you'll learn to love me."

"Never." Caroline vowed. "Not while I breathe."

"We'll see."

He sounded so damn sure of himself, so confident, that she longed to throttle him. Drained, Caroline sank back into her chair. To her horror, tears filled her eyes and fell hot against her cheek. She wiped them aside and sniffled loudly to hold back the flood that lay just beneath the surface. "Paul," she cried softly. "I want to go home. Please."

His mouth grew hard and inflexible. "You are home. The sooner you accept that the better it will be for us both."

With that, Caroline buried her face in her hands and wept until there were no tears left. Her eyes burned and her throat ached.

Paul felt the weight of Denali pressing against his back. Dear God, he prayed he was doing the right thing. He could deal with her harangues, even her feisty anger, but her tears were another matter. They brought all his doubts to the surface. A month—he had promised himself a month. If things weren't better by the end of October, he'd send her back to Seattle. Looking at her now, bent over, weeping as though she hadn't a friend in the world, he felt an overwhelming compassion build up in his heart. It would be so easy to love her. She had spunk and character and was more woman than he had ever dreamed he would find.

By midafternoon, Caroline had read one adventure novel, written her two maiden aunts a scathing letter, destroyed that, and had drawn several pictures of a distorted Paul with a knife through his heart. She couldn't help it; after eight hours of complete monotony, she felt murderous.

Toward evening, Paul handed her her parka. "Are you ready to go back to the cabin?"

Was she ever! But she'd be damned before she'd let him know that. With a regal tilt of her chin, she reached for her jacket and slipped her arms inside the warm, thick sleeves.

She hadn't spoken a word to Paul in hours and he hadn't the decency to reveal the least bit of concern. Well, she could hold out longer than he could. By the time she returned to Seattle, he'd be so glad to be rid of her, he'd give her the divorce without so much as an argument.

A thick layer of snow had fallen during the day, and although the cabin was only a short distance from the pumping station, they needed snowshoes to trek their way back. It was the first time that Caroline had ever worn them, and she was forced to squelch her natural delight.

Again, dinner had been left on the stove. Tonight it was a roast with onions, potatoes and carrots simmered in the juice. Caroline wondered who did the cooking, but she refused to ask Paul a thing.

As he had the night before, Paul placed the silverware on the table and delivered their meal from the stove. A couple of times Caroline felt his gaze on her, but she was determined to swallow her tongue before she'd utter a word.

"I must admit," Paul said, halfway through their dinner, "that I prefer the silence to your constant badgering."

"Badgering!" Caroline exploded. "I do not badger. All I want is out of this despicable marriage."

Paul grinned boyishly. "Has anyone told you how expressive your eyes are?"

Caroline pressed her lips together and stabbed her meat with unnecessary force. "I wish that was your heart. Oops, my mistake. You don't have one."

Paul laughed outright at that. "But I do, love," he said gently a few minutes later. "And it belongs to you."

"I don't want it," she cried, struggling to hold back tears of frustration. "Didn't you say you'd received lots of letters in response to your ad for a mail-order bride? Those women all *wanted* to be your wife. Let me go, Paul. Please let me go. I'll repay you the money you've already spent. I swear I will, and I'll..."

"Enough!" He slammed his fist against the table with such force that her water glass toppled. "I'm sick of your pleading. For the last and final time, we're married and we're going to stay married. I refuse to discuss the matter again.''

"Yes, your Majesty," Caroline returned, just barely managing to regain her composure.

Neither one of them ate much after that. Caroline toyed with the food on her plate, but her appetite had vanished, and with it her will to fight.

Standing, she carried her plate over to the sink and scraped it clean. Paul brought over his dishes and they worked together silently, cleaning away the dinner mess.

"Paul," she said, after he'd wiped the last dish dry, "do you play Scrabble?" Her question was asked with a hint of practiced indifference. He must; she'd seen the game on his shelf.

"A bit. Why?"

"Could you and I play? Just to help pass the evening."

"I suppose."

For the first time in two days, Caroline's smile came all the way from her heart. Her two aunts loved Scrabble and had taught it to her as a child. With such expert tutoring, she was practically unbeatable. Her whole world turned brighter. "It would be far more interesting, though," she added with a feigned thoughtful look, "if we played for something, don't you think?"

"How do you mean?"

She brought the game down from the shelf and unfolded the board. "Simple. If I win I am granted one request from you and vice versa."

"And naturally you'd ask for a divorce. No way, love."

"No, not a divorce." She would work up to that.

"If not the divorce, what would you request?"

"Privacy."

"Privacy?"

"Yes, I want to sleep alone."

Skeptical, he eyed the recliner. "For how long?"

She'd go easy on him. "One night."

"Agreed." He pulled up a chair, twisted it around and straddled it. "And on the off chance I win?" He could see the mischief in her brilliant blue eyes. She clearly expected to beat him.

"Yes?" She regarded him expectantly. "What would you want?"

"A kiss."

"A kiss?"

"And not a peck on the cheek either. I want you to kiss me so good it'll turn my insides out." With her sweet mouth, that wouldn't take much, he mused.

Caroline hesitated. "But nothing more than a kiss, right?"

"Nothing more. Agreed?"

With a saucy grin, she stuck out her hand. "Agreed." They shook on it and Caroline laughed. It felt so good to laugh again; she hated the constant bickering. Besides, this was going to be like taking candy from a baby.

"Let the games begin," Paul said, grinning back at her.

For a moment, it was hard to take her gaze off him. His eyes were smiling and although she couldn't see his face through the beard, she felt he must be a handsome man. His eyes certainly were appealing. Playfully, she held up her hand and flexed her ten fingers.

"You draw first." In gentlemanly fashion, Paul handed her the small velvet bag with the mixed letters of the alphabet.

Caroline inserted her hand and drew out an A. She gave him a triumphant look and set it on her letter holder. "I go first."

"Right."

It wasn't until they were a couple of plays into the game that Caroline recognized Paul's skill. He was going to give her some stiff competition. In fact, their scores remained close throughout the match. Caroline was down to her last five letters when Paul gained a triple word slot, added up his score and beamed her a proud look.

"Paul!" Caroline glanced at the board and gasped, unable to hold back her shock. "That's a four-letter word! A dirty four-letter word!"

"I'm well aware of that, love."

"You can't use that. It . . . it's indecent."

"It's also in the dictionary. Would you care to challenge me?"

She knew if she did, she would immediately forfeit the game. "No," she grumbled. "But I consider that word in poor taste."

Paul's response was a soft chuckle. "You can challenge me if you wish."

"What's the score?" Five letters left . . . If she could use them all she might be able to pull into the lead.

"Three hundred and twenty to two eighty-eight," Paul informed her gleefully. "Do you concede?"

"Never!"

"I'm afraid you must. I'm out of letters."

"You won," Caroline said, almost in a daze. She had lost only one game of Scrabble since her junior year in high school. She had played brilliantly, yet Paul had outdone her.

"Yes, love, I won."

Caroline was so stunned that for a minute all she could do was stare at the board in shocked disbelief.

"Love? I believe you owe me a kiss."

She should object to his calling her "love," but she was too bemused to voice her disapproval. "You beat me in Scrabble," she said. "And I'm a good player. Very good."

"I'm fairly well versed at the game myself," Paul added. "There's not much else for Walter and me to do on those long winter nights."

Caroline's eyes narrowed. He'd hustled her into this match, knowing full well that he had a good chance of winning.

"I believe you owe me a kiss," he repeated.

"You cheated," Caroline cried. "You used a four-letter word and . . ."

"Don't tell me you're a poor sport, too."

As fast as she could, Caroline removed the wooden pieces from the playing board. "You mean in addition to being a liar and a thief."

"I didn't mean it like that," Paul said soberly.

"Well, you needn't worry, I'll give you what I promised, but I still think it's unfair that you used that despicable word."

"You'd use it too," Paul said, folding up the game and placing it back on the bookcase.

"I wouldn't!"

"If you were down to four letters and that word placed you on a triple word score and it would guarantee you a win, then I don't doubt you'd use it!"

"Well," Caroline hedged, a smile lifting the edges of her mouth. "I'd be tempted, but I don't know that I'd stoop that low."

"Yes, you would. Now own up, love."

Reluctantly, Caroline stood and rounded the table to his side.

"A kiss that will turn my insides out," he reminded her.

"I remember," she said ruefully. She stood in front of him and Paul's arm circled her waist, pulling her down onto his lap. She offered him a weak smile and gently placed her hands on his shoulders. His palms slid around her back, directing her actions.

She twisted her head to the right, then changed her mind and moved it left. Slowly, she bent forward and placed her parted mouth over his. His lips were moist and warm and moved lightly, brushing over hers in a slow, sensuous attack. Playfully, Caroline darted her tongue in and out of his mouth, then moved more deliberately until she felt him melt in her arms. His tongue skimmed the inner lining of her mouth as he took command. He kissed her with a wildness that was so much a part of this untamed land. Erotically, he moved his head from side to side, his tongue probing, searching, until she gave him what he wanted—what she wanted.

They broke apart, panting and weak.

"Oh Caroline," he breathed against her neck. Their mouths fused again. Although she'd initially had no intention of giving him more than the one kiss he'd bargained for, she was as eager for the second as he.

Again his mouth nuzzled her neck. "Another game, love? Only this time the stakes will be slightly different."

tion of arrival just more than the one Kiss he'd bargained for, she was waiting for the second as it

began the manipulation her neck . . ." Another game, love?" Only this time the stakes will be slightly different!

Chapter Five

"Another game of Scrabble?" Caroline repeated, feeling utterly content.

Dream or not, her memory served her true; Paul Trevor was one fantastic kisser. Caroline's eyes flew open and she jerked herself free from Paul's arms. Mere hours before she'd vowed to freeze him out and here she was sitting on his lap with her arms around his neck, kissing him with all the fervor in her young heart.

"Our Scrabble days are over, Paul Trevor," she said hotly, placing her hand against the table to help maintain her balance. She brushed the hair from her temple and felt a heated flush in her cheeks.

"You mean you're quitting because I'm a better player than you?" Paul returned with a low chuckle.

"Better player, my foot!"

The whole affair appeared to amuse him, which only served to further anger Caroline. She stormed into the bedroom and sat on the end of the bed, sulking. Until she'd met Paul, she'd considered herself an easygoing, fun-loving person. In two days' time he'd managed to change all that.

With her arms crossed, she fumed, contemplating a hundred means of making him suffer.

It wasn't until they were in bed, Paul sleeping at her side, that Caroline acknowledged the truth: she was more furious with herself than Paul. He'd played an honorable Scrabble game, except for that one four-letter word, and had won their wager fair and square. What infuriated her most was her overwhelming response to his kiss. She didn't want him to be tender or gentle; it was far too difficult to hate him when he was so caring and so loving.

In the morning, Paul woke her. "Time to get up, sleepyhead," he whispered softly in her ear.

Caroline's eyes fluttered open. Paul sat on the edge of the mattress, smiling down on her. "Coffee's ready," he told her.

"Paul," she pleaded, using her blue eyes to appeal to his better nature. "Do I have to go to the pumping station with you again? It's so boring. I hate it."

"I'm sorry, love."

"I promise I won't pull any tricks. On my mother's grave, I vow I won't do..."

His gaze grew cold and he stood. "No, Caroline, you're coming with me."

Arguing would do no good, she realized with a frown, and dutifully tossed aside the heavy quilts to climb out of bed, grumbling as she did so. Paul left her to dress on her own, and she was grateful for the privacy. God knew there was little enough in this tiny cabin.

Caroline prepared herself for the long, tedious hours. She took with her a deck of cards, some reading material, and a pen and paper.

As he had the day before, Paul joined her at the desk beside her own a couple of hours into the morning. He offered her a gentle smile and pulled out the ledger.

She waited to be certain she wasn't disturbing him before speaking. "Paul, who does the cooking for you?"

He didn't look up from the ledger as he spoke. "Tanana Eagleclaw; you met her the day of your arrival."

"There were so many," she explained feebly.

He grinned, but didn't tease her about her memory lapse.

"Paul," she tried again. "I'm a good cook." That may have been a bit of an exaggeration, she added silently, but anything was better than sitting around this infernal pumping station ten hours every day.

"Hmm." He barely acknowledged her, finding his ledgers more compelling.

"Really, if you must know, I'm an excellent cook." She was getting desperate now. "I could prepare our meals. In fact, I'd like to do it."

"Tanana does an adequate job."

"But I want to do it!"

"You can't."

"Why the hell not?"

"Because you're here with me, that's why not."

"Do you mean to tell me that you're going to drag me here with you for the rest of my life?"

Paul sighed expressively. "We're going over the same territory as yesterday. You'll stay with me until I feel I can trust you again."

"Wonderful." He might begin to trust her sometime close to the millennium. A lot of good that did her now.

A week passed and each morning a sleepy Caroline traipsed behind Paul to the pumping station and each night she followed him home. She hated it and Paul knew it, but no amount of pleading could get him to change his mind. He wanted her where he could see her every minute of every day.

The mail was delivered twice a week and a letter was sitting on the table addressed to Mr. and Mrs. Paul Trevor when they arrived back from the station during Caroline's second week in Atta.

"A letter!" Caroline cried, as excited as a child on Christmas morning. Contact with the outside world. A tie with the past. She hurriedly read the return address. "It's from my aunts."

Paul's smile was gentle. "The two schemers?"

Eagerly, Caroline tore open the envelope. "The very ones." She hadn't quite forgiven them for their underhanded methods of getting her to Alaska, but she missed them dreadfully.

"What do they have to say?" Paul coaxed, watching the smile work across her face as her eyes wove their way over the page.

"They asked me how I like my surprise. In case you don't know, that was you."

"And?" he prodded with a soft chuckle.

"And what?"

"How do you like me?"

It was Caroline's turn to laugh. "I find you...surprising."

"Typical."

"Aunt Mabel, she's the romantic one, says she feels in her heart that we're going to be happy and have...oh my goodness."

"What?"

Color seeped up from Caroline's neck and flushed her cheeks. "She predicts twelve children, which is how many my great-great-grandmother had as a mail-order bride."

"I'm willing," Paul informed her with a toothy grin.

"Be quiet, I'm reading. And Aunt Ethel..." She hesitated, her eyes scanning the remainder of the page. "It was nothing." With her heart pounding frantically, and hoping to appear nonchalant, she refolded the letter and placed it back inside the envelope.

Paul joined her at the kitchen table. "What did she say?"

Caroline dropped her gaze. "It wasn't important."

"Shall I read the letter myself?"

"No..." she said, and hid it behind her back. He could easily have forced her to hand it over, but didn't, although his cutting gaze reminded her that the letter had been addressed to them both and he had every right to read it. "She told me that Larry Atkins unexpectedly dropped by when...when he couldn't get ahold of me. Aunt Ethel said she took great delight in telling him I was a married woman now.''

"I see," Paul said thoughtfully.

"I'm sure you don't." Caroline braced her hands against the kitchen counter as she battled down a bout of self-pity. Her relationship with Larry had been over weeks before she had come to Alaska. It shouldn't hurt this much now, but it did. Her heart yearned to know why he'd contacted her and how he'd reacted to the news that she was married to Paul. She yearned to let Larry know that it wasn't a real marriage—not the way theirs would have been.

Gently, Paul placed his hands on the rounded curve of her shoulders. "Caroline, here." He turned her into his arms and held her quietly. It wasn't the embrace of a lover, but that of a caring, loyal friend.

She pressed her face against his chest and drew in a wobbly breath. His hand was in her hair, cradling the back of her head as he rubbed his jaw across her crown in a soothing, comforting motion.

"Do you still love him?" he asked after a moment.

Caroline had to analyze her feelings. She'd been crazy in love with Larry for months. They had taken delight in being so different from each other. She missed him, thought about him, wished good things for him. But did she love him?

Paul decided that holding Caroline was like sampling a taste of ambrosia. He'd barely touched her in a week, wanting to give her time to know him. He yearned to woo her, to court her. Their relationship was in an awkward stage; he wasn't convinced he could trust her yet. From her own mouth he'd been informed that the first time he left her alone, she'd run away, and with winter coming on, he couldn't leave her until he was certain she wouldn't try to escape. He yearned to hold her and kiss her until he felt he'd go mad. His successful restraint was sure to make him a candidate for sainthood. He regretted that he hadn't made love to her on their wedding night.

From her ramblings that night, Paul knew about Larry. The situation was far less than ideal and he'd played the role of the patient husband to his own detriment. She'd been with him nine days, and yet it had aged him a hundred lifetimes to have her softness pressed against him, knowing her thoughts were on another man.

"Caroline," he pressed, needing to know. "Do you still love him?"

"I...yes," she answered truthfully, her voice strained and low. This was difficult. Paul was her husband, in fact if not in deed, although that remained questionable; and she had no desire to be cruel to him. "You don't stop loving someone because they've hurt you," she told him softly, relishing the comfort of his arm. "I'm trying not to love him.... Does that help?"

Tenderly, Paul kissed the side of her face. "It makes it easier to accept. I appreciate what it cost you to be honest."

A polite knock at the door drew them apart reluctantly. A shy and very pregnant Indian girl walked in. Her face was dark and round and when her deep, rich eyes fell on Caroline, her smile was almost bashful, as though she felt she had intruded on their lovemaking. "You sent for me, Mr. Trevor?"

"Yes." Paul slipped his arm around Caroline's waist. "Caroline this is Tanana Eagleclaw. Tanana, my wife, Caroline."

"How do you do, Mrs. Trevor?" the girl said formally, dropping her gaze.

"Fine, thank you, Tanana. When is your baby due?" From the looks of her, it could have been any day.

"Six weeks." Again the Indian girl smiled shyly, obviously pleased with the pregnancy.

Caroline guessed that she couldn't be any more than eighteen. "You're a good cook."

"Thank you."

Paul said something to her in her native tongue and the girl nodded eagerly, her gaze briefly moving to Caroline. She left soon afterward.

"What was that all about?" Caroline asked.

"You said you wanted to meet the girl, so I had her come over."

"But that wasn't the only reason. What did you say to her?"

"When?"

"Just now." Caroline gave him a bewildered look until she realized he had purposely played dumb. "Never mind. You obviously don't want me to know, so forget it." She did understand one thing; Tanana's feelings would be hurt if Caroline were to take over the cooking. Perhaps when her baby was born, Caroline could assume the task without there being any loss of pride.

That night, sitting in front of the fireplace, Caroline wrote her aunts a long reply. She told them that in the beginning she was furious over what they'd done, but gradually she'd changed her mind. Paul was a good man, a decent man, and they had chosen well. There was no need to disillusion the two romantics with the truth. She couldn't tell them that she hoped and prayed that, given time, Paul would see fit to let her return to Seattle. That kind of information would only cause the pair to fret. Nor did she tell them that if she was going to be a bride, she wanted the opportunity to choose her *own* husband. When Paul sent her back, and Caroline believed he would, then there would be time enough to explain everything. For now, she would play their game and let them think they'd outsmarted her and that she was a happy, blushing bride. It could do no harm.

That night, Caroline fell into bed, exhausted. Paul joined her soon afterward and as she did each night, she pretended to be asleep when he slipped his body beside her own.

"'Night, love," he whispered gently.

She didn't respond and a few minutes later drifted into a natural, contented sleep.

A noise woke her up and she stirred, chagrined to note that she was sleeping with her head on Paul's hard chest. His arm secured her to him.

"Is it morning yet?" she murmured, closing her eyes again, reluctant to leave the warmth pressing against her.

"In a few minutes."

Paul rose before her every morning to stoke the fire and put on the coffee. Caroline had no idea if she touched him in her sleep and feared that she would wake one morning in his arms and embarrass them both.

"Do I do this often?" she asked, only a little flustered.

"Not near enough," he returned. His hand ran down the length of her spine, stopping at the small of her back as though it was torture to do so. He paused and inhaled sharply.

Caroline realized it was that soft rumble from his throat that had awakened her. The knowledge produced a lazy smile. Still she didn't move. He felt incredibly good—warm, strong . . . male.

Five minutes passed, then ten. Caroline knew she had to pull herself away; each minute was more pleasant than the one before.

"I'll make the coffee this morning," she murmured, easing her torso from his.

Paul stopped her. "There's no rush. Go back to sleep if you like."

"To sleep?" She lifted her head enough to search his face. "Aren't you going to the station?"

"I'll be there, but you won't."

Caroline was sure she'd misunderstood him.

"I asked Tanana to spend the day with you," he explained. "She's going to introduce you to the other women in the village and show you the ropes."

For a moment, Caroline was too stunned to realize what he was saying. "Paul, oh Paul, do you mean I don't have to go to the station?" Without thought, she wrapped her arms around his neck and, laughing, dropped her mouth over his, covering what she could of his bearded face with a series of tiny, eager kisses.

Paul's hands found her head and guided her mouth to his for a kiss that was long and hard. Leisurely, their lips moved against each other's. Without her being certain how it happened, Paul reversed their positions with such ease that she lay on her back, staring up at him. Their eyes met in the dark, and slowly, as though he couldn't resist her a minute longer, he lowered his mouth to capture hers in a kiss that stirred her heart and her soul. Caroline couldn't have denied herself that kiss to save her soul. Her hands sought the side of his face, luxuriating in the feel of his beard.

Paul broke off the kiss and, with a sigh that came all the way from the marrow of his bones, buried his face in the hollow of her throat.

Caroline entwined her arms around his neck and released her own sigh of contentment. She was shocked at how right it felt to have Paul hold and kiss her. Her heart raged to a pagan beat and her body throbbed with a simmering passion. She didn't want to feel these things. When she left him, she didn't want to be weighted down with regrets.

He raised his head then, and compelled her gaze to meet his own, but she turned her head away. "You're going to be late."

"Right."

No time clock waited for him, and they both knew it. He eased his weight from her and sat on the edge of the bed a moment to gain his strength. Caroline made him weak in ways he didn't fully understand. By rights he should have taken her. She wanted him; he could almost taste her eagerness.

Exasperated, he plowed his fingers through his hair. He'd be patient a little longer, but he wasn't going to be able to withstand many more of her kisses. She drugged him. Fascinated him. Captured his heart and held it in the palm of her hand with as much concern as she would an unwanted sweet.

Although it was midmorning, Caroline was barely up and dressed when Tanana arrived. Again the Indian woman knocked politely at the door before stepping inside.

"Morning, Mrs. Trevor," she said shyly.

"Morning, Tanana. I was just fixing myself some breakfast. Would you like something?"

The Indian woman shook her head. "You come now, please?"

"Now?"

Again Tanana grinned and nodded.

"There isn't time for breakfast?"

"No time."

Muttering disparaging words under her breath, Caroline removed the skillet from the stove and placed the eggs back inside the refrigerator while Tanana grabbed Caroline's fur-lined boots and parka.

"Where are we going?"

"To meeting hall."

"The other women are already there?"

"Many wait."

Caroline hadn't a clue as to what they were waiting for, but she was so pleased to be able to talk to another human being that she wouldn't have cared if they were only going to sit around and drink weak coffee.

As Tanana had promised, there were several women gathered inside the large hall that served as the heart of the small community. Smiling, round faces greeted her when they walked into the room and Tanana led an astonished Caroline to an empty chair that stood in the center of the room—obviously the seat of honor.

She soon recognized that the women were giving a small party in her honor, something like a bridal shower. One by one, each woman stepped forward and offered her a gift. Only some of the women spoke English, but Tanana acted as translator. The gifts were mostly homemade, displaying such talent and skill that Caroline's breath caught in her throat at their beauty. She received a thick hand-knit sweater, slippers made from sealskin, several pieces of intricate scrimshaw with scenes that depicted Indian life in the frozen North, as well as smoked salmon, deer, moose and elk meat. Caroline watched in wide-eyed wonder as they each came to her. They had so little and she had so much, yet they were lovingly sharing a precious part of their lives. A tear gathered in her eye and she swallowed down a thickness forming in her throat, not wanting them to see how much their kindness had affected her.

When they'd finished, Caroline stood and went to each one to personally thank her. Later, after they had served lunch, the women gathered their yarn together and started to work.

"What are they making?" Caroline asked Tanana.

"Sweaters for the tourists."

"Atta gets that many tourists?"

The Indian girl cupped her hand over her mouth and laughed. "No, the stores in Fairbanks, Juneau and Anchorage sell them."

"Oh." Caroline felt like an idiot.

"All the women of the village work on the sweaters in wintertime," Tanana continued. "Each day we gather in meeting hall."

"I knit," Caroline said, broaching the subject carefully. She wanted to be a part of this community. Although her skill might not have been at the level of these women, she could learn. They'd been so kind to her that she wished to return some of their thoughtfulness.

"Would you like to join us?" Tanana asked politely.

"Please." Almost before Caroline knew what was happening, she was handed a pair of needles, several skeins of thick yarn, and with Tanana to guide her, was set to work.

That night, Caroline was bursting with excitement. So much so that she could barely contain it. By the time Paul walked in the cabin door, she practically flew across the room.

"Hi," she greeted, her voice excited. It required a great effort for her to contain her joy and enthusiasm. "Did you know about the ... party?"

His smiling eyes delved into hers. "Tanana told me about it last week. She said that it was time I let you out of bed long enough to meet the village women."

Caroline decided to ignore the comment. "They're wonderful people."

"I know, love." He had removed his parka and hung it in the closet when Caroline grabbed his hand and led him into the bedroom. She'd placed the nonfood items on top of the quilt for him to examine. He picked up each piece and nodded his pleasure at the village's generosity. When he came to the oddly shaped piece of knitting, he regarded it skeptically. "And what's this?"

"Oh, yes, I nearly forgot. The women knit, but I guess you already know that. Well, anyway, they let me sit and work with them this afternoon. Of course I'm not nearly as good as they and my poor sweater wouldn't be anywhere near good enough to sell to the tourists. We laughed about that. It's amusing that some tourist would buy a sweater they assumed was knit by an authentic Indian only to discover it was crafted by a Seattle nurse." She giggled at the memory. "At the end of the afternoon, I think Tanana was afraid of hurting my feelings so I asked if I could do something else with this first effort."

"And what was that?"

"I told them I wanted to knit this sweater for you."

"What did they say to that?"

"Oh, they were pleased, but then they would be, since they probably couldn't sell it." She waltzed out of the bedroom and into the kitchen. "And I made dinner. Tanana looked so tired that I offered. Naturally, she argued with me, but not too strenuously."

"So you had a good day."

"I had a marvelous day!" She turned her back to him to stir the simmering gravy. All day she'd been trying to come up with a way of approaching Paul about joining the women on a daily basis. He'd been so unyielding in other matters that she dreaded a confrontation now.

"I suppose you want to go back?"

Caroline whirled around, her heart in her eyes. "Can I?"

"I think that's more your decision than mine."

She understood what he was saying, but swallowed down a ready reply while she took the thick slices of meat from the oven and placed them on the table.

"Unless you trust me again," she said softly, her eyes holding his, "I know I won't ever be able to prove that I'm trustworthy."

"Then do as you wish."

Caroline was so pleased that she was hard-pressed not to throw her arms around his neck and kiss him the way she had that morning. It wasn't until after they'd eaten that she realized how much she actually wanted to kiss him, and quickly pushed the thought from her mind.

Later, she found herself humming while washing the dinner dishes, and paused, surprised with herself. She was happy—truly happy and content. She turned to find Paul watching her and they shared a smile.

Once again they played a heated game of Scrabble, but without any wagers. To her delight and disgust, Caroline won.

"You'll note that I didn't use a single dirty word," she told him with a proud snicker.

Paul chuckled and reset the board for a second game.

That next afternoon and for several more that followed, Caroline joined the Indian women for their daily knitting session. The first few days, the women were shy and didn't say much to her. Gradually they opened up and she was privilege to the village gossip. More than one of the women seemed to find something about Caroline highly amusing. Every time they looked in her direction, they leaned over to the woman next to them and whispered something that the other found comical. Finally, when Caroline's curiosity got the better of her, she asked Tanana about it.

The Indian girl blushed. "They say you are fortunate woman."

"Fortunate? I don't understand."

"Yes, you have Paul for your lover. They are envious that at night he sleeps at your side and holds you in his arms. They say you will have many healthy babies with Paul. He is . . . I don't know English word."

"Never mind," Caroline returned, her fingers tightening around the knitting needles. "I know what you mean." Did she ever! So Paul was a virile male who had sampled the delights of the village women before her arrival.

By the time she arrived back at the cabin, Caroline was so furious that she paced the small enclosure, ready to give her husband a solid piece of her mind the instant he returned home. She'd never dreamed, hadn't thought he'd ever do anything that low. No wonder he wanted a wife. From the looks the Indian women had been sending her way, the Athabascans had probably started fighting over him. Well, they could have him. She was finished with him, through. Nothing could keep her in Atta now. She didn't care what it took, she was leaving Paul and the sooner the better.

When the wooden door opened and the howling wind whirled around the enclosed cabin, it was only a spring breeze compared to the ice caking Caroline's heart.

"Hi," Paul greeted her with a ready grin, but one look at her contorted, angry features and his smile quickly faded. "What's wrong?"

She didn't wait for him to remove his coat. Her index finger found its mark in the middle of his chest. "You are despicable. You are lower than a snake. You are..." Words failed her as hot tears blurred her vision. "I can't find the words to tell you how much I despise you!"

Paul didn't look particularly concerned. "Was it something I said, or are you still mad about that four-letter word I used in the Scrabble game?"

Chapter Six

"**Y**ou think you're so clever, don't you?" Caroline flared. Her outrage got the better of her and she picked up a book from the end table and hurled it at him.

With a dexterity few could manage, Paul caught the book and the saltshaker that immediately followed. The amusement drained from his eyes. "Caroline, what's gotten into you?"

"You . . . animal!"

"For God's sake, tell me what I did."

"You . . . *beast*!" The pepper shaker whizzed past his ear.

"Caroline!"

"You . . . you . . . virgin-taker!"

Stunned, Paul watched as she stormed into the bedroom and viciously slammed the door. For a minute he did nothing but stand with a book and saltshaker in his hand, too bemused to move. Beyond her explosive fury, what shocked Paul most was the incredible hurt he saw in her eyes.

"Virgin-taker?" he repeated in an astonished whisper.

Inside the bedroom, Caroline sat on the edge of the mattress. Stinging tears threatened to run down her face and she rubbed the heels of her hands against her eyes in a futile effort to restrain their salty release. Damn it all, she was falling in love with him—head over heels in love with a man without morals or conscience. If she didn't love him, then knowing what he'd done wouldn't hurt this much. Caroline cried harder. She didn't want to love him. In time, he'd realize their marriage was a terrible mistake and would send her back to Seattle. Caroline wanted to leave Paul and Alaska without regrets. A hiccupping sob ripped through her throat and she buried her face in her hands.

Her crying had an overwhelming effect on Paul. He'd thought to wait until her anger had fully dissipated before trying to reason with her, but he couldn't. Every sob felt like a vicious punch in his abdomen.

"Caroline," he called softly from the other side of the door. "Can we talk about this?"

Silence.

"Caroline, believe me, I haven't the foggiest idea what you're talking about."

"I'll just bet you don't!"

"I don't." He tried the knob, but she'd locked the door. "As your husband, I demand that you open this door immediately."

She snickered.

"Caroline, I mean it." When she didn't respond, he rammed his hands in his pants pockets, not knowing what else to do. "Are you angry about our wedding night? Is that it?" Standing directly in front of the door, he braced his hands on each side of the jamb. "I can see it isn't going to do the least bit of good to try to talk to you now. You're in no mood to be reasonable."

With that, the bedroom door opened so unexpectedly that he almost fell through the doorway.

Caroline glared at him with renewed animosity. "Do you mean to tell me that . . . that on the night we were married you . . . you took advantage of me?"

"Caroline, if you'd listen . . ."

"O-o-h." Her clenched fists pommeled his rock-hard chest until her fingers felt numb with pain.

"That's enough." Paul caught her wrists and quickly pinned her against the wall. Her shoulders heaved with exertion, and tears streaked her face and brimmed in her wide, blue eyes.

Trembling, she collected herself and drew in a ragged breath. Briefly, she struggled to be free, but Paul's hold tightened. His fierce look held her as effectively as his hands. Caroline met his glare with open defiance.

"Love." His voice was a hoarse whisper of bewilderment and confusion, his face mere inches from her own. "What is it?"

He spoke with such gentleness, such caring that it would be so easy to forget what he was and what he'd done. "Let me loose," she begged, her rage gone now, replaced by a far deeper, more crippling emotion—sorrow.

Paul saw the pain in her eyes and was filled with such perplexity that he reacted instinctively. In an effort to comfort, his mouth sought hers.

"No," Caroline cried, twisting her head from side to side, but her renewed struggles were a puny effort against his far superior strength. With his muscular torso, he anchored her body against the wall.

"Yes," he returned. His mouth was insistent, demanding, relentless, moving over hers with practiced ease. Caroline wanted to fight him, but the battle was one she couldn't hope to win and against her will she found her lips parting to meet his with an eagerness that rocked her soul. Their mouths twisted and turned almost cruelly against each other's in an urgent, fiery tempest of uncertainty and confusion. Gradually they relaxed, the crucial need abated. Paul loosened his grip, but continued to hold her wrists to the wall. His torso, warm from the struggle, secured her against him and Caroline became aware of the heavy thud of his heart while her own pulsed with a frantic rhythm.

They breathed in unison. Paul's gaze searched her face, looking for any clue that would help him understand her irrational behavior. Hot color stained her cheeks, but he didn't know if it was from her anger or her attempts to be free of him. Her lips were moist, dewy from his kisses, and he dipped his head to sample again their intoxicating sweetness. When he finally drew back, they were both trembling.

He released her hands and Caroline dropped them to her side. "I was with the women today," she began, in a voice so fraught with pain that Paul wrapped her securely in his arms. "And they told me . . ."

"Told you what, love?"

"That . . . you're a fantastic lover."

He frowned. "Ah," he whispered slowly, and cupped her face with his hands, kissing her briefly. "And you assumed they meant it literally?"

"How else was I supposed to take it?"

"Love, you must remember their culture is different from our own. I've been with them several years now. They know me well enough to favor me with certain attributes they *believe* I possess."

Caroline's gaze hungrily searched his, seeking the truth. "They sounded so . . . so knowledgeable."

He grinned widely. "Love, I'm only one man. I couldn't possibly have had that many lovers."

"Have you had . . . even one?" Her intense gaze locked with his.

"By everything I hold dear, I swear to you that I've never had a single lover from Atta." Paul had assumed that she would welcome his assurance, but his words produced the most uncanny response; tears flooded her eyes and streamed down her face. Caroline hugged him fiercely, burying her face in his sweater. Half laughing, half crying, she lifted her head then and spread eager kisses mingled with salty tears upon his face. Gently, Paul held her, wondering if he'd been so long outside civilization that he'd lost his ability to understand women. He sighed; perhaps he had.

Their relationship altered after that night. The changes were subtle ones and came about so naturally that Paul could only guess their meaning. The first thing he noticed was that Caroline had placed her suitcase under the bed as though she had finally accepted her position in his life and planned to remain. He yearned for her to do away with the idea that someday he would release her and she'd return to Seattle.

He knew she spent a lot of time with Tanana and apparently the two had worked out an agreement concerning dinner since Caroline started cooking all their meals. She'd once told him she was an excellent cook and he found that she hadn't exaggerated. She was clever, inventive and resourceful. It wasn't every woman who could make dried eggs edible.

Everyone was her friend; even Walter Thundercloud had become her ally. Paul had been in the village six months before the old man had fully accepted him. Walter's acceptance was typical of the love given Caroline by all the natives of Atta. The children adored her; Caroline couldn't walk out the door without two or three of them running to her side, their eyes wide and curious. More often than not, Caroline had something in her pocket just for them—a stick of gum, a marble or two or a whistle. One day Paul discovered Caroline in the meeting hall, skipping rope with the sixth-grade girls. Another day he found her involved in a heated soccer game with the junior-high boys.

When an old woman had a toothache, she came to Caroline. A feverish baby was brought to her as well. A little boy with a side ache showed up unexpectedly one afternoon. The medical clinic was open once a week when a team from the Public Health Department flew in for appointments, but it was Caroline whom the villagers came to.

She was gentle and kind and Paul was so much in love he thought he'd die from wanting her. To rush her into love-making now would be foolish. She was so close to recognizing she loved him, and when that day came it would be right and beautiful, although he often wondered how much longer he could hold out. He endured the sweetest torture each morning when he woke up to find her in his arms. At night, the agony was far greater; he dreaded her touch and at the same time craved it.

That evening after dinner, Caroline brought out a large box and placed it on the ottoman in front of him.

Paul lowered the two-day-old newspaper and raised questioning eyes to his wife. "What's this?"

"Open it and see." Her face revealed her anxiety. She'd worked so hard and so long on this sweater that if it didn't fit, she'd burst into tears. "I probably should have saved it for Christmas, but..." It was silly to be this nervous, but she so wanted to please him and the holidays were a full six weeks away. Besides, she didn't know what else she could do to tell Paul she loved him.

"But what, love?"

"But I thought you deserved it now." For calming her angry tirades, for being so patient with her, for his gentleness and a hundred other admirable qualities. And because she longed to be his wife in the truest sense of the word.

Carefully, Paul removed the top from the oblong box and lifted out the Irish cable-knit sweater. "Caroline, I'm...stunned; it's a fine piece of work."

"If it doesn't fit, I can redo it." She couldn't believe she'd made that offer; the pattern was both difficult and complicated. If it hadn't been for Tanana's and the other women's help, she would have given up and thrown the sweater away weeks before.

"I'm sure it will fit perfectly." To prove his point, he stood and placed it over his head, slipping his arms into the long sleeves. "Where did you get the yarn?" he asked, running his hand over the finely crafted garment. It was a lovely shade of winter wheat and far lighter than the material the village women used.

"I mailed away for it. Mary Finefeather had a catalog."

"How did you pay for it?" She'd never come to him for money, although he would have been more than pleased to give it to her. They had little need for cash in Atta. The supply store and grocery mailed him monthly accounts and his paychecks were automatically deposited in the Fairbanks Savings and Loan.

"I used my traveler's checks."

He nodded and kissed her lightly. "Thank you, love. I'll always treasure it."

Caroline's returning smile was weak, as though she was greatly disappointed by his response. Paul watched her leave and wondered if he'd said something to offend her. He began to doubt that he'd ever understand her.

Hours later, Paul lay at her side. His even breathing convinced Caroline he was sound asleep as she lay on her back wide-eyed, staring at the ceiling. She was now convinced that she was a terrible failure. For two weeks, she'd been trying to tell Paul that she was ready to be his wife in *every* way. How one man could be so completely blind was beyond her. If it hadn't been for a few occasional looks of longing he'd secretly given her, she would have abandoned her cause. She made excuses to be close to him, touch him. The signals she'd been sending him would have stopped a freight train! The sweater had been her ace in the hole and even that had failed. In return, he'd kissed her like an affectionate older brother.

Ah well, there was always another day. Maybe if she wore the fur-trimmed nightgown her aunts had given her... She smiled and her eyes drifted closed. She couldn't get any more obvious than that.

The next day was a busy one. The small town was holding an early Thanksgiving feast, and it seemed half of Alaska had been invited. People had been arriving from the outlying areas all morning. Caroline and Tanana were responsible for decorating the meeting hall and the two of them made a comical sight. Caroline wouldn't allow Tanana, who was in the advanced stages of pregnancy, to climb the ladder to hang the crepe paper streamers, so Caroline wrapped them around her neck and hauled them up herself.

"This isn't fair," Tanana complained. "All I'm doing is holding the ladder for you."

"I'm not going to let you stand on this rickety old thing," Caroline muttered, stretching as far as her limbs would allow to stick the thumbtack into the beam.

"If Mr. Trevor ever saw this, he'd be plumb mad."

"He isn't going to know, and you're not going to tell him—right?"

"What will you bribe me with?"

Caroline laughed. Her young friend was quickly learning the ways of the world. "Hush, now, and hand me another streamer." She climbed down a couple of steps and Tanana gave her the next set of bright red crepe paper strips.

When they had finished, the two women looked about them, proud of their accomplishment. It was amazing what a little bit of color did to add to the festive spirit.

Mary Finefeather, a foster grandmother to many of the village youth, delivered sandwiches to Caroline and Tanana. Typical of the older woman's personality, Mary spoke in choppy one-word sentences.

"Eat," she said with a toothy grin.

"I think that's an order," Caroline commented, and looked to Tanana, who smiled in reply. The younger girl had lost much of her shyness now and Caroline considered her a valued friend.

"What you getting Mr. Trevor for Christmas?" Tanana questioned, studying Caroline with dark, soulful eyes.

"I...don't know. I gave him the sweater last night." She wished she hadn't; with the holidays fast approaching, she had wasted her best gift—seemingly for naught.

"I know what Mr. Trevor wants."

"You do?"

Tanana placed her hand on her swollen abdomen and stared at her stomach. "Mr. Trevor wants son."

Caroline nearly swallowed her sandwich whole. "Oh?"

"You'll give him many fine sons?"

Embarrassed, Caroline looked away. "Someday."

"Soon?" the girl pressed.

"I...I don't know." Caroline couldn't very well announce that she and Paul had never made love, at least not so as she could remember.

Caroline worked for part of the afternoon, then returned to the cabin, frustrated and tired. She'd slept poorly the night before and tonight would be another late one as well. Before she could talk herself out of the idea, she climbed on top of the bed and closed her eyes, intending to rest for only a few minutes.

Paul found her there an hour later, barely visible in the soft light of dusk. He paused in the doorway of their bedroom and experienced such a wave of desire that he sucked in a tight breath. Her blouse had ridden up to expose the creamy smooth skin of her midriff. Her ripe breasts were cupped in a mere piece of white lace. Paul's hands clenched at his sides with the intense yearning to weigh her breasts in his hands and know for himself the taste of their delicate pink crests. He'd been patient, more than patient. Blood pounded in his head and his feet seemed to move of their own accord, taking him to her side. Just to see her like this was enough to make him tipsy with desire.

His gaze lingered on the smooth slant of her brow and a smile briefly touched his intense features. She could make a clearer statement with an arch of her eyebrow than some women said in twenty years. Her nose was perfect and her sweet, firm lips were enough to drive a man insane. She tasted of honey and wine and one sampling was never enough. He thought about the last time they'd kissed and how, for hours afterward, he'd been in a foul mood, barking at Walter Thundercloud and the others until Walter had suggested that Paul do something to cure whatever was ailing him.

Caroline was ailing him. She was in his blood, a cancer that was eating away at him inch by inch. She was his wife, and by God, he'd...

Caroline yawned and rolled over.

Paul jumped away from her as though he'd been burned. His knees felt like pudding, his heart like slush in a spring thaw. On unsteady feet, he walked over to the dresser.

"Caroline, it's time to get up." He hardly recognized the strained, harsh voice as his own.

Slowly, she opened her eyes. She'd been having the most incredibly wonderful dream about giving Paul the son Tanana claimed he wanted so badly. One look at her husband, who stood stiffly on the other side of the room, was enough to return her into the cold world of reality. His back was to her.

"Hi," she said, stretching her hands high above her head and yawning loudly.

"Hi," he returned gruffly. He didn't dare turn around. If her midriff had been showing before, God only knew what he'd glimpse now. He felt himself go weak all over again.

Caroline frowned at his abruptness. "Did you have a good day?"

"Sure." He pulled open the top drawer and took out a clean T-shirt. "You'd better get dressed or we'll be late for the party."

"What time is it?"

"Five."

Caroline's frown deepened. No one was expected before seven. "We've got plenty of time."

No, we don't, Paul wanted to shout. He, for one, was at the end of his rope.

"Paul, what's wrong?"

"Nothing." He slammed the drawer shut with unnecessary force. "I just happen to think it was time you got out of bed."

"Are you angry because I took a nap?"

"No," he barked.

She rose to a sitting position and released a long sigh. "Sometimes I don't understand you."

"That makes two of us."

"Will you please turn around? I don't like talking to your back." She made the request softly, confused by his harsh mood. She'd never known Paul to be so short-tempered and illogical.

"If you don't mind, I'm busy."

Caroline blinked, stunned. The conversation with Tanana played back in her mind and a heaviness settled on her shoulders. She loved Paul and yearned to give him a child, but instead of growing together they seemed to be drifting apart. Sudden tears misted her eyes. She'd thought that once she acknowledged that she was in love with him everything would be perfect. Instead, it had gotten worse—much worse.

Paul tossed his sweater on the bed. "Good grief, don't tell me you're crying! One day you're hurling saltshakers at me and the next you're weeping because I tell you to hurry and get ready for a party you've been working on all day."

Her eyes rounded with determination to hold back the tears. "I'm not crying. That's ridiculous. Why should I be crying?"

He threw up his hands. "God only knows. I've given up trying to understand you."

The party was a grand success; the meeting hall burst to the rafters with friends and loved ones from nearby communities. The dinner proved to be scrumptious and Caroline received rave reviews for her apple pies and decorating efforts. Although she smiled and made all the appropriate responses, she couldn't seem to get into the party mood.

When the tables were cleared and the dancing began, Caroline noted how Paul seemed to dance with every woman in the room but her. Not that Caroline was given much time to notice. One partner after another claimed her hand for a turn around the floor. After an hour, she pleaded exhaustion and sat down, fanning her flushed face with one hand.

To her surprise, Paul joined her, sitting in the chair beside her own. His mouth was pinched, his face grim. "I imagine you're pleased to have every man for a hundred miles panting after you."

Caroline's mouth fell open at the unjust accusation. Quickly, she composed herself, stiffening her back. "I'm going to forgive you for that remark, Paul Trevor, because I owe you one. But from here on we're even." She stood and purposely walked away from him. Blinded by confusion, she nearly stumbled into Walter Thundercloud, and glancing up at him, hurriedly stammered an apology.

"Didn't you promise me this dance?" Walter said.

Still unable to find her tongue, Caroline nodded.

Studying her, the Athabascan guided her onto the dance floor. A waltz was playing and Caroline lightly slipped one arm around the older man's neck and placed her hand in his.

"All right, girl, tell me—what's made you so unhappy?"

Caroline's mouth formed a poor excuse for a smile. "Paul. I don't know how any one man can be so stupid."

"He's blinded with his love for you."

"I sincerely doubt that's it." Caroline gazed directly into the blunt Indian features. "I have the feeling he's ready to ship me back to Seattle." There had been a time when she'd prayed for exactly that, but now her heart ached at the mere thought of leaving him.

Standing by the punch bowl, Paul watched her. Caroline could feel his dark gaze on her back. With every passing minute, his eyes grew darker and more angry.

Walter chuckled, the sound coming deep from within his throat. "Paul would rather cut off his arm than send you away. Have you told him you love him?"

Caroline's shocked gaze clashed with the man's wise old eyes. "No."

"Then do it, and soon, before he makes an even bigger fool of himself."

When the dance ended, Walter delivered her to Paul's side and quietly left them. Caroline and Paul stood glaring at each other until the music started.

"Shall we?" Caroline asked, glancing toward the crowded floor.

"Why not? You've seen fit to dance with every other male here tonight."

"Paul," she whispered. "Are you jealous?"

He didn't answer her, but she noted that his features were as grim and tight as she'd ever seen them. His hold on her was loose, as though he couldn't bear to touch her.

Caroline swallowed her pride. "There isn't anyone here that I'd rather dance with more than you."

Still, he said nothing. His eyes were focused straight ahead and there wasn't so much as a flicker in his rock-hard features to indicate that he'd heard her, or if he had that her words had had any effect on him.

"When I first came to Atta, I hated it."

If possible, his mouth grew harder, more inflexible.

"But . . . things changed and I realized I was happy here. There's a wildness to this land. A challenge that makes people strong and wise. I've seen that in you and admired your patience and gentleness."

Momentarily, Paul dropped his gaze and studied her as though he didn't quite trust what she was saying.

Caroline thought her heart would burst with pain when he quickly glanced away, dismissing her claim.

"You idiot," she hissed and brought her shoe down hard on the top of his foot.

Paul let out a small yelp of pain.

"I'm trying to tell you I love you, but you can forget it. And while you're at it, you can forget about our son, too!" Forcefully, she broke away and left him holding up one leg like a flamingo while he nursed his injured foot.

At the door, Caroline grabbed her boots and parka and stormed out of the meeting hall, too angry for tears, too frustrated to think what she was doing. She knew only that she had to escape.

"Caroline!"

His frantic call came to her before she reached the cabin door. With stiff resolve, she chose to pretend she hadn't heard him.

"Damn it, Caroline, would you wait?"

She ignored his pleading as well. By the time he arrived home, she was sitting in front of the fireplace with a book in front of her face, studiously focusing her attention on the fine print.

"Caroline...what did you just say?" He was breathless, his voice rushed and uneven.

"It was nothing."

"It was everything," he whispered in awe. "Do you love me? Caroline, for God's sake would you kindly look at me?"

"No."

Paul felt like he was going to explode with happiness. "And what was that crazy remark about a son?"

She turned the page of the novel and glanced with keen interest at the beginning of the next chapter, although she hadn't a clue as to the story line.

Paul fell to his knees at her side and removed the book from her stiff fingers. Her eyes refused to meet his, although his looked demanded it of her. "Caroline..." He breathed her name with a heart overflowing with expectancy and hope. "Oh God, are you telling me you're ready to be my wife?"

"I couldn't have made it any plainer. I've flaunted myself like a hussy in front of you all week. I gave you the sweater...hoping... Paul Trevor, you're an idiot! For days, I've been throwing myself at you and you...you've been so blind and so stupid."

"You have?" Paul was flabbergasted. "When? Days?"

"Weeks!"

"Weeks?" Dear God, he had been blind, but no longer.

His hands framed her face as he guided her lips to his, kissing her with such hungry intensity it robbed her breath. Without her being aware of how he managed it, he lifted her from the chair, cradled her in his arms and carried her into their bedroom. He laid her upon the mattress and knelt over her, studying her once more to be sure this wasn't some dream.

Caroline stared into his hungry eyes and twined her arms around his neck, bringing his mouth back to her own to kiss him long and ardently. "You idiot," she whispered.

"No more, love."

Their lips met again and again as though each kiss was sweeter and more potent than the one before. Holding back nothing, Caroline surrendered to him with joyful abandon. He explored her face and her neck, charting undiscovered territory with his lips as he helped her undress. Finally they were both free of restricting clothes and Paul kissed her until she responded with a wantonness she didn't know she possessed. They broke apart, winded and panting.

"Caroline," he murmured, his features keen and ardent in the moonlight. "Are you sure?"

"I've never been more sure of anything in my life."

Utterly content, Caroline lay with her cheek pressed against her husband's chest. Her silken leg stroked his and she sighed her happiness. There was no turning back for them now; they were truly husband and wife, their commitment to each other complete.

Paul's hand smoothed the tumbled hair from her face. "Are you happy, love?"

"Very." Her nails playfully scraped at his curling chest hairs. "Why didn't you tell me it was this good? If I'd known, I would have demanded my wifely rights." She lifted her head to kiss the strong, proud line of his chin. "The Athabascan women were right; you are a fantastic lover."

Paul opened his mouth to answer her when there was a loud knock on the front door. Caroline gave him a look of dismay; no one would come unless there was trouble.

Paul rolled to his feet, his body tense and alert. "I'll be right back." He reached for his clothes and was gone before she could protest.

Caroline dressed in a rush, anxious now. When she joined Paul in the living room, she found him speaking hurriedly to Thomas Eagleclaw, Tanana's young husband.

"Tanana's gone into labor," Paul explained. "Her mother is with her, but she wants you."

Caroline nodded. "I won't be a minute."

Chapter Seven

By the time Caroline arrived at Tanana's cabin, her heart was pounding, not with exertion from the long walk, but with excitement and, she admitted, anxiety. Her experience had been limited to a sterile hospital delivery room with a doctor, other nurses and all the necessary emergency equipment. None of that existed in Atta, and Caroline had never felt more inadequate.

Thomas, Tanana's husband, led the way into their cabin, which was even smaller than Paul's. Tanana lay in the center of the double bed, her face glistening with perspiration, her eyes wide with pain. The Indian girl held her hand out to Caroline. "Thank you for coming."

"When did the pains start?" Caroline asked, sitting on the edge of the mattress.

Tanana lowered her gaze. "This afternoon."

"Why didn't you tell me?"

"I wasn't sure they were true."

Caroline understood. Tanana had mentioned twice that week that she'd been experiencing "twinges" in her abdomen. Caroline had explained that those were normal and the girl needn't worry.

The older Indian in the bedroom rose to greet the latest arrival. Caroline had met Tanana's mother previously and the older woman smiled her welcome and returned to her rocking chair, content to let Caroline assume the role of midwife. Wonderful, Caroline mused dryly, returning to the kitchen to wash her hands. Silently, she prayed this would be an easy birth, routine in every way.

It wasn't. Hours later, both Caroline and Tanana were drenched with sweat. The girl was terrified. Caroline, although outwardly calm, was equally frightened. Tanana's mother continued to rock, offering an encouraging smile now and again. Certainly the old Indian had delivered countless babies, Caroline thought.

"It shouldn't be long now," Caroline said, smoothing the hair from Tanana's brow and wiping her face with a cool washcloth.

The Indian girl tried to smile, but the effort was too great. "Rest as much as you can between pains," Caroline instructed.

Tanana nodded. She closed her eyes and rolled her head to the side, ruthlessly biting into the corner of her lip as another contraction took hold of her young body.

"Don't fight it," Caroline said softly. "Try to deal with the pain."

Tanana's death grip on Caroline's fingers slacked and Caroline relaxed as well. "You're doing great, Tanana. I'll check you with the next contraction and we'll see how far things have progressed."

Caroline's worst fears were confirmed; the baby was breech. The knot of fear that clogged her throat was palpable. Didn't this baby realize she had only limited experience in this area? The least it could do was cooperate! "I'm going to get some fresh water," she told Tanana, and stood to leave the bedside. Tanana's eyes revealed her fear. "Don't worry," Caroline said with a reassuring smile, "I'll be right back."

In the next room, Paul was playing cards with Thomas, although it was easy to see that neither man's attention was on the game. One look at Caroline's distraught eyes and Paul stood and moved to her side at the kitchen sink. "What's wrong?"

"The baby is breech. Paul, I'm frightened. This is far more complicated than anything I've ever handled. Good Lord, I've worked in a doctor's office for two years; you don't get much experience in delivering breech babies in an office building."

"Tanana needs you."

"I know." Paul was referring to strength and confidence, but she couldn't offer the poor girl something she didn't have herself.

"If it becomes more than you can cope with, we'll call in a plane and fly her to Fairbanks."

That would take hours and they both knew it. "I'll...do my best."

"I know you will, love." Gently, his hands cupped her face and he kissed her, his lips fitting tenderly over hers, lending her his own strength. A whimper from Tanana broke them apart and Caroline hurried back to her friend's side.

The hours sped by, but Caroline was barely aware of their passing. She was busy every minute, talking softly, encouraging Tanana. Her friend's fortitude and inner strength amazed her. Several times, Caroline thought Tanana would succumb to the pain and fear. When the squalling infant was released from the young girl's body, unrestrained tears of happiness filled Caroline's eyes.

"You have a son," she said, gently placing the baby atop his mother's stomach.

"A son." Tanana's wide smile revealed her overwhelming delight and with a cry of joy, she fell back against the pillow, content for the moment.

A few minutes later, Caroline entered the kitchen, carrying the crying infant in her arms. Her eyes met Paul's as the two men slowly rose to their feet.

"A boy," she said softly.

Thomas let out a hoot of exhilarated happiness and paused to briefly inspect his son before he rushed past Caroline to join his wife.

Paul looked down at the small bundle in her arms. His eyes softened at the wrinkled face and tiny fingers protruding from the soft blanket. "You must be exhausted," he said, studying Caroline.

Lightly, she shook her head. She'd never experienced such a wondrous feeling of excited bliss in her life. It was as though she'd labored for this child herself and he had been born of her own body. "He's so beautiful." Unabashed tears filled her eyes and she kissed the baby's sweet brow.

"Not half as beautiful as you, love," Paul said tenderly, his heart constricting at the sight of a babe in his wife's arms. The day would come when they would bear a child of their own and the thought filled him with happy anticipation.

An hour later, when both mother and baby were resting comfortably, Paul took Caroline back to their cabin. Now that the first surge of high spirits had faded, Caroline realized how weary she was. "What time is it?"

"Noon."

"Noon? Really?"

Paul led her directly into their bedroom and sat her down on the bed where she fell back upon the rumpled sheets and heaved a sigh, closing her eyes. Smiling down on her, Paul removed her shoes.

"Paul?"

"Hmm?" He unzipped her jeans next and slid them from her long legs. A surge of desire shot through him and he forced himself to look at her face and remember how exhausted she was. Given the least amount of encouragement, he would have fallen into bed beside her.

"Tanana told me you wanted a son." Her eyes were closed and she felt weary and lethargic, as though someone had drugged her.

"A daughter would do as well."

"Soon?"

"Sooner than you think if you don't get under those covers," he grumbled, lifting the thick quilts over his wife's inviting body.

Caroline smiled, feeling warm and unbelievably secure. "I love you," she murmured dreamily.

The words rocked Paul. He stood at the edge of the bed, unsteady. "You love me?" He'd only dared to dream her love would come this soon. She didn't answer him and he knew that she was already asleep. His heart swelled with such joy that he felt like shouting and dancing around the small room. Instead, he bent down and gently kissed her temple. To remain with her now would be torture and although it was a different kind of agony, Paul left the room and curled up on the recliner, meaning only to rest his eyes.

Caroline found him there several hours later. "Paul," she whispered, lightly shaking his shoulder.

With much reluctance, he opened his eyes. When he saw it was Caroline, he grinned sleepily. "Did you rest?"

"Like a baby. Why are you curled up out here?"

"Because you needed your rest, love." His arm circled her waist and brought her into his lap where he nuzzled her neck. She felt incredibly good in his arms, soft, feminine, his—all his. He owned her heart now. Larry was in the past and gone forever.

Paul thought of his life before she'd come to him and wondered how he'd managed all those years without her. She was as much a part of him now as his own heart. She was his world, his sun, his pride all in one. All these weeks she'd led him down a rock-strewn trail, but every minute had been worth the wait. She was more than he'd ever dreamed.

Her hands directed his mouth to hers and she kissed him hungrily. He didn't need to tell her why he'd slept on the recliner; Caroline knew and loved him all the more for his thoughtfulness.

"Oh Lord, Caroline," he groaned, his mouth repeatedly rubbing over hers. "Do you know what you're doing?"

She answered him by unfastening the buttons of his shirt and slipping her fingers inside to stroke his chest. The wild sensations he aroused in her were so exquisite, she wanted to weep.

The soft gentle sounds of their lovemaking filled the cabin. Whispered phrases of awe followed as Paul removed her blouse and freed her breasts.

"Caroline," he moaned, his voice low and husky. "If we don't stop right now, we're going to end up making love in this recliner."

"I'm not willing to stop. . . ."

In the days that followed, Caroline was astonished that they'd waited so long to become lovers when everything was so extraordinarily right between them. Now they seemed to be making up for lost time. His desire for her both delighted and astonished Caroline. They made love every night and often Paul couldn't seem to wait until their usual bedtime. In the middle of a Scrabble game, she found him looking at her with a fierce gleam in his eye.

"Paul?"

He glanced toward the bedroom and arched his brows in question.

"It's only seven o'clock," she said, laughing with a hint of disbelief.

His look was almost boyish as he dropped his gaze. "I can wait."

Caroline smiled, stood and walked around the table to take him by the hand. "Well, I can't."

They never finished playing Scrabble. Instead they invented new games.

Some nights, Paul was barely in the door when he wanted her.

"What's for dinner?" he would ask.

She'd tell him and catch that look in his eye and automatically turn down the stove. "Don't worry, it can simmer for an hour."

Their dinner simmered and they sizzled. This was the honeymoon they never had and Caroline prayed it would last a lifetime.

She yearned to get pregnant, but the first week of December, she discovered sadly that she wasn't.

"If the truth be known," Paul said comfortingly, "I'd rather have you to myself for a little while."

Caroline nestled close to his side, her head in the crook of his arm. "It may not be so easy for me. My mother had a difficult time getting pregnant."

"Then we'll just have to work at it, love."

Caroline laughed; if they worked any harder, they would drop from sheer exhaustion. Paul kissed her and held her close. "I never thought I'd find such happiness," he told her.

"Me either." He wasn't a man of many words, not one for flowery speeches. Nor did he shower her with expensive gifts. But his actions were far more effective than mere words. He loved her, and every day he did something to let her know how much he cared.

One morning after Paul had left for work, Caroline realized that she'd nearly let all this happiness slip through her fingers. The pain of Larry's rejection had nearly blinded her to Paul's love. When Larry had left, Caroline had almost died inside. Now she realized how mismatched they had been. They'd been friends, good friends, and erroneously had assumed a friendship as strong as theirs meant they would automatically be good lovers. It wasn't until she and Paul became lovers that Caroline could acknowledge that a marriage to Larry would have been a terrible mistake. Only Larry had recognized the cold hard facts.

Undoubtedly, Larry was torturing himself with guilt. Her aunts had mentioned his visit in a letter and although his name was only brought up briefly again, Caroline knew that he'd been back to visit her aunts, hungry for word of her.

In an effort to ease her friend's mind, Caroline decided to write Larry a letter. It was the least she could do. He'd feel better and she could tell him herself how happy she was. She wished him the best and was eternally grateful that he'd had the wisdom and the courage to keep them both from making a colossal mistake.

Caroline had originally intended her letter to be brief, but by the time she'd finished, she'd written five notebook pages. She told him about Paul and how much she loved her husband and thanked Larry for being her friend. She added bits and pieces about her life in Alaska and how marvelous the land was. Come summer, Paul had promised to take her hiking and fishing and she joked with Larry because he got queasy at the sight of a worm. When she'd finished, Caroline read the letter and realized that her happiness shone through like a beacon. Larry would have no more doubts.

After stuffing the five pages into an envelope, Caroline carried the letter over to the supply store that also served as the local post office.

"Good afternoon, Harry," she greeted the proprietor with a ready smile.

"Mrs. Trevor," he returned formally. "Nice day, isn't it?"

"It's a beautiful day." She handed him the letter.

"This all I can do for you?"

Caroline hedged. "It is unless you can sell me a pizza. I've had the craving for a thick, cheesy pizza all week."

He chuckled and rubbed the side of his jaw. "Unless there's a frozen one at the grocery, I'd say you're out of luck."

"I had that feeling," she grumbled, and with a cheery wave, was gone.

Paul rounded the corner of the supply store just as Caroline disappeared. "Afternoon, Harry. Was that my wife?"

"Yup, you just missed her. She came to mail a letter."

Paul's gaze sought Caroline out, but she was too far away from him to shout.

"Thick letter too, now that I look at it. She might be needing an extra stamp. I best weigh it."

Paul nodded, hardly hearing the man. "She's fond of those aunts of hers."

"Her aunt has a funny name then: Larry Atkins."

The name sliced through Paul as effectively as the serrated edge of a knife. He attempted to hide his shock and anger from Harry, but doubted that he had. Without bothering to buy what he'd needed, Paul left soon afterward and returned to the pumping station. He tried reasoning with himself that it was only a letter, then he recalled all the times Caroline had walked letters over to Harry, preferring to deliver them herself, claiming she needed the exercise.

His anger only increased when he remembered how she'd sat at the desk across from his own and vowed to find a means of escaping him. Her voice had been filled with conviction and vengeance. In his callowness, Paul hadn't expected her to be so deceitful. Once he was putty in her hands, she'd silently slip away.

"That's ridiculous," Paul said aloud. "No woman is that good an actress."

All the talk of a child. Dear Lord, she knew his Achilles' heel. He sat at his desk and slumped forward, burying his face in his hands. He couldn't condemn her on such flimsy evidence, but he couldn't trust her either. She'd taught him that once when she'd walked out on him with Burt Manners, but it seemed he was a slow learner.

By the time Paul arrived home that evening, he was, to all appearances, outwardly calm.

Caroline whirled around when he entered the cabin. "Guess what I'm making for dinner." Her smile was brighter than the sun had been all day.

"What's that, love?"

"Pizza."

"Pizza?"

"Well, a close facsimile. I didn't have a round pan so I'm using a square one. And I didn't want to make bread dough, so I'm making do with biscuit batter. And last but not least, we didn't have any sausage so I'm using ground caribou."

"A caribou pizza?"

"How does it sound?"

"Like we'll be eating scrambled eggs later."

"Oh, ye of little faith."

Paul laughed shortly; she didn't know the half of it.

Dinner was only partially successful. To her credit, the caribou pizza wasn't half bad. He managed to eat a piece and praised her ingenuity.

"What's for dinner tomorrow night? Moose Tacos?"

She laughed and promised him fried chicken.

While Caroline did the dishes, she watched Paul. He sat in the recliner with the paper resting in his lap as he stared into space. His face was so intent that she wondered what could be troubling him.

"Paul."

He shook himself from his reprieve.

"Is something wrong?"

"Nothing, love. I was just thinking."

"About what? You looked so pensive."

"Life." His grin was wry.

"Life?"

"It's taken an unexpected turn for us, hasn't it?" He eyed her carefully, hoping to read her heart and know for himself the truth. He saw the love and devotion shining from her eyes and called himself every kind of fool.

"Tanana let me watch Carl for her this afternoon," she announced, smiling. "He's growing so fast."

"You love that baby, don't you?"

"As much as if he were our own."

Tenderness wrapped its way around his heart, suffocating his doubts. He had Caroline as his own, loved her more than life itself. If she were playing him for a fool, then he was the happiest idiot alive. He planned to hold on to that contentment, hug it against his breast and treasure every minute she was with him for as long as it lasted. She might dream of her precious Larry, she might even write the bastard, but it was in the curve of his arm where she slept. It was his body that filled hers and gave her such pleasure that she wept with joy. It was his name she bore and later, God willing, it would be his children her slim body gave life to.

When they made love that night, it was like a storm of passion that had overtaken them. Electricity arced between them, the current more powerful than lightning. Each caress became a fire only their love could extinguish. Gradually their love play crescendoed into a rhapsody that rose ever upward, building, mounting until it seemed that all the instruments in the world had joined together for one joyous song. Afterward, Caroline lay limp and drowsy in her husband's arms. Her cheeks were flushed with the gentle blush of pleasure, her breath uneven. Paul closed his eyes, wondering how he could have ever doubted her. He buried his face in her hair, savoring the fragrance, and held her close until he recognized the even meter of her breathing and knew she was dreaming.

Caroline wasn't sure what woke her. One minute she was asleep and the next awake. It took her a moment to realize Paul wasn't asleep.

"Paul, what's wrong?"

"Not a thing, love."

She slipped her hand over his ribs and buried her face in his throat. He'd been so quiet this evening and their love-making had been a desperate act of passion. Paul wasn't himself and Caroline wondered what had happened to bring this about. "I've failed you in some way, haven't I?"

He hesitated. "No, love, I fear I may have failed you."

"Paul, no. I'm happy, truly happy."

"Do you miss Seattle?"

"I miss my aunts," she admitted. "I wish you could meet them; they're a delight. And now and then I think about my friends, but there's nothing for me in Seattle now that I'm with you."

"I love you, Caroline."

She smiled and kissed the side of his mouth. He'd shown her his love in a hundred ways, but he'd never said the words. "I know."

"You're laughing at me, aren't you?" His grip on her tightened as though he wished to punish her.

Caroline jerked away from him with a gasp. "Paul, what's gotten into you?"

He held himself rigid and didn't speak for an interminable moment. "I told you I loved you and I know you were smiling."

"I...was happy." She lay on her stomach, her hands buried under her.

Another long minute passed. "I'm sorry, love. I didn't mean to frighten you."

She nodded and rolled away from him. Their happiness was shattering right in front of her eyes and she was powerless to change it.

"Caroline," he said at last, reaching for her. "I talked to Harry after you were in the store today. I saw the letter you'd written to Larry Atkins."

Her brows arched. "It's obvious you didn't read it."

"Why?"

"If you had, your reaction would be altogether different."

"Have you written him in the past?" Paul hated his jealousy. All day he'd been brooding; furious with himself and unreasonable with Caroline. If love did this to a man, he wanted no part of it, and yet he wouldn't, couldn't give her up.

"This is my first letter to him."

"Why did you feel it was necessary to contact him now?"

"To thank him."

"What?"

"It's true. You mean this is what's been troubling you all day?"

He didn't answer, ashamed of his behavior.

"Why didn't you ask me earlier? I would have told you all about it. I wrote Larry to let him know he'd done me a gigantic favor by standing me up at the altar."

"You told him that?"

"Not exactly in those words, but basically that was what I said."

"Why didn't you tell me about writing him?"

Caroline expelled her breath on a nervous sigh. "To be truthful, I didn't think about it. My mistake. Are you always going to be this irrational?"

"When it comes to my wife contacting another man, you're damn right I am."

"It isn't like you're making it sound."

"I have only your word for that."

Caroline fumed, and rather than argue, she turned her back on him. "Good night, Paul," she grumbled. It wouldn't do any good to talk to him now. In the morning things would be better.

For two days they put the incident behind them. Their happiness was too complete to be destroyed over a silly letter and they each, independently, seemed to realize it. On the third day, Paul arrived home two hours before his usual time.

"You're home early." In the midst of writing out Christmas cards, she was delighted to see her husband.

He sat at the table across from her. "I've got to fly into Fairbanks for a few days."

"Oh, Paul, Fairbanks? Oh, heavens, I can hardly wait! The first thing I'm going to do is order a real sausage pizza with extra cheese and then I'm going to shop for twelve hours nonstop. You have no idea how much I wanted to buy Tanana and the baby something special for Christmas and there just doesn't seem to be anything in the catalogs. Why didn't you say something earlier?"

"Because..."

"And you know what else I'm going to do?" She answered her own question before he had the chance, her voice animated and high-pitched. "I'm going to soak in a hot bubble bath until my skin wilts, and watch television. Doesn't that sound silly?"

"Caroline," he said gruffly, his gaze just avoiding hers. "This is a business trip; I hadn't planned to bring you along."

Chapter Eight

It took a full minute for the words to sink into Caroline's baffled mind. "You're not taking me with you?" With deliberate patience, she set the pen down and pushed the Christmas cards aside. "Why?"

Paul refused to meet her probing gaze. "I've already explained that it was a business trip."

"That's not the reason and you know it, Paul Trevor." She'd thought they'd come so far, but the only one who had moved had been her. She'd walked into his arms and been so blinded by her love she hadn't recognized the chains that bound her.

"I don't know what you're talking about."

"Like hell!"

"I go to Fairbanks every other month or so...."

"Every other month?"

"You can go another time."

"I want to go now."

"No!"

"Why not?" She grew more furious by the moment.

"Because—"

"Because you saw that stupid letter to Larry and are absolutely convinced I've made arrangements to escape."

"Don't be ridiculous." But her accusation was so close to the truth that Paul's heart pounded hard against his ribs in silent objection.

Caroline's smile was sad. "Since I'm your prisoner, you might as well lock me in a cell."

"You're my wife!"

"I'm the woman who was forced into staying married to you. What we have isn't a marriage!" She saw him open his mouth to contradict her, then close it again. "It takes more than a piece of paper signed by the proper authorities to constitute a marriage."

"Caroline, you're making too much of this."

"Yes, master," she said, staring straight ahead, refusing to look at him. "Whatever you say, master." She gave him a mocking bow, folding her hands in front of her and bending low.

"Caroline, stop that."

"Anything you ask, master." He wanted a slave. Fine! She would give him one. She'd speak only when spoken to, bow to his every wish, smother him with her servitude.

Her unflagging calmness shocked her. It was as though the sun had come out in full force, revealing all the glaring imperfections of their relationship. She stared at the flaws, appalled and saddened. She'd come to love Paul and Alaska. She'd found happiness with him only to discover it was marred with imperfections. She was no better off now than she had been that first week when he'd forced her into becoming his shadow. The only difference was that she'd grown more comfortable in her cell.

Another thought came to her and she forgot her resolve not to speak. "How...how do I know you don't have a lover in Fairbanks?"

Paul stood, pushing back the kitchen chair with such force that it threatened to topple. "That's ridiculous. I can't believe you'd even think such a thing!"

"Why? I've lived with you these last two months, I'm well aware of your appetite for..."

"The only lover I have is you!" He shouted the words and stuffed his hands inside his pants pockets.

"If you can't trust me, there's nothing that says I have to trust you." She didn't think for a minute that Paul did have another woman, but she wanted him to sample a taste of her own frustration. "The fact you don't want me along speaks for itself. It's obvious you're hiding something from me." She arched her brows speculatively. "Another woman, no doubt."

Paul's mouth was tight. "That thought is unworthy of you."

"It's only tit for tat."

His expression darkened. "I'm leaving for Fairbanks and you're staying here and that's the way it's going to be."

Caroline fumed. "Yes, master."

"Oh, Lord, are we back to that?"

She didn't answer. Instead she walked across the cabin and reached for her parka and boots. "I'm going to see Tanana unless my master demands that I remain here."

"Caroline." He stopped her just before she opened the door, but she didn't turn around and Paul knew that she was fighting back tears. He felt himself go weak; he loved her and yearned to take away the pain, but it was too late to change his plans now. "Never mind," he said gruffly, and turned his back to her.

Caroline nodded and left him, gently closing the door behind her.

Paul paced the room, his thoughts in conflict. Caroline was right; she'd given him everything—her love, her heart, her trust... And yet, he wasn't satisfied; he wanted more.

The cold wind cut through Caroline as she traipsed the frozen pathway that led to the Eagleclaws' cabin. She needed to get away and think. Paul had hurt her; he'd never guess to what extent his doubts pained her sensitive heart. No matter how strenuously he argued otherwise, she was his prisoner in fact and in deed.

Tanana answered the knock at her door and looked relieved to discover it was Caroline. The baby cried pitifully in the background.

"Carl cried all night. I think he's sick."

Caroline didn't bother to take off her parka, but walked directly to the baby's side. Gently, she lifted him from the crib bed. His little face was red and his legs were drawn up against his stomach.

"He might have colic."

"Colic?" Tanana repeated.

"Does he cry after each feeding?"

"And before. All he does is cry."

From the Indian girl's obvious exhaustion, Caroline could believe it. "Then I think you should make an appointment with the medical team for next week."

Tanana agreed with a short nod.

"Lie down for a bit and rest," Caroline said softly. "I'll hold Carl."

"You spoil him."

Caroline grinned and kissed the top of his small head. "I know, but let me."

"You'll make a good mother for Paul Trevor's sons."

Some of the light faded from Caroline's eyes and she quickly averted her face so her friend couldn't read her distress. She spent most of the afternoon with Tanana and the baby, leaving only when she was certain that Carl would sleep and that his mother had received a few hours' rest.

"Send Thomas if you need me," she instructed on her way out the door.

Paul met Caroline halfway back to the cabin. His eyes held hers in a long, steady look. "I'll be leaving in a few minutes."

"Would my master wish me to carry his bags to the airstrip?"

"Caroline . . . don't, please."

Keeping up this charade was hard enough when her heart was breaking. "Carl has colic and poor Tanana's been up two nights with him.'' She tried to cover the uncomfortable silence.

Paul's eyes caressed her. ''You don't need to go to the airstrip.''

She lowered her gaze, already feeling herself weaken.

Walter met them and loaded Paul's suitcase onto the back of the dogsled. He seemed to realize that Paul and Caroline needed time alone.

''Caroline,'' he began. This was hard for him, harder than he thought. ''You're not a prisoner.'' He turned her into his arms and held her close, shutting his eyes to savor the feel of her against him. Their coats were so thick that it made holding each other awkward and he reluctantly dropped his arms.

Caroline swallowed her anger. ''How long will you be away?''

''Four, possibly five days.''

It seemed a lifetime, but she said nothing. His hands caressed her face with such tenderness that Caroline closed her eyes and against every dictate of her will, she swayed toward him. When he fit his mouth over hers, her lips parted with eager welcome. The kiss was long and thorough, making her all the more aware of the seductive power he held over her senses. Of their own volition, her arms slid upward over his chest and around his neck. One kiss and he dominated her will, destroying her weak resolve. Caroline didn't know whom she was more furious with, herself or Paul.

''Oh, love,'' he breathed against her lips. ''Next time maybe you'll come with me.''

Purposefully, she stepped away from him. She was irate, frustrated with herself for being so weak and more so with Paul for not trusting her. ''I'll be happy to go with you if I'm still here.''

The shock that contorted Paul's features and narrowed his eyes caused Caroline to suck in her breath. Abruptly he turned away and left her, marching to the airstrip without a word of farewell.

Caroline didn't know what had made her say anything so incredibly stupid. She regretted her sharp tongue, but Paul had hurt her and she wanted him to realize she wasn't a lifeless rag doll with no feelings.

"Damn!" She stomped her foot in the dry snow. If she'd hoped to build a foundation of trust, she'd just crumpled its cornerstone.

Caroline stood as she was until Paul's plane had taxied away and ascended into the gray sky. Only then did she return to the cabin, disillusioned and miserable. It astonished her how empty the place felt. She remained standing in the middle of the living room for several minutes, hardly able to believe that in the span of a few hours, her entire world could have been jolted so sharply.

That night, Caroline slept fitfully. She was too cold, then too hot. Her pillow was too flat and the mattress sagged on one side. After midnight, she admitted that it wasn't the bed or too many blankets. The problem was that the space beside her was empty. With a sigh, she turned and stared at the ceiling, trying to come up with ways of repairing her marriage.

Paul set his suitcase on the carpeted floor of the Hotel Fairbanks. His room was adequate—a double bed, dresser, chair and television. He stared at the TV set and experienced a small twinge of regret. The sensation multiplied when his gaze fell on the bathtub.

Regret hounded him. Not once in all the weeks that Caroline had been in Atta had she complained about the less-than-ideal living conditions. Yet she'd been denied the most simple of pleasures.

Slowly, Paul removed his parka and carelessly tossed it on top of the bed. He ran his hand over his eyes; he was determined to rush this trip and get back to Caroline and rebuild what his jealous doubts had destroyed.

After he'd undressed and climbed into the soft bed, Paul lay on his back, his arms folded behind his head. It didn't feel right to be here without Caroline. A smile lifted the corners of his mouth as he recalled how quickly she'd dropped her role of servant; she had too much fire in her to play the part with any conviction.

He thought about her being alone in the cabin, curled up and sleeping in his bed, and experienced such an over-whelming surge of desire that his body tightened and ten-sion knotted his stomach. She often slept in that thin fur-lined piece of silk her aunts had given her. Usually it rode up her slim body so that if he reached for her, his hand was met with warm, silken skin.

Paul inhaled sharply at the memory. Her eagerness for his lovemaking had been a surprise and a delight. She hadn't refused him once, welcoming his ardor with an energy and enthusiasm he hadn't hoped to expect. He wouldn't leave her again, wouldn't take another trip unless she could join him. He planned on telling her so the minute he returned to Atta.

Caroline woke early the next morning. As usual it was dark. The hours of daylight were becoming shorter and shorter as they approached the autumnal equinox. More and more of each day was spent in complete darkness. She thought about the summer and what it would be like to have the sun shine late at night. Then she wondered if she'd be in Atta to see it. The thought stunned her. Of course, she'd be in Atta. This was her home now.

No sooner had she dressed and fixed breakfast than there was a knock on her door. Walter Thundercloud stood on the other side, grinning wryly.

"Good morning, Walter."

He nodded politely, stepped inside and looked a bit un-easy.

Without asking, she poured him a cup of coffee and placed it on the table.

"You okay?" he asked gruffly.

"Of course I am."

"Paul asked me to check on you."

Caroline pulled out a chair and sat across from the old Indian. Naturally Paul would want to be sure his prisoner was in her cell. Her hands surrounded the thick mug. "I'm fine. You needn't worry about me."

Walter hesitated. "Paul has been in Atta several years now."

It seemed that her husband's friend was leading up to something. She nodded, hoping that was encouragement enough for him to continue.

"When he first came, he had the cabin built for privacy. The oil company had supplied his quarters, but he wanted something larger and more homelike so he could bring his wife to live with him."

"His wife!" Caroline nearly choked on her coffee. It scalded the inside of her mouth and burned a path all the way to her stomach.

"The woman wasn't his wife yet. She'd only promised to be."

"I see." Paul had been engaged! "What happened?"

"He never told me, but one day a letter arrived and after he read it, Paul left the station and got sick drunk. He never mentioned her name again."

Nor had he mentioned the woman to Caroline. The heat of jealous anger blossomed in her cheeks. The night of her arrival, she'd spilled her guts about Larry. Apparently, Paul had gone through a similar experience and hadn't thought to mention it to her. Talk about trust!

"For many months, Paul was angry. He worked too hard, some nights not sleeping. He scowled and barked and drank more than he should."

"He didn't leave Atta and try to work things out with this woman?"

"No."

Caroline took another sip of her coffee, not surprised. He had an overabundance of pride, oftentimes to his own detriment. "Why are you telling me this?"

"For the first time since Paul Trevor arrived in Atta, he smiles every day. He laughs. Before my eyes I've seen happiness fill him. These changes come when you come."

So Walter wanted to reassure her. She smiled softly and diverted her attention to her drink, not wanting him to know his words only proved how little she knew of the man who was her husband.

"What made Paul decide to marry now after all this time?"

Walter shrugged. "I think Tanana had something to do with that."

"Tanana?" Caroline didn't understand.

"He wants a family."

She nodded. Tanana had told her the same thing.

"He loves you," Walter continued. "I don't believe Paul ever thought he'd be fortunate enough to find such a good woman as you. He put the ad in the paper because he was lonely."

"But why did he advertise for a wife? Surely there were women who would want to marry him. Someone in Fairbanks?"

Walter added sugar to his coffee, stirring it a long time, far longer than necessary. "You'll have to ask him that."

Alarm turned her blood cold. "He has a woman in Fairbanks?"

Walter chuckled and shook his head. "Not as far as I know. He advertised for a woman because he hadn't the time to properly date someone and build a relationship by the usual means. Then, too, I think he feared the same thing would happen to him a second time and she would change her mind."

No wonder he'd been so insistent that they stayed married. "Why is a child so important to Paul?"

"I don't know. I suppose it was because he never had a family himself."

This was another shock to Caroline. Paul had spoken only briefly about his background. He'd been raised somewhere in Texas. As far as she knew, he hadn't contacted his parents about their marriage and now that she thought about it, Paul seemed to change the subject whenever she mentioned anything about his childhood.

The faded eyes brightened. "I'm not telling you these things to stir up trouble." The old man paused and chuckled. "I can see that most of what I've said has been a shock. I don't know that Paul would appreciate my loose tongue, but I felt you should know that he's gone through some hard times. You've been damn good for that boy."

"Our relationship is still on rocky ground."

"I can see that. I was surprised he didn't take you to Fairbanks and when I mentioned it, he nearly bit my head off."

"You were right when you guessed that I love him."

"He's equally smitten. He'd move heaven and earth to see that you were happy. He may have married just so he could have a son, but he loves you."

Another knock sounded, drawing their attention to the front door. Thomas Eagleclaw stepped in without waiting for an invitation. His eyes were round and eager. "Mrs. Paul, please hurry come."

"What is it?"

"Tanana and baby sick."

An exchange of the native tongue flew over Caroline's head as she stood and reached for her coat. Momentarily, her gaze collided with Walter's. The older man reached for his parka as well and followed her to the Eagleclaws' cabin. Even before they reached the small log structure, Caroline had a premonition of disaster. Her chest tightened with dread.

The baby lay in his bed, hardly moving. His round eyes looked up at her and when Caroline felt his skin, he was burning up with fever. "How long has he been like this?"

"Apparently Tanana's been ill as well." Walter answered for the young man.

"Why didn't you come and get me?" Caroline asked Thomas.

"Tanana probably told him not to; she didn't want to trouble you," Walter whispered, standing close at Caroline's side.

"But Carl is very sick."

"Mary Finefeather has fever," Thomas announced.

"Mary, too?"

Caroline turned to Walter. "I'll do what I can here and meet you at Mary's."

Walter nodded, and left.

Tanana's young face felt hot, and the girl whimpered softly when Caroline tried to talk to her.

The young husband stood stiffly by the bedside. "She's much worse this morning."

"Oh, Thomas, I wish you'd come for me," Caroline said, more sharply than she intended.

The young man looked guiltily at the floor.

"How are you feeling?"

He shrugged, still not looking at her.

Caroline pressed the back of her hand to his forehead and shook her head. "Get in bed and I'll be back when I can."

Although she tried to be calm, her heart was racing. She hurried from the Eagleclaws' to Mary's cabin on the other side of the village. Once there, Caroline discovered that the older woman's symptoms were similar to Tanana's and the baby's.

"Walter, contact the Public Health Department and see if they can fly in some help. I don't know what we've got here, but I don't like the looks of it."

Walter's eyes met her own, dark and serious. "In the winter of 1979 we lost twelve to the fever."

"We're not going to lose anyone. Now get on the wire and hurry!"

Paul paused on the sidewalk outside the jewelry store to look at the diamond rings on display. He'd never thought to ask Caroline if she wanted a diamond. She wore the simple gold band he'd given her and hadn't asked for anything more. Now he wondered if she was disappointed with the simplicity of the ring.

He thought about the gifts he'd already purchased her and realized he'd probably need to buy another suitcase to haul them all back to Atta. He smiled at the thought. He'd bought her everything she'd ever mentioned wanting and, in addition, purchased gifts for Tanana and the baby, knowing Caroline had wanted something special for the two. In his own way, Paul longed to make up to her for excluding her from this trip. Never again would he leave her behind. He decided he'd buy her a ring and save it for Christmas. Everything else he'd give her when he arrived home.

Never had he been more anxious to return to Atta.

The Public Health Department flew in a doctor and two nurses the same afternoon that Walter contacted them. The community meeting hall served as a makeshift hospital and the worst of the sick were brought there. Tanana, the baby and Mary Finefeather were the first to become seriously ill. Others soon followed. Within two days, Caroline and the medical staff tended twenty-five patients. The following day it was thirty, then thirty-five.

"How long has it been since you slept?" Dr. Mather asked Caroline on the third day.

Her smile was weak. "I forget."

"That's what I thought. Go rest, and that's an order."

She stiffened her back and shook her head. She couldn't leave when so many were sick and more arrived every hour. The other staff members had rested intermittently. "I'm fine."

"If you don't do as I say, you'll be sick next."

"I'm not leaving."

"Stubborn woman." But his eyes spoke of admiration and appreciation.

Later the same day, Walter brought her something to eat and forced her to sit down. "I think I should contact Paul."

"Don't." She placed her hand on his forearm and silently pleaded with him. "He'd only worry."

"I think he should. You're working yourself into an early grave."

"I'm as healthy as an ox."

"You won't be if you continue like this."

Walter gave her one of his looks and Caroline slowly shook her head. "All right, we'll compromise. I'll go lie down in a few minutes, but I'll have someone wake me after an hour."

Mary Finefeather died early the next morning. Caroline stood at Dr. Mather's side as he pulled the sheet over the proud Indian face, relaxed now in death. Tears burned the backs of Caroline's eyes, but she dared not let them flow. So many needed her; she had to be strong.

"Are you okay?" the doctor asked.

"I think so," Caroline answered in a strangled voice. "What about the baby?" She'd held Carl for most of the night. He was so weak, too weak to cry. He had lain limp in her arms, barely moving.

The doctor hesitated. "It doesn't look good. If he lasts through the day, then his chances will improve."

The floor pitched beneath her feet. She'd known it herself, but had been afraid to admit it. "His mother?"

"She's young and strong. She should make it."

"Anyone else?"

"Two others look serious."

Caroline bit the soft flesh inside her cheek and followed him to the bed of the next patient.

At the end of the fourth day, Paul returned to the hotel, packed his bags, and checked out. He felt as anxious as a kid awaiting the end of the school term. He was going home to Atta, home to Caroline—his wife, his love. After a short trip to a pizza parlor, the taxi delivered him at the airport. If Burt Manners was late, Paul swore he'd have his hide.

The pilot was waiting for Paul at the designated area inside the terminal. Burt rose to his feet as Paul approached him.

"I've got bad news for you," he said, frowning as he eyed the pizza box.

"What's that?"

"We aren't going to be able to fly into Atta."

"Why the hell not?" Frustration caused Paul to tighten his grip around the handle of his suitcase.

"A white-out."

"Damn!" Paul expelled the word viciously. A white-out was dangerous enough to put the finest, most experienced pilot on edge. Visibility plummeted to zero, making a thick London fog preferable. The condition could last for days.

"There's nothing more you can do." Dr. Mather spoke gently to Caroline and attempted to remove the lifeless four-year-old child from her arms.

"No, please," she whispered, bringing the still body closer to her own. "Let me hold her a few minutes longer. I . . . I just want to say goodbye."

The doctor stepped aside and waited.

Caroline brushed the thick hair from the sweet face and kissed the smooth brow, rocking her gently to and fro in her arms, singing the little girl a lullaby she would never hear. Anna was dead and Caroline was sure Carl was next. Tears rained unchecked down her cheeks. She took a moment to compose herself, then handed the child to the doctor. "I'll tell her mother."

A week after Paul had left Atta, he returned. Walter Thundercloud was at the airstrip waiting for him when the plane taxied to a standstill. One look at the deep, troubled frown and sad eyes that marred the Indian's features and Paul knew that something was terribly wrong.

"What is it?"

"The fever came. Five are dead."

Fear tightened Paul's throat. "Caroline?"

"She's been working for three days without sleep. Thank God, you're back."

"Take me to her."

By the time Paul reached the meeting hall, his heart was pounding. Rarely had he moved more quickly. If anything happened to Caroline, he'd blame himself. He'd left her, abandoned her to some unspeakable fate. He stopped in the doorway, appalled at the scene. The stench hit him first; the hall smelled like death. Stretchers littered the floor, children were crying.

It took him a moment to find Caroline. She was bent over an old woman, lifting the weary head and helping her to sip liquid through a straw. Caroline looked frail and fragile and when she straightened, she staggered and nearly fell backward.

Paul was at her side instantly. She turned and looked at him as though he were a stranger.

"I'm getting you out of here," Paul said, furious that she'd worked herself into this condition and no one had stopped her.

"No, please," she said in a voice so weak it wobbled. "I'm fine." With that, she promptly fainted.

Paul caught her before she hit the floor.

Chapter Nine

Caroline struggled to open her eyes; the lids felt incredibly heavy. She discovered Paul sleeping awkwardly in a kitchen chair at her bedside. He was slouched so that his head rested against the back. One arm hugged his ribs and the other hung loosely at his side. Caroline blinked. Paul looked terrible; his clothes were wrinkled and disorderly, his shirt was pulled out from the waistband and half-unbuttoned.

"Paul?" she whispered, having difficulty finding her voice. She forced herself to swallow. When Paul didn't respond, Caroline lifted her hand and tugged at his shirttail.

His eyes flew open instantly and he bolted upright. "Caroline? Oh God, you're awake." He rose to his feet and brushed his unkempt hair from his face, staring down at her as if he couldn't quite believe it was she. "How do you feel?"

The past week suddenly returned to haunt her in technicolor detail. She thought of Mary Finefeather and her abrupt one-word sentences and Anna, the bubbly four-year-old. An overwhelming sadness at the loss of her friends brought stinging tears to her eyes.

"Carl?" She managed to squeeze the name of the baby from the tightness that claimed her throat.

"He's improving and so is Tanana."

"Good." Caroline closed her eyes again because sleep was preferable to the memories.

When she awakened a second time, Paul was sitting in the chair beside their bed. Only this time his head was slouched forward, his elbows resting on his knees, his face buried in his hands. She must have made a sound; he slowly lifted his head.

"How long have I been asleep?" she asked.

"Forty-eight hours."

She arched her eyebrows in surprise. "Did I catch the fever?"

"The doctor said it was exhaustion." Paul stood and poured a glass of water and lifted her head so she could sip from it. When she'd finished, he gently lowered her back to the bed.

Caroline rolled her face away so she wouldn't have to watch his expression. "I want to go home."

"Caroline, love, you are home."

Her eyes drifted closed. She hadn't thought it would be easy; she knew Paul too well.

"Caroline, I know you're upset, but you'll feel different later. I promise you will."

Despite her resolve not to cry, a tear coursed down her cheek. "I hate Alaska. I want to go where death doesn't come with the dark, where children laugh and I can smell flowers again." People had died here—people she had loved, people she had cared about. Friends. Children. Babies. The marriage she'd worked so hard to build wasn't a real one. The only ingredient that held it together was Paul's indomitable pride; he wasn't going to let her go after he'd already lost one woman.

"You don't know what you're saying," he stated, discounting her words as he reached for her hand.

"I want to go home."

"Caroline! Damn it!" He released her hand and she heard him stalk to the other side of the room. "I'll fix you something to eat."

Alone now, Caroline pushed back the covers and carefully sat upright. The room spun and teetered, but she gripped the headboard and gradually everything righted itself.

Suddenly she felt terribly hungry. When Paul returned, carrying a tray of tea, toast and scrambled eggs, she gave no thought to refusing it.

He fluffed up her pillows against the headboard and set the tray on her lap. It looked as though he meant to feed her, and Caroline stopped him with her hand.

"I can do it."

He nodded and sat back in the chair. "Walter said you nearly killed yourself. You refused to leave, or rest or eat. Why did you push yourself like that, love?" He paused and watched her lift the fork to her mouth with unhurried, deliberate movements. "He told me about Anna dying in your arms."

Caroline chewed slowly, but not by choice; even eating required energy. She didn't want to talk about Anna, the fever, or anything else. She didn't answer Paul's questions because she couldn't explain to him something that she didn't fully understand herself. In some incomprehensible way, she felt responsible for the people in Atta. They were her friends, her family, and she'd let them down.

"I can't tell you how bad I feel that you were left to deal..."

"Why didn't you mention her?"

Paul gave her an odd look. "Mention who?"

She glared at him. "You know *who*."

"Oh Lord, don't tell me we're going to go through this again. Should I wear padded clothes as protection against the salt and pepper shakers?" Mockingly he held up his hands, his eyes twinkling.

For a moment, Caroline was furious enough to hurl something at him, but it required more energy than she was willing to expend.

"Caroline, love..."

"I'm not your love," she said heatedly.

Paul chuckled. "You can't honestly mean that after the last few weeks."

"Correction," she said bitterly. "I'm not your *first* love."

Paul went still and his eyes narrowed. "All right, what did you find?"

"Find?" Caroline discovered she was shaking. "Find? Do you mean to tell me that you've got...memorabilia stored in this cabin from that...that other woman?"

"Caroline, settle down..."

"Oh-h-h." It required all her restraint not to fling a left-over piece of toast at him. He must have noticed her temptation because he quickly lifted the tray from her lap and returned it to the kitchen.

While he was gone, Caroline lay back down and tried to compose her thoughts. He'd loved another woman so much that it had taken years for him to commit himself to a new relationship. Caroline was simply filling some other woman's place in his life. What bothered her most was that he'd never mentioned a previous lover. The more she learned, the more imperative it became for her to leave.

He returned to the bedroom, his steps reluctant, almost hesitant. The tips of his fingers were slipped into the back pockets of his jeans. "This isn't the time to talk about Diane. When you're stronger, I'll tell you everything you want to know."

"Diane," Caroline repeated slowly, and vowed to hate every woman with that name. An eerie calm came over her as she suspiciously raised her eyes to meet Paul's. "This...Diane didn't happen to be blond, blue-eyed, about five-five and have an hourglass figure, did she?"

Paul looked stunned. "You knew her?"

"You idiot, that's me!" She grabbed a pillow from his side of the bed and heaved it at him with all her strength.

She was so weak that it didn't even make it to the end of the mattress.

Innocently, Paul raised both his hands. "Love, listen, I know what this sounds like."

"Get out!"

"Caroline."

"No doubt the doctor told you I should remain calm and quiet. The very sight of you boils my blood, Paul Trevor, so kindly leave before there's cardiovascular damage!"

He advanced toward her and Caroline scrambled to her knees and reached for the glass of water. "You take one more step and you'll be wearing this!"

Exasperated, Paul swore under his breath. "How one woman could be so utterly unreasonable is beyond me."

"Unreasonable!" She lifted the tumbler and brought back her arm, making the threat more real. The action was enough to force him to exit the room. Once he'd gone, Caroline curled up in a tight ball and shook with fury and shock. Not only hadn't he told her about Diane, but he'd chosen Caroline because she obviously resembled the other woman. He'd told her often enough that one look at her picture and he'd known. Sure he'd known! She was a duplicate of the woman he'd once loved.... And probably still did.

Blissfully, Caroline escaped into a deep slumber. When she awakened, she felt stronger and, although she was a bit shaky on her feet, she managed to dress and pull out the suitcase from beneath the bed. Her hands trembled as she neatly folded and packed each garment.

"What are you doing?" Paul asked from behind her.

Caroline stiffened. "What I should have done weeks ago. Leaving Atta. Leaving Alaska. Leaving you."

"I won't let you, love," he said after a long, tension-wrought moment. "I realize things are a bit unsettled between us, but we'll work it out."

"Unsettled. You call this unsettled? Well, I've got news for you, Paul Trevor. Things are a little more than just unsettled. I want out. O-U-T. Out!"

"There will be no divorce."

"Fine, we'll stay married if that's what you want. We'll have the ideal marriage—I'll be in Seattle and you can live here. No more arguing. No more disagreements. No more Scrabble." Frantically, she stacked her sweaters in the open suitcase. "Believe me, after this experience I don't wish to involve myself with another man again."

"Caroline..."

"I'll tell you one thing I'm grateful for, though," she interrupted him; talking helped to relieve the terrible ache in her breast. "You taught me a lot about myself. Here I was playing Joan of Arc to an entire Indian village as if I were some heroic soul. I was a real Clara Barton dispensing medical knowledge and good will with the best of them."

"Caroline..."

"I even fooled myself into thinking you and I could make a go of this marriage. I thought, 'Gee, Paul Trevor's a good man. Better than most. Fair. Kind. Tender.' I'll admit that the events leading up to our marriage were a bit bizarre, but I was ready to stick it out and make the most of the situation. Things could have been worse—I could have married Larry." She laughed then, but the sound contained little amusement.

His hands settled on her shoulders and he attempted to turn her around, but Caroline wouldn't let him. "Please, don't touch me." He was warm and gentle and she couldn't resist him. Her eyes filled with tears and Paul swam in and out of her vision as she backed away from him.

"I can't let you go, love," he said softly.

"You don't have any choice."

"Caroline, give it a week. You're distraught now, but in a few days, you'll feel differently."

"No," she sobbed, jerking her head back and forth. "I can't stay another day. Please, I need to get away."

"Let me hold you for just a minute."

"No." But she didn't fight him when he reached for her and brought her into the warm circle of his arms.

"I know, love," he whispered, and felt his heart catch at the anguish in her tormented features. She buried her face in his shirt and wept, her shoulders shaking with such force that Paul braced his feet to hold her securely.

"She died in my arms," she wailed.

"I know, love, I know." His hand smoothed her hair in long, even strokes. Regret sliced though him like a hot knife. He'd left her to face this alone, never dreaming anything like a fever could happen, thinking only of himself. He'd been incredibly selfish.

When her tears were spent, Caroline raised her head and wiped the moisture from her face. Paul's shirt bore evidence of her crying and she guiltily tried to rub away the wet stains.

His hand stopped hers and tenderly raised her palm to his mouth. He kissed the inside of her hand while his eyes held hers. She didn't want him to be so gentle; she wanted to hate him so she could leave and never look back.

"Please, don't," she pleaded weakly.

Paul released her hand.

"Caroline," he said seriously. "I can't let you go."

"Why not? Nothing binds us except a thin piece of paper." He flinched at her words and she regretted hurting him.

"I love you."

Knotting her hands into fists, she raised her chin a fraction. "Did you love Diane, too?"

Paul's face seemed to lose its color.

"Did you?" she cried, her voice raised.

"Yes."

Caroline pressed her advantage. "You let her go. You didn't go after her and force her to marry you and live on this frozen chunk of ice. I'm only asking for the same consideration."

"You don't know..."

"I do. I know everything there is about Alaska and Atta. I know that I can't live here anymore. I know I can't look you in the face and feel I'm your wife and you're my husband. I know I can't bear any more pain. Please, Paul, let me go home.'' She was weeping again, almost uncontrollably.

Paul advanced a step toward her. "You'll feel better tomorrow,'' he said softly, then turned and left the room.

Caroline slumped on top of the bed and cried until her eyes burned and there were no more tears. Spent, she slept again, only to awaken in a dark, shadowless room. Someone, probably Paul, had placed a thick blanket over her shoulders. She sat up and brushed the unruly mass of hair from her face.

Instantly, Paul stood in the doorway. "You're awake."

"Yes, master."

He sighed, but said nothing more.

"I've fixed you something to eat. Would you like to come out here or would you rather I brought it in to you?"

"Whatever my master wishes."

He clenched his fists. "It'll be on the table when you're ready."

"Thank you, master." Her words were spoken in a monotone.

Patience, Paul told himself. That was the key. Caroline had been through a traumatic experience that had mentally and physically exhausted her. She needed to know she was loved and that he would be there to protect her against anything like this happening again. For the hundredth time, he cursed himself for having left her while he'd gallivanted off to Fairbanks.

He ladled out a bowl of rich vegetable soup and set it on the table along with thick slices of sourdough bread. Next he poured her a tall glass of milk.

Caroline changed clothes and brushed her teeth and hair. She looked a sight; it was a wonder Paul wasn't happy to be rid of her.

Paul glanced up expectantly when she entered the room and pulled out a kitchen chair for her to sit down. Unfolding the napkin, Caroline spread it across her lap and stared at the meal. Although it smelled delicious, she had no appetite.

Her lack of interest must have shown in her eyes because Paul spoke sharply. "Eat, Caroline."

"I . . . I don't think I can."

"Try."

"I want to go home."

Paul's fists were so tight his fingers ached. *Patience*, he reminded himself for the tenth time, and she'd only been awake a few hours.

He took the chair across from her, straddled it and watched her as she methodically lifted the spoon to her mouth. "I brought you something from Fairbanks. Would you like to see it?" he coaxed.

She tried to smile, but there was nothing left of her strength. All she could think about was Seattle and her two aunts and how the world seemed to be right there. There was too much pain in Atta. "Will you let me go home if I look at it?"

A muscle leapt in his temple, but he refused to rise to the bait. He stood, opened the closet door and brought her several packages.

"Go ahead and open them," he said eagerly, then changed his mind. "No. You eat, I'll open them for you." From the first package, he produced an expensive bottle of perfume she'd once mentioned enjoying. He glanced expectantly to her, anticipating her delight.

Caroline swallowed down her surprise. He could be so loving and she didn't want him to be. Not now when all she could think about was leaving him.

"Well?"

"It's very nice. Thank you, master."

Paul had had it. His fist slammed down on the table and he shot to his feet. "You will never call me your master again. Is that understood?"

"Yes."

"I wish you'd stop this silly game!"

"Will you let me go home if I do?" Caroline asked and took another spoonful of soup.

Paul ignored the question and from the second package withdrew a huge teddy bear and was pleased when she paused, the spoon lifted halfway to her mouth.

"For Carl," he explained. "You said you wanted something special for him. I thought we'd save it for Christmas."

She nodded, and recalled how close they'd come to losing the baby. Tears filled her eyes.

Paul turned the bear over and ran his hand through the thick fur. "You twist something in the back here and Mr. Bear actually talks."

Caroline's nod was nearly imperceptible.

"Would you like to see what I got Tanana?"

"Not now...please." She looked straight ahead, and felt dizzy and weak. Setting the spoon back on the table she closed her eyes. "Would it be all right if I lay down a minute?"

"Of course." He moved to her side and slipped an arm around her waist as he guided her back into the bedroom. The suitcase was open on top of the bed. Paul moved it and set it on top of the dresser.

Caroline felt listless and tired. "Do I really look so much like her?"

"Her? You mean Diane?"

Caroline nodded.

"Now that you mention it, I suppose there's a certain resemblance, but it's only superficial."

"Why didn't you tell me about her?"

"It's a long story. Too complicated for right now."

"And you think my involvement with Larry wasn't?"

Paul sighed and closed the lid of her suitcase. "The two aren't comparable."

"What about your family?"

Paul went tense. "Who mentioned that?"

"We're married," she said sadly, "and yet you hide your life from me."

"I have no family, love. I was raised in a series of foster homes."

"You tell me about your childhood, but not Diane. I think I know the reasons why."

Irritated, Paul shook his head, his mouth pinched and white. "I love you."

"Then let me go back to Seattle," she pleaded.

"No, now don't ask me that again."

"Yes, master."

Paul groaned and slammed the door.

If Paul thought Caroline would give up her quest to return to Seattle, he was wrong. For two days, she sat around the cabin, listless and lethargic, staring into space. She never spoke unless spoken to and answered his questions with as few words as possible. She wore her unhappiness like an oversized cloak that smothered her natural exuberance.

He tried to draw her out, tried reasoning with her. Nothing helped. By the time they climbed into bed at night, he was so frustrated with her that any desire for lovemaking was destroyed. He longed to hold her, yearned to feel her body close to his, but each time he reached for her, she froze up.

She didn't mention returning to Seattle again. She didn't have to; the misery was evident in her eyes. Her suitcase remained packed and ready, a constant reminder of how eager she was to leave him. He placed it back under the bed once, but she immediately withdrew it and set it by the front door, waiting for him to release her. He let her keep the suitcase there because she'd only put it back if he moved it. He couldn't let her leave Atta; he couldn't lose her.

Each morning Paul promised himself Caroline would be better, but she tried his patience to the breaking point. He had to find a way to reach her and was quickly running out of ideas.

But today, he vowed, would be different. He had a plan.

After dinner that evening, Paul sat in his recliner, reading the Fairbanks newspaper. His mind whirled with thoughts of seduction; he missed Caroline; he missed having the warm, loving woman in his arms. It had been nearly two weeks since they'd made love and if anything could shatter the barriers she'd built against him, it was their lovemaking. He smiled, content for the first time in days.

"Caroline."

She turned to him, her eyes blank. "Yes."

"Dinner was very good tonight."

"Thank you."

"Would you come here a minute, please?"

She stepped toward him in small, measured steps, refusing to meet his eyes, and paused directly in front of the recliner.

"Sit on my lap."

Caroline hesitated, but did as he requested.

His hand massaged her tense muscles. "Relax," he whispered.

Caroline found it impossible to do so, but said nothing.

"Okay, love, place your hands on my shoulders."

She did that, too, with a fair amount of reluctance.

"Now kiss me."

Her eyes narrowed as she recognized his game.

"You're so fond of calling me your master, I thought you might need a little direction."

She didn't move.

"Just one kiss, love?"

Lightly, she rested the heels of her hands on his shoulders and leaned forward.

"Okay, love, kiss me."

Caroline stared at him blankly and gently pressed her closed mouth over his.

"No, love, a *real* kiss. One that will turn my socks inside out."

Caroline rubbed her closed mouth over his in the briefest of contacts.

"I've never known you to be so selfish. It'll be Christmas soon, and even a grinch could do better than that."

With the tip of her tongue, she moistened her lips and slanted her head to press her mouth over his. She felt like this was all a dream and it wasn't really happening.

The kiss was routine. Paul wove her hair around his fingers and placed his hand at the back of her head, holding her to him. His warmth permeated her heart and Caroline felt herself soften.

"I've missed your kisses, love." His eyes held hers. "I've missed everything about you."

Caroline couldn't seem to tear her gaze from his.

"Kiss me again—oh, love, you taste so good."

He tasted wonderful too, and Caroline settled her mouth over his, her lips parted enough so that she couldn't protest. With a sigh, she surrendered, admitting defeat.

Before she even realized what had happened, Paul had removed her blouse and was lazily running his hands over her bare breasts, praising her, telling her again and again how much he loved her.

He continued to kiss her with an urgency that quickly became an all-consuming passion. She felt weak, spent. Her arms clung to Paul and when he ran his hand along the inside of her thigh, she squirmed, wanting more and more of him. Her fingers shook almost uncontrollably as she pulled the shirt tail from his waist band and rubbed her palms over his chest.

"Oh Lord, love, I want you."

Somehow those words permeated the fog of desire when the others hadn't. With a soft moan, she lifted her head from his and stared at him with tear-filled eyes.

"Love?" He reached for her and she moved away as though he held a gun in his hand.

"Paul, please, I can't live here anymore. It hurts too much. Forcing me to stay only makes it worse."

His face lost all color. He could see it would do no good to reason with her, and sighed with defeat. "Alaska is my home."

"But it isn't mine."

"You'll get over this," he promised gently.

"I can't . . . I won't. I tried, Paul, I honestly tried."

He was silent for so long that Caroline wondered if he was going to speak again. "I won't come after you, Caroline. I didn't for Diane and I won't for you."

She nodded numbly. "I understand."

His fists bunched at his side. "I won't keep you against your will any longer."

Tears streaked her face and when she spoke, her voice was low and rusty. "Thank you."

"Shall I arrange for the divorce or would you rather do it yourself?"

Chapter Ten

"Oh, Sister," Ethel Myers said with a worried frown, "I don't know that the brew will help dear Caroline this time."

"We must think, and you know as well as I do that we do it so much better with Father's brew." With exaggerated movements, Mabel Myers poured two steaming cups of the spiked tea and handed one to her younger sister.

"Poor Caroline."

Mabel placed the dainty cup to her lips, paused and sighed. "She sounded so happy in her letters."

"And she tries so hard to hide her unhappiness now."

"Paul Trevor must be a terrible beast to have treated her so..."

"He isn't, Aunt Mabel," Caroline said from the archway of her aunts' parlor. "He's a wonderful man. Good and kind. Generous and unselfish."

Ethel reached for another porcelain cup. "Tea, dear?"

"Not me," Caroline said with a grin, recalling the last time she'd sampled her great-grandfather's brew. Before she'd known what was happening, she'd been married to Paul Trevor and was lying in his bed.

"If he wasn't a beast, dear, then why did you leave him?"

Caroline claimed a seat on the thick brocade sofa and sadly shook her head. "For silly reasons, I suppose."

"Silly reasons?" Ethel echoed, and the two older women exchanged meaningful glances.

"Then, dear, perhaps you should go back."

Caroline dropped her gaze to her lap. "I can't."

"Can't?" Mabel repeated. "Why ever not?"

"There was another woman...."

"With him?" Ethel sounded shocked. "Why, that's indecent. He *is* a beast."

"He loved Diane a long time ago," Caroline corrected hurriedly. "He never told me about her, but when he gave me the ticket home, he said that he didn't go after Diane and he wasn't coming after me."

Mabel placed her hand on top of Caroline's and squeezed gently. "Do you love him, dear?"

Caroline nodded. "Very much."

"Then you must go to him."

Her two aunts made it all sound so easy. Every day since she'd been home, Caroline had thought of Paul. He'd been right. Time had healed her from the shock of losing her friends to the fever. She'd been distraught; the people who had died hadn't been nameless faces in sterile hospital beds, but friends. They had been a part of her Alaskan family and each one had touched her heart in a special way.

"Go to him?" Caroline repeated and sadly shook her head. "No."

"No?" both sisters exclaimed together.

"If he loved me enough, he'd come to me. I need that, although I don't expect anyone else to understand the reasons why."

The doorbell chimed and Caroline stood. "That must be Larry. We're going to a movie."

"Have a good time, dear."

"Oh yes, dear, have a good time."

NO RISK, NO OBLIGATION TO BUY...NOW OR EVER!

GUARANTEED

PLAY "ROLL A DOUBLE" AND GET AS MANY AS FIVE FREE GIFTS!

HERE'S HOW TO PLAY:

1. Peel off label from front cover. Place it in space provided at right. With a coin, carefully scratch off the silver dice. This makes you eligible to receive two or more free books, and possibly another gift, depending on what is revealed beneath the scratch-off area.

2. Send back this card and you'll receive brand-new Silhouette Romance™ novels. These books have a cover price of $2.75 each, but they are yours to keep absolutely free.

3. There's no catch. You're under no obligation to buy anything. We charge nothing – ZERO – for your first shipment. And you don't have to make any minimum number of purchases – not even one!

4. The fact is thousands of readers enjoy receiving books by mail from the Silhouette Reader Service™ months before they're available in stores. They like the convenience of home delivery and they love our discount prices!

5. We hope that after receiving your free books you'll want to remain a subscriber. But the choice is yours – to continue or cancel, anytime at all! So why not take us up on our invitation, with no risk of any kind. You'll be glad you did!

No sooner had the front door closed than Ethel glanced at her sister, her eyes twinkling with mischief. "Shall I get the stationery or will you?"

"Hi." Larry kissed Caroline lightly on the forehead. "At least you've got some color in your face tonight."

"Thank you," she said, and laughed. Leave it to Larry to remind her that she'd been pale and sickly for four weeks. "And you're looking dashing, as usual." It nearly frightened her now to think that they'd almost married. Larry would make someone a wonderful husband, but Caroline wasn't that woman.

"Is there any movie you'd particularly like to see?" he asked.

"You choose." Their tastes were so different that anything she opted for would only be grounds for a lively discussion.

"There's a musical playing at the Fifth Avenue."

His choice surprised Caroline. Musicals weren't his thing. Blood and gore were what thrilled Larry.

"Do you approve?"

Caroline looked up at him and was forced to blink back tears. She hadn't cried since she'd returned to Seattle. Tears were a useless emotion now. She was home and everything was supposed to be roses and sunshine. Only it wasn't, because Paul wasn't there to share it with her. She'd been a fool to leave him and even more of one not to admit her mistake and go back.

"I've said something to upset you?" Larry asked kindly, offering her his handkerchief. It was clean and ironed and so like him that Caroline only wept louder.

"Caroline?"

She blew her nose loudly and handed him back his hanky.

He stared at the wadded mass of white cotton and shook his head. "You go ahead and keep it."

"Paul liked musicals," she explained, and sniffled. "He can't sing worth beans, but he didn't hesitate to belt out a song like Mario Lanza.'' She paused and giggled. ''And then he'd ask: 'Is it live or is it Memorex?' ''

''You really dug this guy, didn't you?''

''He was the only man I ever knew who could beat me in a game of Scrabble.''

''He beat you in Scrabble?'' Even Larry sounded impressed. ''As far as I can see, you two were meant for each other. Now when are you going to admit it?''

''Never, I fear,'' she said and an incredible sadness settled over her.

Ethel Myers sat in front of the antique typewriter and looked thoughtfully toward her sibling. ''Pour me another glass of tea, will you, Sister?''

''Most certainly, Sister.''

They looked at each other and giggled like schoolgirls.

''Caroline must never know.''

''Oh no. Caroline most definitely would not approve.''

''Read the letter again, Sister.''

Ethel picked up the single sheet of linen paper and sighed. ''My darling Paul,'' she said in a breathless whisper, as though she were a great actress practicing her lines. ''I feel you should know that I find myself with child. Your loving wife, Caroline.''

''Excellent. Excellent.''

''We'll put it in the mail first thing tomorrow.''

''More brew, Sister?''

Ethel giggled and held out her cup. ''Indeed.''

A week later, Caroline lay on the end of her bed and admitted defeat. Paul wasn't coming for her. He'd told her he wouldn't so it shouldn't be any great shock, but she'd hoped he would. If he loved her, truly loved her, then he would have forsaken his pride and come to Seattle to claim her as his woman. So much for dreams.

She turned onto her side. Surely, he must realize that she was waiting for him. She needed proof of his love—proof that she was more important to him than Diane had ever been. She was his wife, his love. He'd told her so countless times.

A sour taste filled her mouth. Admitting she was wrong wouldn't be easy. Look how long it had taken her to realize how mismatched she and Larry were.

Caroline sighed expressively and closed her eyes. Carl would have his first tooth by now. She missed the baby, and Tanana and the long talks they'd shared. She missed the women of the village and the authentic Indian sweaters she used to knit for the tourists. She missed the dusk at noon and the nonstop snow and even the unrelenting cold.

Most of all she missed Paul. He might have been able to live without her, but she was wilting away for lack of him.

With the realization that Paul's pride would keep him in Alaska came an unpleasant insight; it was up to her to swallow her considerable pride and go to him.

Within twenty minutes, her luggage was packed. She'd waited five weeks and another day was intolerable. She'd go to him. She hated the thought, but her love was too strong to give her peace.

"Are you going someplace, dear?" Aunt Mabel asked as Caroline descended the stairs, a suitcase in each hand.

"Alaska."

"Alaska?" Mabel cried, as though Caroline had suggested outer space.

Immediately Ethel appeared and Mabel cast a stricken gaze toward her sister. "Caroline claims she's going to Alaska!"

"But she can't!" Ethel cried.

"I can't?" Perplexed, Caroline glanced from one addled face to the other. Only last week the pair had suggested she return.

"Oh, dear, this is a problem."

Ethel looked uncomfortable. "Perhaps we should tell her, Sister."

"Perhaps we should."

Caroline knew her lovable aunts well enough to realize they'd been plotting again. "I think you'd better start at the beginning."

Fifteen minutes later, after hearing all the details, Caroline accepted a cup of the brew. She needed it. "Paul will come," she murmured. Never having one of his own, Paul wanted a family.

"He'll come and then you'll be happy. Isn't that right, dear?"

Her aunts gave her a look of such innocence, she couldn't disillusion them. "Right," Caroline said weakly.

"You were going back to him," Ethel pointed out.

"Yes." But this was different. At least if she returned to Atta, Paul would have his pride intact. But now, he would believe he'd been tricked again, and that wouldn't set right with her husband. Her aunts' meddling once was Paul's limit.

"You're not unhappy, are you, dear?" Mabel queried softly.

"I'm happy," she replied. "Very happy." Briefly, she wondered how long she could disguise the fact that she wasn't pregnant.

Her aunts returned the teapot to the kitchen while Caroline remained in the room off the entry that her aunts insisted on calling the parlor. The doorbell gave a musical chime and, still bemused from the tea and her aunts' schemes, Caroline rose to answer it.

The man who stood outside the door was tall and well built. Strong and muscular. Caroline glanced up at him expectantly and blinked, finding him vaguely familiar.

"Caroline, I know..."

"Paul?" She widened her eyes to study him and her mouth dropped open. It was Paul, but without a beard. Good grief, he was handsome! Extraordinarily good-looking! Without realizing what she was doing, she lifted her hand to his clean-shaven face and ran the tips of her fingers over the lean, square jaw.

"May I come in?"

For a moment, Caroline was too flabbergasted to react. "Oh, of course. I'm sorry." Hurriedly, she stepped aside so he could enter the Victorian house, and then led him into the parlor. "Please sit down."

He wore gray slacks, the Irish cable knit sweater she'd made for him and a thin jacket. Everyone else in Seattle was wearing wool coats and mufflers and claiming it was the coldest winter in fifty years.

"How are you, Caroline?"

She was starving for the sight of him and so incredibly pleased that she couldn't take her eyes off his smooth jaw. "Fine," she said absently. Then she remembered what her aunts had told him and frowned. "Actually, I haven't been well, but that's to be expected." She placed her hand on her stomach and hoped she exuded a pregnant look. "How are you?" No doubt the news of her condition had come as a shock.

"Fine."

Having forgotten her manners once, Caroline quickly tried to right her earlier lack of welcome. "Would you like some tea?"

"Coffee, if you have it." He paused and looked at the ornate frames on the mantel that pictured her two aunts and added, "Just plain coffee."

"But you drank your coffee with cream before."

"I meant with cream. It's the other things I'm hoping to avoid."

Her bewilderment must have shown in her eyes. "I don't want any of your aunts' brew."

"Oh, right."

Caroline rushed into the kitchen and returned with a cup of coffee for Paul and a tall glass of milk for herself. He'd insist that she eat right if she were pregnant. Her two aunts joined her and when the small party entered the room, Paul stood.

"You must be Ethel and Mabel," he said politely.

They nodded in unison.

"He's even more handsome in person, don't you think, Sister?"

"Oh, most definitely."

"Caroline," Paul grumbled when the two older women showed no signs of leaving the parlor. "Could we go someplace and talk?"

"Oh, do go, dear," Ethel encouraged with a broad grin.

"Someplace *private*," Mabel whispered, and the way she said it suggested a hotel room. Even Caroline blushed.

Paul escorted her to the car, a rental, she noted, and opened the passenger door for her. She couldn't stop staring at him. He looked so different—compelling, forthright, determined.

Once she was seated inside, he paused and ran his hand over the side of his face. "I feel naked without it."

"Why... why did you shave?"

He gave her an odd look. "For you."

"Me?"

"You once said you refused to stay married to a man when you couldn't see his face."

Caroline remembered his response, too. He'd told her to get used to his beard because it was nature's protection from the Alaskan winter. He'd adamantly refused to shave then, but he'd done it now because this "pretend pregnancy" was so important to him. She should be the happiest woman alive, but unexpectedly Caroline felt like crying.

"I said several things," she answered, her gaze lowered to her clenched hands in her lap. "A lot of them weren't necessarily true." She dreaded telling him there wasn't any baby and wondered how long she could pretend. This was no way to negotiate a reconciliation. "How's Tanana?" she asked, changing the topic.

"Much better. She misses you and so do the others. Carl's growing more every day."

"I... miss them too."

"Do... did you miss me?" he asked starkly.

He sounded so unsure of himself, so confused that finding the words to tell him everything that was on her mind was impossible. Instead she shook her head vigorously.

"I know that I've made some bad mistakes.... I know that I haven't any right to ask you to reconsider the divorce, but I love you, Caroline, and I'll do whatever you want to make things right between us again."

"I know," she said miserably.

"If you know that, then why are you acting like my being here is all wrong? It's that Larry fellow, isn't it? You've started seeing him again, haven't you?"

"Yes...no. We went to one movie and I cried through the entire comedy because I was so miserable without you. Finally Larry told me to get smart and go back to you where I belonged."

"He told you that?"

She nodded again.

"Is it Alaska, love? Would you rather we lived elsewhere?"

"No," she said quickly. "I love Alaska. It was the fever and the exhaustion and everything else that caused me to believe otherwise. You were right—a week after I arrived here I knew Seattle would never be my home again. My home is with you."

"Oh, love, I've been stir-crazy without you. Nothing is good anymore unless you're there to share it with me." Although it was awkward in the front seat of the car, Paul gathered her in his arms and kissed her with the hunger of a five-week absence. His mouth moved over hers slowly, sensuously, as though he couldn't believe she was in his arms and he half feared she'd disappear.

Caroline wrapped her arms around his neck and kissed him back with all the passion of the lonely weeks. Tears dampened her face and she buried her nose in his throat, heaving a sigh. "There's something you should know."

"What's that, love?"

"I...I didn't write the letter."

He went still. "What letter?"

"The one that told you I was pregnant."

Caroline could feel the air crack with electricity. The calm before the storm; the peace before the fury; the stillness before the outrage. She squeezed her eyes closed, waiting.

"You're not pregnant?"

"I swear I didn't know my aunts had written to you. I can only apologize. If you want, I..."

"Love." His index finger under her chin raised her gaze to his. "I didn't receive any letter."

"You... What? No letter?"

"None."

"You mean... Oh, Paul, Paul," she squeezed his neck and spread kisses that tasted of salt over his face. She kissed his eyes, his nose, his forehead, his chin and his mouth.... Again and again she ministered to his mouth until they were both winded and exhilarated.

"I didn't ever think I'd be thanking the postal service for their bi-weekly delivery," Paul said, and chuckled.

"You love me more than Diane." She said it with wonder, as though even now she wasn't sure it could possibly be true.

"Of course, love. You're my wife."

"But..."

"Diane was a long time ago."

"But you saved things to remember her by?"

"Only her letter. She decided she wasn't the type to live in the wilds of Alaska. She said that if I loved her, I'd be willing to give up this craziness and come to her."

"But why keep the letter?"

"To remind me that it takes a special kind of person to appreciate the challenge of Alaska. The land's not right for every woman, but it's right for you, love."

"Because you're right for me." Her face shone with her love. She was incredibly happy.

"I can't promise you that there won't be fevers, but I vow that I'll never leave you to face them alone and I'll never doubt you again."

"Nor I you." She felt like singing and dancing and loving this man until "his socks were turned inside out." She placed her head on his shoulder and sighed. "Can we go home soon? I miss Atta."

"Yes, love. Whenever you want."

"Is today too soon? Oh, Paul, I had the most marvelous idea about getting some additional medical training so that we could open a clinic."

"Love," he chuckled. "I sent for a mail-order bride, not a doctor."

"But I could have done so much more when the fever broke out if I'd had the proper supplies."

Paul's hand slipped under her sweater to caress her midriff. "I have a feeling you're going to be too preoccupied for quite some time to be thinking about doing any studying."

"But I can, can't I?"

"Yes, love. Anything you want."

"Oh, Paul, the only thing I want or need is you. Thank you for loving me, thank you for coming for me, and thank you for Scrabble."

"No, love," he said seriously. "Thank you."

With a happy, excited laugh, she hungrily placed her mouth over his.

* * * * *

A Note from Heather Graham Pozzessere

This has always been one of my favorite books because Venice is one of my favorite places in the world. The city is magic.

I was married right out of high school, and went to college with my husband. We were both eager to travel and longed to see the places our grandparents had been born: Ireland and Scotland on my side; Italy on my husband's.

Our first opportunity we headed off to Europe. They were naturally lean days, but we had a wonderful time buying bread and cheese from small shops for our meals, visiting cathedrals and museums.

Venice was beyond a doubt one of the most romantic places we visited. We splurged on champagne, and the gondolier tied the bottle behind his little vessel to keep it cool in the water as we traveled along the exotic canals. We returned to Venice when my oldest son was two years old, and I'll never forget watching him run across St. Mark's Square with the birds flying everywhere and the beautiful old buildings rising out of the water.

Mysterious. Quaint. Exquisite. Venice is all of these.

My love for the city and the sweet memories it always brings regarding my own marriage keep it special in my heart, and I hope you will feel a bit of that magic when you read *The Di Medici Bride*.

Heather Graham Pozzessere

THE DI MEDICI BRIDE

Heather Graham Pozzessere

Prologue

Oh, no... where the hell was she?

The question pounded in Christina's mind along with the throbbing pain that viciously attacked her temples.

And it was really a ridiculous question. She knew she was at the Palazzo di Medici, in Venice. She was a guest there, of course. A guest of the old contessa... and of Marcus di Medici....

Marcus...

She opened her eyes slowly, cautiously.

The first thing she saw was her own hand, lying beside her face on the silk-covered pillow. For some reason her long fingers appeared very delicate there. Even her nails, with their polish of soft bronze, seemed vulnerable against the deep indigo of the sheets.

Indigo...

Her fingers clutched convulsively against the smooth sensual material of the pillowcase. The silk in itself was not alarming. Marcus di Medici preferred the feeling of cool silk to cotton; all the beds in the palazzo were garbed in silk.

It was the color of the silk that was so chilling.

Christina opened her eyes wider. Without daring to twist her head, she further surveyed the room. Soft Oriental rugs lay pleasingly against a polished cream Venetian tile floor. The walls were papered in a subdued gold that lightened the effect of the deep indigo draperies and mahogany furniture. Across a breezy distance, highlighted by the morning dazzle of the sun streaming through French doors, was a large Queen Anne dresser, its only ornament a French Provincial clock.

Chris closed her eyes and swallowed miserably. Memories of the past night returned in fragments to compound the ferocity of her headache. Marcus...exercising his considerable charm. But she should have known.... No, that wasn't being honest with herself. She *had* known. She had been as suspicious as he. She had sadly overrated her own competence and confidence with the male of the species.

Not with just any male. With Marcus di Medici.

She had been certain she could be just as charming...and just as evasive. But she had played out her hand—and lost.

Lost what? She didn't want to remember, but she had to.

Panic gripped her for a moment. She had no doubt that she was lying in his bed. But when she refocused her eyes on her hand, she felt a tingling of relief. A white lace cuff rimmed her wrist. She was dressed.

Her relief faded. How had she come to be dressed this way? She had left the palazzo in a black cocktail gown.

She remembered him, waiting at the foot of the stairs, elegant and overwhelmingly male in a black tux. He wore it so well. His shoulders were so broad, his waist and hips so arrestingly trim. His tanned olive complexion had looked almost copper against the crisp white of his shirt; his hair was a jet deeper than the fabric of his suit.

And from beneath the dark arched brows, his eyes had been a startling arresting blue. A deep blue. So deep that they, too, could appear black.

Or indigo. . . like the sheets.

But last night they had been alight with charm and suave pleasure at the sight of her. Still, she hadn't doubted for a moment the measure of cunning beneath the civil facade of the beast. She had been careful, so careful. But not careful enough.

She clearly remembered the walk around St. Mark's Square. She remembered laughing and cleverly avoiding his questions. She could see them now as they tossed bread crumbs to the pigeons that thronged before the ancient cathedral.

And she could clearly see them in the gondola as they skimmed along the canals, listening to the subtle music of the gondolier.

She remembered the restaurant, the aroma of the masterfully prepared appetizers. The mussels, the clams Casino, the scungilli, tiny squid prepared so tenderly in garlic and oil that they were the sweetest delicacy to the tongue.

Chris closed her eyes tightly. She could recall exactly how his arm had rested leisurely on the back of the booth behind her, his hand so relaxed. Yet she had already known its strength. His palm was broad, but he had long tapering fingers that could tighten like talons or touch with tenderness. His hands were tanned to the same golden color as his sharply handsome features, and they had gleamed against the white sleeve that peeked from beneath the black jacket.

She even remembered the look of his blunt black-banded watch against his wrist. The last time she could remember noticing had been 10:05 P.M.

Perhaps it had been the wine. He had ordered a vintage as smooth as the silk of his sheets, and she had been nervous, yet trying not to betray her wariness. Perhaps she had imbibed too freely. She had only thought herself watchful because he had known all along that she was watching him. She had meant to charm and seduce him, but instead he had charmed and seduced her. She had been a fool, easily manipulated. Twice a fool. She had thought herself so competent, confident, bright and sophisticated, a worthy player of the game. But she had known that she was out with a well-dressed panther, one with a frightening veneer of charisma and cordiality.

Sophisticated... Oh, what a fool she had been! He had taken her out and given her wine, and she had been as easy to handle as a girl of sixteen. She had thought herself strong and determined enough to trick a murderer, to expose the secrets of the past! She had played with Marcus di Medici....

Her last memories were still a blur she could scarcely straighten out even now within the confused confines of her pain-racked mind.

Another ride along the canals. A hushed stop at the dock of a crumbling old cathedral. Strange, but she could vividly remember the frescoes on the high, gracefully arched ceilings....

He had whispered to her. Murmured gently and tenderly. He had clutched her fingers firmly but without painful pressure as he had led her along. Her hand had appeared so starkly pale and fragile against his strong dark ones.

Snatches of Italian and some other language—perhaps Latin?—haunted her memory, but they had been spoken so rapidly that she couldn't recall a word.

And then, try as she might, she could remember nothing more. Nothing more...

Nothing! Except the sound of her own laughter, a mocking echo in her ears.

Chills suddenly raked through her, sending ice and fire hurtling with erratic speed and fever along the length of her spine. He was in the room. She knew it. When she opened her eyes once more and turned, she would find him leisurely leaning against the frame of the French doors. But there would be nothing truly leisurely about him. Even in moments of repose, he was still full of leashed tension. Always he was the panther, stalking, ready to strike. He had been playing with her, toying with her from the very beginning. But now it was time for the kill, time for the sophisticated beast to show his face.

Chris tightened her eyes in a moment's frenzy of fear, anger and reproach.

The man might very well be a murderer, but she had been so sure of herself! She'd thought herself a Mata Hari, and now she was paying the price, lying in a murderer's bed.

No! an inner voice shrieked. *Not Marcus!*

What a fool she was. Even now, when she couldn't believe the price she had paid, she wanted to defend him. She wanted to believe in him.

There was a slight movement in the room. A whisper of sound in the air. He was watching her, Christina knew. Watching her, and waiting. He could afford to wait with amused and taunting patience. She had nowhere to run, nowhere to go.

She didn't want to open her eyes; she didn't want to turn to him. She didn't want to face the consequences of what had passed between them in the misty oblivion of last night.

She heard the quiet ticking of the clock on the dresser. It was persistent. Monotonous. And yet it seemed to grow in volume, mocking her, and suddenly she could bear it no longer. He was there, and the force of his presence caused her to open her eyes and turn . . . and meet his smoldering indigo stare.

He was leaning against the doors, as she had suspected, dressed in a caramel velour robe. The V neck of the haphazardly belted garment bared the breadth of his chest with its profusion of crisp dark hair. A gold St. Christopher's medallion seemed to emphasize the masculinity of copper flesh and muscle.

His legs, too, were bare beneath the knee-length hem of the robe. Long sinewy calves, covered seductively with short black hair, gave way to bare feet. Chris even noted the particulars about his feet. They were long no-nonsense feet, planted squarely on the floor.

"*Buongiorno. Buongiorno, amore mio.*"

The soft taunt of the words brought her eyes back to his. There was no pretense of charm within those dark-blue depths in the demanding light of day, only smoldering fire. Something that warned that the harnessed tension and electricity that seemed to vitalize the air about him could explode too easily.

He began to stalk slowly toward the bed. His full sensual lips were curled into a slight mocking grin of cold amusement. Chris curled her fingers tightly around the bunched-up sheets, her eyes on him with mounting wariness and a fear she couldn't subdue despite her staunchest efforts. She waited to fling harsh questions at him. No, not questions. Demands. But she couldn't seem to form the words she wanted to say.

Because, despite everything, despite the horrible web of deception that had brought her here, she was fatally attracted to him. Like a moth to flame. There was a strength about him that could not be resisted. He mesmerized; he seduced; he wielded an indomitable power with the flick of an eye, a wave of the hand.

He had her cornered. She had to fight, had to resist.

He stood still before her, then calmly sat beside her on the edge of the bed. The faint scent of his after-shave assaulted her senses and warned her afresh of the raw masculine strength that was inherently a part of him. She narrowed her eyes and stiffened, preparing to do battle.

But before she could lash into him, he chuckled, the sound dry and biting. One dark brow rose with cool mockery and cutting amusement.

"What? Can she be angry? Dismayed? How so, my love? You wanted a di Medici man. You said so often enough. Well, you've gotten one. I could resist the temptation no longer. But perhaps you feel that you brought the wrong di Medici to the altar?"

Fury stabbed through her. She raised a hand swiftly toward his ruggedly hewn features, but he moved more swiftly, catching her wrists with a cold gleam of triumph in his eyes.

She felt him as she might a fire. His touch seared her, warmed her, frightened her as she had never known fear before. He was so close, so intimate, so demanding. . . .

She cried out inwardly again. No! Marcus could not be guilty of blackmail—or murder. Not Marcus. For all that she sometimes hated and feared in him, she could not accept that Marcus could be evil, or that he could harm her. She just couldn't believe it. Not in her heart nor her soul. Not when, beneath everything, she was falling in love, and that love just wouldn't allow her to see evil. . . .

Because it wasn't there. Not in Marcus. No matter how dangerous he could appear, no matter what the evidence led her to see, she knew inside that it couldn't be Marcus.

But . . . she had married him. The fragments of the dream that she didn't want to accept were true. She had been conned.

"Why?" she breathed, incredulous and furious and achingly aware of him against her. And as his handsome features came nearer, she hollowly echoed the question within her own heart.

Why? She had always believed that he wanted her. She had also believed that he despised her. So why did he have such a seductive power over her?

Like now. When the triumph faded from his eyes, she caught a glint of sorrow, of tenderness. Like fencers, they had often circled around one another. Like the moth and flame, they had too often come dangerously close together.

What exactly had he done? What had *she* done? Last night . . . could it have been real?

"*Cara* . . ." he murmured, and the tenderness remained, an apology he would not put into words. He meant to play his hand to the end. "Why? Because it was your wish, of course."

He had duped her. Cunningly. With carefully planned intent. Why? Had it been love, he would never have had the need. The money?

"*Cara...*" he repeated, touching her cheek tenderly with his knuckles. Chris jerked from his touch, lowering her head as tears stung her eyes. He stood up impatiently. "We have both known that something had to happen between us. Did you take me for a saint? I have only given you what you wished. Or perhaps," he said mockingly, "it was truly Tony whom you wished to captivate. He is the more malleable, is he not? But, alas! As you Americans are so fond of saying, you have made your own bed. Now you shall lie in it."

He had added insult to injury. Anger washed through her like a raging tide, and she hurled her silk-covered pillow in his direction.

He started to laugh. "Another cliché, but you're truly beautiful when you're angry."

"Why?" Chris raged.

An elite brow rose. "Why? You were there, too, my love. Oh, I admit, we were neither of us completely lucid, but... that is the course of love, my sweet."

It was a lie. He had planned the entire thing. The dinner, the wine, the gondola... the wedding.

But why?

He started to open the door. Chris leaped from the bed, racing toward him. "Wait! What are you doing? We have to do something about this. Surely we can arrange an annulment—"

"An annulment?" He kept smiling, but she sensed his anger, his controlled tension. He caught her shoulders, his grip a shade too tight.

"*Cara*, I am on my way downstairs to make the announcement to the family." His eyes narrowed. Warningly. "If you have any sense, Christina, you will keep your mouth shut. You will give the appearance of a sheepish—embarrassed, perhaps—but very happy bride. For God's sake! Haven't you the sense to stay alive!"

His grip tensed as their eyes clashed in anger. She was certain that he wanted to shake her. He released her instead with a little shove. He opened the door and exited, closing it sharply behind him.

Christina swore vehemently.

The door opened again. He was smiling. "Don't fret, *mia moglie*. I'll come back to you... quickly." His voice was husky, tinged with laughter. She would gladly have struck him.

Mia moglie. My wife.

Christina started to shake.

Why? she screamed to herself in a raging silence. She closed her eyes. Again, despite her anger and confusion, she couldn't bear to condemn him. Perhaps... perhaps he *had* married her to protect her. It wasn't love, but perhaps it was, at least, protection. Caring. Perhaps he knew just as she did that things were very, very wrong, that someone near them was guilty of holding deadly secrets. Someone was guilty of blackmail.

And someone was guilty of murder.

Chris bit down on a knuckle, trying hard not to become hysterical. She sank in confusion back onto the bed.

How had she come to this? Trapped in a web that was not of her own weaving, cast into this game where she didn't begin to know the rules.

Falling in love with a man she often thought she hated at the same time.

Hated... and feared.

She should have stayed away from Venice. From Contini and the di Medicis. She'd intended to do just that. Chris had never thought she harbored a determination to flush out the roots of her past....

Until the mime troupe had come to Venice. Until Alfred Contini had sought her out, and brought her to the palazzo.

And begged her to help him, right before dying in her arms.

Chapter 1

Twilight was coming, and with it a sudden breeze swept through St. Mark's Square. Chris Tarleton looked around, and smiled slowly.

The lights had come on. The last vestiges of a red-and-gold dusk were combining with the soft artificial light to create a shimmering splendor all around the ancient Basilica, the bridges, the Venetian-Gothic elegance of the Doge's Palace and, of course, the water. The Grand Canal rippled and sparkled behind her with the brilliance of a thousand gems. It was a spellbinding moment for her; this was Venice, in all its artistic glory, in all its magical mythical beauty.

Then she shivered, touched by a strange feeling of déjà vu. She had loved the place before she had come here. Before she had seen the multitude of pigeons that flocked to the Square, and the toddlers who screamed with delight and laughter as they chased the birds. Before she had ever raised her head to see the two great granite columns at the water's edge with their respective figures of St. Theodore and the winged lion of St. Mark. Before she had felt the magic that was Venice by night…the laughter and the excitement. This was not just Italy, it was Venice. It was the Renaissance, the Far Eastern influence that had come here in the days of Marco Polo. It was beautiful and totally unique—and by nightfall, absolute magic.

But it was not strange—Chris knew that it shouldn't have been. She had been born here, but until yesterday, when her mime troupe had arrived to prepare for this evening's performance in the Square, she would have said with all honesty that she had absolutely no memory of the place. But then, she thought wryly, she had left when she was four and grown up in Detroit, Michigan—far, far from this world of gondolas and canals and ancient architecture that spanned the centuries and led back to a distant different time.

A shiver ran up her spine again, another whisper of breeze swept by, and near her, a group of the ever-present pigeons burst into flight. Venice. Her parents had seemed to hate the place. And in her conscious mind, she'd harbored no great wish to return to the city. But when she had learned that it was on their schedule, she had been fascinated; she had experienced the first of the shivers, as if she had known she would come back, as if she had been compelled, as if the performance were merely an excuse for her coming here. Venice was her city; she had known it as soon as she had seen it.

"Christina, you are ready, yes?"

Chris started, then turned to smile at Jacques d'Pry, the head of the school in Paris and the leader of a prestigious corps of mimes. Jacques had been a favored pupil of the great Marceau, and he was a rigid taskmaster, an absolute disciplinarian. Chris had never minded the discipline or the hours and hours of physical exercise—sometimes abuse! she added to herself, with humor—that led to the perfection of her craft. She had always felt lucky, even blessed, to have been accepted as a student at the school. She had been stunned to have been chosen as a member of the professional corps that traveled across Europe each summer.

"*Oui*, Jacques," she murmured, tensing and flexing her fingers again and again. The fingers were, Jacques often stressed, perhaps the mime's greatest tool. There had been many sessions of total concentration, total silence, when they had done nothing but draw the thumb to the forefinger isometrically, so that when the performer reached for an individual string, the audience saw the string and felt its pull.

"Then come, please, we begin the show."

Jacques led the way through the milling crowd at the water's edge to a section of the Square, paved with marble and trachyte, that had been roped off for the performance. Tomas and Georgianne Trieste—two Parisian mimes who had fallen in love with the romance of silence—followed behind Chris, and behind them came the last of their group, Roberto Umbrio, a very dedicated and impassioned young man from the Basque Provinces. None of them spoke. Once they had started their approach to their "stage," the law of silence was in order.

A little girl cried out something in Italian and grabbed at Christina's white-gloved hand. Chris restrained a smile, widened her reddened mouth into an "O," and brought her other hand up to it in surprise. The child laughed delightedly, and Chris felt a familiar warmth fill her. The laughter of a child made the often dreary monotonous hours and hours of work worthwhile.

Moments later she was on, into her secret world. The lights, the beauty of the Square, were still there, as were the whispers of the audience, mainly in Italian but spattered with the excitement of many tongues. But they were all part of an outer world. Tonight she played Jacques's wife, alarmed at the prospect of his anger when he discovered a naughty escapade of the children—Georgianne, Roberto and Tomas. There was a door to be locked against him, and then she had to discover that she had locked herself in, rather than him out. There were invisible pulleys to work with, invisible chairs and stairs. And then there was the inevitable confrontation with her "husband," and her efforts to escape his wrath. But, of course, the husband intended no harm to his wife. All her fiascoes were her own, and he was left to shake his head at her foolishness and the disaster she brought upon herself.

There were two men in the audience who had not come to see the show; they had come to see Christina Tarleton.

One was an old man, older than his years. He was short and slim, balding, and the fringe of hair that remained had faded from black to snowdrift silver. His cheeks were gaunt; lines were deeply etched around eyes that defied time—brown eyes, deep and warm, yet sharply alert. And anxious now. Eyes that were focused intently on the girl on the pseudo stage.

It was easy to see that she was slim, as agile and graceful as the cats that haunted the streets of Rome. She was clad all in black: black tights, black flowing skirt, black knit top, black slippers. Only her hands were in white—white gloves. And her face was powdered with white to enhance the eyes, the expression and the mouth. Perhaps that was why he could see the color of her eyes so clearly. They were tawny, part green, part gold. Like the sun, they were alive with expression and warmth, and thickly fringed with honeyed lashes that matched the color of her hair. Her hair was pulled back, and it was neither blond nor brown; rather, it was a tawny shade of sun and honey somewhere in between. The old man was fascinated by her lithe movements, by the elegant strokes of her hands and fingers against the air, by the practiced twists and turns of her supple body.

Fascinated and . . .

Hurt. He clutched his hand to his chest suddenly; the pain, guilt and remorse went deep. For a moment he felt dizzy. She did not have her father's coloring, only his height and slim build. She did not look like James at all, and yet there was a look of him about her.

And standing there in the crowd, with the show proceeding before him, he wanted to reach out. To touch her. Did he feel that he could vindicate his sins against her father? he asked himself sharply. Something inside him cried, and he stared up at the Basilica suddenly, crossing himself and murmuring beneath his breath, "Blessed Jesu, forgive me."

He closed his eyes. In a minute the dizziness left him. He felt the same restlessness, the same *need* he had experienced when he had first seen the paper and read her name in the list of performers. He would make it up to this girl, and sweet, sweet Jesu, it was possible that the girl could help him. He was too old to go on as he had. His conscience could no longer bear the weight of his lie.

She was a Tarleton. A part of the trio. The name Tarleton belonged beside those of Contini and di Medici.

His lips, faded against the weathered wrinkles of his face, relaxed into a smile. A sudden peace had settled over his soul. Now he could watch the show; he knew what he would do at its conclusion.

But in time his smile slipped away. He wondered what she had been told about Venice—and what she might remember. Remember? Bah! She had been but a child.

Still, it was her heritage he intended to give her.

The second man who stood in the crowd assessed the girl with a cool sweep of sharp startling blue eyes. He was not at all old, and though his exact age might be indeterminable, he was obviously in the prime of his life. He was tall, and though his shoulders were broad, he gave the appearance of being a lean man. His suit was designed with impeccable taste; it hugged his trim form. And, despite a certain relentlessness, if not ruthlessness, about the firm square line of his jaw, he was a handsome man. More than handsome. He exuded an assurance that was a power unto itself. When he spoke, it was with the inner knowledge that his quiet words would be taken as a command; when he moved, it was never with any question of where he was going. He was capable of an absolute stillness, of listening, watching and waiting. His intelligence was shrewd; his thoughts were seldom known, for an invisible shield could fall over his eyes with a blink, and the true import of his words could be hidden in a deadly fashion.

Tarleton.

Like the old man, he had seen the name in the papers, and if curiosity had not drawn him here, the suspicion that the old man was coming would have brought him anyway.

He watched the girl and he watched the old man, wondering at the pained expression in the old man's eyes. Something seemed to light a quick fuse to his temper. Contini was an old man now. Old and weary. The Tarleton girl had no right to be here, dredging up painful memories that had been best buried by time.

Marcus di Medici lifted his eyes from the old man to the stage, and he felt as if anger sizzled and seared in each and every one of his nerve endings. His father had died so senselessly all those years ago—at the hands of a Tarleton. And now *she* was back. The sound of her name in his mind ripped open old wounds; the sight of her made him remember until he felt all the pain again, just as if he were once more a boy of twelve. . . .

He crossed his arms over his chest, adjusting his stance, and his lashes fell briefly over the agate of his eyes. He closed his heart and his mind took over objectively. She was good. Lithe, smooth, graceful, like a young animal, composed of fluid sinews and vitality. She seemed to move with the ease of the wind or flowing water.

And then he discovered uncomfortably that he was looking at her too objectively—as a woman. A heat ran through him that had nothing to do with temper, anger, regret or the past. For a moment every thought was washed from his mind except one. She was, in the black mime's outfit that clung so tightly to her supple form, the most desirable woman he had ever seen. She was beautiful. And that beauty was demonstrated in every movement. He discovered that he was wishing he could hold her, feel the vibrance of the liquid curves and hollows of her body beneath his hands, strip away the fabric and the makeup and make fevered love to the woman beneath.

Startled, Marcus gave himself a little shake and smiled dryly at the intimate path his imagination had taken. A comedy was taking place on stage, nothing risqué.

His smile faltered. She was the daughter of a murderer. And not just any murderer. She was the daughter of the man who had killed his father.

For a moment his every muscle went rigid, and then he forced himself to relax. She had come to Venice with the mimes. She would leave with the mimes. She would be gone, and the past would fade into memory once again.

Marcus gazed at Contini, then returned his attention to the show. Without his knowledge, a smile curved his lips again, small and a little crooked. He was suddenly remembering her as a child. Even at four she had been a pretty thing. Willful, spoiled and pert, determined and stubborn. She had driven him crazy. But when he had been half-ready to kill her, she had looked at him wide-eyed, her tawny gaze filled with tears, and his anger had melted away.

He could even remember thinking that James Tarleton was going to be in trouble by the time his daughter reached her teens. At four she had known how to wield her power. A little imp—a practiced seductress with the flutter of her lashes. Pretty and as bright as a star. She'd had an almost uncanny command of both English and Italian—and the powerful ability to use all her feminine wiles.

Marcus sighed, slipped his hands into his pockets and turned away although the show wasn't over. The sins of the fathers, he reflected, did not fall upon the offspring. Contini, Marcus was certain, intended to approach her.

And if he asked her to the palazzo, Marcus decided firmly, he would be courteous. He would make her welcome but hope that she did not stay long enough to rake up the ashes of his past.

"And so ends another season!" Jacques muttered happily in English. He had just shaken hands with the last child waiting in line to meet them; he had only to meet with the producers of the show and the summer's work would be officially over.

Chris smiled a little secretively, watching her teacher and employer with affection and amusement. In class Jacques spoke French exclusively. On tour he spoke English. He was, however, a master of at least five languages.

"What shall we do with the evening in celebration?" Georgianne asked excitedly, laughing. "The night is young, and so are we! And this is Venice!"

Her husband grinned dryly at Chris. "Doesn't she sound just like 'An American in Paris'?"

Chris laughed. "Well, she's right, you know. We're off. We should be doing something."

Jacques lifted a hand to them, then wandered off to finish his business with the show's producers. Only Roberto seemed brooding and intense, as usual, as they waited near the lightly rippling water.

"We've got a month off," he reminded them all. "Tomas, Georgianne, what do you plan to do with the time?"

Georgianne smiled. "Party! We're going to go back to Rome—we did throw three coins in the fountain, you know. Roma, Napoli and then Nice and Monte Carlo." She grimaced very prettily. "We want to gamble away some of our hard-earned money. And you?"

"I will go back to school early and work to improve my craft," Roberto said reproachfully. The others exchanged quick smiles, but said nothing. Georgianne linked an arm with Chris.

"And you, Chris? What will you do? You are welcome to keep company with Tomas and me."

Chris laughed. "No thanks. I can't imagine joining a pair of honeymooners." She sobered. "I was thinking about going home. Jacques wants me to teach next year, you know. And I'm not sure what I want to do. I have been 'An

American in Paris' for three years now. And I have to start
deciding what I really want to do with the rest of my life."

"Oh, to the devil with the rest of our lives!" Tomas proclaimed. "I say we find a lovely spot for dinner, indulge in
rare and delicious wine, dance and—"

"Tomas!" Georgianne murmured, interrupting. "Look,
that old man over there is watching us most peculiarly."

"Yes, he is," Tomas murmured. He looked at Chris.
"Why don't you go over there and find out what he wants?"

"Me!" Chris exclaimed, startled.

"Of course!"

"I don't speak Italian!"

Tomas frowned. "I thought you said you were born
here?"

Chris sighed. "Tomas, I left Italy when I was four. And
that," she added wryly, "was over two decades ago. I never
had much occasion to use the language on the streets of
Detroit, and I've only managed to make my French halfway decent this year."

"It doesn't matter," Roberto interrupted tensely. "The
man is coming to us."

The man was coming to them, straight to them, Chris realized. And then she experienced another one of her déjà vu
sensations. Before he took another step, she knew that he
was coming to her. And although she didn't actually recognize him, she knew that he was Alfred Contini.

Tingling sensations raced through her, and she was left to
wonder again if she had really come to Venice because of the
mime troupe, or if her coming had really been preor-
dained. For a brief second she was afraid. And then the fear
was gone.

She wanted this; she wanted this confrontation. Just as
she had wanted to come back to Venice. She was curious—
no, damn it, *compelled*—to find out the truth. What had
driven her parents from Venice, a city they once had loved?

Contini was old, Chris thought, as he walked toward her.
Very old—much too old for her to have remembered him.

If she did have a memory of him locked away in her mind, just as she had of the Piazza San Marco, it was a memory that was twenty-one years old. And unlike granite and marble, a man would change drastically in that amount of time.

Small and slim, he still had a look of strength about him like stone. Until he had almost reached her. And then something tender and a little bit...frightened?...seemed to crumple his old face as he reached out a frail hand to her.

"Christi?"

A quick chord of distant memory caused her to shiver briefly. Christi. Contini's name for her.

She smiled and accepted his hand warmly, strangely touched by a flood of emotion for this worn and aged man who was reaching out to her.

"Alfred!" she replied softly.

"Ah, Christi! So you do remember me?"

"No!" Chris laughed and shook her head. "But I knew who you must be if this is Venice—and it is."

Christina quickly introduced him to the rest of the group. Alfred replied graciously, but his attention was completely for her.

"Christi, you will do an old man the honor of having dinner with him?"

Georgianne cleared her throat, apparently somewhat suspicious of the elegantly dressed, elderly Venetian. "Christina, do you remember our plans?"

Chris hesitated for a second, suddenly and deeply aware that her answer was going to mean everything to her life. She could almost see herself standing at a crossroads....

Ridiculous, she told herself impatiently. She couldn't pretend that she wasn't haunted by the past, and she had never gotten over the vague dream that she could completely solve the mystery of why her parents had left Venice with such sadness in their hearts.

She had known that she herself would seek out Contini.

Chris turned to Georgianne with a bright smile. "Georgianne, I hope you all will excuse me. I haven't seen Signor Contini since I was a small child. Do you mind?"

Tomas shrugged. The two years he had known Chris had proved to him that she was an adult. Charming when she chose to be, competently assertive when she did not.

Chris felt a little like laughing. She could see the emotions darting quickly through their eyes. Suspicion, worry, and then that mutual shrug. What on earth could happen to her in the company of such an old man?

She felt a tug of affection and appreciation for their protective attitude. It was nice to have such caring friends. Their ensemble work made them more than professional associates, perhaps more than friends. A little like family.

"You know how to get back to the pensione, right?" Tomas asked her.

"Yes, yes, thank you Tomas," Chris said.

"Miss Tarleton will be perfectly safe, I assure you," Alfred Contini interjected. "I will see to it. Christi?"

"I'd love to have dinner," she said brightly, and she waved to the others as she moved away with him. "Would you mind, though, if we returned to the pensione for a moment first?" She grimaced. "I'd like to remove this makeup."

"Certainly, certainly!" Contini said agreeably.

Chris would have taken one of the vaporetti, the mass transit boats that moved through the canals, but Contini was already raising a hand to summon a gondola—much more expensive. She would have protested had she been on a date, but she swallowed her words. From Alfred's finely tailored suit, it appeared that nothing much had changed from what little she had learned from her grudging mother. Contini was a very affluent man, able to hire all the gondolas he might wish.

He watched her after they had taken their seats in the small boat. Then he grimaced apologetically. "Forgive me. When I saw your name, I could not help but come."

Chris smiled ruefully. "I believe I would have come to you if you hadn't come to me."

He hesitated a moment. She couldn't see his features clearly, because they had suddenly passed from light to shadow.

"What do you know of the past, Christi?"

"Only what my mother told me," Chris answered honestly.

"And that is—no, no, never mind. We will wait until we sit over dinner, *si*?" He cast a quick glance toward their gondolier.

Chris smiled at him. *"Si."*

Soon they turned off the Grand Canal and followed one of the smaller waterways that led to her pensione. Contini pointed out a number of the grander buildings, and told her the names and histories of a number of the crests on the red-striped poles that guarded many gondolas in their berths.

When they reached her pensione Chris quickly washed her face, then glanced at Contini's very expensive suit. She excused herself and hurriedly changed into a white silk blouse and black velvet pants.

Then they were out on the water again, soon following the Grand Canal to an elegant waterside *ristorante* near St. Mark's Church and the Doge's Palace. It was a very lovely spot, with each table secluded by shrubbery. Theirs was right by the water, with a wrought-iron fence separating them from the brilliance of the canal, sparkling in a multitude of colors beneath subdued lighting.

Contini asked if he might do the ordering for them. Chris lifted her hands, laughed and agreed. The old man was absolutely charming—a perfect escort.

He told her that they would begin with antipasto, enjoy a bowl of scracciatelli, have cappelletti for their pasta, and then veal for their main course.

Chris laughed and told him that in the States, the pasta would be the main course. He grimaced, then suggested a deep red Valpolicella. The antipasto and soup were accompanied by light conversation, and then, when their waiter had left them in their secluded corner, Alfred smiled again and looked at her as he toyed with his soupspoon.

"The show was very good. I enjoyed it. You are a talented young woman. What made you choose to become a mime?"

Chris finished an olive, took a sip of her wine and shrugged. "First, thank you for the compliment. As to being a mime...well, I started out at about eight wanting to be a gymnast. But I was behind the kids who had started out at four, five and six, and some of the vaults scared me a little. A few years later my mother was determined that I should have dance lessons—"

"Ah," Contini interrupted with affectionate laughter, "yes, Joanne would have wanted her daughter in dance! She always wanted her little girl to be such a lady, such an angel!"

Chris couldn't help but respond to his warm reference to her mother with a feeling of warmth herself. And though her mother had warned her to stay away from Venice—"it just wasn't a good place for a Tarleton"—she had always seemed sad to have left, sad to be forced into hating people who had once meant so much to her.

"Mother can be a bit much, can't she?" Chris asked ruefully. "And I take it I wasn't exactly an angel?"

"Ah, certainly an angel!" Contini said, his dark eyes sparkling. "But an angel with the devil in her soul! You were...spirited."

Chris raised one eyebrow. "Not at all sweet and mannerly?"

"Only when you thought you would get your way. And how is your mother? Well, I hope?"

"Very well. She remarried when I was in college. A very nice man. He's a ranger at a national park out west, in Montana. He and Mom are very happy."

"That is good. That is very good," Alfred Contini murmured, looking down at his soup. "Please, tell me more about your work."

Chris shrugged, paused for a minute, then continued. "I started taking dance. Then we went to Chicago one weekend when I was a senior in high school, and Marcel Marceau happened to be making an appearance. At the time," Chris said with a laugh, "I didn't even want to go. But once I had seen him, I was hooked. I knew I wanted to be a mime. Mother—" Chris paused to exchange a wry glance with Alfred "—had in her heart and mind decided that I needed a complete liberal education, but I was able to combine the two by finding a college in California with a wonderful, wonderful department for the performing arts. Anyway," she said, grinning, "I managed to make a great deal of money with some friends doing street theater, and I came straight over to Paris to audition for the school there. I was very lucky—I was accepted. And so here I am now."

"And what will you do now? The tour is over, isn't it?"

"Yes. I've been offered a teaching position for the fall. I have about a month to think it over."

Contini nodded, but said nothing. Their waiter had returned to clear away their plates and replace them with the pasta dishes. Contini refilled Christina's wineglass.

"So," he said then, "what do you know of The di Medici Galleries?"

"Very little," Chris admitted. "Only that you and my father and Mario di Medici went into business together. And that the galleries are now world famous. And—" she hesitated briefly "—that Mario di Medici died, and my father chose to leave the company and return to the United States."

Contini shrugged. "Yes, simply put, but all true." His dark eyes took on a distant look, as if he were suddenly lost in a mist of memory. "I met your father at the end of the war. And Mario...well, I'd known Mario most of my life. Your father and I were working on certain..." He paused, waving a hand as he searched for the English word.

He'd been talking about the war. "Reconstructive projects?" she asked.

"*Si, si.* He was a wonderful man. He had the power and the enthusiasm to bring men together. And he could sell canal water to a Venetian!"

"He provided the sales and business know-how," Chris murmured.

"Yes. And I—I had the money. I had never liked Mussolini, or his association with Hitler. I'd taken my money out and put it into Swiss francs in a Swiss account long before the downfall of our country. And Mario . . . well, the di Medicis are one of the oldest and most respected families in Venice. Mario's was a bastard branch of an old family, perhaps, but centuries have a way of forgiving such a thing, you understand."

Chris nodded, hiding a smile. She did know that the di Medicis had been counts of Venice since the Renaissance— certainly long enough to be forgiven an indiscretion!

"Mario gave us his . . . class. Ah, Mario! He was both a gentleman and a gentle man. He knew art; he had an eye for the truly beautiful and antique. It was a wonderful partnership."

Chris set her fork down and swallowed her wine, feeling a slight tingling sensation that warned her that she was about to ask a question to which she wasn't sure she wanted an answer.

"What happened?"

"The statuette," Contini murmured.

"What?" Chris pressed him softly.

"There was a statuette in the galleries, and it disappeared. Suddenly we were at one another's throats, old friends such as we. Then we determined to talk it out aboard the *Trieste*, di Medici's yacht. We were all there that day. Mario and his wife, your father and mother. Sophia and I. Genovese, Joe, Antonio, Marcus . . ."

He was wandering, Chris realized. She leaned forward slightly. "Alfred? Please, what happened then?"

He looked at her suddenly, as if startled by her presence. But then he smiled sadly.

"Mario was lost. He...disappeared. They found his body days later. They pulled it out of the sea."

"And my father left."

"Yes, soon after your father left."

He drank his glass of wine quickly, seemed to shudder a bit, and then smiled again.

"Christi, you say that you have some time now. Please, would you think about coming to the palazzo to spend some time? To...to vacation with us? The galleries, they are your heritage, too, you know."

Chris didn't answer him right away; the waiter had returned to whisk away the pasta plates and serve the veal. She felt absurdly as if she were at a crossroads again—that her life might be deeply changed if she agreed.

But something might be lost if she did not. She was so curious to discover what had happened. She felt the pull of Venice, the irresistible draw that had affected her when she had stood in St. Mark's Square.

And she felt her heart beating furiously. There was a mystery here. It had to do with her life, her past, and she longed to solve it.

"Christi?"

She had taken a bite of her veal; startled by the pleading in the old man's voice, she looked up into his eyes, into a dark pool of misery.

"*Per piacere*, Christi! *Per piacere*. I am an old, old man, Christi. I need you."

"Need me?" she murmured.

"To be my friend."

"I—I am your friend, Alfred."

"Then you must come. You must come to the Palazzo di Medici!"

Chris frowned, setting down her fork. "Forgive me, Alfred, I don't mean to be rude. But I assume that the palazzo actually belongs to Mario's widow and his sons—"

"And they will greet you for me, I promise, Christi." She looked uncertain, and he waved a hand in the air. "The palazzo is very big . . . and it has been my home for decades. And Mario's sons, they are decent men. The palazzo belongs to Marcus . . . he is the eldest and the most responsible. Antonio, he is a little bit too much for the fun of things. You remember nothing about them? As a child you followed them both about and taunted them mercilessly!"

Chris shook her head. "I'm sorry. I was only four. I really don't remember much of anything."

She wondered why she was hesitating and putting this poor man through such anxiety when she knew she wanted to go to the palazzo. Perhaps being there would be like being in St. Mark's Square and her memories would come back to her.

She was determined to find out just what had happened to make any mention of Italy a painful thing in her family for so many years.

"I could come to the palazzo," she said slowly, and Alfred clapped his hands like a boy, then reached out to grasp her hand with a surprising strength.

"*Grazie, grazie*, Christi! I am grateful, I need you . . . to know your heritage."

His eyes seemed fevered; Chris felt a shiver of fear grip her for a moment. Why was he so fervent?

She closed her fingers around his, trying to reassure him. "It will be fun, Alfred."

She smiled, tugged lightly at her hand until he released it, and picked up her fork once again. She returned her attention to her food, then paused as the strangest sensation crept along her spine—an uncanny feeling of being watched.

She looked up and was stunned to encounter the bluest eyes she had ever seen. Crystal eyes, ice eyes. And they were locked on her intently.

She didn't realize that she gasped, but the man looking at her was so arresting that he could make a woman's heart falter, then race madly, her breath catch, then sweep through her lungs too quickly.

He was tall. And except for those eyes he was dark. Jet-black hair and brows, handsome features made up of rugged angles and planes turned almost copper from the sun. His suit was dark and extremely well tailored, enhancing a form that appeared lean, yet was well muscled. His shoulders were broad despite the trimness of his waist and hips. He was responding to a question from the maître d', and he almost appeared indolent. But Chris knew, from that very first glance of him, that he would never be truly indolent. If he were to walk slowly, it would never be because he didn't know exactly where he wanted to go. His gaze, she was certain, was a shrewd one, taking in all that could be seen by the naked eye—and some of what could not. He was dressed impeccably and seemed comfortable in his formal attire. She had the strangest feeling that he would be equally comfortable walking through a jungle in worn denims. There was something intangible about him. . . .

A sense of danger, Chris mused, irritated that she shivered at the thought. And yet it was true. His looks—the jet hair, the startling blue eyes, the rugged tan on hard-cut masculine features—were not his greatest attraction. It was something about the way he stood, the way he moved. He could probably be a very ruthless man, Chris thought, and a relentless one. He would go where he wished to go, do what he wished to do with an implacable will and drive. And it was disturbingly exciting even as it was frightening, to feel his eyes on her. Chris thought that he would probably be as charming and as civil as his handsome attire; she was equally certain that, should he be crossed, he could strip away that charm as easily as the suit. And beneath it he would be a man of raw power, as impassioned and determined as a tiger freed from a cage.

"Christi, what is it?" Alfred asked.

"Pardon? Oh! I believe we're being watched. Rather, I know that we are."

Contini smiled. Christi was very beautiful, graceful and sophisticated. If she had not noticed that all eyes constantly turned to her, he certainly had. But he turned around with a frown, then murmured, "Ah, but it is Marcus!" He turned back to Chris. "The women, you know, they worry about me. And Marcus, well, he knows that a man of my age cannot cause much trouble, but he is the responsible one, so they send him!"

Marcus di Medici . . .

Chris felt her heart race once again as he began to move toward them. He was not a stranger who would wander off into the crowd and leave her merely to ponder the strength of the impression he had left upon her. He was Marcus di Medici, and if she was going to the palazzo, she was going to his home. The closer he came to their table, the more aware she became that he exuded something seductive, something dangerous.

Something on a very primal level, despite his sleek allure, which warned her to be on her guard. . . .

Chris shivered. The man was almost upon them; she felt hot one minute, chilly the next.

Stop! she commanded herself furiously. The chills subsided. She intended to be in control of the situation. She had long ago decided that if she wasn't beautiful, she had health and youth, and by the grace of those two, she was passably attractive. And she was certainly no teenager; she had toured half of Europe, was well educated and well traveled and—she thought with a quirk of humor—she even knew which fork to use.

She could be charming herself when she so chose, and if she planned on getting any answers about the past, Marcus was the man she would have to question, possibly haunt.

He had reached the table. He nodded curtly in her direction, but addressed Contini. "Alfred, I'm sorry for interrupting you. The household has been worried. It's quite late."

"Yes, yes, I suppose it is. You haven't interrupted me, Marcus, I'm very glad you're here. Miss Tarleton has just agreed to stay at the palazzo."

"Has she?"

Chris felt his eyes on her again. She forced a smile to her lips, wondering what to say. She had another strange premonition—though of what, she didn't know—as Marcus pulled a chair up to the table and took a seat, then signaled for a glass so he might pour himself some wine.

"Christi! Do you remember Marcus?"

"Not at all," she murmured sweetly, watching the man.

"Christi, Marcus di Medici."

She extended a hand. "It's a pleasure to meet you, Mr. di Medici," she said quietly, almost screaming when his hand touched hers. The pressure was firm, the touch as vibrant as a blazing fire.

He released her hand, sipped his wine and smiled. The smile seemed very, very dangerous. "Since I *do* remember you, Miss Tarleton, let me say that it is a pleasure to see you again."

"Thank you," she said simply.

"So?" He arched one dark brow. "You are coming to the palazzo? When?"

"I—"

"Tonight, Christi!" Contini said. "You must come tonight! Marcus, please, you must tell her that she is welcome, that she must come tonight."

Marcus turned to her and smiled, once again with little humor. "You are welcome," he told her cordially, and she knew that he was lying. "And I see no reason why you should not come tonight. But Alfred..." His eyes turned to Contini, and Chris was certain there was warmth in them then. "You must go home. I can see to Miss Tarleton. Genovese has the boat at the piazza outside the main entrance; please, allow him to take you home."

Contini listened, then sighed. He grimaced ruefully to Chris. "Marcus is right, *cara* Christi. My apologies. You will not mind if I go home to my bed? An old man needs his sleep. You will not mind if Marcus escorts you?"

I mind like hell, Chris thought dryly, but she kept smiling. "Of course not."

Marcus rose along with Alfred Contini, helping the older man. Alfred smiled at Chris one last time. "We will see one another in the morning."

"Yes," she murmured.

Marcus watched him until he was greeted at the entrance by a short wiry Italian man of an indeterminate age. Genovese, Chris assumed. But then Marcus was sitting again, his eyes touching her, openly assessing her with no thought of apology, and she felt tension—and anger. His gaze was very nearly insolent, and yet he gave no indication of reacting to what he saw.

"Would you like coffee, Miss Tarleton? Espresso, tea or cappuccino?"

"Coffee, please," she replied.

He signaled to the waiter and switched easily to Italian to order. A second later they were served.

"Why are you coming to the palazzo, Miss Tarleton?" he asked at last, lighting a cigarette to go with his coffee and leaning back slightly in his chair, his eyes raking blue fire over her once again.

"Curiosity, Mr. di Medici. Is that so unusual?"

"No. And neither is it really unusual to see a very young woman on the arm of a very old man. It's hard to tell what is what these days."

Chris felt her fury growing, but she allowed herself to do no more than flick her lashes briefly.

"Meaning, Mr. di Medici?"

He shrugged, rather eloquently, Chris thought. "Merely that Contini is an old man—and a rich one. Are you out hunting a fortune, Miss Tarleton?"

The question was very smooth, and painstakingly polite. His voice, like his eyes, could touch her with husky velvet—and with fire.

Chris forced herself to smile. "It's quite hard to tell these days, isn't it?"

He laughed and she felt the sudden warmth of it, for it was honest laughter.

"So you intend to leave me in wonder," he said, musing.

"I haven't left you in anything, Mr. di Medici. Whatever you choose to think will be your affair, won't it?"

He smiled and lifted a hand for the check. He signed it with a pen from his inner pocket, and Chris again caught herself thinking about him. He was made for a three-piece suit; he was lean, sleek and dark, like a panther. Negligent, and yet vibrant.

Dangerous.

Not really. *She* intended to be dangerous—if he crossed her.

"Are you ready, Miss Tarleton?"

She nodded uneasily, again noticing in his polite tone and sweeping gaze a sense of his hostility. Leashed, as his tension was leashed. Very, very controlled.

"Then come. The palazzo awaits."

He helped her from her chair. His hand was against her spine as he escorted her from the restaurant, and she felt as if she had been seared through the silk of her blouse. But then, it felt as if his eyes had already stripped her to the soul, as if he could bare both her heart and flesh at will.

"We'll hail a gondola," he murmured, "since Genovese and Alfred have taken our launch."

Soon they were seated in the small boat, moving along the Grand Canal. As had happened earlier, it seemed to Chris that they moved too quickly from light to shadow, back into light, then into shadow once again. Sitting beside the man, Chris again felt the tension in him, the vibrancy, and against her will she felt fear and excitement. He didn't speak, but she watched his face and when he turned to her, she was startled once again by the hostility in his eyes.

"Mr. di Medici," she said, refusing to flinch from his stare. "I cannot imagine what I might have done to you at the age of four. And yet I'm certain that you really don't wish to 'welcome' me into your home at all. Why?''

He shrugged, then leaned away from her, crossing his arms over his chest. She couldn't see his face or his eyes for a minute, only a formidable, very male shape. His voice came from the darkness.

"It's rather hard to welcome the daughter of a murderer," he said casually.

"What?" Chris gasped.

"Surely you knew." His voice grated harshly. "Your father was accused of murdering mine."

Chapter 2

"**W**hat?" Chris gasped again, and this time she leaped to her feet to confront him, causing the gondola to sway precariously and the gondolier to gasp something himself.

"Sit down!" Marcus commanded, reaching out for her and sweeping an arm about her waist to bring her crashing gracelessly back down beside him. "Do you wish to swim at night? I promise you, the water can be quite cool!"

"Let go of me!" Chris seethed, tearing herself away from his touch but being careful not to rise again. The gondolier said something in rapid Italian and Marcus answered him with a laugh, but when he turned to look at Chris, the laughter faded and his eyes looked like cobalt fire in the night.

"Can you please behave rationally?" he asked, his words low and crisp with irritation. "He's asking me if we would care to be put ashore to finish this lovers' quarrel."

"Lovers' quarrel! Tell the man that you just accused my father of murder and ask him how he would feel!"

He didn't respond to her anger. He stared off to the left bank of the Grand Canal and said with a sigh, " I am not the first to accuse him, Miss Tarleton."

"Then—" Chris swallowed and lowered her tone to match his, despite an inner turmoil that seemed to make her motions those of a puppet, jerked on a string, and her speech rapid. "If my father were guilty of murder, he could not have returned to the States!"

"I said that he was accused, not convicted."

"Then what—why—"

He spun toward her sharply. She felt the sweep of his cobalt eyes and shivered involuntarily. "Miss Tarleton, it is not a subject that I care to discuss. If you want more information, you'll have to speak with Alfred."

"Wait a minute!" Chris declared hotly. "You can't say something like that and refuse to explain yourself."

"I can, and I intend to," he said briefly. "Where is the pensione?" he asked her.

"Off the Via Pietà," Chris murmured distractedly. "You're wrong!" she insisted. "I knew my father, and I don't know what you think, or why, but he couldn't possibly have committed a murder! I'm telling you—"

He wasn't listening to her; he was giving the gondolier directions.

"Marcus di Medici!" Chris insisted. "You are not listening to me! I'm telling you—"

"You can't tell me anything," he told her with a tired sigh. "You were a child of four when all this happened, hardly equal to the task of sorting the facts. The matter is best left alone. James was dismissed for lack of evidence; there was no trial. He was not forced to leave Italy. He chose to do so. Let's leave it at that. The past is best buried."

"No! Not when—"

"I believe we are here, Miss Tarleton," he interrupted quietly, and Chris realized that the gondola was indeed standing still at the piazza by the pensione. Marcus stood to help her from the boat. He spoke to their gondolier; she assumed he was asking the man to wait for them. The boatman chuckled, and Chris was further infuriated to realize that he assumed that they were indeed in the middle of a lovers' quarrel, which Marcus—the male, the rational member of their duo—would quickly solve, putting her—the female, the irrational one—in her place.

"You needn't tell him to wait," Chris said, fighting for control over her temper and to achieve a cool tone. "I don't care to go back with you, Mr. di Medici. Perhaps you do not care to welcome the daughter of a man you saw fit to condemn when a court of law did not do so. And *I* do not care to enter the household of the man who condemned him!"

He stared at her for several seconds in a way that made Chris wish she could back away from him. He had one foot on the seat of the gondola, one foot on dry land, and though the canal rippled below him, he was perfectly comfortable, perfectly balanced. He was so agile, shrouded in darkness, only his eyes alight with that blaze that subtly invaded her being, causing her to shiver, to remember that her first impression of him had told her that he could be a dangerous man.

He moved suddenly, taking a single springing step with no sound that brought him next to her, staring down at her again, and leaving her feeling decidedly at a disadvantage. But she tightened her jaw and tilted her chin in challenge, determined not to back away from him.

"Do you wish me to give a message to Alfred?" he inquired softly.

She was somewhat stunned, having assumed that he would fight her decision. But why should he? she wondered. He had said he didn't want her at the palazzo.

"Yes. Tell Mr. Contini that I'm very sorry. Tell him that I found you to be intolerable, rude, insolent and arrogant and that I have no wish to 'vacation' beneath your roof."

She thought she saw a smile briefly curve his lips, and his lashes fell momentarily over his eyes. She hadn't insulted him, she had amused him.

"Do I frighten you, Miss Tarleton?"

"Certainly not! You offend me."

"There is no reason for you to refuse to come because of me. The Palazzo di Medici is large, very large. I spend a great deal of time working." He lowered his eyes for a second, and his tone changed; she sensed a sudden warmth and caring in it. "And Alfred Contini is an old man, Miss Tarleton. He wishes to have you there."

"Perhaps he does not believe my father to have been a murderer!" Chris snapped.

"Perhaps not," Marcus agreed coolly. "But that is not the point, Miss Tarleton. Alfred is old and ill; if he wishes to have you at the palazzo, then I do, too."

"No matter what your own feelings, I take it," Chris said dryly.

"I apologize. I never should have spoken."

"But you did!" Chris cried passionately. "Your apology does not change your feelings—"

"Then," he interrupted smoothly, "perhaps you have to come, Miss Tarleton. Since you are your father's passionate defender, perhaps you can change my feelings."

"I really don't give a damn about your feelings," Chris muttered.

He arched a brow, and she realized he was still amused by the entire encounter. "If I were you, Miss Tarleton, I would be very interested in discovering the truth."

His voice seemed to rake over her soul, rough and intimate velvet. She longed to push him backward, right into the canal. But she realized with sinking dismay that he was right; she had to go to the palazzo. It was no longer a matter of curiosity; she *was* her father's "passionate defender."

He was still watching her; she didn't know if it was with tolerance and scant interest or a great intensity. All she knew was that she felt his strange power once again; there was something primal and raw beneath the immaculate tailoring of his suit. She shivered, all too aware that his sexuality was a part of the danger he represented. He didn't need to touch a woman to make her tremble; all she needed to do was see him, inhale his subtle scent, feel the brush of his words or his eyes....

She smiled, like a tiger released from a cage herself. He was ready to condemn her father, but she was not. She was suddenly determined to discover the truth and then rub his nose in it. And she'd use him—and any member of his family—in any way she had to in order to discover that truth.

"If you'll wait here, Mr. di Medici, I'll get my things," she murmured coolly.

"If you wish some assistance—"

"I do not." Chris smiled grimly, then left him.

In her room, Chris hurriedly assembled her things, then paused to write a note to the others, explaining that she was going to the Palazzo di Medici to stay with old family friends. She added cheerfully that she hoped they all enjoyed their vacations, and that she would see them in the fall.

Chris was about to hurry back downstairs when she paused and walked down the hallway to the single window that overlooked the small canal. She could see Marcus by the poles of the piazza, talking with the gondolier. He laughed at something the other man said, shrugged, then paced across the piazza, obviously impatient and curious as to what could be taking her so long. Moonlight cast a cold glow over the piazza. She realized then that he really didn't walk at all; he stalked. Fluidly, smoothly, like a shadow through the night, or a sleek beast through the jungle. He lifted his head suddenly, staring up toward the window as if he knew she was there. Chris ducked back quickly, but she kept her eyes on him, studying him, trying to determine what it was that made him so compelling. Perhaps it was the lean form that touched chords of both primal excitement and fear; perhaps it was his face, the angles and lean planes so masculine, strong and striking.

She didn't know. She gave herself a little shake and reminded herself that she was going to beguile Marcus di Medici into doing her will—and make him swallow his own words like muddy canal water.

She forced her eyes from him and hurried downstairs. He saw her as soon as she stepped outside, and he moved toward her, silently taking her suitcase. "It's very late," he muttered. "I hope Alfred asked that a room be prepared for you."

"I'm sure I can prepare my own room," Chris replied dryly. They were at the gondola, and she tried to step ahead; she felt his arm at her elbow, steadying her anyway. She sat as far from him as possible. The gondolier was grinning again. Chris sat in silence until she lost her cool.

"Oh, good heavens! Will you tell the man that this is no lovers' quarrel—and not at all amusing!"

Marcus laughed. "Why spoil his evening?"

Chris fell silent and once again watched the magnificence of the buildings they passed in the moonlight. Baroque palaces, Gothic palaces, one after another. And then they were passing St. Mark's Square again, and Chris could have sworn that the winged lion, high on its granite column, was laughing down at her. They passed beneath the Bridge of Sighs, then turned and traveled beneath a number of small bridges, the pedestrian highways of Venice.

Suddenly she swallowed and caught her breath. She would have sworn she never would have recognized it, but she knew the Palazzo di Medici as soon as the gondola swung along the canal. It was huge, rising several stories out of the water and, unlike the majority of its neighbors, it did not sit wall-to-wall with the next building. Venice was a city created of islands; the Palazzo di Medici was an island in itself. An expanse of marble steps led to it from the water; it was set back, separated from the canal by those white gleaming steps and a garden enclosed by a wrought-iron fence. There were four graceful columns on the landing of the stairs, and the overhang formed an inverted V, with the family crest of the di Medici—St. Mark's winged lion in the center, Neptune rising to the left and a thorned rose to the right—fixed on a huge bronze shield in the center of the V. Chris allowed her gaze to sweep southward; she knew that she would see a bridge leading from the second story of the piazza across a slender waterway to the back of another building, similarly fenced, and of the same baroque design. The second building was where the galleries were housed.

"You do remember it," Marcus observed.

"No, I don't," Chris replied curtly.

She felt Marcus shrug. She wasn't on the right side of the gondola to escape unassisted to the landing, so she silently accepted Marcus's touch once again as he helped her out. He paid the gondolier—tipping him well, Chris assumed from the man's fervent thanks.

"*Prego, prego!*" Marcus murmured, her suitcase in one hand, the other coming resolutely to her waist once again to usher her up the steps.

Despite Marcus and her own stalwart determination, Chris felt a twinge of unease as they started up the stairs. Alfred Contini wanted her here but did anyone else? If the general consensus was that James Tarleton had murdered Mario di Medici, it was unlikely that his widow would be glad to see Chris. Or that Tony, Marcus's younger brother, would be thrilled to pieces, either.

She heard her own footsteps on the marble stairs. They seemed to echo loudly. How many steps were there? Fifteen, sixteen, seventeen . . .

She was still three steps from the landing when the intricately carved wooden entrance door swung open. From inside a massive chandelier cast a glow over the entryway.

There was a woman standing there, tall, dark and slim, and very proud, judging from her posture. For a moment Chris thought that she was young, and she wondered if either Marcus or Tony had married and Alfred had neglected to tell her so. But Marcus kept ushering her along, and she saw the woman's features. She was very beautiful, with a slim heart-shaped face and huge deep-set dark eyes. But she was not young; she was, Chris thought, either in her late forties or early fifties.

"Sophia," Marcus murmured, and Chris frowned fleetingly. The name had touched a chord in her memory.

"Ah, Marcus, Miss Tarleton, you have arrived," the woman said, and Chris could discern nothing from her voice. There was no warm note of welcome, but neither was there anything hostile in the words.

"Come in, come in. Genovese will take the bag."

They stepped into the grand entryway of the palazzo. The short slim man of indeterminate age whom Chris had seen helping Alfred Contini earlier was quickly at their side, taking the suitcase from Marcus.

"*Grazie*, Genovese," Marcus murmured.

"*Prego*," was the muffled response. Genovese left them, striding across the marble-tiled entryway to a curving staircase that led to the second landing. Chris gazed up at the chandelier. It hung from a majestic cathedral ceiling adorned with frescoes.

"So, you are Chris Tarleton. You've grown a great deal since I saw you last."

Chris started, then stared at the woman. She smiled sweetly. "I left twenty-one years ago. I certainly hope I've changed."

"You are a performer, Alfred tells me."

Chris lowered her lashes quickly. It was obvious that Sophia—whoever *she* was—thought that performers were of a lower class than average citizens.

"I am a mime," she replied.

"A very talented one, Sophia," Marcus said from behind her, startling Chris again. She spun around to look into his enigmatic cobalt eyes.

"You were at the show?" she asked him.

"Yes," he said, and for some reason she shivered again, knowing that he had watched her when she hadn't been aware of him.

"Ah, there you are at last!"

The cry came from a male voice at the top of the stairs. Chris gazed upward to see a handsome young man with a dazzling white smile staring down at her. "It's about time, Marc! I've been dying of curiosity to see our mystery guest—our prodigal daughter!"

Marcus laughed. Chris glanced his way and felt suddenly warm. There was open amusement in his eyes, and his smile was as full and inviting as his brother's. His teeth were white against the copper of his features, and when he met her gaze with a teasing light in his eyes, she knew that he was definitely capable of being charming.

"Come down, Tony. Miss Tarleton, my brother, Antonio. Tony, Miss Christina Tarleton."

Tony quickly came to them, offering Chris his hand. His touch was warm, his smile genuine, and she almost felt like crying. At least someone besides Alfred was glad to see her.

"Hello, Tony," she murmured.

"Hello yourself, gorgeous!" Tony laughed. He was in jeans and a blue denim shirt; his eyes were blue, but a lighter shade than his brother's. He was very handsome, and he seemed . . . fun. Not at all like Marcus, with his underlying elemental streak of danger.

He kept her hand and swung around to Sophia. "She did turn out just beautiful, but then, you're the one who always said she would!"

"Yes," Sophia remarked dryly.

Tony slipped an arm around the older woman. "It takes a beautiful woman to judge another, *si*, Sophia?"

"*Grazie*, Antonio," Sophia said, slipping from his embrace. "Since you two are here, I will beg leave to retire. I haven't the energy of your youth. Marcus, there is coffee in the rear courtyard, if you wish, and I've had the crystal room prepared for Miss Tarleton. If you'll excuse me, I'll say goodnight."

"Of course, Sophia. It is very late. Good night," Marcus said.

She waved to him as she started for the stairway, seeming to sail regally.

"Thank you, thank you very much," Chris called after her.

She received a dismissive wave in return.

"Where's Mother?" Marcus asked Tony. "Sleeping?"

"Yes, she said she'd have to see Chris in the morning," Tony replied. Then he grinned broadly at Chris again. "Are you up to coffee?"

She could feel Marcus standing behind her. She gave Tony a brilliant smile. "I'd love some coffee."

He caught her arm in his and led her through the grand marbled entryway. "Do you remember the palazzo, Chris?"

"No, not really," she replied.

"Then I'll tell you a bit about it so you don't get lost! The music salon and den are to the left; the dining room and kitchen are to the right. You can reach the courtyard by going either way. All of our rooms are on the second floor, Alfred and Sophia are on the third. There's an elevator at the rear of the stairs. The bridge to the galleries is on the second floor, but you mustn't use it now; it's in urgent need of repair! There are subterranean tunnels, too, but again, you really mustn't use them. Marc is busy saving them—and everything else in Venice!—from the sea."

Chris turned around a bit. Marcus was following them, but he was at a distance. She frowned and lowered her voice, bringing her lips close to Tony's ear. "Please, Tony, help me quickly. Who is Sophia? I don't remember her."

Marcus was closer than she had thought. Either that, or he had closed the distance between them with uncanny speed.

"Sophia Calabrese has been the housekeeper here since my father invited Alfred into the house," he answered for Tony. "Don't you remember her? She lived here when you were born."

"She seemed familiar," Chris murmured. "Of course. The housekeeper..."

Tony broke into soft laughter. "Marc! Chris is an American, a worldly woman. Sophia is Alfred's *mistress*. She has been so for thirty years. Not that I think much can go on between them anymore."

"Tony!" Marcus said sharply.

Chris laughed, linking her arm more tightly through Tony's. She was aware of the beautiful hallway they were passing through. It was wide enough to be a room in itself, and lined with chairs and love seats, pedestals, statues and paintings. And then they came to a huge room with four sets of French doors, all standing open to a beautiful tiled patio. Chris could see a circular table there, set with a snowy cloth, a silver coffeepot, cups, saucers and plates.

"Sophia must have thought we needed supper!" Tony laughed, very gallant as he led Chris onto the patio, seated her and handed her a napkin with a flourish, and poured her some coffee. Marcus silently took a chair opposite her.

Chris looked up at Tony and returned to their earlier topic of discussion. "Sophia has been Alfred's mistress for thirty years? Now that's definitely Italian! Why didn't he marry her?"

"I don't really know—" Tony began.

"Nor is it any of our business, is it?" Marcus interrupted. He sipped his black coffee, watching Chris pointedly over the rim of his cup.

She shrugged, then smiled at Tony again. "People are fascinating, aren't they, Tony?"

Tony seated himself and caught her hand and her eyes across the table. "*You're* fascinating, Christina."

She laughed, quickly retrieving her hand. She wanted to taunt Marcus di Medici, but with his eyes on her, she only dared to go so far.

"Thank you, Tony," she said a little breathlessly, then allowed her eyes to roam over the courtyard. "This is the most land I think I've seen in Venice. All the other buildings are built so close together."

"Oh, most of them have courtyards," Tony said. "I guess that we do have more property than most, though. But there isn't much space, you see. It's a bit like New York City—"

"You've been to New York?" Chris interrupted.

"Oh, yes, of course. We—Marcus and I—travel extensively. It's necessary to keep the galleries going." He started lifting the silver domes from the serving platters on the table. "Pastry, cookies and cakes. What would you like, Miss Tarleton?"

"I liked 'Chris' better," Chris told him, "and I really don't care for anything at all. I had a huge dinner."

Tony didn't press her. He selected a large anise cookie himself and eyed it as he continued to talk to her.

"We're opening a gallery in the States soon," he told her.

"Really?" Chris inquired politely, a little annoyed that they traveled so frequently and had never bothered to check into the state of her welfare or her mother's.

"Yes. We've already opened a place in Paris, and one in London. Next year will be the States."

"Where?" Chris asked.

"We haven't decided yet. Either New York or Boston," Tony replied.

"And it probably won't be next year," Marcus contradicted his brother. He glanced at Chris as he lit a cigarette. "We've just opened a new exhibition here. Something quite different."

"You'll love it!" Tony assured her.

"Actually, it's more of a show than an exhibit. We're using robotronics, something that's pretty widely used in some of your American amusement parks."

Tony snapped his fingers. "Like the Hall of Presidents!"

Marcus grinned tolerantly at Tony. "Something like that," he agreed. "Only we depict Venetian life through the centuries, and the costumes and jewels on the animated figures are real."

"It sounds fascinating," Chris murmured.

"Oh, you'll see for yourself," Tony assured her, munching his cookie. "In fact, I'll take you through tomorrow—"

"No, you won't," Marcus interrupted smoothly. "You're going to Florence tomorrow, remember?"

"Ah, Marcus! You could go! You really should go; you know the tapestries much better than I."

"You know them well enough, Tony. And I can't go. The workmen are coming to look at rot in the catacombs. And I have an appointment at the bank at eleven. *And* the engineer is coming from the computer company to work on the latest figures."

Tony grimaced, but gave in gracefully. He winked at Chris. "Alas! We get a beautiful guest—and I'm out on my ear. But I'll make it up to you, Chris, I promise."

She smiled. "I'm sure you will. How long will you be gone?"

He shrugged. "Two days, three at most. Whatever the gorgons upstairs and this whip-cracker do to you, see that you wait for me!"

"Gorgons?" Chris queried, frowning.

"He's referring to Sophia and our mother," Marcus said with a sigh. "And I'm sure they'll be very gracious."

"But of course," Tony said to his brother. "Chris is here because of Alfred, isn't she?" There was something peculiar—amused, but nevertheless resentful—in his tone.

"Yes," Marcus said simply. He crushed out his cigarette and sat back in his chair as if he were removed from the group, an observer only.

"Ah, well then, Alfred will be wanting your company."

"And she his," Marcus commented dryly.

"Whatever for!" Tony laughed. "She'll spend hours sitting in the courtyard . . . oh, perhaps it will not be that bad. We have a very unique pool on the roof. Do you swim?"

Chris nodded. She felt suddenly very wary of Marcus; she knew he was watching her carefully.

"I believe she wishes to be with Alfred," he said lightly. "After all, it is at Alfred's invitation that she has come." He looked straight at Chris and smiled, but spoke to Tony. "She might be after his money, you know."

Tony laughed. "Are you?" he asked Chris.

She returned Marcus's blatant stare. "Oh, possibly, Tony. I haven't decided yet."

Tony was taking the entire thing as a joke. He laughed again. "Well, you needn't bother with Alfred. Seduce Marcus here—or better yet, seduce me! We've both got a share in it all."

Chris set down her coffee cup, still eyeing Marcus carefully. There was nothing to be read in his cobalt gaze, yet she still shivered at his undaunted perusal of her. She smiled slowly and turned to Tony. "What a lovely idea. If I fail in coercing the whole thing from Alfred Contini, I'll just have to con a share of it from one of you."

Tony's eyes were a dazzling shade, like a summer sky, as he laughed again. "Marriage, my dear Miss Tarleton. Take us for all we've got."

"I'm certain she'll try," Marcus murmured.

Chris cast him a quick hostile glance, then grinned sweetly at Tony. "Do you think I should? Go after one of you, that is."

"Why certainly! And, Marcus, think of the gain to us! Anytime one of the robots went out, we'd have a mime, talented flesh and beautiful blood, to slip into the show! We wouldn't have a worry in the world."

Marcus smiled politely. "I think we'd still have plenty of worries, Tony. Most assuredly more." He rose suddenly, as if he had tired of a game. Perhaps he had, Chris thought; he had tired of the game of watching her.

"Miss Tarleton, I'll show you the galleries myself tomorrow." He raised a dark brow in his brother's direction. "I have a few papers to go through before the morning, and I'm sure Tony will be happy to show you to your room."

"I'd be happier to show her to mine," Tony commented.

Chris laughed, but Marcus was not amused. "Antonio!" he said rather sharply. "Miss Tarleton is Alfred's guest."

Tony glanced at Chris and shrugged sheepishly. "I'm sorry for the comment. I can't help the thought."

"You're forgiven," Chris said flippantly. Marcus was behind her; she could feel his eyes, like blue fire. Good. Let him think she'd be willing to hop into his brother's bed. At least Tony hadn't greeted her by condemning her father.

"*Buona notte*, Signorina Tarleton," Marcus murmured. His voice was low, a brush of raw silk. When she turned to reply, he was gone.

"Sinister chap, isn't he?" Tony inquired affectionately, referring to his brother.

Chris spun back around, looking at Tony with surprise. He laughed. "Marc sometimes takes life a bit too seriously," he told her. He lifted his shoulders and allowed them to fall, then grinned. "Marc had to grow up very suddenly—at twelve. My father was gone, and your father was gone, and even then Alfred was ailing. It all fell to Marc. He did a remarkable job of keeping things together through the years. So forgive him if he's a bit brusque at times. He's also... well, he's used to speaking and being obeyed, you know. And..."

"And what?" Chris pressed Tony.

He gave her his infectious grin. "Half the time he doesn't need to speak to be obeyed." He shook his head as if grasping for an elusive answer, then laughed. "Women! It's a pity I wasn't the son to inherit that dark charisma of his. I could have taken it much, much farther! Marc loses interest so easily, you see. If he inclines his head to get them, he inclines his head once more when he wishes them gone! Ah, to have been the eldest!"

"I'm sure you do quite well on your own," Chris told him dryly.

Tony chuckled. "I do try."

"Tony," Chris murmured, suddenly very serious. It was all well and good to joke with Tony and goad Marcus, but that wasn't why she had come to the palazzo, nor was it to take anyone's money. She swallowed suddenly. "Tony, please..."

"Christina! What is it?"

He lost his lighthearted manner very quickly; his question was caring and concerned, and Chris decided that although Marcus might be a thorn in her side, she liked Tony di Medici very much.

"Tony, Marcus said something to me tonight that was very upsetting. He said that my father murdered yours."

Tony instantly withdrew from her; a pained expression flashed through his eyes as he leaned back in his chair.

"Chris, *per favore*, leave the past alone."

"Tony! I can't. I can't believe that my father was a murderer! I knew him, Tony. He was gentle and kind, and any mention of Venice was like stabbing him with a knife."

"Chris, Chris!" Tony moved forward again, taking her hand in his. "Whatever happened, I'm certain James did nothing on purpose."

"But what happened?" Chris almost screamed.

"I—I can't tell you. Don't ask me this, Chris, please. I can't say anything. I was barely eight at the time. Please, Chris, I can tell you nothing. I will tell you nothing."

There was an implacable look in his eyes, very similar to his brother's. Chris sighed and cast herself back into her chair. "I've got to find out somehow, Tony."

He hesitated uncomfortably. "Christina, please, if you have any mercy, don't speak of this to my mother."

She closed her eyes and shook her head wearily. She didn't want to make promises that she couldn't keep.

"Christi, *per favore!*"

The soft entreaty brought her eyes open again. Tony smiled a little ruefully. "I—I really can't tell you anything, Chris." The teasing light returned to his eyes, and he suggested, "Plague Marcus if you must; he was older at the time. More aware of what was going on."

"Marcus..." Chris murmured bitterly. "It's like talking to a granite wall."

Tony laughed, his easygoing nature apparently restored. Or perhaps he felt that he had put himself in the clear; if Marcus chose to answer her, that would be his privilege.

"I've heard my brother accused of being many things, but never as cold as a granite wall!"

Chris merely lifted a brow, then stared at her coffee cup again, suddenly bone weary. It had been a long day, and an even longer night.

"Ah, Christi! *Bella, bella*, Christi! You could melt the strongest wall! Charm Marcus."

"Umm," Chris murmured dryly. Then she offered Tony a weak smile. "Would you mind showing me to my room now? I'm very tired."

"Of course, of course! Come." He stood and courteously pulled back her chair. He led her in silence back through the hallway and up the stairs. Chris noticed curiously that the stairs here were wooden when most of those she had seen in Venice were constructed of marble, granite or some other type of stone.

"What's the matter?" Tony asked.

"The stairs...they're unusual."

"Unusual, and a pain," Tony agreed. "We're always fixing them. I don't know what got into our ancestors. I don't even know where they got the wood!" He sighed. "These old palaces, they eat you alive. What with the constant battle with the sea and the salt in the air..."

"I guess it is very hard to preserve things," Chris said.

"Very. But it's fascinating." He smiled. "We're active in a group to preserve all of Venice. The sea threatens to engulf us, and it is only in modern times that we have realized this. Marcus or I will show you some of our efforts one day."

"Thank you," Chris said. "I'd enjoy learning."

Tony grasped her face lightly between his hands and kissed her cheek. "*Buona notte*, Christi," he murmured. Then he pushed open the door they stood in front of and switched on the light.

"*Buona notte*, Tony."

He smiled and left her. Chris turned around and immediately understood why it was called the crystal room. The chandelier was almost as large as the monster in the entryway. Enormous, and beautiful. The swirling pink-and-white tiles on the floor gave the bedroom a feeling of being even larger than it was. There was a huge old bed with a massive carved headboard in the dead center of the room; to either side were French doors leading to an outer terrace or balcony. The white muslin drapes flowed in the night breeze. There was a breakfast table, as well as a gateleg table and two large dressers to match a huge wardrobe. A door to the far left, Chris quickly discovered, led to a modern bathroom.

Her suitcase lay on the foot of the bed, and she moved to it quickly, undoing her blouse as she went. The abject weariness that had struck her when she was sitting with Tony remained with her. All she wanted to do was bathe and fall asleep . . . and stop wondering how she could prove that her gentle kindly father had never murdered anyone.

To sleep . . . and forget the disturbing effects of her confrontation with Marcus di Medici.

She opened her suitcase and smiled absently at its contents. One nice thing about living in Paris had been the acquisition of a marvelous lingerie wardrobe. Her nightgown was a gauzy fluted pink silk. It went perfectly, she decided, with the elegance of the room.

But she could really come up with little appreciation for anything at the moment. Her mind was spinning on a terrible course: how could they be saying these things about her father? Even Tony, who had been so ready to greet her, seemed to believe that James Tarleton had killed Mario di Medici. And no one would even talk to her about it.

She set her lips grimly as she ran a quick bath. There would be ways to find out. She'd study her Italian dictionary until she had a strong enough command of the language to check the newspaper morgue, the city records and whatever else she could get her hands on. Damn them all! She would find out the truth.

Chris sank into the warm water and tried to relax, but soon gave up. She washed quickly and slipped into her nightgown, feeling refreshed in body, if not in mind. She pulled back the embroidered spread and literally slid into bed. The sheets were pink silk, just like her gown.

"What a match," she murmured aloud, then she doused the antique bedside lamp and determined firmly that she was going to sleep.

"Charm Marcus," Tony had told her. But how should she set about charming a man with a deadly fascination of his own? He was capable of being completely courteous—and completely intractable, implacable and as hard and cool as stone. He could look at her and light a fire in the very center of her being.

She tossed and turned and discovered that she was sliding again on the sheets. Damn! she thought. They didn't go with her gown at all!

Concentration was the name of the game, she reminded herself. And as she had learned in several classes, she started contracting her muscles tightly starting with her toes, then forcing them to relax. Finally either the exercise worked or exhaustion took over, and she drifted into a deep sleep, one from which she was awakened with a startling jarring thud.

Chris's eyes flew open. It was dark except for the moonlight. Still night. Then why...?

She sighed. She had awakened because she had fallen to the floor. Sleeping on silk in silk was like being on a slip 'n' slide. The top sheet and spread were tangled around her, and she was a disheveled mess on the tile. Probably bruised in a dozen places, she decided ruefully.

"What are you doing, Miss Tarleton?"

The deep husky voice was so startling in the night that Chris gasped. She stared at the doors leading to the terrace and saw a tall form there. A man. Marcus di Medici.

He moved into the room silently and turned on the bedside lamp. Light flared all around her and Chris realized that a nightgown was hardly the attire she wanted to greet someone in, especially him. His eyes were raking over her in amusement and no sign at all of humble apology. He was still in his suit. His arms were crossed casually over his chest, and his lips were curved in a wry smile.

"I fell!" Chris snapped, but when she tried to rise, she discovered that she was too tangled to do so. He laughed and reached for her hands, pulling her from the welter of bedding. Chris found herself swallowing as she was set on her feet—too close to Marcus, too aware of his lean sinewed physique and his heated sensual power. He smiled as he held her there for a moment, and suddenly she was also all too aware of her own lack of clothing. The nightgown cut a deep V between her breasts, and the material hid little if anything from his imagination.

He kept smiling. He still had her hands, trapping her just inches away from him. "I'm sorry. We have nothing but silk here. It seems so cool when the air is hot."

She wasn't really touching him, yet she could have sworn that she felt the entire hard length of his body against her own. Suddenly she broke the searing contact of his eyes and tore her hands away.

"Where did you come from, anyway?" she demanded irritably, dragging the sheet and spread from the floor and hugging them in front of her. His lashes flickered and his grin deepened as if he were completely aware that her action had been caused by an uneasy fear.

"My room is next to yours. The terrace connects them. I heard the crash and came to see if you were all right."

"I—I'm fine. I'll just have to learn to sleep in the center of the bed."

He laughed huskily. "Or without the nightgown."

"Yes, quite. Well, if I con one of you fascinating di Medicis into marriage, I won't have a worry in the world, will I?"

She had the pleasure of seeing the amusement fade from his features. But then she was sorry that she had been so flippant because his hands were on her again, drawing her to him, and this time the length of her body was crushed to his, and she did feel all the strength of his well-muscled shoulders, arms and thighs.

"Christi, *cara*, take heed. All the di Medicis do not care to be conned."

His breath warmed her cheeks, and violent tremors, hot and insistent, ravaged the pit of her abdomen. She was about to do something, anything, to escape his touch when he released her, brushing her cheek with his knuckles in a surprisingly tender gesture.

"Again, Miss Tarleton, I wish you *buona notte*."

And then he was gone, silently disappearing into the night.

Chapter 3

They were talking about her when Chris came down to the courtyard the next morning.

She hadn't the least idea what they were saying because they were speaking very rapidly in Italian, and it was only her name that she caught, assuring her that she was indeed being discussed.

She had been walking along the same great hallway she had followed the night before, and she paused when she reached the large inner patio. She wanted to get her bearings before joining the group.

Marcus and Tony were both there. Tony was talking excitedly; Marcus was reading a newspaper and sipping espresso, apparently paying little heed to the discussion. Alfred was at one end of the table; Marcus at the other. Tony was to his brother's left, while Sophia was near Alfred. The other woman at the table had to be Gina di Medici, Mario's widow. The hardest of the lot to face calmly, Chris decided.

No, Marcus would always be the hardest of the lot to face calmly.

There were two girls who appeared to be little more than teenagers serving the group. The offerings seemed to be coffee, rolls, fruit and cheese. Breakfast, Chris realized, was not a major meal to Italians. But then, she had accustomed herself to nothing but coffee and croissants in Paris.

She cleared her throat and moved into the morning sun. All talk immediately stopped, and she was glad she was also accustomed to being stared at, since it seemed that everyone was staring at her now.

"*Buongiorno,*" she murmured, stepping forward confidently.

"*Buongiorno*, Chris, *buongiorno!*"

Bless Tony! He was instantly on his feet, rushing around to greet her. Marcus closed his newspaper more slowly and stood; Alfred would have done so as well, but Chris quickly begged him to remain seated.

"Christi," Alfred said to her as Tony seated her on his other side, "Sophia tells me you met last night; now you must meet Gina di Medici and you'll have no strangers in this house, eh?"

Chris nodded. No strangers! These people were strange even for strangers. But she smiled down at Gina di Medici, praying fervently that Gina would accept her smile at face value.

Gina di Medici was a striking woman and, like Sophia, she had aged very well. It was difficult to believe she could have grown sons, except that it was quite obvious that Marcus and Tony were her sons. Gina's eyes, too, were a beautiful blue—a shade more like Tony's than Marcus's—and stunning in their clarity. But whereas Marcus and Tony had hair as dark as midnight, Gina di Medici was fair. Her hair remained a true blond, with no hint of gray. Her face was a lovely oval, hardly touched by the lines of age.

She smiled at Chris in return, and yet it was as if she wasn't smiling at all. Rather, it seemed that she had curved her lips in an automatic gesture. There was no malice in her eyes when she looked at Chris, but something that hurt far more deeply: sorrow, and the deepest remorse.

"Christina, child," she murmured softly. "It is good to see you again."

Chris swallowed, fully aware despite the gentle words that Gina di Medici wasn't happy to see her at all. To Gina, Christina's presence was like having gravel scraped over an open wound.

Chris decided right then that she could make a promise to Tony never to harass his mother with questions. She would never intentionally hurt Gina.

"*Grazie*, Gina," Chris murmured, lowering her eyes. When she raised them, she found Marcus staring at her. Strangely, it was he who looked away first.

"Does the palazzo bring back memories, Christi?" Alfred boomed out.

"I'm, uh, not sure yet," Chris murmured. She shook her head. "I don't think so."

Sophia was rising. "What would you like, Christina? Tea, coffee, espresso, cappuccino?"

"Coffee, please," Chris said. Sophia lifted a hand and murmured something in Italian. One of the girls brought Chris a delicate china cup and filled it with pitch-black coffee. Tony pushed back his chair, glancing at his watch. "I've got to go. Christi, don't forget, wait for me!" he teased her. He kissed her hand, then moved around the table to kiss his mother's cheek.

"Marcus, if you decide we need anything else, call me," Tony told his brother.

Marcus replied with another of his rare genuine smiles. "I'll be lucky to find you in, Tony."

Tony laughed, waved to the group and left. Alfred asked Marcus something about the workmen who were coming, and Gina di Medici leaned across the table a little to talk to Chris.

"How is your mother, Christina?"

"Fine, thank you," Chris replied. She told Gina about her mother's remarriage, then paused awkwardly. She didn't really know what to say to Gina.

Sophia said something a bit sharply in Italian. Chris looked at her blankly, and thought that Sophia was smiling a little smugly. "Christina, answer me!"

She shook her head. "I'm sorry, I can't. I don't speak Italian."

"But it was your first language!" Sophia exclaimed.

"Sophia!" Alfred remonstrated with a frown. "Leave the girl be."

"I never knew it was my first language," Chris said a bit stiffly. "And I haven't had occasion to use it since I left, I suppose."

Marcus stood, tossing his newspaper down again. "Mother, Sophia, Alfred, have a good day. Christina, I'll be back for you right after lunch."

"Back for me?" Chris murmured with more confusion than she would like to have shown him. But there had been something a little less disturbing about Marcus seated than Marcus standing. Looking up at him, all Chris could remember was the way he had touched her last night, and she wasn't at all sure whether she disliked the man, or was totally fascinated by him.

Strangely, though, she already felt as if she had known him for a long, long time. As if their relationship had been formed on a distant intangible level where all that mattered was an elemental heat.

His lips curved just slightly, and she wondered if he was aware of her disturbing reaction to him.

"The galleries, Christina. I told you I would show you the galleries. Will two this afternoon be all right?"

"Fine, thank you," she said, glad to have regained a cool voice and her senses. Marcus, she reminded herself, was going to have to be the direct line of her attack.

He gave them all a brief wave and disappeared in Tony's wake. Chris felt as if both Sophia and Gina were watching her. Alfred started talking again as soon as Marcus had disappeared from view.

"Would you care to join me on the roof this morning, Christi? You can bathe in the pool while enjoying the sun."

"Certainly," Chris told him.

"You haven't eaten anything, Christina," Gina commented. "You must eat something."

Chris automatically reached for a roll. Gina smiled at her again, and Chris felt that Gina was trying very hard to get past her memories in order to make her feel welcome.

Alfred asked Chris about Paris as she ate, and Chris was glad to talk about her time in that city. It seemed like a safe subject.

She had a second cup of coffee while Gina and Sophia agreed that Rome offered more than any city on earth, to which Chris made no comment. But when they all rose at last and Chris returned to her bedroom to change into her bathing suit, she let out a long sigh of relief.

She had survived her first morning at the Palazzo di Medici.

Survived. It was a strange word to use, but that was exactly how it felt, she mused.

The pool on the roof was unlike anything Chris had ever seen, and she loved it immediately. It was tiled all in black, red and gold, and the family crest was set in the center beneath the water, shimmering in the sun. The pool was surrounded by a little wall, making it entirely private. There was a Jacuzzi in one corner that created a cascading waterfall running into the main body of the pool. It was wonderful, and Chris was pleased to stay there, swimming lap after lap and convincing herself that she had rid herself of what she was beginning to think of as the "di Medici tremors."

At length, though, she pulled herself from the water to lay out a towel on a bench at Alfred's side.

"How was your swim?" he asked her, his dark eyes sparkling with happiness. Chris was amazed that her presence could mean so much to him.

"Wonderful," she said, smiling. "This—" she waved a hand around to encompass the palazzo "—is wonderful. Thank you so much for inviting me here."

He gazed at her, and his smile slowly faded. "You did not come just to amuse an old man," he told her.

Chris shook some of the water out of her hair and smiled. "I'm very glad that I've met you, Alfred—as an adult, that is. And I'm very happy if I'm making you happy. But you're right; I came because I want to know what happened."

He shrugged, looking uncomfortably upward. He stared at the sun when he spoke. "Can it matter now, Christi? Can any of it really matter now?"

"It matters to me," she said quietly. "Alfred, you didn't tell me that my father had been accused of killing Mario di Medici."

Alfred lifted a slim hand, then allowed it to fall helplessly back to his lap. "It was so long ago. And . . . and I do not blame your father, Christi. I—I do not believe that he killed Mario."

"Alfred, won't you tell me about it?" Chris pleaded. "I need to know what happened. I can't make any sense of it if I don't know what went on!"

"Sometimes I think it is best that family skeletons remain locked away," he murmured. "And then . . ."

"Alfred," Chris pressed him urgently.

He shrugged. "It was that damned statuette!"

"Why was one little statue so important?" Chris demanded.

"Because its value would be immense—if it was what we thought it was. A Michelangelo, Christi! It was, we believed, a working model for a tomb relief."

"And it just . . . disappeared?"

"Yes, but the statuette was not what really mattered in the end. It merely brought on the clash of tempers on the ketch that day and—"

"Mario di Medici died," Chris finished. "But, Alfred, it sounds like there were a number of people on board that boat. My father and mother, Gina and Mario, Sophia and you. Genovese . . . and didn't you say there were others, too?"

"*Si, si*, Christi. Fredo Talio and Giuseppi—Joe—Conseli. They are . . . they are still with us."

"Still with us?"

"Yes, they work for Marcus. Or the galleries." Alfred closed his eyes and leaned back. "Marcus heads it all now. I have no more interest. Too many deaths . . . Christi, what of your father? What happened to him?"

Chris looked down at the brick deck that rimmed the pool. "He died of a heart attack right after my thirteenth birthday. It was . . . instantaneous, they told us."

"That would be God's way to depart this life," Alfred murmured. "God knew him to be innocent."

"Then he was innocent! Alfred, help me prove it!"

He sat up suddenly, staring at her intensely, then looking all around them like a startled rabbit. "Christi," he murmured, and she was concerned because it suddenly seemed that he was breathing much too fast. "Christi, we will not talk about it here, *per favore?* Even the air, it has ears. The walls here, they listen. Didn't you hear that?"

"Hear what?" she asked him.

"The sound . . . someone coming. Christi, swear to me that you will not talk about it here!"

His face had grown very flushed, and Chris could still sense his too-rapid breathing.

"I swear, I swear!" she promised solemnly. "Please, Alfred, *per favore*, don't upset yourself! I won't say another word."

Slowly he seemed to relax. At long last he smiled again and swept out an arm to encompass Venice.

"Venezia! Ah, Christi, once she was the jewel of the sea. All merchants knew Venezia! Marco Polo brought back his gifts and crown jewels from Kublai Khan. It was from here that he left for his journeys, and it was here that he returned. Ah, what a great city! The doges kept power, but the merchants were princes! She was a city where people lived and breathed and laughed and knew the beauty of song and the great artistry of her Italian sons! But we weren't always 'Italian.' Did you know that Venice belonged once to the Austrians?"

"No," Chris murmured, watching him and smiling but feeling as if his sense of unease had become hers. She had the horrible feeling of being secretly watched.

"We were a young state once. A Venetian republic, Romanized in the third century, of course! The French put an end to our independence in 1797, and we were provisionally assigned to Austria. We joined the new kingdom of Italy in 1866."

Though Chris was listening to him, she felt as if she were in a fog. The unreasoning uncanny fear remained with her. And it was absurd. They were on the roof. There was only one place where someone might be—in the marble archway that protected both the new elevator shaft and the ancient winding stairway to the roof.

Chris looked quickly to the arch and swallowed.

Gina di Medici was there, standing with the breeze catching her hair and her skirt. She might have been a young girl, anxiously looking for her lover. She shielded her eyes from the sun with her hand.

"Alfred! Christina! You must dress for lunch!" she told them.

"Coming!" Chris tried to call, but the sound that came out of her mouth was more like a croak.

How long had Gina been standing there, watching her and Alfred?

Chris rose and Alfred did the same. She started toward the arch ahead of the old man, forcing a smile. She almost started violently when she realized that Sophia was there, too, hidden in the shadows behind Gina.

Gorgons. Tony had called the two women gorgons. Perhaps that was just what they were, like the multitudes of imps that guarded Notre Dame in Paris, these two guarded the Palazzo di Medici and all its secrets.

Chris gave herself a firm mental shake. They were two middle-aged ladies, very attractive at that, and she was the intruder here, not the two of them.

"How was the pool?" Gina asked her.

"Lovely!" Chris replied, and she wrapped her huge towel about her like a cape and hurried past the two women.

She felt a hand grasp her elbow just before she could enter the elevator. Startled, Chris spun around. It was Alfred, anxiously looking back over his shoulder.

"Christi. Meet me at the galleries at closing time on Friday."

Friday was three days away. She wondered what his message was, and why he was willing to wait so long before passing it on.

"Friday, Christi."

"Yes, yes, Alfred. Whatever you wish."

"I need you, Christi. I need you."

"Alfred, I..." She wanted to demand to know what made him so nervous. She wanted to clutch his hand, pat it and assure him that everything was all right.

"I can—" He looked around again, lowering his voice. Chris saw that Gina and Sophia had walked out on the brick deck to stare out to the sea. "Christi, I can tell you about your father then. The galleries, right after closing time. I'll see that the main door is open."

"I don't even know where they are yet!"

"You'll know. Marcus will show you today."

She did squeeze his hand then. "I'll be there, Alfred. Don't worry, I'll be there."

"Bless you, Christi."

She frowned, then squeezed his hand again. "And I promise you, Alfred," she said softly but very firmly, "I will help you."

He smiled. She felt like an angel—for the moment, at least.

Alfred wasn't at the courtyard table when Chris came down to lunch. Sophia told Chris that he had decided to eat a light lunch upstairs; he intended to spend the afternoon resting. It sounded natural enough; a number of Italians, like Spaniards, liked to rest during the heat of the afternoon and work or stay active in the evening.

But it did leave Chris alone with 'the gorgons' for lunch.

Whereas breakfast at the palazzo was small, lunch seemed to be a meal that could fill Chris up for the next two weeks. There were endless antipasti, as well as soup, cannelloni and rigatoni, and a choice of fish or veal for the main course. Chris was sure she'd never get to the main course, but she surprised herself by being almost famished. It had been the swimming, she decided, and determined not to turn into a blimp during her stay.

She was also glad of the food because it gave her something to talk about when she was trying to stay away from uncomfortable subjects.

Halfway through lunch, though, Chris found that she didn't have to keep the conversation going. Sophia was determined to do so.

"Christina," she said, pointing to one of the young dark-haired girls who were serving the meal, "this is Liggia; that is her sister, Teresa." Chris smiled warmly at the girls, who gave her shy tentative smiles in return. But she realized quickly that she wasn't being given a casual introduction when Sophia spoke next, sighing dramatically.

"Liggia and Teresa are our only live-in help these days. The world... it is not what it was. We have a service to do the floors and furnishings once a week, but otherwise..." She paused and stared pointedly at Chris. "I do hope you understand, Christina. You will help."

Chris smiled very sweetly. "I love to clean."

"Sophia!" Gina di Medici gasped. "You mustn't ask Alfred's guest—"

"Guest! She's James Tarleton's daughter, isn't she? She is a part of all this. She shouldn't mind giving—"

"Sophia!" Gina di Medici could put quite a ring of authority into her voice when she chose, very much like her elder son. "I am the Contessa di Medici, and the last I heard, this is still the Palazzo di Medici! You'll not ask a guest—"

"Please! Please!" Chris interrupted, somewhat stunned by the sudden hostility between the two women. "Gina, I'm quite accustomed to looking after my own things and my own surroundings, which is what I believe Sophia is asking. And I'd rather not be a noncontributing guest. Really, I don't mind at all!"

Both of them were silent for a moment, staring at her as if they had just remembered that she was there. Sophia sighed first. "I am sorry. I shouldn't have spoken. If Marcus would just hire more help—"

"Marcus can't afford more help," Gina interrupted impatiently.

"Can't afford! Alfred would gladly—"

"Marcus will not accept Alfred's money for use in his private concerns," Gina said flatly.

"His reasons make no sense to me!" Sophia said, and then she continued speaking in rapid Italian that left Chris completely out in the cold. She turned her attention to the espresso she had chosen for after lunch and picked at a piece of cheese. Should she admire Marcus for refusing to take Alfred's money for his 'private concerns'? No, she thought dryly, why should she? Who else was there to eventually inherit everything—the Swiss accounts and the galleries—except for Marcus and Antonio di Medici?

Chris wondered a little sourly if the whole thing might be a show, put on entirely for her benefit. Perhaps the di Medicis wanted her to think that they were in the midst of financial difficulties. Exactly why, she wasn't sure. Maybe Marcus wanted her to think he was broke... just so she wouldn't go hunting for a di Medici husband! It was hard to believe that any of this lot were really facing poverty!

"What a lovely discussion for luncheon... with a guest in attendance!"

The words, drawled in icy English, stopped both Sophia and Gina cold. They—and Chris—stared up in horror at Marcus, who was making a swift entrance across the courtyard.

He ignored them, and their obvious discomfort, as he sat down and smiled at Teresa. "Teresa, espresso, *per favore*."

The girl bobbed to him and ran to do as she'd been told. He thanked her warmly, then caught Christina looking at him. She couldn't read the expression in his eyes; they were simply as sharp as midnight gems as he smiled slowly. "Well, it seems you have had a wonderful introduction to the palazzo. I assure you, we are not customarily so rude."

He was apologizing to her, and yet she felt that he was angry—also at her. Because he had heard the remarks regarding his finances?

Chris swirled the espresso in her cup, withdrawing her eyes from his. "I am just that, Marcus: a guest. I shouldn't interfere with the family."

"Marcus, I—" Gina began to say, but he waved a hand in the air. "*Per favore*, let's drop it! Christina, how was your morning."

"Lovely," she replied. "The pool is just beautiful."

Marcus stared down at his own espresso. "It *is* beautiful," he murmured. Then he looked at her. "Your father designed it."

"He did!"

"Yes, he was able to tell the workmen how to create it from an existing fountain and small fishpond."

Chris heard the sound of a chair being scraped back. She glanced up quickly to see that Gina di Medici was rising.

"Marcus, Christina, you'll excuse me, please. I—I've acquired quite a headache."

Marcus was instantly at his mother's side, speaking to her softly in Italian. She smiled at him; he kissed her cheek and she left the courtyard.

"I really do not mean to give offense, Christina," Sophia said, "but it was terribly cruel of Alfred to ask you to this house."

"Sophia!" Marcus snapped.

Perhaps because Chris had had it with the accusations—unfounded, as far as she could see—being thrown so easily at her father, she was ready to fight her own battles.

She leaned across the table and gave Sophia a straightforward glare. "Perhaps it will prove to be a very good thing for the contessa that I am here. Maybe she has been blaming the wrong man for all these years. At any rate, Sophia, I am here, and I cannot leave until I understand it all—or until Alfred, or the contessa, ask me to!"

Sophia stared at her in return, apparently stunned. Then she emitted a furious oath, which Chris didn't understand, since it was in Italian. She did, however, get the general meaning.

Marcus said something very sharply. Sophia threw her napkin on the table and stalked back to the house, her high heels clicking loudly on the tiles.

Chris lifted her hands a little helplessly. "I, uh, I'm sorry. I really am causing quite a disturbance."

He laughed and sat down beside her again, idly drawing a finger over the back of her hand. "Perhaps, as you say, disturbance is good."

"But your mother..."

"My mother has lived too long with her memories. And I do not think that she blames you. Mother would not find fault with a child."

Chris was absurdly tempted to wrench her hand from the table because his touch was both lulling and far too evocative. She felt herself tensing, so she forced herself to relax and smile sweetly. She was out to win Marcus to her side, one way or another, and charm had been his brother's suggestion.

"It would be nice to prove that my father wasn't to blame, either," she said softly.

He grunted impatiently and pushed back his chair to rise. "Are you ready to leave?"

"Yes. I just have to get my purse. Shall I meet you at the bridge?"

"No, meet me back here. We'll walk."

"Walk?"

"Yes, we'll go the long way, since the bridge has been closed off for repairs. The galleries are actually on a little peninsula."

Chris nodded and hurried back through the house. She ran up to her room and grabbed her handbag, then paused briefly at her mirror. She'd chosen a short candy-striped halter dress with a wide band around the waist, hoping that the outfit would emphasize the nice color she had picked up that morning. It was summery, casual and, she added hopefully, smiling at her image, alluring. Her hair was freshly washed, full of sun and the light rose scent of a French shampoo. Unwilling to ponder her seductive powers or possible lack thereof, she quickly hurried out of the room and raced back downstairs.

Marcus was still standing in the courtyard, waiting for her. When she reached him, she was a little breathless. He smiled and took her elbow to lead her down a long set of steps to a slim pedestrian pathway marked, Via di Medici.

"You have your own road?" Chris asked.

"We've even got a canal," he replied lightly.

"Umm. Your mother said that she was a contessa. Does that make you a conte?"

"Yes, but it doesn't mean anything these days. Except—" he grinned down at her "—that we do get invited to have tea with the Queen when we're in London."

Chris laughed. He could be charming when he chose. Frighteningly so.

She walked in silence at his side for several seconds, noting that they passed a small flower stall, a cheese shop, a bakery and a boutique. Then they turned a corner, crossed over a small bridge and were in a square with the inevitable church to their left and the di Medici galleries before them and to the right.

Chris gasped softly. The building was, she thought, even more magnificent than the Doge's Palace. Eight massive columns decked the porch; row upon row of elegant terraces ringed each floor, evidence of a heavy baroque influence. The length of the roof was lined with colorful flags.

"My God, it's grand!" Chris murmured.

"Do you think so?" Marcus inquired politely. "We grow rather accustomed to such things here."

Chris laughed. "In Paris I grew accustomed to Notre Dame. But it's still grand. And so is this."

He smiled. Tolerantly, she thought. "Come on, I'll show you what I can. The left wing holds the pieces that are for sale. The right wing is a museum. The new exhibit is there. I'm sure that will interest you."

They started with the left wing. Chris wished she had a better education in art than she did. As Marcus pointed out several of the more valuable paintings, lithographs and sketches, the only names she recognized were Picasso and Dalí. Hoping to sound intelligent, she asked Marcus why such works were for sale and not in the museum.

He shrugged. "Because we have to keep the place afloat," he told her. Then he smiled again. "Our crowning glory here is a very unique Rembrandt. And we have a number of small sculptures made by the students of Michelangelo."

They walked through another gallery filled with tableware: flatware in both silver and gold, china and crystal. Another room featured love seats, a third bedroom furnishings.

"And this is all for sale?" Chris murmured.

"Of course. We acquire to sell. Only when a piece is extremely unique can we afford the luxury of adding it to the museum. But come, you'll see our private treasures now."

After crossing an inner courtyard to the right wing, they were stopped by a rotund jovial man. Marcus greeted him quickly in Italian. When the man turned to Chris, grinning like an old friend, Marcus quickly introduced her in English. "Christina, you probably don't remember Joe—Giuseppi Conseli. He has been with us since the galleries were opened. Joe, Christina Tarleton, all grown up."

Joe broke into a quick spate of excited Italian, then apologized profusely. "Chris, little Chris! But of course, you were so little! You cannot remember old Joe, eh?" He took her hand between both of his, then sighed, glancing at Marcus. "Ah, all will be well now, perhaps. The three names are joined again: Contini, di Medici and Tarleton. Christina, it is a pleasure!"

"Thank you," she told him, wincing a bit at the pressure of his handshake. "It's a pleasure to see you." And it was definitely a pleasure to see someone who was pleased to see her.

He smiled at her warmly again. He was almost completely bald and his head gleamed like a dime.

"Marcus, I do not like to disturb you, but can you come?"

"Yes, of course." He turned to Chris. "Why don't you go through the history display with the robotronics, Chris? It takes about twenty minutes, and I will be back by then."

She frowned. "Is there trouble?"

"I need to see the workmen below," he told her briefly. Then, to her surprise, he kissed the top of her head and hurried away with Joe.

She stood there watching his agile broad-shouldered form walk away. Stood there shivering inwardly, fascinated by his touch.

She forced herself to turn and find the historical exhibit. It was not an auditorium, as she had imagined it would be, but rather a theater-in-the-round. The center stage was alive with light, while all around there was shadow. Chris watched the figures, fascinated. There were Roman soldiers, medieval knights, the doges or duces of the Dark Ages and Renaissance, elegantly dressed ladies, milkmaids and even several of the more notorious courtesans.

The exhibit was marvelous. The figures were incredibly lifelike as they moved on their pedestals and spoke in soft Italian.

When Chris left the exhibit she immediately ran into Marcus again. The rotund Joe was still at his side, as was another taller and swarthier man.

"How did you like it?" Marcus asked her quickly.

"Breathtaking," she told him.

He turned to the swarthy man with the very lean face and very dark eyes. A man, Chris decided, right out of an Edgar Allan Poe poem.

"Chris, I wanted you to meet Fredo Talio. He and Joe are my most valuable assistants. Fredo, like Joe, has been with us since the galleries opened."

Chris said hello and discovered that the swarthy man was capable of a decent smile. Even so, he made her uneasy.

She wondered why, then realized that Alfred Contini had told her that both these men had been aboard the sailboat the day that Mario di Medici had gone overboard and died. She was anxious to know them . . . and also frightened.

They stood for several seconds talking to the two men; then Marcus took her arm again. *"Con permesso,"* he murmured to the two. "You will excuse us. I wish to show Chris the gem salon before the galleries close for the day."

Fredo and Joe quickly moved out of the way, murmuring that they had things to do before closing. Marcus led her quickly down a long hallway that opened onto an immense room with only five or six waist-high cases. A massive glass skylight let in what remained of the afternoon sun and caused the jewels in their cases to sparkle with rainbow brilliance.

"Dear God!" Chris gasped, and Marcus laughed.

"No, Chris, we do not own all of these. Most are on loan from the Italian government. These are all crown jewels from various principalities and duchies."

She couldn't help but ooh and aah as they walked past the various display cases. She didn't consider herself much of a jewelry fanatic, but these were magnificent. Crowns with every conceivable stone: diamonds galore, rubies, sapphires, emeralds. Opals and pearls, aquamarines and other semiprecious stones. Bracelets, medallions, necklaces—even a set of toe rings that had belonged to a Renaissance Veronese duchess.

Not until they reached the last of the exhibits, the one directly in the center of the room beneath the skylight, did she realize that Marcus was watching her. And then, as she stared at the tiara and medallion in the case, something registered in her mind. The emblem on the medallion, the coat of arms, was familiar. The winged lion was in the center, a thorned rose to the right, and Neptune rising to the left.

"di Medici!" she proclaimed, and Marcus grinned.

"Yes," he said simply. "We do own those."

He led her out of the salon and toward the stairs to the courtyard and main entrance. "Would you like to have dinner out?" he asked her casually.

She glanced up at him. "Would I like to have dinner out... or would you prefer not to return to your own palazzo?"

He laughed. "All right, I'd just as soon not go back right now. Do you mind?"

Chris lowered her eyes quickly. "Not at all," she told him quietly.

"There's a small...intimate...place right around the next corner," he told her.

She forced her eyes up and kept smiling. From where they stood, she could see the bridge that led from building to building, from the di Medici Galleries to the Palazzo di

Medici. Marcus was holding her arm, and she could feel another onslaught of tremors, hot and cold, thrilling and weakening. She spoke quickly. "Did things work out well?"

"Things?"

"With the workmen?"

"Oh, yes. They believe it's quite safe. Only minor repairs."

"What?"

"The tunnel . . . and the catacombs, of course."

"What's down there?"

His lips curved slightly; his eyes held a definitely wicked cast, all the more beguiling as the sun slipped lower and the sky was bathed in orange and scarlet. "Family secrets and skeletons," he told her. "What else would a di Medici keep buried below the earth? If you have the courage and heart, Chris, I'll take you one day."

She laughed, shaking off his macabre tone. "Oh, I've got the heart. And in daylight, I'm loaded with courage." She frowned then. "What was Joe saying when we first met him, when he was talking so enthusiastically in Italian?"

He watched her for a moment, his eyes partially hidden by the darkness of his lashes. "He was saying that you had grown like a flower. Like a rose. Very beautiful."

"Oh!" Chris murmured.

"A thorny rose, I told him."

"Did you?"

"Of course." He paused for just a minute, then smiled dryly. He started walking again, pulling her close, and murmuring to her in a warm stirring whisper. "You are beautiful, Christina. But then, you know that, don't you? You're relying on that fact to wheedle every bit of information out of me that you want."

"What!" she demanded, wrenching away from him. His tone had been so seductive that she hadn't realized for several seconds that she was being mocked.

He appeared undaunted by her anger, only challenged. He pulled a pack of cigarettes from his inner jacket pocket and lit one, watching her over the flare of his match.

"I told you, Christina, I do not care to be conned. But..." He shrugged, then smiled slowly, and in the darkness she couldn't tell if the smile was sardonic, or merely amused. "But perhaps I will not mind being charmed. We will have dinner alone, away from the palazzo, and perhaps I will tell you why your father was accused."

"Perhaps!" she snapped. "You owe it to me! Damn it! Someone owes me an explanation."

"Don't tell me what I do or do not owe, Christina," he warned her quietly, but she sensed the granite behind his words, the warning ... or threat.

She didn't feel like backing down, even if she was shivering again, outwardly and inwardly. And she didn't know if it was with anger or the sense that she had fallen prey to something beyond common sense or logic.

Fallen prey to Marcus. His excitement and danger.

He didn't allow her time to answer. He slipped an arm around her, pulling her close to his body, its strength and riveting heat. "You're cold," he told her. "Let's get to the *ristorante*. Because I choose to, I'll explain what happened. Though you really should know."

"How could I?" Chris cried out.

He hesitated again, and she could feel him looking down at her, his cobalt eyes raking over her. She cast her head back to meet those eyes, now cold as the moon.

"Because you were there," he said softly.

Chapter 4

"*What?*"

"Could we go inside, please? You're shivering again. And I'd appreciate it if you'd quit shouting."

"I'm not shout—"

He laughed, bringing his hand from her shoulder to clamp it lightly over her mouth. "You were shouting. *Per favore!* Can we go inside?"

Chris nodded, and managed to maintain a tense silence while he led the way into a restaurant called Le Grotto. The place gave the appearance of a cave—or a cellar, at the very least—but it was decorated with warm wood and plants, and each of the booths was very private, in its own little enclave. They were seated immediately, and when the waiter spoke ingratiatingly to Marcus, he glanced at Chris.

"Wine?"

She shrugged. "When in Rome..."

"This is Venice," he reminded her.

"Close enough."

He spoke to the waiter in quick flowing Italian, then faced Chris again, his hands folded on the table. "You really have no memory of Venice?" he asked her.

"No, not really," Chris murmured, wondering suddenly if that meant that Marcus intended to lie to her. "Just ... images now and then. A sense of déjà vu. When I got to St. Mark's Square I knew what it was going to look like, although I didn't really remember it, if that makes any sense."

The wine arrived, and the waiter poured a small amount in Marcus's glass. He tasted it and nodded. A glass was poured for Chris, and small crisp loaves of Italian bread were set before them. Marcus caught the waiter before he could leave, asking Chris quickly if she liked shrimp.

"Yes," she told him.

"It's their specialty. Shall I order?"

Why did she feel that it wasn't really a request? Because it wasn't, she decided. It was an assumption that she would comply. He was just showing a facade of courtesy.

She lifted a hand. "It makes no difference."

He placed their order, and the waiter moved away. Somewhere a violinist was playing, but it seemed that they were very much alone. They were across the table from one another, but her kneecaps kept brushing his and even that contact seemed to start her heart racing.

"Would you care to go on?" she asked him, watching him over the rim of her wineglass. He raised one brow, but kept silent. "Would you please go on?" she murmured with a saccharine edge, smiling as she added, in a softly warning tone, "Before I start shouting again and leap across the table to strangle you."

He chuckled, a warning in itself. "Why do I doubt, Christi, that you could do such a thing?"

She ignored the comment. "All right. Alfred Contini and Sophia were there on the yacht that day. My parents and your parents. Genovese was there ... and Joe Conseli and Fredo Talio. Right?''

"Yes. And so were Tony and I ... and you."

Chris took an overlarge drink of her wine. The dry liquid burned her throat and abdomen. She swallowed a second time and set her glass down, wanting to watch him but unable to. She traced a finger around the rim of her wineglass.

"So why my father, Marcus? All those people were there ... yet it's pinned on my father. How? Why?''

"Because your father was the last person to see him alive."

"The last person to admit to seeing him alive!" Chris exclaimed indignantly.

"Because," Marcus said, and his voice seemed to grate impatiently, "they'd been fighting."

"Fighting?"

"Yes. They'd come to blows. Your father had a black eye and a cut lip. He told your mother that my father looked worse." He was silent for a minute, then added bitterly, "And, oh, he did! By the time they found him, he was hardly recognizable."

The waiter came over then, leaving a typical antipasto tray piled high with olives, small tomatoes, celery, anchovies and slim pepperoni. Chris looked at the platter, feeling a little ill.

The waiter moved away.

"You're not eating," Marcus commented.

She stared up at him furiously. "No, I'm not. And you've got no right at all to condemn my father on such slim evidence!"

"Slim evidence?" he asked quietly as he selected a piece of pepperoni.

"Damned slim ... and even an Italian judge thought so, too!" Chris exclaimed. "All right, they'd been fighting. But like two men, Marcus. My father came in with a black eye, not with a denial. He didn't do anything cold-blooded or conniving. He got into a fight. Where is your sense of reason? Obviously someone else killed your father!''

"Who?" Marcus demanded flatly, and she felt the full blue flame of his gaze. "Myself? Or Tony? You? Perhaps you're up to strangling men these days, but you were only four at the time. Your mother? She never left the cabin."

"You're neglecting Alfred, Genovese, Joe and Fredo, and Sophia," Chris said stiffly. "And your own mother."

His hand shot out across the table, encircling her wrist in a painful vise. "You would accuse a woman who has lived in a tomb herself since his death? My mother?"

"Why not?" Chris demanded heatedly, ignoring the burning hold around her wrist and meeting his gaze with fury of her own. "You accuse my father."

He emitted an impatient curse and practically threw her wrist from him. "You refuse to face the facts, Christina," he said wearily. "Your father left. The rest of us...we have all been together for the past twenty-one years. I'm sorry. Everyone believes that your father killed mine. If he hadn't, somewhere in all these years, something would have come up. Some type of evidence or proof of guilt. It has not."

Chris took a deep breath. "You're wrong about one thing, Marcus. Not everyone thinks my father was guilty. Alfred Contini doesn't think my father killed yours."

She had the supreme satisfaction of seeing stunned surprise filter across his customarily guarded and implacable features.

"What?" he demanded with a quick harsh breath.

"You heard me."

"Alfred told you this?"

"Yes, quite flatly." Chris smiled, picking up her wineglass to swirl the liquid around. "It's rather amazing, isn't it? All these years, Alfred Contini has been cared for into his old age by the powerful di Medicis. His loving mistress stays by his side . . . but he came to me, a near stranger, to ask for help."

"He asked for your help?"

"He said that he needed me." Chris just stopped herself from telling him that Alfred intended to meet her alone at the galleries to talk to her and impart secrets that he didn't want the "walls" or the "air" to hear. She wanted to rub Marcus di Medici's nose in his own arrogance, but she reminded herself that Marcus could be the very "walls" or "air" that Alfred had meant.

Marcus lowered his head. A lock of his jet hair fell across his forehead, and when he raised his eyes to Chris once again, they were filled with amusement. The candlelight was caught in his eyes, making them look like blue diamonds, and something about his expression caused Chris to catch her breath and reminded her with a little shock that she should never have forgotten her first impression of the man. He was elementally dangerous on many levels, not least of them sexual.

Her hand lay on the table. He reached out to touch it again, but this time without painful strength. She found that she was staring at his fingers as they stroked her flesh. The nails were neatly bluntly cut. His hands appeared slimmer than they were because his fingers were long. Long, and filled with a shocking strength . . . and stunning tenderness. Now his touch grazed lightly, almost absently, over her knuckles, and he warned her with humor, "I wouldn't take anything that Alfred has to say too seriously. His health is poor, and I think that he is often bored with life these days."

"Bored, perhaps, but not senile," Chris objected quietly. Her eyes were still drawn to his fingers where they stroked her hand. She could snatch it away, she knew, but some part of her refused to do so. She couldn't help it; she had never pretended to herself that she had been anything but fascinated by him from the first. If he had walked away she would have been fine. But instead he had become, within hours, the focal point of her life.

"Then, Christina," he murmured lightly, "perhaps you should be very careful. If any of what you are saying is true, Alfred could well be casting you straight into the fire!"

Her eyes flew to his. "What?" she demanded.

He shrugged. "Oh, Christina! I wasn't being serious! Alfred is old and lonely. Perhaps he craves a little intrigue or excitement in his life, and perhaps he also feels this is a time for peace. He has you here; he does not want you hurt. It's very possible that his plan is simply to give you a sense of well-being so that in your mind, and your heart, you can clear your father."

"I don't . . ."

She paused when the waiter arrived, and watched as their pasta and shrimp were served. The pasta tonight was a spaghettini with a light sauce. The shrimp had been broiled in oil and garlic, then topped with crispy cheese and bread crumbs. Everything smelled delicious, and Chris hoped she could find an appetite.

Among other things, she was acquiring a headache. The white wine that Marcus had ordered was extremely potent.

The waiter refilled their glasses, and apparently asked Marcus if there would be anything else. Marcus glanced to Chris. She hadn't understood many of the words, but she had grasped the question. She smiled at the waiter.

"No, *grazie*."

He left them. Chris picked up her fork to poke at the shrimp. She started when she felt Marcus's hand on hers again, and when she looked into his eyes this time, she felt as if something as haunting as Venice itself swept through her being. There was, she thought, guarded concern in his eyes, something gentle where there was so often anger and mockery.

"Christina, let it all lie," he told her quietly. "Let the past go. You are here, you are welcome. Enjoy Venice, enjoy the galleries. My father is dead, so is yours. Let them rest."

"I . . ."

She wanted despertely to break his spell over her. She tossed back her hair and offered him a very cool smile. "Have you forgotten? I'm really after Alfred's money."

He slowly withdrew his hand from hers, and she saw the ice rise in his eyes again. "Ah, yes. Alfred's money. Or a di Medici husband, didn't you say? Actually, we're not worth much . . . financially."

"Oh, but you must be! All those gems! Those paintings!"

He smiled, white teeth flashing in the candlelight, copper features harsh and drawn. "The galleries and the palazzo, they are hungry, Christina. They consume money like sharks prey upon the weak."

Chris chewed a shrimp and deliberately ignored his comment. "This really is delicious, Marcus. And you needn't worry too much. I'll go after Tony, I believe. He has a much sweeter disposition."

"Really? Perhaps I should try to exude a greater charm."

"You could try," Chris murmured noncommittally, and she began to wonder what she was doing besides playing with fire.

He seemed to be thinking the same thing. Smiling laconically, he reached across the table, grazing her cheek with his thumb.

"The irony of it, Christina, is that I do find you fascinating," he murmured, and a flash of pure heat assailed her. "So if you choose to flirt with fire, *cara* Christi, see that you do not do so carrying casks of petrol, eh?"

Chris caught his hand and placed it on the table, smiling sweetly. "I always flirt carefully, Marcus."

He laughed, freeing her from his spell.

"Eat your shrimp, Christina. *Manga. Manga.*" Smiling with a slight curl of his lips, he tapped her glass.

"Bicchiere," he said, and she smiled, finding herself repeating him. *"Pane."* He picked up the bread, then pointed to her shrimp. *"Frutti de mare."*

"Fruit of the sea?" she asked.

"Literally, yes. Seafood."

Chris did manage to eat as the meal turned into a lesson in the Italian language. And—the déjà vu again—many of the words rolled off her tongue very easily.

Despite the fact that the evening had begun with tense anger and rigid determination, she discovered that she had a nice time. She laughed, smiled and was, she was certain, charming... to an extent, at least.

But then, he had already told her all that he could. Or had he? She didn't feel like dealing with it anymore that night. Her headache had become light-headedness, and the idea of playing with fire had become very seductive.

By the time they left Le Grotto Ristorante a full moon had risen over the city. Chris smiled slightly as she stared up at it. Venice, Venezia... it was a city of romance, touched by the years and by the future. She loved the water, the bridges, the gondolas and everything about the city.

And Marcus...

Dark, handsome and intriguing. The perfect host when he chose to be. Courteous, charming, polite.

But always... mysterious. It was his eyes, she decided then. So deeply, deeply blue against his dark complexion. His features were so ruggedly defined, his movements so smooth. What was it about the man? She liked the casual touch of his hands, the feel of the fabric of his suit. His casual laughter, his negligence and...

And his intensity. It was always there, lurking beneath his smile or his laughter. In the way he looked at her, touched her with his eyes.

The narrow roads were almost empty as they sauntered slowly back to the palazzo. She didn't mind his arm about her at all, and that thought made her smile again.

She was going to have to watch out for the local Venetian wines. They were a potent brew.

It seemed that he could read her mind. As they neared the palazzo steps he asked her, "Did you like the restaurant?"

"Yes."

"The shrimp?"

"Yes."

"The wine?"

She wrinkled her nose. "It was a little dry."

"Ah, well, there is a similar sweeter vintage," he murmured.

"I'll have to try it sometime."

"Yes," he murmured. He opened the gate and locked it behind him. Then, in the shadow of the steps, shrouded by vines and shadowed by the moon, he pulled her into his arms.

Startled, Chris stared upward into his eyes. She felt his palms grazing her bare shoulders, then fitting themselves to the base of her spine, pulling her hard against him. His lashes fell briefly over his cobalt eyes, darker than the night, hypnotic, and then he returned her gaze with a probing depth.

"If it's Antonio you're after," he whispered, "I'll have to sample what I might be missing . . . now."

Chris knew that she should resist him, yet she had no desire to. She watched his eyes as they came closer and closer to hers, then disappeared altogether as she closed her own and felt the hot provocative touch of his mouth, firm against hers. Ah, yes, she had charmed him. Done such a wonderful job that she was in his arms, losing sight of everything but the perfect feeling of being there. This kiss was no mild thing, stirred and fanned to grow deeper; it began as a tempest. She felt that she melted at the steel of his arms about her, fusing to his length. And yet she was real and alive, and aware that as he held her, she pressed her length to his, arching to appease the hunger of his mouth and her own. His tongue moved wickedly, fluid and demanding; his hand moved to her cheek, then caressed her throat. Blue fire sizzled within her, sweet and urgent, lapping along her spine, burning into her limbs. She played with the dark hair at his nape, touched his cheek, savored the scent and taste of him, barely aware that in all her life, she had never been kissed like this. So deeply, so passionately. Never had a man made her feel so alive, so hungry herself.... She felt the warmth of him beneath his jacket, the taut musculature, rippling, powerful beneath her fingers. The feeling grew that this was something wild and beautiful, as old as original sin, but absurdly right.

It was the full moon over Venice, she decided vaguely. Erotic, romantic, decadent...casting a light of intrigue and fascination. But no, it wasn't the moon or Venice, she admitted somewhere in her heart. It was the man. Marcus di Medici. Tall, sleek and sinewed, unleashing his power, the intangible strength of the sensuality she had known she would find and shiver beneath since she had first seen him....

His mouth drew gently away from hers, and his hands tangled in her hair as he held her close, kissing her cheeks and her throat, holding her, feeling the erratic racing of her pulse. Then, at last, he stepped back and she almost fell; he righted her, then released her.

And smiled.

"Christina..." he murmured, and the sound of her name had never sounded so raw and exotic before. But then a cloud passed over the moon, and when she could see his face again, it was cast in shadow and his eyes were elusive indigo. He smiled, and even before he spoke, she knew that the cloud had taken something away, that he had changed.

"It's a pity," he said lightly, "that you're after money...and I really have so little."

She was dying to slap him, but she knew he would be amused, and prepared to stop the gesture before she could complete it.

She managed to smile very icily instead. "Don't worry about it. I still find Tony by far the more...charming...of the brothers di Medici. *Buona sera*, Marcus. *Grazie*, for dinner—and for the...entertainment."

Chris was pleased with her control, proud of her dry reply and relieved that she had held her temper in check.

But she was raging inside.

She walked up the steps and across the courtyard with slow and amazing hauteur...but she ran up the steps to her room, and hurled her purse onto the bed with a streak of pure violence.

Marcus di Medici...she would truly love to strangle him. Just what the hell was his game?

Her anger fled suddenly, leaving her so weak that she sank down onto the bed.

His game...

Yes, Marcus was playing a game. But there was something deeper here, too. Something that went beyond their words, beyond circumstances. Words could easily be lies, and yet...

It was no lie that he wanted her. That, too, she had known from the first time their eyes had met.

And yet he was like a dark panther. Accustomed to stalking, accustomed to the kill. Aware of his own strength. Wasn't she just like any other prey that he had set his eyes upon?

Chris took a deep breath and began to pace her room, riddled with confusion, doubt and fear. Half the time she was certain that he despised her. But then he would smile, or he would laugh...or he would touch her. And she would feel again that his touch couldn't be a lie, that the electricity that had sparkled between them and flourished at every new meeting was flaring toward an explosion that was inevitable, that she could never deny. That she would never want to deny. He made her ache with anticipation, made her long to delve past the mysteries or ignore them, just to be with him.

Chris sank back onto the bed again. Mysteries. The palazzo was filled with them, shadowed by the past. Guilt was the family skeleton.

But already, absurdly, her heart was rebelling against her mind. There might be evil somewhere, but Marcus could not be that evil.

He was innocent. Totally.

Innocent of what? she asked herself.

Then a sense of foreboding settled over her so chillingly that she had to rise again, running her hands over her bare shoulders and hugging herself for warmth.

Something was going to happen. She had come here to find out about the past. Well, she had found out. And now she was going to prove that her father had never been a murderer.

Chris smiled grimly to herself. So what if she was fascinated by Marcus—he had admitted to being fascinated in return. She would be damned if she would be a pawn; he would be forced to play that position.

Determined, Chris showered and changed for bed, then crawled between the silk sheets, very carefully remaining dead center. She assured herself that she would find out the truth. Alfred Contini would be able to give her all the information she needed.

If Alfred said that her father was innocent, then it seemed very obvious to Chris that he was.

But proving it wouldn't be that easy. As she tossed about—carefully—trying to get comfortable so that she could fall asleep, she realized that she had acquired a very real sense of fear. Of foreboding.

And she couldn't shake it until sleep at last claimed her.

Chris awoke in the middle of the night, wondering why she had done so. Then she was touched by the chilling feeling that someone was in her room, watching her.

She opened her eyes carefully. Moonlight was pouring in from the terrace in a soft glow. She could easily see everything but the farthest corners of the room. She didn't realize that she had been holding her breath until she exhaled shakily with relief. There was no one there.

She hesitated for a few moments, then crawled from the bed, carrying her pillow with her. She wasn't sure why, since a pillow wasn't much of a weapon. But even when she checked out the corners and the bathroom, there was nothing to imply that anyone had ever been in the room or anywhere near her.

Puzzled, Chris sat on the corner of the bed, trying to fathom the strange feeling that had assailed her. She had been so certain. . . .

But why would anyone in the di Medici household want to come in and stare at her as she slept, anyway?

She shrugged, then stood and walked slowly, as if drawn, to the terrace. She had never been out on it before; she knew it connected her room with Marcus di Medici's.

The gauze drapes drifted around her as she stepped into the night air. The moon was still shining beautifully. There were no clouds, and it was a silver orb hung against black velvet. Or indigo velvet, really. A blue darkness just like . . .

Chris took a few steps along the terrace, her bare feet silent. The French doors to Marcus's room were open. Curiosity compelled her to step closer to them. She hesitated when she reached them, then peered around one door. Was Marcus, too, out on a silent stalk in the night?

The moonglow filtered into the room. She saw his bed, placed against the opposite wall. The sheets, a striking masculine indigo, were drawn back invitingly, but there was nobody in the bed. She gazed at the drapery beside her hand. Indigo.

But the Persian area rugs that lay scattered about the floor were light, and there was a white French Provincial clock on his heavy dresser. It was a striking room, much like its occupant.

But where, Chris wondered, was Marcus di Medici? Had he been in her room, silently moving about? Looking for something? What?

She inhaled deeply, then exhaled. She shouldn't be here. She had been disturbed by a possible covert invasion of her privacy, but wasn't she doing the same thing? It was ridiculous to be here, barefoot and scarcely clothed, peeking into a man's room.

Chris turned to tiptoe back to her own room, but from the other side of the door a hand shot out, capturing her arm, spinning her back around. Terrified, she screamed—but her scream was choked off by a hand quickly clamped over her mouth. Shivering with dismay, she heard Marcus speak just as she looked up and saw his eyes, devil dark, yet blazing where they caught the moon's glow.

"Will you shut up—unless, of course, you wish to explain to the entire household why you were sneaking about my room in the middle of the night."

Rigid, she shook her head. He released her and planted his hands on his hips. Chris noted that he, too, was barefoot. And clad only in a belted knee-length robe. A gold chain around his neck gleamed. She followed its line down the V of his robe to a medallion nestled in a thick mat of dark hair on his chest.

"If you had knocked, I would gladly have let you in," he drawled insinuatingly.

Chris instantly decided to go on the offensive. "What were you doing in my room?" she demanded.

"*Cara*, this is my room."

"But you were in mine!" Chris declared.

"Doing what?" he demanded impatiently.

"I—I don't know. Standing, sneaking around . . ."

"I believe I just caught *you* sneaking around."

"That's exactly the point. You were hiding behind the door—"

He sighed with exasperation. "I was behind my door because I heard someone prowling around the terrace."

"I wasn't prowling..." Chris began to protest, then she asserted, "Someone was in *my* room!"

He laughed. "Christina, I promise, if I'm ever in your room, you'll definitely be aware that someone is there...and that it is me."

"Oh, go to hell!" Chris muttered, turning to walk back along the terrace to her own doors. She entered her room, then turned around to give the moon one last suspicious glance. Instead she started, gasping as she crashed into Marcus.

"Shhh!" he warned harshly, bringing a finger to his lips, holding her bare arm with his other hand.

"What are you doing?" she whispered a little desperately. Not only was she half-naked, but so was he. And he was so close that she could feel the coarse hair on his chest teasing the flesh of her breasts through the silk of her gown. A trembling heat, the sensation that engulfed her when he came too close, threatened to overwhelm her.

"We'll check out your room," he told her.

"I already did," she murmured.

Nevertheless he released her, then moved around the room, a stealthy silent shadow. For a moment he disappeared into her bathroom, then reappeared, hands on his hips once again, one brow laconically raised. "Your door is locked, isn't it?"

"Yes."

"Are you quite certain that you don't have strange imaginings?" he asked her. "Or fantasies?"

"Will you get out of here, please?" Chris demanded irritably.

He chuckled softly. "Certainly, *cara* Christina..." He didn't touch her again. But at the doors, he paused and gave her an amused grin. "I do like your 'prowling' mode of dress, Christina. In fact, I'm growing very fond of that gown."

She was glad that she was in the darker shadow of the room, because a flush rose to burn her features. There was nothing to her gown. She had known it last night; she knew it now. Sheer, spaghetti-strapped and long, but with high slits along each leg.

She had no reply; he wasn't expecting one.

Chris crawled back into bed, determined that she was going to get to a boutique in the morning and purchase some puritanical neck-to-toe cotton nightgowns.

And then, of course, she wondered why she should be so determined. How many more clandestine meetings was she expecting to have with Marcus di Medici?

"I should lock those damn terrace doors," she muttered to herself. But it didn't occur to her to get up again and do so.

It was almost eleven o'clock by the time she went downstairs the next morning. Once she had fallen asleep again, she must have slept like a rock.

There was no one around when she reached the courtyard, but the snowy tablecloth, with a single flower and place setting for her, waited invitingly. Chris wandered to the serving cart to pour herself coffee.

"*Buongiorno*, Signorina Tarleton."

Startled, Chris spun around. Genovese was coming across the courtyard toward her.

Chris studied the man. He was no more than five-foot-eight and slim, but wiry. His eyes were dark, and his dark hair was untouched by silver, but seeing his weathered olive face up close, Chris knew he was either in his late forties or early fifties. But of course. He couldn't really be a young man. He had been with Alfred Contini for at least twenty-one years.

"*Buongiorno*, Genovese," Chris murmured a little awkwardly, taking a sip of her coffee. "I, uh, I'm sorry to be late. I appreciate the coffee you've kept for me."

"There are croissants in the basket," Genovese said, his English heavily accented.

"*Molto grazie*," Chris told him softly.

He smiled, then chuckled. "No, signora. *Molto bene*, as in food, eh? *Mille grazie*. A thousand thank-yous."

Chris laughed, too. "Thank you for the lesson, Genovese. Maybe one day I'll get it all right."

He pulled out her chair. "Once, when you were a little, little girl, you had it all right."

Chris sat, wondering why she felt so uneasy to have the man behind her. Alfred trusted him implicitly. But it seemed that since she had come to Venice and the Palazzo di Medici, she didn't like having her back turned to anyone.

"Strange, isn't it?" she murmured. "Some things are easy to remember ... and some things are not."

He was still behind her. "You remember nothing of your years in Venice?"

Did she? Yes, bits and pieces, a fragment here and there ... or perhaps it was only the pretense of memory, something totally subconscious that surfaced without her command.

"No, absolutely nothing." She lied cheerfully. "Where is everyone?"

"Alfred and Marcus are out on business; Tony has not returned from Firenze. Sophia has gone shopping; Gina is in the chapel."

"The chapel?"

"*Si*, she ... meditates."

"In other words, she wishes her privacy?" Chris asked him.

"Ah...yes," Genovese murmured, at last moving around the table. "If there is anything that you need ..."

"There is nothing at all that I need, Genovese. *Mille grazie*."

"Then I will leave you," he murmured.

Please do! Chris thought silently, and was angry at herself for allowing the man to make her uneasy. He'd never been anything but perfectly courteous and polite. She was allowing herself to become frightened, and that bothered her.

Chris was glad to be alone. She ate a croissant and sipped two cups of coffee, then decided to spend the afternoon following the path she had learned last night. She would find that boutique and purchase new nightgowns. She would also find a bookstore and buy herself a good English-Italian dictionary. Then, if Alfred couldn't help her, she would find out what newspaper morgues and record offices she could get to so she could study the media coverage of Mario's death and see what had been written about the involvement of her father, and everyone in the household.

So decided, she ran upstairs for her purse, then found Genovese in the hallway and told him that she'd be gone for most of the afternoon.

He was like a very concerned parent, offering to accompany her so that she didn't get lost. Chris assured him that she was a seasoned traveler, and that even if her command of the Italian language was close to nil, she knew enough to get around the streets.

He still appeared unhappy when she left.

But Chris loved her afternoon out. She found exactly what she wanted in the boutique: nightgowns so all-encompassing that only her face and hands were left bare. On impulse she also bought a stunning black cocktail gown that had been greatly reduced in price.

It was fun to wander around. She adored all the alleyways and little bridges and the beautiful old churches she came to on almost every corner. She stopped at a little sidewalk café and bought herself cappuccino and some bread and cheese for lunch, and tried to think out all of the things she had learned since coming to the palazzo.

But uneasiness settled over her again, the feeling that something was about to happen. Ridiculous, she told herself. It was just Venice. She was allowing herself to get wrapped up in the past, and it was nothing less than ridiculous.

But she was convinced that someone had been in her room last night. Marcus? He had been up; he had caught her as easily and stealthily as if he had been waiting for her....

No, he wouldn't lie. Why not? she charged herself. Because he was Marcus. Because she...

Was falling beneath his spell. Thinking about him in the bright sunlight made her shiver, then grow hot.

Impatiently, Chris paid her bill and started to wander back toward the palazzo. Alfred would tell her something on Friday, she was convinced. She would prove her father's innocence, then bow regally out of the picture and return to Paris, where she could decide what she wanted to do with the rest of her life.

Thinking about her life reminded Chris that she had spent a day with no exercise at all. When she returned to the palazzo she hurried straight to her room, changed into a leotard and worked out on the floor to limber her muscles.

When she decided she had practiced long enough for a seasoned mime on vacation, she was thirsty. Not trusting her system to Italian tap water—even in Paris, she drank only bottled water—Chris decided to find the kitchen and get a drink. She drew a skirt on over her leotard and tights and hurried down the stairs in her dance slippers, remembering to follow the arched hallway to the right.

She found the formal dining room—a huge place containing a grand old table with enough chairs for twenty people—and knew the kitchen must be right through the archway behind it.

But at the archway, Chris paused.

People were arguing in the kitchen. Violently. Two voices were rising in very rapid, very vehement Italian.

One of the voices belonged to Alfred Contini. The other, Chris realized slowly, belonged to Genovese.

She paused for several seconds, then decided that she didn't want to be caught eavesdropping, even if she couldn't understand a word. She hurried back through the dining room to the entryway, then decided to wander out to the courtyard. There might be something to drink set out on one of the serving carts, and she hoped that Alfred would make an appearance, and possibly explain something about what had been going on.

But Chris never reached the courtyard. She noticed a wrought-iron gate in the center of the hallway that she hadn't registered before. She paused, then walked toward it.

It led to a sweeping set of marble steps that went downward into darkness.

There was something about the steps that touched a chord in her memory. Wide white marble going downward into darkness. They were probably like a hundred others in Italy, Chris reminded herself, leading beneath the main level of the palazzo to the catacombs . . . and the chapel, she assumed. Gina had been down there earlier, wanting privacy. But that had been hours ago. Marcus had warned her that the subterranean tunnels weren't safe, but surely the chapel was or else Gina would not have been there.

Chris shrugged a little uncomfortably. None of it really mattered. She knew she was going to go down the steps. There was simply something there that . . . beckoned to her.

She opened the gate and started down, her footsteps very silent in her slippers. Her breath came quickly, and yet she wasn't frightened at all, just very curious and anticipatory.

Darkness quickly fell around her, but then she saw light ahead of her coming from one side. She reached the last step. It was cavernous here; great unadorned arches swept away in perfect symmetry to her left. They faded into darkness, and Chris knew that they marked the tunnel that led beneath the water to the galleries. To the right, from where the light came, was the chapel.

She walked quickly to it.

It was a simple chapel; there was an altar with a large gold cross, and several pews. The ceiling was frescoed, and various religious paintings lined the walls. Chris walked forward to stare at the altar, shivering a little. She knew that she had been here before.

"You recognize our chapel?"

The question was softly voiced. Chris spun around. Gina di Medici was kneeling in the last pew. Chris hadn't seen her because she had been hidden from view by the doorway.

"Yes," Chris answered Gina. Then she added, "I'm sorry to disturb you. I—I didn't think you'd be here so long."

Gina smiled—sadly, Chris thought—and stood to walk up to Chris.

"When you were a child you loved to come here to play. We tried to tell you that it was a place for sanctity, but you did not care to listen. Someone told you that the original di Medicis claimed to have built their altar with a tiny bone fragment belonging to St. Mark at its center. You wanted us to tear up the altar so that you could see the bone."

Chris grimaced. "I'm afraid I must have been a rather irreverent child."

Gina waved a hand in the air. "All children are irreverent, yes?"

"I hope," Chris murmured. Gina's words were quiet, and they seemed friendly. But her eyes, so crystal blue, held the sadness that never failed to touch Chris. Suddenly she wanted to leave as desperately as she had wanted to come.

She backed away from Gina. "I'll leave you now, Gina. Truly, I didn't mean to intrude."

"Christina . . . wait. A moment, please."

"Yes?" Chris murmured, forcing herself to stay still. It seemed as if the chapel were shrinking, closing in around her.

"I—I want you to know that I am glad to have you here. I missed you very much when you were taken away. I had no little girl of my own to dress up and your mother and I . . . we were very close. I—I apologize for my manner. I do not seem to be able to let go. . . ."

Chris paused, holding her determination to clear her father in check. "Gina, for yourself and no one else, you must let go. You're a beautiful woman; there can be more happiness."

"Yes, so they say. It was just that Mario..." She hesitated and her eyes were astute as they stared bluntly into Chris's. Her voice was very soft when she spoke. "Marcus is very much like his father. You will know what I mean."

"Both of your sons are wonderful, Gina. You should be very proud."

She smiled dryly. "Tony... he is a fine son. I bless God each time I see him. But you cannot deny that you feel the strange power that belongs to Marcus. It is a power that compels women, yes? He is a man who harbors his secrets, and not even I know him well. He is intense, and perhaps there lies the fascination. Such a man was Mario. I loved him with all my heart, with all of me, and I have not found that which I lost with him yet. But, Christina, you are welcome here."

"Thank you," Chris murmured, but more than ever she wanted to flee. The candlelight in the chapel was flickering; for a moment Gina's eyes seemed very wild and Chris wondered if she hadn't lost a bit of her sanity. Any woman who spent hours and hours closeted in an ancient chapel...

She began backing away and Gina was still smiling.

"I'm terribly thirsty," Chris murmured. "The stairs just seemed to beckon...."

"There will be lemonade in the courtyard," Gina told her.

"Thank you," Chris said, nodding. She tried a brilliant smile, then turned and walked away from the chapel. She didn't even look to the left, to the dark subterranean tunnels, as she hurried to the steps.

But once she was halfway up the marble steps she started to feel ridiculous again. She had literally almost run away from Contessa di Medici, gentle lovely Gina.

Chris shrugged as she turned to reclose the gate.

Had she really been frightened? Or had she, perhaps, been merely ill at ease because Gina had seen—and commented on—her reactions to Marcus di Medici.

Oh, God! Just what was her reaction to the man? Yes, he was compelling; yes, he was intense. Yes, he could touch her and make her feel as if her blood sizzled and her soul drifted on clouds....

And he was secretive, too. Dark and intriguing. She didn't trust him; he made her wary. She was also willing to swear that he was innocent when she didn't even know of what he might be accused!

She emitted an aggravated little sound to herself and hurried down the hallway to the inner terrace, then out to the courtyard. She smiled then, because Alfred was sitting at the table, alone. His old head was leaned back, the waning afternoon sun shining on his bald spot. His eyes were closed as if he were resting.

Christina walked over to him. She was about to speak when he murmured something in Italian. She frowned, thinking he had dozed and was talking to himself. Then he murmured aloud in English. "Blackmail, blackmail... never pay a blackmailer."

He seemed very disturbed; his face was growing a mottled color. Chris knelt at his side, loosening his tie.

"Alfred! Alfred! Wake up, you're distressing yourself!"

His eyes flew open. For a moment he appeared absolutely panicked. Then he saw who was there, and his color faded back to normal. "Christina," he said, sounding relieved. He caught her hand and patted it.

"Alfred, what's wrong? You said you needed me. Let me help you."

"Never pay a blackmailer, Christi. Never live with a lie."

"Tell me about it, Alfred."

He lowered his voice. "I will, I will, at the galleries Friday. When we are alone. Absolutely alone!" He was looking over her head. Chris spun around quickly.

The house had seemed so empty for so long. But now, it seemed, everyone was coming to the courtyard.

Gina was smiling and heading toward them. Sophia was right behind her with Genovese, apparently giving him instructions in Italian. And behind them was Marcus di Medici.

His eyes, dark and intent, stared searingly—warningly?—straight into her own.

Chapter 5

Fifteen minutes later Chris was still trying to decide just who in the household frightened Alfred Contini.

They were all seated around the table, sipping drinks, lazily watching the sunset. Alfred was querying Marcus about a trip he had made that afternoon to an old church, and Sophia—all friendliness and charm this evening—was asking Chris numerous questions about the United States. Genovese had served the drinks, then disappeared.

It seemed to be nothing more than an easy social gathering.

But each time Chris looked at Alfred Contini, she thought the old man was still disturbed. It made her unhappy to see that; in the little time that she'd had with him, she'd come to like him very much.

Blackmail...

He'd been muttering away about blackmail. Who would be blackmailing him and why?

Unless, she thought fleetingly, it had something to do with Mario di Medici's death. Someone might know that James

Tarleton hadn't murdered Mario. And that same someone might know who had. And they could be blackmailing Alfred....

She shook her head unconsciously. Why blackmail Alfred...unless Alfred had been the murderer. She couldn't accept that any more than she could accept the accusation that her father had been the murderer. Was he protecting someone, then?

Who?

There was a rustle of sound from the gate to the Via di Medici. Dressed in their solid business suits, Joe Conseli and Fredo Talio were coming to join the group. Fredo's smile was wide across his robust face. Next to him, the sallow Joe seemed saturnine even though, Chris realized, he was smiling, too.

"Fredo, Joe!" Sophia rose to greet them, linking arms with both men and bringing them to the table. Gina also rose to accept kisses on the cheek. Both men greeted Chris cordially, then apologized and began to speak quickly in Italian to Marcus. Apparently the discussion was strictly business. And then everyone was speaking Italian. Chris was glad to realize that she was beginning to recognize some of the words. It was obvious to her that they were discussing the galleries. First, something about one of the figures: it seemed that a costume had been completed for Catherine di Medici. Second, the tourist board had asked that the galleries be kept open on a certain night in August for a student affair. Chris was rather proud of herself for having followed the conversation that far. But apparently it wasn't quite good enough, because Alfred lowered his voice to speak in an aside to her.

"You must study your Italian, Christi! Study it well."

"I will," she murmured, again getting the feeling that Alfred Contini—the de facto patriarch of the family—was desperate.

Who frightened him? she wondered again. Was it Genovese? After all, Alfred had been arguing with Genovese earlier. But he had also clammed up when he had seen Sophia and Gina. And if he did need help, one shocking question remained: why not go to Marcus or Tony?

"How did you like the galleries, Miss Tarleton? Did you have a chance to view them all?"

The question came from Joe Conseli. It was politely asked, but she had the strangest feeling that it wasn't a casual question, that he was listening intently for her answer.

"I saw a lot, and of course, I was wonderfully impressed," Chris told him. "I suppose it would take days to really see it all."

"Ah, yes, of course! To study each piece!" Fredo said.

"I'm sure she'll get the chance to study everything as thoroughly as she chooses," Marcus said, and Chris found his speculative gaze on her.

She smiled. "I do plan to study everything," she told him levelly.

He smiled briefly in return. Then Fredo asked him about something, and he replied in Italian.

Chris suddenly felt like screaming. Everything that was said, every glance in her direction, seemed filled with intangible undercurrents. Was it just her? she wondered. Or had all this been going on for years?

"Would you care to come?"

"What? Pardon?" Chris murmured, startled. The question had come from Marcus. For once she had been completely unaware of his eyes raking over her.

"I said, would you like to come with me?"

"Uh, where?" Chris murmured uneasily, fully aware now that everyone at the table was staring at her.

Gina di Medici laughed suddenly. "Christina, where have you been? Gathering wool? Marcus has been talking about the Church of the Little Flower."

"Oh? I'm sorry. I suppose I was lost in thought. What is the Church of the Little Flower?"

"Just what it sounds like: a church," Alfred said with a grunt. "A sinking church, at that. But Marc is on a committee that tries to save old buildings."

"You really should go with him," Sophia purred, smiling at Chris with rather icy eyes. Chris assumed that Sophia would love to see her anywhere except there.

"Yes," Gina said, suddenly grasping Chris's hand. "Go with him. You will enjoy the trip."

You *are* both gorgons, Chris thought fleetingly. Both Sophia and Gina were looking at her as if they were sending her off to be fed to a dragon and were very pleased with the idea.

Or were they? Perhaps they were just being polite. The "dragon," in this case, was Gina's son.

And Gina knew that something was going on between Chris and Marcus. Did she approve, or disapprove?

She seemed a lot like Marcus, welcoming her and repelling her, all in one breath.

"Christina?"

Marcus was on his feet, waiting. Chris shrugged. Marcus was behind her, pulling out her chair. "We go by the front," he murmured, so she waved goodbye to the others, feeling that they were all relieved to see her go.

Chris started to walk ahead, then decided it was too unnerving not to know where he was. She paused and turned, only to discover that he was right at her elbow.

"Where are we going?" she asked him.

He laughed. "Down to the Grand Canal, and then we take a left."

Chris smiled. He opened the carved front doors and caught her hand to lead her down to the di Medici *pali* that guarded the boats.

"The motor launch," he told her, and she felt lighthearted for a change as he led her to a small motorboat. He hopped in, caught her about the waist and brought her down to him. She sat on a plank at the rear of the boat, by the tiller.

Chris stared out at the buildings they passed. Venice was beautiful by day, she thought, but it was magnificent by night. Even the shabbier palaces appeared beautiful, cast in soft light. The water shimmered, and the air seemed exceptionally cool and fresh, and subtly exciting.

And Marcus...

As ever, he held his own excitement and fascination.

They turned into a small canal, and a moment later he murmured. "There she is, the Church of the Little Flower. What do you think?"

"What do I think...?" Chris murmured, and she stared at the church as they approached it. The architecture appeared to be Venetian Gothic. It was a pretty church, with numerous coats of arms displayed along the rooftop. It was small, though, and the steps seemed particularly close to the water.

"It's... nice," Chris murmured.

He smiled at her. "Take a closer look."

She did, and he waited, killing the motor and letting them drift toward the building. "The walls! They're crumbling... and the steps are too close to the water."

"Exactly," Marcus murmured. Then the double doors—richly carved with saints, but with warping wood—swung open.

"Conte di Medici! Marcus! *Buona sera*."

There was more, spoken in a deep male voice, but Chris lost the flow of words. It was a young man who spoke, about the same age as Marcus or Tony. He kept up a smooth flow of words until he saw Chris; then he broke off suddenly. Chris could follow his next words. He asked Marcus who the beautiful woman might be. She smiled a little dryly. Italian men did tend to be flirts.

"*Una Americana. Parli inglese*, Salvatore."

"Hello, hello, hello!" Salvatore said, reaching to help Chris from the boat. She liked the firm grip of his hand, his flashing dark eyes and his smile.

"Hello, Salvatore," she said with a smile. She instantly felt Marcus's hand at her waist; he had lost no time moving behind with a single lithe step from the boat.

"Sal, Chris Tarleton. Chris, Sal Astrella. A very old friend."

They smiled at one another. "Come, come, and see what you think," Sal said, ushering them into the church.

Chris followed them, not at all sure what they were looking for as they walked around the small building. The sides of the room were lined with small altars, and there was, of course, the main altar. There were numerous beautiful paintings, and a magnificent pulpit near the main altar, but like the facade of the building, it appeared to be rotting. The stone floor was worn smooth.

"Eh, *mi parla*, Marcus!" Sal murmured at last.

Marcus looked at Sal with a grimace. "The committee has refused to take it on?"

Sal nodded.

"I can see why. The costs will be atrocious."

"I'm willing, if you are."

"What are you talking about?" Chris asked at last.

Both men turned to her and laughed. "We both belong to a committee that works to preserve our buildings," Sal told her.

"But the committee has refused to take on this church. They say it is too far gone."

"So you see, sometimes Marc and I try to save buildings ourselves."

"But usually," Marcus murmured, grimacing once again, "we do so to resell."

Sal laughed. "Often to Americans at that, those who wish to have a second home in Italy."

"But you can't resell this time?" Chris asked.

Sal slipped an arm around her shoulder and walked her toward the main altar. "Christina, see that altar? Cardinal Valotti of the sixteenth century is buried within. He is a saint to these people! You see, this is a parish. Father Donato came to me when the building was condemned. The people do not want to lose their neighborhood *chiesa*."

"I see," Chris told him, and she did. It would be a terrible thing to see people lose a place they held so very dear.

Sal turned around. "Well, Marcus?"

He shrugged. "It will need pilings. All the wood has worm rot. The frescoes must all be refinished. There is nothing that doesn't need work."

Sal grinned. "I know. Well?"

"It's a challenge."

"Then you agree?"

He shrugged. "Why not? You'll put me in the poorhouse yet. When the Palazzo di Medici starts to sink into the sea, I hope you'll be there to bail me out!" He smiled as he approached them, spoke lightly to Sal and caught Chris's hand to pull her back to his side.

"*Bene, bene!*" Sal laughed. "Shall we celebrate with something?"

"Chris?"

"Why not?" she murmured.

They left together, and Chris was glad of Sal's company. He was serious, but young and entertaining, and she liked to see the easy repartee he and Marcus enjoyed.

It was, she decided, the first time she had ever seen Marcus appear so young himself. He smiled frequently and relaxed.

They went to a slightly rowdy bistro. Pop music was being played loudly, most of it American or English. Chris learned that Sal was an attorney, that he didn't really know a thing about art, and had no association with the galleries. She liked him all the more because of it.

She told Sal that she was a mime, and he demanded a demonstration so beseechingly that she laughed and tried to teach him the principles of pulling a string. He was hopeless using only his fingers.

"Sal!" She laughed. "You must bring down the wrist first, and allow the hand to follow."

She showed him again, and he shook his head, watching her admiringly. "You must be very good."

"She is excellent," Marcus said softly, and Chris was amazed by the tenor of his voice; his words were spoken with no mockery, and nothing danced in the cobalt depths of his eyes except for what appeared to be honest admiration and affection.

They ordered German beer and thick Italian pizzas, the original pies baked in pans and loaded with tomatoes, fresh cheeses, oregano and parsley. Chris danced with Sal, and then she danced with Marcus. As it happened, the music slowed for them; it was an Italian love song.

With one hand he clasped her fingers to his chest; he rested the other at the base of her spine. Her cheek leaned against the fabric of his jacket, and she felt her heart beating painfully.

There were things going on at the palazzo; intrigue shrouded in the shadows of the past was surfacing again. She knew it. Marcus was a part of it all, a dark and dangerous part. Twenty-one years ago there had been a murder of which her father had been accused; this very afternoon Alfred Contini had cried in his doze about blackmail.

But here, held so close to Marcus, feeling the heat and hardness of his body, letting the arresting male scent of him flow over her, Chris could only believe what her heart cried out.

Whatever it was, Marcus was innocent.

She heard his words whispered in her ear as his head dipped to hers. "You move like a gazelle, Christi.... Did you know that? Or a cat, ever graceful. Or a floating swan."

She tilted her head back and smiled, dazzled by the warmth in his eyes. "No, Marcus, *you* are the cat. A panther, stalking in the night."

He laughed, startled by her comparison. "Do I stalk you, Christina?"

"I don't know," she replied honestly.

His slightly secretive smile remained on his lips; he lowered his head slowly, and his lips touched hers lightly. She didn't think to twist away; his mouth was warm and fascinating, and it was the merest brush of a kiss, gone very quickly yet leaving her aching for more of that almost speculative and musing—but tender—touch.

His eyes touched hers with their intriguing glitter. Before either of them could speak he pressed her head back to his chest, and they swirled with the dance.

"How are you doing with Alfred?" he asked her.

She stiffened a bit, angered by his caustic tone—especially since he had just kissed her. "How am I doing?" she asked sharply.

"Have you convinced him to leave all his money to you?"

Was he teasing her? she wondered desperately. She was so easily lulled by him. She had to remain on guard against him. "I'm trying," she said sweetly.

"Umm," he murmured noncommittally. "It will be a pity if he leaves it to you. Then you will not need to try for a di Medici husband."

"A pity?" she demanded, casting her head back again. "But I told you, I would opt for Tony, anyway."

Chris thought that his smile was very grim. The music hadn't stopped, but he led her from the dance floor. Sal had ordered another round of beer, and the evening remained pleasant, but Chris felt as if a special warmth she had touched upon briefly had disappeared before she'd known it was within reach.

They dropped Sal off in front of the church. He said something in Italian to Marcus, and Marcus shrugged, then spoke. Chris thought he said that Sal should say to someone named Anna whatever he wished.

Sal told Chris that he hoped he would see her again soon; Chris echoed the sentiment, and then she was alone with Marcus once again as he steered the boat toward home.

"Who is Anna?" she asked lightly.

He cast her a noncommittal glance. "A friend," he said briefly. Chris fell silent. She felt as if a tension were growing within her, getting stronger the closer they came to the palazzo. Suddenly she wanted to challenge Marcus. She desperately needed to know where he stood about things.

"I think that Alfred Contini is being blackmailed," she said flatly—and calmly, she hoped. "Do you have any idea who might be doing such a thing to him, or why?"

"Blackmail?" He frowned as he gazed at her, as if drawn from his own distant thoughts. "Good Lord, no. Who would blackmail Alfred? And as you say, for what?"

Was his surprise genuine? she wondered. Or had his eyes narrowed a little suspicously?

"I don't know," Chris said, looking out at the water and wondering if she weren't a complete fool. "Something that happened in the past, I would think."

"Think!" Marcus muttered with annoyance. "Christina, your imagination is wild. You play in the field of illusion so frequently that you see things that do not exist."

"I do not! And my father didn't kill your father, which means that someone else did. And maybe Alfred knows who and—"

"Damn it, Chris, stop it! Stop it, do you hear me?" His hand left the tiller to catch her chin and tug it around roughly so that she met his eyes, harsh now as they reflected the water. "Don't run around with your idle accusations."

"Why? If they *are* idle, what do I have to fear?"

He began to swear vigorously in Italian. Chris pulled her chin from his grasp, feeling ridiculously close to tears. She barely noticed as the boat docked; she only became aware of where they were when he stepped over her, reached for her hands and practically dragged her to the steps.

"Let go of me," she muttered.

"No, not until you listen to me. You cannot change what happened; you can only cause trouble. Keep your mouth shut, Christina."

"I—"

"Just what are you out to do, Chris? Is this to be a form of vengeance? Do you feel that your father was cheated, and so you will torment us all? Are you after Alfred's money? Or perhaps you really have determined that having a di Medici husband would be the best vengeance for the wrongs supposedly done the Tarletons!"

"What?"

"What are you up to, Christina?"

"I'm trying to find out the truth!" she raged. And then she wrenched her hands from his. "*Buona sera*, Marcus. Thank you for the outing."

Chris left him and hurried to the elaborately carved doors of the palazzo. She wrenched them open and hurried up the steps to her room.

She changed into one of her new ultramodest gowns and lay down to go to sleep.

But sleep was elusive. All she could think of was Marcus's dark eyes. The threat in them, and the barely leashed intensity of his anger. And the warmth that had burned so briefly...

And Alfred. Muttering so disturbingly about blackmail.

When she did sleep, it was restlessly. She woke sometime during the night and opened her eyes slowly. She almost started when she realized that someone was definitely at her terrace doors. She was so frightened at first that she couldn't move or scream, and then she didn't want to.

It was Marcus. She recognized his tall dark form, the silence of his movement. He walked across the room and checked the lock on her hallway door, then paused briefly to glance at her. Chris hurriedly slitted her eyes, watching him from the shadow of her lashes.

He seemed to accept the fact that she was sleeping peacefully and turned to disappear onto the terrace.

She lay awake for a long time again, afraid to wonder if his anger had been a bluff... and if he might really be concerned for her safety.

With the morning sun pouring through the terrace doors, Chris stretched and slowly wakened, a frown furrowing her brow.

The loud strains of a rock song by Duran Duran seemed to be shivering through the very walls of the palazzo.

Duran Duran? Chris smiled, hurried out of bed and decided on a light knit dress for the day since it was Friday at last, and she would finally get to meet Alfred at the galleries. Then she hurried downstairs to find out why the house was filled with music.

As soon as she reached the courtyard she knew. Tony had returned from Florence.

He was sitting at the table, rocking to the beat with a knife and spoon. He saw Chris when she entered, grinned like a minor-league devil and jumped up to give her a hug.

"Christi! You waited for me to return. You didn't let any of the demons or gorgons chase you away."

Chris laughed and hugged him in return, then stepped away from him, lifting a brow to indicate the music that filled the courtyard. "A bit loud, isn't it?"

"Only a bit. Eh, Christi, the gorgons are all out. I can blare to my heart's content and offend no one. Unless, of course, it's bothering you?"

Chris shook her head. Tony poured her a cup of coffee and extravagantly pulled out a chair.

He smiled at her as he pulled his own chair close. "You see, the palazzo only looks as if it's old enough to sink into the sea. It's been totally rewired—except, of course, below—and Marcus and I put in sound systems and speakers years ago. I mean, it's as necessary as indoor plumbing these days, you know."

"Umm, sure," Chris murmured. The Duran Duran tape ended and something by David Bowie began. "How was Florence?"

"Lovely... except that her name is Angela."

"Oh, and you had me languishing away here with the gorgons!"

He teased the back of her hand with a playful finger. "Ah, but I lost you before I ever had the chance to meet you, didn't I?"

He spoke softly, looking over her shoulder. The music danced around her with a rhythmic sensual beat, yet that wasn't what made her tremble.

The song playing was called "Cat People." Chris thought it was rather apropos.

She spun around. As she had expected, Marcus was standing there, hands in his pockets, watching her and Tony. He was in dark jeans and a navy denim work jacket that was dusted with a little plaster. How long had he been standing there? she wondered. Not long, she decided, as she realized he was walking over to them. But his movements...it seemed as if he moved in step to the sexual beat of the music, as if he could turn into a black panther at any minute and continue after his prey.

"Hey, Antonio, are you coming down?" he asked his brother, passing them and going to the serving cart to pour himself some orange juice. He didn't sit at the table but leaned against it, nodding at Chris and giving her a crisp, "Good morning."

Tony grimaced. "Yeah, I'm coming. What have the workmen said so far?"

Marcus shrugged. Chris watched the ripple of his shoulder muscles. "They say it's not as bad as we thought. The tunnel is good, and the construction is sound there, and in the foundations for both the galleries and the palazzo. We have no leaks. There's just one section they say should be reinforced, down beneath the galleries."

"The land of deep dark family secrets!" Tony teased Chris.

"Come help, Tony," Marcus prompted his brother irritably. "I've got to get to the galleries and take a look at the books; we do have a problem somewhere. You've—"

"Trouble with the books?" Chris interrupted him. Did he suspect embezzlement?

He sighed. "Chris, it isn't your concern. Just something that I have to look into." He turned back to Tony, dismissing her query. "Tony, you've got to be there by this afternoon to check in the tapestries that you bought in Florence. Right now the workers are plugging up some holes in the inner wall and the tunnel. They could use some help and supervision . . . to make sure it will be done."

"Okay, okay!" Tony grinned. "No rest for the weary!" he groaned to Chris. "Eh, Marcus. Let's do something tonight, shall we? You could give Anna a call, and Chris and I—"

"I think you'd better give that a little thought, Tony," Marcus interrupted him, grinning. "Katrina Loggia has called the galleries at least five times in your absence. Once to tell me I was aiding and abetting your wanton life-style by sending you out of town so frequently." He paused a minute. "Maybe you'd better call Katrina. She's the best woman you've found yet."

"Ah, but I can't leave the 'Bella Christi'!"

"You won't. Chris and I will come with you."

"What about Anna? Shall we allow her to lie languishing?"

"Anna never languishes," Marcus said dryly.

"Hey, hey!" Chris interrupted. "I'm an adult. They told me so when I turned twenty-one, and that was several years ago. You both go out with your friends. I'm perfectly capable of taking care of myself. And good heavens," she teased, smiling as she looked at Tony, "if I'm going to con Alfred out of all his money, I'm going to have to spend some time with him."

"True, true," Tony mused, responding to her teasing. "But, in case all fails with Alfred—"

"And you wish to entrap a di Medici husband," Marcus interrupted, rising fluidly, coming behind her and playing gently with her hair, "then you should be working on the di Medicis."

"Seriously," Chris murmured, very aware of his touch, of his presence behind her, "I've . . . got some shopping to do this afternoon. If I went out it would have to be late."

"Everything is late in Italy," Tony told her.

"Yes, as in work," Marcus reminded him.

"I'll be right down. Can I just finish my coffee, master?" Tony asked his brother, grinning.

"If you can drink fast," Marcus replied, chuckling.

"I could help," Chris offered.

"And delve into the family closets? Never!" Tony said. "No, Christi. When it's all fixed up, you can come through."

Chris turned around with a strange feeling. Marcus was gone.

"He's like a damned panther!" she muttered. He could move without a sound.

Tony laughed. "Brother Marcus, you mean? No sound upon the step and all, eh?"

"Umm. Stealthy."

"And the eyes . . . kind of searing?"

"Deadly and dangerous," Chris agreed with dry solemnity.

Tony laughed again, truly enjoying her comments. "Well, if you're handling a black panther, you'd better pull out your whip and chair! And I'd better get down there." He reluctantly pulled out his chair to rise, then said, "Chris, I almost forgot. Alfred left you a note. It's on the serving cart. Ah . . . here it is."

"Thanks," Chris murmured, accepting the note. She glanced at it a bit quizzically. It was in an envelope, and though the envelope hadn't been ripped, it looked as if it had been opened and resealed. She opened it quickly herself, waving absently as Tony murmured again that he had to get below.

"*Cara* Christi," it read. "Make it the gem salon, six-thirty this evening. *Per favore*. I'll see that the doors are open. Alfred."

Something made Chris call out quickly to Tony. He paused just before entering the inner terrace, shading his eyes from the sun with a hand as he looked back to her.

"Tony, who has been around this morning?"

"Around?" He sounded mystified.

"Yes. Around the courtyard. Besides yourself."

"Marcus, of course. Sophia, Genovese. My mother. Oh, Fredo and Joe were even by." He shrugged. "Everyone, I suppose. Why?"

"Oh, nothing. I was just wondering." She smiled sweetly. "If you all want to go out later, nine or ten o'clock would be fine with me."

Tony nodded and waved again. Chris sat pensively at the table for a while, drank her coffee without tasting it, then went back upstairs.

She spent an hour exercising, then paused without really knowing why and looked around her room.

Things seemed . . . different. Nothing major, and nothing seemed to be gone. But a brush seemed to be placed at a different end of the dresser. She had tossed her handbag on the pillows after making the bed; now it was below the pillows.

Chris shrugged, but tingles burned along her neck and down her spine. She stood and looked through the drawers. Her things were all in order, but they, too, seemed . . . different.

Uneasily she showered, redonned her knit dress and determined to leave the palazzo. Until it was time to meet Alfred and find out what was going on, she didn't want to be around the di Medicis or their home.

Chris took herself on a sight-seeing trip, visiting a number of art galleries, museums and cathedrals. She also went into one of the tourist offices and asked about getting access to public records. The friendly girl on duty gave her a map and a list of libraries and offices, and Chris decided that her day had been well spent.

She had been using public transportation—the vaporetti—and they hadn't been running exactly on time. By the
time she reached the square in front of the galleries—the
Piazza di Medici/Contini, she noted dryly—it was closer to
seven o'clock than it was to six-thirty.

And it was growing dark.

Chris hurried up the steps to the main entrance; not until
she was almost there did she slow her pace.

There were lights within the galleries, but they were pale
and muted. The ancient building suddenly seemed sinister
beneath the moonlight.

What am I getting myself into? Chris wondered belat-
edly. She had never really stopped to think about personal
danger, even though it seemed that Marcus was constantly
warning her to be careful. Was that because he *did* know
something she didn't?

Chris gave herself a serious shake. She had come this far
because she wanted Alfred to talk to her, to confide in her
and let her help him. There was nothing sinister about a
building. Even an ancient building, filled with cavernous
passages and shadowed archways and the secrets of the
centuries. . . .

"Quiet!" she warned herself aloud, and hurried up the
last of the steps. But she found herself looking around when
she reached the main doors. The piazza was empty except
for a few pigeons. In the distance on the water, a pair of
gondoliers were shouting to one another. In the other direction, down the via from the piazza, a couple of lovers
were disappearing arm in arm down an alleyway.

Chris pulled at the door; as Alfred had promised it was
open. She slipped inside.

It was even eerier to be inside the galleries at night than it
was to look at them. She inhaled deeply and the sound
seemed to echo. She held her breath, then exhaled very
softly.

She could have sworn she heard her heart beating like
thunder.

The inner courtyard was in front of her with its empty concierge stands, shadowed marbles and tiles, statues and archways. Chris closed her eyes for a minute, leaning against the door. It would be after seven o'clock now. She was lucky that Alfred hadn't chosen to leave.

She might be uneasy—she refused to even think the word "frightened"—but she might also be within an inch of clearing her father's name.

With that in mind Chris straightened and headed for the left-hand stairway. The banister felt like ice beneath her fingers. And despite all her reasoning, the higher she climbed, the more furiously her heart seemed to beat.

She passed the doors to the historical exhibit. They were open, and as she glanced in she shivered. All the figures stared out at her from the darkness, posed, eyes wide, arms outstretched.

Almost as if they were beckoning to her to join them.

Chris shivered, then was furious again with herself for being ridiculous.

She hurried on. The gem salon would be next.

But as she neared those doors she slowed her pace, then came to a dead standstill. Someone was whispering in the salon, and someone else was replying furiously. They were speaking in Italian, low but vehement.

She should run, get the hell out of there, Chris thought. But logic didn't seem to have much control over her actions. Without conscious thought she moved closer to the doors, until she was staring into the salon.

Alfred was there, standing right in front of the case with the di Medici jewels and directly beneath the skylight. Moonlight pouring in like quicksilver displayed his features clearly. They were strained and angry, and tinged with an unhealthy pallor.

But despite the moonlight, Chris couldn't see the features of the other person at all. She couldn't even tell if it was a man or a woman. It might have been a gargoyle that had crawled down from the ceiling for all that she could tell; the figure was clothed from head to toe in a hooded cloak.

"No, no, *no!*" Alfred exclaimed, slamming a fist down on the glass case. Chris flinched, expecting it to shatter. But it didn't and she noted that a piece of paper floated to the floor, unseen by either Alfred or the hooded figure. What was it? Chris wondered. The subject of the argument?

Alfred threw his hands up and stalked to the left side of the room. The figure followed. The words were coming more and more quickly between them, more and more vehemently. Chris swallowed, certain that her presence would break up the argument. She should just burst in with a cheerful "hello" and a broad smile on her lips.

She started to do just that, but suddenly Alfred stood dead still and shouted in English to the figure, *"Murder! Blackmail! Where and when does it end!"*

Chris was halfway across the room. Something about his words warned her of imminent danger. Instinctively she pitched to the floor and rolled silently until she was hidden behind the case containing the di Medici jewels. How well she was hidden she didn't know, because the moonlight was almost like a flashlight on her, streaking through the skylight.

With her heart pounding at a fevered pitch, she crept to her knees to look beyond the case and a scream froze in her throat. Alfred was screaming, *"No!"*

And the moonlight, powerful, glowing quicksilver, was reflecting off the blade of a raised knife.

"No!" Alfred shouted again, and then he was running past the cloaked figure and out of the salon. The figure followed him with a whirl of flowing fabric. Chris heard their footsteps clattering on the stairs; she heard the great front doors being thrown open and falling shut.

She left her hiding place behind the case with little thought and tore down the stairs herself, not realizing until later how foolish the action had been. But Alfred was out there being chased by a figure in a flowing robe who was wielding a knife.

She didn't notice a thing about the courtyard as she raced through it; she, too, yanked open the doors with a vehemence. Heaving, panting, she raced down the steps to the piazza, and there, right beside a little fountain, she saw Alfred suddenly pause in flight, clutching at his heart.

The cloaked figure was nowhere to be seen.

"Alfred!" Chris screamed, and sobs tore from her along with her breath as she raced to him.

"Alfred! Alfred!" She curled her arms around him, trying to help him stand. The piazza was absurdly empty in the glowing moonlight. He was too heavy. He began to sink to the ground; she sank along with him, trying to protect his head and keep him warm with her own warmth.

"Help!" she screamed to the night.

"Christi, Christi..." His eyes were open, dazed, but deep-brown and luminous, staring into hers. "Help me...."

"I'm here, Alfred, I'm here. I'll help you. I have to attract someone—"

"Oh, God, Christi! The sins of the past. They catch us all." With a sudden burst of energy he grasped her shoulder, his fingers painful and desperate. "Careful, Chris, careful. It was my fault. I paid. I hid the truth. Be careful. Marcus—"

His voice broke off. A terrible chill swept over Chris. Was he telling her to be careful of Marcus or to go to Marcus for help?

"Alfred, don't try to talk. I've got to get help!"

At last, Chris saw people emerging from the alleyway. A man, a woman and a child, chattering as they ambled along in the night.

"Help!" Chris screamed, hoping the fear in her voice would atone for her lack of Italian. She racked her memory furiously for the right words. *"Attenzione! Attenzione! Dove un medico? Per favore, un medico!"*

The woman began to cry something excitedly to her husband. The husband raced toward Chris, while the woman started to scream, *"Polizia! Polizia, un medico!"*

The hand that was grasping Chris's shoulder slowly began to relax. She stared into Alfred's eyes again, tears blinding her own. "Christi, *bella* Christi, I brought you into danger. Find the new will. I tried to make reparation.... But watch out. Watch out for—"

"Alfred, don't worry! Rest easy, help is coming."

He shook his head and tried to moisten his dry cracking lips. "Come closer!" he gasped, and she could barely hear him. She lowered her head to his mouth. "I took care of you, Christi. Find the will. You must be careful...you know the truth. Your father didn't kill Mario...you know he didn't. It was my fault. All my fault. And now the years have caught up with us all. They've—"

"Alfred! Stop!" Chris begged. "I'm getting help." She couldn't understand his ramblings; all his words managed to do was steal his remaining strength.

"Christi...watch out for..."

There was nothing more. Numb with pain and fear, Chris raised her head. Alfred was still staring at her. But his eyes were completely glazed. She realized that his chest was moving no more. "No, Alfred!" she cried, and she pressed her ear to his chest.

There was nothing. Not even the faintest beat of hope.

The Italian man was standing beside her; she tried to nod that she understood when he told her that the *polizia* were coming.

And then there was a big commotion on the piazza. It seemed that people were springing from everywhere. Chris could only stare at the ground. She saw a pair of feet and black jean-clad legs coming toward her.

A man bent down beside her, taking Alfred's head from her lap and placing it very gently on the ground. She looked around, still dazed, and saw that it was Marcus. "Goodbye, old friend," he murmured softly. For once his indigo gaze held nothing but tenderness, caring and sadness. His dark features were drawn and strained, his hands, on Alfred and on her, were gentle.

"He is gone, Chris," Marcus said. And he reached to close the lids over the dark-brown eyes of Alfred Contini. When that was done he set his arms around Chris and helped her rise. She was staggering. He drew her very gently against him and smoothed back her hair with a deep protective tenderness.

She broke into tears and turned her face into his chest. "Marcus, he was murdered," she garbled out.

She felt his body stiffen, but barely noticed. "No, Chris, it was a heart attack. Chris, a heart attack."

"No," she murmured.

"Hush! Christina, before God! Hush!"

Swift sizzling fear swamped her senses. Dear God, she couldn't tell anyone what she had seen. If the murderer—the cloaked figure with the gleaming knife who had pursued Alfred until his heart gave out—if he or she knew what Chris had seen . . .

She began to shiver. There were shrill whistles and a flurry of activity. The police came, and a doctor, and a stretcher. A million questions were being thrown at Marcus in Italian; he was answering them all calmly. Chris vaguely heard him explain that she was an American, Alfred's guest, his guest. And she vaguely heard the respect for Marcus in the voices of the officers; she heard them addressing him by his title—and they believed every word he said, and didn't pressure him once. Someone asked something about Alfred, and he hesitated several seconds, then softly said, *"Sì."*

Alfred Contini was gently swathed in a giant sheet, then taken away. The piazza began to clear.

Chris watched, shivering. She buried her face in her hands, and of all things, absently realized that she had lost an earring. What could an earring matter when Alfred had died . . . ?

Marcus gave Chris a little shake.

"Alfred is gone, Chris. We must go home. You must rest from the shock, and I . . ." He inhaled deeply and exhaled sadly. "I must tell my mother, and Sophia."

Chris nodded again. Somehow she was able to walk beside Marcus.

Marcus . . .

Oh, God! What had Alfred been trying to tell her? Was Marcus truly her friend, or was he the dark and sinister danger that she should be fearing?

Marcus . . .

She closed her eyes and swallowed a new rush of tears. Now, feeling his touch, his warmth, his tenderness and his strength, she could believe no evil.

It was strange. With shock and pain foremost in her heart, still she was comforted, and yet trembling again in another way. It felt right to be with Marcus now. But it had always felt somehow right to be with Marcus. Since that first night when she had seen him she had felt the draw, so powerful. . . .

Was she falling in love with him?

Or falling into a trap—from which there would be no escape?

Chapter 6

Three days later Alfred Contini was taken down the Grand Canal one last time.

His gondola was shrouded in black; behind the coffin, keeping a silent vigil, were Sophia Calabrese and Gina di Medici. They, too, were shrouded in black.

Chris, in the next boat between Marcus and Tony, realized that she was more a part of the scene than she would perhaps have been willing to be had she not spent the hours and the days following Alfred's death in an absolute daze.

Like Gina and Sophia, she was clad in black. And she wore a low-brimmed black hat with a black veil.

Everything had been draped in black: the galleries and the palazzo, even the small *chiesa* or church near the galleries where Alfred had attended Mass almost every Sunday for thirty-odd years.

Contini had been a name of importance in his city of merchant princes. And his city had turned out for him. As the parade of gondolas and launches in funeral black traveled along the canal, people lined the streets to throw flowers into the water and murmur prayers for his soul.

Bells were chiming across the city; they seemed to toll heavily upon Chris's heart.

In the days of Alfred's wake she had carefully withdrawn. Sophia had not cried; she had retired to their quarters, begging to be allowed to grieve in private. Gina had cried; Chris had been impressed by her earnest emotion. Alfred Contini had enjoyed one true friend in life, at least.

Tony had been uncustomarily somber; Marcus had been quiet—and completely efficient. He had closed the galleries for several days so that the last of their original founders could be mourned.

The gondolas came to the little *chiesa*. Chris slipped into a pew, between Marcus and Tony once again.

Only Gina could be heard, weeping during the long service and the Mass. Sophia held to her silence.

When it was over the mourners filed from the church. Chris could see a workman tearing at the stones of the floor to the left of the altar; Alfred would be interred in the church he had patronized, as he had planned during his lifetime.

The gondolas, still shrouded in black, began their slow journey back to the palazzo.

But this night no one would be grieving in private. The numerous friends and acquaintances of Alfred Contini would all be pouring into the palazzo. Food and wine would be served in abundance, and Alfred would be eulogized by one and all.

Chris had never felt so lost in a foreign land in all her life. There were so many people there, and they were all speaking in Italian. Marcus never faltered as a host; Chris was introduced to everyone. She noticed that a number of people stared at her peculiarly when they heard her name. Why not? They all assumed that she was the daughter of a man who had murdered a di Medici—it probably did seem strange that she was in the household.

One name in particular caught Chris's attention: Anna Garibaldi. The woman appeared to be in her late twenties; she was very confident in herself and in her movements, which made sense because she was beautiful in a fashion that only an Italian woman could be, Chris thought. Her deep-brown eyes were huge and hidden by luxurious lashes. Her waist was tiny; her hips and breasts flared like any man's fantasy.

Although none of her actions was overt or the slightest bit in bad taste, it was obvious to Chris that she knew both Marcus and Tony very well, and that she was warmly welcomed by Sophia and Gina.

Perfect wife material? Chris wondered, and she couldn't help but feel a horrible stab of jealousy. She didn't really know Marcus at all; she should mistrust him like a snake. He seemed unwaveringly positive that her father was a murderer and Chris wasn't at all certain that he didn't really totally dislike her.

But, she decided, watching him move smoothly among his guests, exchanging quiet words here and there, she must be in really bad shape. No matter what logic said, no matter how sternly she warned herself that he had more reason to be her enemy than her friend, she could not stop her feelings. In her heart she was sure that Marcus could be trusted.

Chris sipped a glass of dark dry wine, wondering if anyone would notice—or care—if she escaped to her room. But right when she was feeling so lost and lonely that she was ready to fly to the stairs, Sal came to her, kissing her cheeks and smiling in warm greeting.

"Chris, how very sad this is for you. I hope you are bearing up all right."

"Yes, yes, I am. Thank you, Sal."

"What will you do now?" he asked her.

She hadn't really thought about it. She should leave; Alfred had asked her here, but now Alfred was dead. Yet how could she leave when she knew he had been murdered and that he had been paying a blackmailer?

Yet how could she stay? she wondered with a shiver. She hadn't been asked to talk to the police. They had simply assumed that he'd had a heart attack while she was with him.

Chris hadn't told a soul about the figure with the knife. Instinct had warned her that her life might depend on her silence.

She hadn't even tried to talk to Marcus. He had been extremely remote. And in the darkness of the night she had begun to doubt herself. Marcus was a di Medici. He had been awfully close—and come awfully quickly—to the scene of the crime. And he needed money.

No, no, no. Marcus would not hide behind a hood and cape; he would not sink to blackmail. He would never have raised a knife against an old and ailing man like Alfred....

But who, then? The deeper she went, the less sense any of it seemed to make.

"Christina?"

"Oh, Sal, I'm sorry. I was thinking, I guess. I—I'm really not sure what I intend to do yet."

"Well, you've got to stay a week, at least."

"For what?"

"The reading of Alfred's will."

"Why? What could it have to do with me?"

Sal smiled. "Alfred was my father's client for years and years. Right after your father left the company, he set up a small trust fund for you."

"Oh," Chris murmured. Then she quickly asked, "Sal, Alfred murmured something to me about a new will once. Does that mean anything to you?"

Sal frowned. "Yes, come to think of it. Last week he called my father at the office and asked him a lot of questions about wills. Dad told him that his was all in order, and Alfred asked what he had to do to legally constitute a new will. But as far as I know he never made one out." Still frowning, he turned around. Chris paled as she saw that

Marcus was right behind him. "Marc, did Alfred say anything to you about making out a new will?"

Indigo eyes immediately fell scathingly on Chris. They flickered over her features briefly. "No, he said nothing to me. But that isn't to say that he didn't. Why? Did you manage to persuade him to bequeath his money to you after all, Christina?"

"He mentioned a new will right before he died, that's all," Chris said, stiffening, but keeping her voice sweet. She smiled at Sal, who appeared ill at ease and startled by the animosity between them. "I assume that the di Medicis inherit the majority of Alfred's holdings?"

"A majority, yes. Sophia, of course, receives her pension. And, as I mentioned, there are various trust funds and the like."

"You'll have to remain on the prowl for a di Medici husband then, Christina," Marcus said blandly, then added, "Excuse me, I believe Tony needs some assistance with the wine."

He nodded, stiff and straight, dark and immaculate and as cold as the moon, and joined Tony behind a serving cart.

Anna wandered over to him. Chris saw his smile flash brilliantly, and she wished she could throw him—bound and gagged—into a canal.

She turned back to Sal and handed him her wineglass. "Sal, I've got a terrible headache. I don't think I'll be missed here. I'm going to try to slip upstairs."

Very nicely, he lifted her fingertips and kissed her hand. "I will miss you, Christina. But go, get some sleep. I'll see you soon."

She smiled her thanks and made a quick disappearance up the stairs. In her room she quickly pulled off her hat and flowing veil and stripped off the depressing black dress.

When her own father had died she had worn light purple. Her father had hated black. And her mother had ordered the church filled with white lilies, smiling through her tears to say that James had always told her that death was but a new life, and she must always think of it that way.

Tiredly, Chris crawled into a white gown, but she couldn't sleep, so she prowled around her room. She stopped in front of her dresser, puzzled as to why she was staring down at it. Then she realized that she was looking at a single earring—a pearl that dangled on a long loop.

There was only one earring because she'd lost the other on the day Alfred had died. She had barely thought about it at the time . . . how could she, when a man had died?

But now it disturbed her, and as she stared at its mate, she slowly understood why.

She had lost it the day Alfred had died. But she could remember playing with it absently on the vaporetto that had taken her to the galleries. She'd had it on then.

And both earrings had bounced against her cheeks when she hurried up the steps. Yet she had realized it was gone just before she walked back to the palazzo with Marcus.

Dizziness swept over her. There could have been only one place where she might have lost it. In the gem salon, when she had pitched to the floor and rolled.

Chris caught her breath, suddenly remembering the sheet of paper that had fallen right by the di Medici jewel case. Right where her earring would be. What had been on the paper? Something to do with the blackmail . . . or the murder?

She shook her head vehemently. She would love to have the paper, but the earring mattered more. If the cloaked figure got into the jewel salon before she did, her earring would be found. And the wielder of the knife, who had sent Alfred running terrified to his death, would know that she had seen everything.

She had to get into the salon and find her earring.

Chris forced herself to lie quietly and tried desperately to figure out how. She couldn't very well ask for a key.

She lay there, closing her eyes tightly, trying to visualize the galleries. All she could see in her mind was the skylight and the moonglow reflecting on the di Medici jewels.

Restlessly she tossed and turned until she realized that the skylight was her only chance. She was a mime, with training in gymnastics. If she was careful she could climb to the roof and descend through the skylight, then find her earring and scurry back up.

The idea terrified her, but it was her only chance.

By the next morning it seemed that the household was beginning to return to normal. The galleries were still closed, but when Chris came downstairs—as late as possible, in the hope that she would be alone—she learned from Genovese that Marcus and Tony had gone to direct some workmen at the Church of the Little Flower.

She thanked Genovese, and felt a little unnerved when he hovered near her. She thought that he was about to say something, but Gina came out to the table. Genovese seated her, then left.

Chris tried to talk to Gina, but Gina wasn't in the best of moods. Or perhaps she had dropped all pretense of courtesy for the day. She looked at Chris and murmured, "It is surprising how people die when you're around, isn't it, Christina?"

Chris excused herself immediately. She left the house and searched the streets until she found a shop where she could buy some strong cord and a grappling hook.

Chris waited until midnight, feeling all the while that she was an idiot. She was going to dress in dark clothing and break into the di Medici galleries like a sneak thief. It was a truly idiotic plan—it was just that she couldn't see any other way. She wanted to trust Marcus; she just didn't dare. She didn't dare let anyone know that she had been in the galleries the night Alfred Contini had died.

She wasn't expecting anyone to be up and around at that hour, but she still planned her exit carefully. The stretchy black outfit she wore could have been street clothing; it was composed of a leotard and knit pants. And her gym slippers could have passed for regular shoes. Her hair was bound at her nape so as not to get in her way, and she carried her rope and grappling hook in what could have passed for a large leather purse.

But she needn't have feared for her appearance as she left the palazzo. She didn't pass a soul when she crept out of the still crepe-decked mansion.

Once she reached the via Chris felt a real case of nerves coming on. Not only was she going to try to scale walls and avoid the alarm system of the galleries, she was walking through streets that were darkly shadowed and might be plagued by an ordinary mugger.

Chris grimaced as she hurried along, closely hugging to the walls. It would be just her luck, she decided, to be knocked out cold before she ever reached her real destination, to get into real trouble.

But if she didn't go back...

If the cloaked figure with the lethal knife discovered the earring that was so easily identifiable as hers...

She started to shiver again, then took a deep breath and gave herself a mental shake. She was on her way; all she had to do was carry through. Get into the gem salon, get out again.

It would probably make more sense to get out of Venice.

But she couldn't leave. Not now. For her father, for Alfred Contini, the truth had to be known. Even if that truth might include Marcus di Medici.

Chris blocked her mind to all but the task at hand when she reached the square and stared up at the galleries. Even the flagpoles were still draped in black crepe.

She stared at the columns, but knew she didn't want to go in by the front. On the side near the water was a workman's scaffold; she could climb that to the first-floor overhang, scurry up to the skylight, secure the rope on one of the gargoyles facing the canal and lower herself to the floor. Easy?

So easy that she was shaking again once she had climbed up the scaffolding. She looked below her. The canal was dark; no gondolas were slipping by in the night. She couldn't hear a sound from the square. Inhaling, then exhaling, Chris stared at the overhang that would take her to the skylight. It wasn't particularly steep, she assured herself. If she fell, well, she would be one American lost in a Venetian canal. But she wasn't going to fall. She was going to hold tight to the roof tiles until she reached the skylight.

Chris began to climb. She felt grit on the tiles and was glad, because it gave her a better hold. She didn't look down. Inch by inch she edged along, a hand, a foot, a hand, a foot. And then she was there.

She hurried along the roof, forced herself to slow her pace, and then pulled the bag from her shoulder to secure the rope around a particularly macabre gargoyle—one with its tongue out and twisted—before moving to the skylight. The hinge was stubborn, but there was no lock on it. With a little grunting and maneuvering Chris managed to pull it open. She lowered herself through, wincing as she felt the rope tighten around her body. She had judged things just a little short; her feet dangled about six inches from the floor.

She freed herself from the rope and dropped those six inches with a little thud. Just like a cat, she thought, a cat burglar! Oh, don't! she wailed to herself. Find the paper, find your earring, and get back out!

It was dark in here again tonight; the only light in the room was from the moon. Chris looked up. With the skylight open she could see the moon itself, still almost a full circle.

She had landed less than a foot from the case with the di Medici jewels. Starting to feel a little frantic again, she began to crawl around on her hands and knees. The floor felt a little strange, she thought. As if it were made of wood here, instead of marble. But the jewel case sat on a rich throw rug, so it was impossible to see what was beneath. And did it matter? All she needed to do was find the—

Paper. There it was. It had fallen to the rear. Chris reached for the note. She had to stare at it hard in the moonlight, and then she saw what was written. She didn't have to know Italian to understand it. Alfred's name was on it, and an unsigned demand for umpteen million lire.

Chris couldn't begin to compute the sum in American dollars; she only knew that it was vast.

A cloud moved over the moon, blocking some of the light. Chris hurriedly tucked the note into her waistband, then kept crawling around. Here, right here, was where she had been the other night. The earring had to be here.

And then she saw it, too. Almost directly beneath the case. In the almost complete darkness that shrouded the place now that the moon was covered, Chris could see the gleam of gold. She stretched her fingers far beneath the case.

And then suddenly she screamed in amazement and terror as the floor opened directly beneath her. She vaguely heard a snap, as if a hinge had given way.

And then she was falling, rolling, sliding helplessly through what seemed to be an absolutely endless chute, so amazed and totally stunned that she couldn't even scream again as she desperately tried to stop her wild flight.

She gasped for breath as the chute began to level off; then she gasped again as even the chute disappeared and she went into a free-fall.

But not a long one. In total darkness she landed hard on a cold stone floor.

Shocked, shaken, shivering and trying to regain her breath, Chris closed her eyes while the question of where she could be raged violently through her head. She opened her eyes. Oh, God, was it dark! She closed them again. When she opened them a second time she could make out shapes in the darkness. Boxes, it looked like, with something on top of them. Long rectangular boxes.

She shivered and swallowed, testing her limbs carefully for breaks or bruises. She seemed to be okay. There was a scuffling noise near her, and she bit her lip, panicking at the thought of rats or snakes or other creatures. She moved, and gave a little scream as something soft and clinging brushed her face.

Spiderwebs! Chris clawed them from her face with a vengeance, shivering as she wondered what might be crawling through her hair. Then she warned herself that she was about to panic and she closed her eyes, shuddering one last time, and yelling silently at herself that if she was ever going to get out of wherever she was, she was going to have to figure it out first.

She groped her way to her knees, then crawled up to the nearest box. It wasn't a box. It was some kind of stone. She ran her hand over the thing on the top, and then paused, another scream forming in her throat.

The box was a tomb—and the "thing" on top was a sculptured relief of whoever was lying inside.

All the boxes were tombs. Ancient tombs, carved by stonecutters in centuries long past.

She had fallen into the family crypt.

A spider crawled over her hand where it lay on the stone breast of a long-deceased di Medici count. Chris did scream then; she tried to rise, only to bump her head against the low archway of the catacombs.

And then she thought that she would have a heart attack herself; her blood seemed to congeal, her breath to stop, and her muscles to become paralyzed.

She heard a long low chuckle from the darkness. From the graveyard of the di Medicis.

A blinding light flared in her eyes, and a husky male voice murmured, "*Buona sera*, Christina. What an odd way for a guest to spend her evenings."

"Marcus!" Chris screamed, and heedless of anything but the desperate desire to escape the dank aura of death, she hurled herself into his arms.

He stiffened immediately, holding her from him. "Christina, what are you doing here?"

"I lost my earring," she babbled quickly.

"You lost your earring, so you broke into the gem salon?"

Oh, God! He doubted her! He was going to force her to stay down here; he sounded so terribly remote, and in the artificial gleam of the flashlight his eyes seemed like blue flames, filled with an implacable fire.

Marcus... perhaps Marcus couldn't have murdered his own father. But he did need money. He had been in the square just seconds after Alfred had died. She didn't want to believe him guilty, but someone in his household was. Why not he? Just because she was a woman who had fallen foolishly in love?

The way he was looking at her right now... as if he'd gladly crack her over the head with his flashlight and leave her to reside among his ancestors forever after...

"I swear to you, I lost an earring, nothing more. I wasn't trying to steal any gems."

"Then why didn't you just ask me to let you into the salon?" he demanded pleasantly.

"Because, because..." She couldn't tell him it was because she hadn't been sure that he hadn't been the one running around in a cloak and brandishing a razor-edged knife.

She swallowed quickly, thinking desperately. "Because of Alfred's death. I—I didn't want you to open the galleries. You haven't been particularly talkative lately, you know." She tried to add a tremor—not difficult—and a great deal of sweet plaintiveness to her voice. Georgianne had once given her a great French philosophy: when all else fails, flirt like hell.

He didn't seem at all ready to let her off the hook. He leaned casually against one of the tombs, resting the flashlight on top of it and crossing his arms over his chest.

"You might have killed yourself, you know," he told her flatly. But then he smiled, and in the eerie surroundings of the tomb his smile was both disturbing and frightening. She might truly have met a demon among the dead. "But what the hell, if you're missing one earring, scale a wall and a roof and drop twenty feet from a skylight. No big deal. Especially when you might have just asked."

Chris carefully ducked from below the arch and moved closer to him, moistening her lips and trying to avoid staring at the symmetrical rows of ancient sarcophagi. "Marcus, please get me out of here. If I was almost killed anywhere, it was coming down that chute from the trapdoor."

He shrugged. "You wouldn't have been killed." He smiled again. "The fall down that chute isn't a lethal one. Scary, and a little bumpy, but certainly not lethal. I pulled the trap."

"You!"

He hiked a brow curiously, still as relaxed as if they were carrying on their conversation at a sunny kitchen table. It was absurd, Chris thought, that he could still appear so absolutely arresting, so dark and fascinating, when she wasn't at all sure that he didn't mean to leave her there and when he was telling her that her predicament was his fault.

"Tell me, if you thought you had a sneak thief in a position to be snared, what would you do? Trapping the thief would seem an intelligent thing to do, don't you agree?"

Chris didn't respond. She forced herself not to back away from him. "What—what are you doing here yourself?"

He patted the stone relief beneath him. "Visiting Great-Great-Great-Great Uncle Francis?"

"Marcus!"

He smiled again, coldly, and picked up the flashlight, throwing its glow to the right. There was an archway there, but it had been bricked in. The di Medici crest was on the bricks.

"There were a number of decades somewhere in the 1500s when my ancestors didn't have such neat and tidy burials. They were simply laid upon vaults." He shrugged. "The masons are coming tomorrow to work again, and I must decide what to do about that section of the crypts.''

''At—at one A.M.?'' Chris asked weakly.

He smiled. ''We're a late-night people.''

''I don't believe you.''

''*You* don't believe *me*? I catch you breaking into the gem salon, and *you* don't believe *me*? Christina, the palazzo is mine. I have a right to be wherever I choose within it.''

''In the crypt?''

''It's my crypt!''

Chris let out a long breath. He had moved the flashlight again. She could see the full body relief on the stone where he sat. It was a man with carved stone boots, medieval leggings and a thin crown around his curling stone hair. His eyes were closed; his arms were reverently crossed over his chest. His facial structure was very similar to Marcus's. There was a thin silver spiderweb over his face, stretching to the sword he held against his form.

She found that she wasn't breathing very well. ''Marcus . . . could we please get out of here?''

He paused, staring at her in the strange and macabre light. Then he sighed. ''You're not going to tell me what you were doing, are you, Christina?'' he asked her softly. A trembling sensation danced all along her spine at the sound of his voice, echoing slightly.

''I told you—''

''Yes, you dressed up all in black and went out scaling the walls. And wound up trapped—by the di Medici jewels.'' He stood, and she moved backward slightly, bumping her head against the arch again. He smiled grimly, but made no move to touch her. ''You should have continued your pursuit of a di Medici husband. Wives do get the jewels, you know.''

''Marcus, please.''

''Ah, yes! Marcus, please! Good thing to say right now, isn't it?''

''I didn't even know where I was—or what these . . . things were.''

He sighed. "Good heavens, Chris, what do you think one is going to find in the catacombs?" Still smiling sardonically, he reached for her. Chris couldn't help but allow a small gasp to escape, and he laughed. "I'm trying to help you. Watch out. Some of the tombs are low, and you can trip."

She had never really known just how warm his hand could be, until she felt his touch in the cold dampness of the catacombs. She felt her fingers curling tightly around his, and at that moment she would gladly have followed him anywhere, as long as it was out of the catacombs.

It seemed to take them forever to leave the tombs. Before they came to a floor-to-ceiling grate Marcus halted suddenly and trained his flashlight on the wall. It was simple gray marble, with a number of brass plates. Chris realized that it was the "modern" section of the tombs and that the name on the last plate was Mario di Medici.

Chris felt as if an ominous silence was about to explode into something far worse.

Marcus started moving again. Now there were just walls and archways and the occasional squeak of a rat. In another moment her heart began to beat with relief. She could see light coming from the chapel, and the stairway that led to the main floor of the palazzo.

But Marcus stopped before they reached the stairway, turning to stare at her harshly.

"You told me the other night that Alfred had been murdered. He died of a heart attack, Christina. What were you talking about?"

"Nothing," she murmured quickly.

"Christina . . ." The pressure of his fingers increased on hers.

"Nothing! Nothing, I swear it," she babbled. "I told you, I lost my earring and—please, please, Marcus, let's get out of here. If I want the jewels I'll shoot for a di Medici husband, I swear it. Please, Marcus."

She was startled when he pulled his hand from hers, slipped an arm around her and bent to lift her into his arms. "You're shivering, Christina," he whispered to her.

She couldn't hide it; he was holding her very close. She could feel the strength and tension in the rippling muscles of his shoulders. He surely knew that she was terrified.

Suddenly she decided to tell him about the blackmail note, to enlist his aid—or taunt him into an admission that something was going on. Perhaps something in which he was involved. No! But if he *was* involved, wasn't she a fool to speak when she was in his arms, alarmingly at his mercy?

"Alfred was being blackmailed," she declared in a rush, attempting to pin his eyes with her own. "There was a blackmail note. I saw it. I *have* it."

His brows drew tightly together in a wary frown. "Where is this note?"

Chris reached into her waistband, but the note was gone. She closed her eyes with a sinking sensation. She must have lost it before plummeting through the trapdoor.

"I don't have it anymore. I swear it was there, Marcus. You have to believe me. You have to."

"You have to get your nose out of places where it doesn't belong, Christina," he whispered hoarsely, refusing to release her. He smiled. "You're still trembling."

"Marcus, let's go back and look for the note," she said, ignoring his comment.

"Chris!" he snapped, aggravated. "You're shaking like a leaf, and I'm not crawling around through spiderwebs all night to look for some figment of your imagination!"

"Marcus!"

"If there is such a thing, it will still be there later! Come on," he said more gently. "I'm getting you out of here."

She didn't reply. She held an arm about his neck and kept her gaze locked with his as he started up the steps. He carried her through the long marble hallway, past the entryway with its subdued chandelier, and down the hall to the kitchen, where he set her on the counter. He smiled a bit vaguely, dug a towel out of a drawer, soaked it with warm water and came back to her.

He gently began to clean her cheeks. "You're much prettier without the webbing about the face," he teased lightly.

He walked away and took a little bottle from a cabinet, shaking a pill into his hand. He poured her some water.

"Take this."

"What is it?" she asked suspiciously.

"Aspirin. It will help you to sleep tonight if you have aches and pains, or cold clammy dreams about dead contes and contessas," he teased.

Chris still wouldn't take the pill. He sighed with an effort at patience and pulled out the vial. "Look, Chris, they're all exactly alike! It's aspirin, I swear it! I wouldn't be trying to poison my entire family, would I?"

Chris realized that she was still nervous. And she wouldn't sleep without some kind of help. She dutifully swallowed the pill.

"Marcus, why wasn't Alfred buried here?"

"Alfred was not a di Medici, remember? Not that that would really have mattered; he was family. But he wanted to be interned at the church." He grimaced. "I can't say I'm fond of the idea of spending eternity in this place myself."

Chris smiled, but then she sobered. "Marcus, what's going on here?"

"I don't know what you're talking about."

But he did. She could tell.

"Are you protecting someone in your family?"

"If they need protection," he said dryly. "It would seem that they do, with a jewel thief in their midst, wouldn't you think?"

Chris fell silent. It was useless trying to talk to him. Tonight, at least. If she could get him alone again, far from the house, if she could get him to relax...perhaps ply him with wine, she thought, holding back a laugh.

He left her to pull a pair of snifters from a cabinet. From another he took a bottle of French brandy. "I think you need a drink," he told her. He came back to her, standing right before her as he handed her a brandy.

"Should I? After that pill . . ."

He grinned indulgently. "I wouldn't advise emptying a wine barrel, but a few sips won't hurt you. You're as pale as the 'relations' I left behind," he told her, tilting her glass in her numbed fingers so that she was forced to drink.

She smiled wanly. "Contini *was* being blackmailed, you know."

Had she struck home? she wondered. His expression gave nothing away, but she remembered that several days before he had mentioned something about going through the books—and had snapped at her when she had asked about it. Had large sums of money been disappearing?

"He said he made out a new will," Chris said impulsively.

Marcus shrugged. He was so close to her that his chest was almost against hers, and his hips were wedged between her legs where they dangled down the counter. The warmth of his body was like the sun. Powerful. Searing. Undeniable.

He plucked the snifter from her hand and set it on the counter. She could only stare into his eyes, aware of what was coming and glad of it, eager for it.

He moved even closer. She felt the strength and warmth of his body as his arms came around her, holding her tightly, holding her close. His lips touched hers slowly, as if tonight he had decided to explore and savor sensation. His mouth moved lightly over hers, then drew away, and he looked at her again. His eyes held a heated sizzle, but also more. There was a tenderness in his gaze that was almost shattering.

As if he shared the attraction . . . and the caring, too.

Finding no resistance in her eyes, he swept his arms about her once again, and his lips touched hers with a greater passion, hungry, persuasive. He tasted of the brandy, and his scent was like a potent musk, reminding her that she was falling in love with him, that she was enchanted by the probing of his tongue, moving against her teeth, then finding her tongue and all the little crevices of her mouth. She ran her hands down his back, and shivered deliciously, convulsively as his hands ran along hers, before moving between them to caress her breasts. He found her nipples easily against the knit of her leotard top, grazing them to hardened peaks. An ache rose within her; she didn't want to lose him, not the scent, the taste or the touch of him. The wonder of being held and caressed beguiled her.

His lips drew slowly from hers. His whisper was gentle as his lips brushed her cheek. "Go to bed, Christina," he told her.

She lowered her eyes quickly from his. Her lips were moist from the kiss; her body still seemed to sizzle from the heat of his. She closed her eyes for a minute, trying to still the reeling sensation of wanting him.

She needed answers. She was supposed to be the seductress, yet she was getting so emotionally involved. She had to learn to control the sensations of her body and her heart!

He wanted her; she knew it. But she was going to have to learn to play her role with greater appeal—and far greater finesse—closing her soul against his power over it. He could be tender...very tender. And gentle. Yet she couldn't let that sway her....

She raised her eyes. His were very dark, hard and mysterious. "Go to bed," he repeated softly. He lifted her from the counter. "I've got to go out."

"Where?" she challenged him.

He placed his hands on his hips and cocked his head slightly. "If I'm harboring a jewel thief, I need to get rid of the evidence."

Chris lowered her eyes again, then raised them with a sweet smile. "Marcus...do you think we might get out of here...together...alone...for an evening?"

He stared at her for several seconds. "Yes, I think that we might."

"Tomorrow?"

"Yes. Now go to bed."

Chris kept smiling sweetly as she hurried out of the kitchen and through the entryway to the stairs. In her room, she locked the door carefully before running to the shower to wash away the last of the spiderwebs from her hair and body.

When she crawled into bed she was more confused than ever. Marcus just couldn't have been blackmailing Contini. But Marcus had been right there when Contini died, and he had been in the catacombs tonight. He had a flair for being in strange places....

She was always throwing thinly veiled accusations his way—which he denied. She couldn't help but think that he was protecting someone. If only he would talk to her. If only she could trap him in some way.

It was difficult when you loved the man you were trying to trap. Loved him and distrusted him. And sometimes hated him.

Chris slept very restlessly.

And again she woke up in the night, certain that someone was in her room. But she didn't really feel that she was awake; perhaps she was only dreaming.

In her dream she opened her eyes carefully, keeping her lashes lowered.

It was Marcus. In a short robe, he was standing by her dresser. It seemed that he was going through her things.

She wanted to call to him, to stop him, to accuse him. But it was only a dream, and she couldn't say anything; she couldn't stop him or accuse him. She was too groggy to do so.

Chris blinked. Marcus wasn't there. It *had* been a dream. She rolled over and fell quickly back to sleep.

When she woke up in the morning she wasn't so sure that it had been a dream. She had been so tired! And she had taken the pill ... and had the brandy.

Angrily Chris crawled out of bed and hurriedly washed. She was going to march straight downstairs, find Marcus and demand that he explain what he was up to.

She hurried down the stairs and through the hallway to the courtyard, but paused before exiting the inner terrace. There was another family argument going on.

Genovese was standing at the head of the table. Sophia was screaming something at him, and Tony was laughing. When Sophia turned on Marcus in anger he merely lifted a brow and shrugged, then said something very calmly.

Gina watched everyone silently, her eyes darting from her sons to Sophia to Genovese.

Chris decided she might as well make her presence known.

She walked out onto the patio, her skirt swinging, her smile cheerful. She pretended not to notice that a dead silence had followed her entry. She poured herself a cup of coffee, saying, *"Buongiorno."*

Marcus moved forward to crush out a cigarette; then he leaned back in his chair, watching her with a polite smile. "It is a good day for you, Christina. Genovese tells us that he has found Alfred's new will."

"Oh?" Chris tried to sip her coffee with nothing more than polite interest. Her heart was beating painfully.

"Yes. It seems that Alfred's funds have been distributed evenly. Half to you, half to the di Medicis—and Sophia, of course."

"Half!" Chris gasped.

"Oh, yes, and you're the executor. In charge of the pensions and so on. There are legacies for Genovese, Joe Conseli and Fredo Talio. Also a few other friends and servants and distant relatives."

"I...doubt if it's legal," Chris murmured uneasily. Dear God, they were all staring at her as if they would like to throttle her. Except for Tony and Marcus. Tony was amused. Marcus was...almost disinterested.

"Ah, what a pity!" Tony teased, catching his brother's eye. "Now she'll no longer need a di Medici husband."

Marcus shrugged. "Maybe she wants it all?"

Chris thought that he was smiling. The two of them were crazy.

Tony chuckled again. "We should think this one out, Marc. I would say that one of us might need a Tarleton wife."

Gina stood up and excused herself, then quickly left the table. Sophia followed suit, throwing her napkin on the table and muttering, "It's disgraceful!" She glared at Chris and walked away.

Genovese cleared his throat. He spoke in Italian to Marcus, but Chris understood his words: "What shall I do?"

"Take the will to Sal's office, please. He can handle it from there. Oh, take the launch. It will be quickest."

Genovese nodded and left, too. Chris gazed after him uneasily. Certainly Genovese couldn't wish her any harm; he had discovered the will and presented it. He could have just torn it to shreds. . . .

But something about him made her uneasy. He often appeared weasely and ageless, his eyes colorless. When he looked at Chris, he made her uncomfortable.

Marcus stood up abruptly. "I have things to do at my own office."

"Wait!" Chris cried. "I want to talk to you."

"It will have to wait. I'll be home early." He smiled slightly, and she wasn't sure if it was with mockery or not. "We'll be seeing each other all evening, remember?"

He started to leave the courtyard, heading in the direction of the steps to the via.

"Damn . . ." Chris began.

"Give up," Tony advised. He pushed back his own chair. "I'd best get to work myself." He kissed the top of her head. "Something's bothering him about the books. That's why he's so brusque. Don't let him bother you. I'll bring him home for lunch, I promise."

Tony left, too. Chris sat alone at the table for a while, then decided she might as well work off her aggravation and fear with some exercise.

She did. She went upstairs and worked out for a long while, trying not to wonder what the new developments meant. Marcus in her room at night...Alfred Contini leaving half his money to her. Well, if things had been left to her, she was damned well going to get into the galleries and find out what was going on with the books.

Chris glanced at her watch and saw that it was almost lunchtime. She showered quickly and dressed, determined to corner Marcus and find out what he had been doing in her room.

Just as she was brushing out her hair, she heard his voice from the grand entryway below. She stepped out onto the balcony and glanced down. He was talking to Genovese, but he seemed to sense her presence. He looked up at her expectantly.

"Stay there, Marcus, please!" Chris called.

He smiled, his eyes a dazzling fire. "I'm here."

Chris whirled from the balcony banister, moved toward the stairs with firm steps and started down.

But on the fourth step the floor suddenly gave away. The wood of the step groaned and shattered beneath her weight.

Chris fought valiantly for her balance, but her shoe was stuck in the cracked wood. She jerked at her foot and went catapulting down the rest of the stairs, a scream tearing from her throat.

She landed with a hard crash on her head. She stared upward. The chandelier danced like a trillion suns above her.

"Christina! Christina!" It was Marcus's voice that she heard, his arms that she felt around her. His eyes were fire, she decided. A blue blaze. But like the crystals of the chandelier, they began to dim.

Bit by bit the light faded, and then was gone completely. The pain in her head had been like a large black bird, spreading its wings over her eyes, over her mind, and she slipped silently from consciousness, murmuring, "Marcus..."

Chapter 7

Even in the realm of her subconscious, it was dark.

Chris dreamed she was in the catacombs. The walls were dank and musty and she could hear a roar, as if the water of the canal surrounding the tunnel was rushing like a full sea in turmoil. All the archways were deep and darkly shadowed, yet she had no choice but to run from one to the next, toward the crypt.

She was being pursued.

She kept telling herself that her pursuer could not be Marcus, but when she turned in flight she saw him, tall, dark and as mysterious as the shadows, not running after her but maintaining a steady pace. He was stalking her. And she knew that when he passed from one archway to the next he could change, if he so chose. He could become St. Mark's great winged lion, or he could become a panther, as black and deadly as the night.

She kept running until she found herself in the crypt. She banged against the gate. Marcus was calling her, and she looked back. But in the darkness she couldn't tell which he had become, the winged lion or the panther. Was he trying to hurt her, or help her? She didn't know, so she forced her way through the gates. And then she remembered that all she would find at the end of the tunnel was the walled tomb where dozens of di Medicis lay together in the sleep of eternity. She wanted to turn back, but someone was pulling on her wrist. She stared at her hand, trying to scream. The stone reliefs from the tombs had become flesh, and those long-dead di Medicis wouldn't allow her to escape.

"Christina! Stop it! You will wrench the needle from your arm."

Her eyes flew open and came into immediate contact with hard blue ones. "Marcus!"

"Yes, of course," he murmured, and she realized that his large bronzed hands were on her shoulders, pressing her back against a pillow. A cotton-covered pillow.

"Where am I?"

"In the hospital. You've suffered a slight concussion. Not a bad one, but bad enough to keep you here a few days. But you're going to be all right. Or you will be, if you'll settle down."

Dazed, Chris sank back against her pillow. She gazed at her hand; it was bandaged, and a tube was feeding a colorless liquid into her veins. She turned to Marcus. He was in a blue-and-white striped, short-sleeved knit shirt and jeans; she could see the hard muscles of his bronzed arms, very dark against the stark white of the hospital sheets. His eyes were very blue—and fathomless. His features were drawn, his jaw very rigid.

Chris closed her eyes for a minute. The step had broken, and she had fallen. A step that a half dozen other people used daily had happened to fall apart when she stepped on it.

She had fallen through the step soon after Tony had laughingly informed her that she was rich—very soon after. *Too* soon after.

She felt a tender touch against her cheek and opened her eyes. Marcus was smiling. "You're really all right."

She lifted the tubed and bandaged hand. "Then what is this?"

"This is because you've been out of it a while. They will keep you here a few nights to observe you."

"I don't feel too bad." Chris moved and winced. She did have a headache.

"You'd feel worse if you tried to stand up right now," Marcus murmured. He was sitting beside her on the bed and appeared very comfortable. Chris was startled when someone moved beyond him. It was Tony, sitting in a chair. He came up to the other side of the bed and smiled before bending to brush her forehead with a kiss. "You have a bruise on the head, you know. A concussion."

"Tony, call the doctor. He wanted to know as soon as Chris came to," Marcus instructed.

Tony smiled encouragingly, tapped her nose playfully with a knuckle and left, calling to someone in the hallway.

Marcus leaned close to Chris, very tense. "You need to get out of Venice. I'm still not sure quite what you're up to, but this city does not seem to be healthy for you."

"What do you mean?" Chris said with a gasp, lowering her voice quickly as a stab of pain shot through her head. "Marcus! What are you talking about? Was this done to me on purpose?"

"No, of course not. That wooden stairway... it has always been a problem."

"Marcus, did you go back to the galleries? Did you find my earring? Did you—"

"Shush, Christina, you are not to be excited. Yes, I went back to the galleries. I got rid of your rope and your grappling hook. But..." He hesitated, and she felt his probing stare for long seconds. "I didn't find any earring. Nor a 'blackmail' note."

"You didn't find an earring, or the note...but Genovese did find a new will," Chris muttered bitterly, closing her eyes again.

"Yes, and it appears as if you did come out the heiress. Suspicious, isn't it? You come to Venice to charm the old man, he drops dead of a heart attack and voilà, the money is yours."

"I *am* suspicious!" she flared, staring at him furiously again. "And I'm the one in the hospital!"

He waved an arm in the air. "An accident of time and place."

"You don't believe that, Marcus di Medici. You know that Alfred was being blackmailed. Marcus, you know what's going on."

"Christina, you are being hysterical."

"I am not!" She closed her eyes immediately after her denial; her head had begun to ring like the bells of St. Mark's on Sunday. It was foolish to argue with him; she knew it. She opened her eyes and smiled at him sweetly. "Marcus...I need your help."

"My help?" he murmured sardonically. But he went no further, because the doctor entered and shooed both him and Tony out of the room. The doctor was a pleasant man with a heavy accent, who was ready to cheer on all Chris's attempts at Italian. Somehow they stumbled along together; he assured her that she looked fine, that she would be all right—and that she was lucky that she apparently knew how to break a fall. He promised to see her in the morning to release her.

When the doctor left, only Tony returned to the room. Chris lifted a brow and Tony smiled, taking a seat beside her on a chair, rather than intimately on the bed as Marcus had done. He picked up her hand, the one without the intravenous, which the doctor had promised would quickly be removed, and played idly with her fingers. He sighed. "What a week."

"Yes, it has been, hasn't it?" Chris murmured. "Tony, where did Marcus go?"

"To shoot the staircase, I think," Tony teased. "No, seriously, he had to get it fixed immediately. He wanted to talk to the doctor, and he said that he had a few things to take care of at the galleries. Why? Am I bad company?"

Chris smiled. "No, you're not. I just don't ever seem to be able to pin your brother down these days."

Tony's cheerful smile faded. "He has been a bit mysterious, even for Marcus. But don't worry about it. You'll be out of here soon enough."

"And then what?" Chris murmured, closing her eyes.

"Well, then you'll have to start learning all about the galleries. You're an owner now, you know."

Why? Chris wondered fleetingly. Why had Alfred done this to her? She didn't want the galleries, and she didn't want all these people hating her. All she wanted to do was find out what was going on—what *had* gone on so many years ago.

"Tony?" she said softly.

"What is it, Chris?"

"Do you . . . hate me because of Alfred's will?"

Tony was silent for a second; then he burst into laughter. "Good God, no! Why should I?"

"Because it should have gone to you . . . or to your family. Or to Sophia. I'm an outsider."

"Yes, and the most fascinating thing I've seen in years." Tony chuckled agreeably. "Chris, the di Medicis were never dependent on Alfred, despite my dear brother's constant harping about money. I like to think that both Marcus and I are brilliant businessmen."

"I think that someone does hate me," Chris said lightly. She expected Tony to deny her words immediately, but he didn't. He hesitated again.

"Maybe you should get out of Venice for a while, Chris," he murmured. "For a few days. See Rome, or tour Florence. Or go to the Riviera and get a nice tan."

"Tony, are you worried about me being in your house?" Chris demanded tensely.

"Don't be silly," he said, but she sensed that he was lying. Tony was worried, and if Tony was worried . . .

"Ah, Chris! Here comes the nurse with your dinner. Maybe I can charm her into bringing me a tray, too." His eyes twinkled as he cocked his head slightly. "Want to make any side bets?"

"Against you? Never," Chris murmured.

She was glad she hadn't bet against him, because the nurse did bring a second tray. During dinner Tony turned the conversation around to the galleries, trying to give her an education on various Renaissance painters. Chris realized that he could be charmingly stubborn when he chose; he wasn't going to talk about the will nor imply in the least that her mishap on the stairway could have been anything but an accident.

"What about your mother?" Chris asked in the middle of a discussion on Michelangelo.

"What about her?"

"She resents me."

Tony shrugged. "I don't think so. I think she's getting over it." He paused, then grimaced. "I think that Mother is falling in love again."

Chris gasped. "You're kidding!"

He shook his head. "Every Tuesday she goes to the church for parish work. And she's been staying out for dinner afterward. I think it has something to do with a retired banker named Umberto Cellini. I think he'd like to make it more serious. Perhaps she would, too. She's been a widow a long time."

Chris digested that bit of information slowly. "And what about Sophia? What will she do now?"

"Stay on, I guess. She really is a marvelous housekeeper—a great supervisor, I should say. But that will be up to Marcus. The palazzo is his, you know."

"And what about you?"

He laughed. "Don't worry about me. We have various properties, a number of which are mine. I don't have any younger-son syndromes, if that's what you mean."

"I didn't," Chris murmured. But did she? She didn't know what she thought about anything or anyone anymore. "It is curious that Alfred never married Sophia."

Tony shrugged. "No, it's really not so strange. You forget, Alfred was an old man—from the old Italy. I think he always thought himself a class above his mistress. But he must have loved her. He never left her. C'est la vie!" he added in French.

Tony stayed with her until eight o'clock; then he kissed her forehead and left, promising to see her in the morning.

Chris closed her eyes, trying to sleep, but it seemed impossible. Someone, she was convinced, had tried to kill her. Someone had tampered with the steps. She couldn't believe it was Tony; she couldn't believe it was Marcus....

She opened her eyes and almost screamed out loud. Genovese was standing half in and half out of the doorway, staring at her with his dark but colorless eyes.

"Signorina Tarleton, a thousand pardons!" He came quickly into the room, running his fingers over the brim of a worn fedora. "I didn't mean to startle you."

Chris tried very hard to smile. "That's all right, Genovese. Thank you for, uh, coming to see me."

He shook his head solemnly. His voice became a whisper. "I came to tell you that you must be careful, that you should get away from Venice immediately!"

Chris felt shivers race along her spine. "Why, Genovese, do you know something?" she demanded.

"Si..."

He stopped when he heard a slight sound at her doorway. Chris looked beyond him. Marcus was standing there.

Quiet, calm, straight and tall. He was in a dark vested suit, watching them both with shielded eyes. He moved into the room, passing Genovese with an absent smile and coming to Chris. He sat beside her on the bed and took her hand in his.

"How are you?"

"Fine. I'm quite certain."

His eyes moved to Genovese; his smile was polite, his gaze speculative. "It was good of you to come see Chris, Genovese."

"Yes, I just wished to see how she was." He bowed his head a little nervously. "I'm leaving now. *Buona sera*, Signorina Tarleton."

He was out of the room before Chris could respond. She stared at Marcus furiously. "Why is he afraid of you?"

"Afraid of me! He isn't—that I'm aware of."

"Well, it's curious, isn't it, that everyone is warning me to get away from Venice?"

Marcus seemed to start. He released her hand and paced nervously to the window, like a cat on the prowl. He lit a cigarette as he stared out into the night. "Perhaps you *should* leave Venice for a while, Christina."

"Why? Because you know that something's going on? You know that my father didn't murder yours—"

"I know nothing of the kind!" he proclaimed, turning to her in anger. He stalked to the door of her room. "Go to sleep, Chris. I'll come to get you in the morning."

Tears stung her eyes as she saw him walk out of the room. There seemed to be no one to turn to. She wanted to trust him so badly, yet she couldn't.

And she didn't want to sleep. She didn't want to dream about righteous winged lions and silent black panthers stalking through the catacombs.

Chris stayed awake, staring up at the corniced hospital ceiling for a long, long time. She determined then that she would not be frightened away. She would be careful, but she would get to the bottom of things. She would quit accosting Marcus and start trying to charm him again. The answers were somewhere. . . .

The galleries, she had to get back to the galleries again. Her earring had to be there, along with the note. If she could just find the note...

Then she could prove to Marcus that everything she was saying was true. Except that...except that she already thought he believed her, no matter what he said. He *did* know that something was going on.

Chris let out a little sob. Marcus...Marcus was the worst of it all. Insanely, she was falling in love with him. Sometimes she hated him, and she was afraid to trust him. But she was falling in love with him.

Marcus...if she could just sway him to her side. If she could only get him to talk to her...

While Chris finally drifted into a restless sleep, Marcus paced the doctor's office below. Dante Rosellini was an old family friend, and Marcus trusted him, but he was still worried. He had already spoken to Dante—enough for his friend to know he felt there was a great deal wrong. But now this! These damn pills were going to derail his plans of making Christina sweetly, deliriously, *pliantly* tipsy.

His left hand was in his pocket as he moved about pensively; in his right he clutched a small container of white pills.

"Does she have to take these, Dante?"

Dante Rosellini frowned. "No, Marcus. She does not *have* to take them. They are only a mild tranquilizer...to take the edge away from things. But they are not necessary. Why?"

Marcus grimaced. "I was anxious to take her to dinner tomorrow...and to ply her with a little wine. She really is all right?"

Dante arched a knowing brow. "She is fine. I have kept her here purposely to assure it. And, Marcus, there is nothing wrong with you taking her to dinner. Nor with 'plying her with a little wine.' But if you intend to do so, then do not let her take the pills. But I don't understand this. I've never known you to have the need to coerce a woman to your will!''

"I have a need to protect this particular woman," Marcus responded quietly. "And I'm afraid I'll have to coerce her to do it."

"I'm not so sure I like this."

"I don't like it myself, Dante. Trust me. I have her very best interests at heart!"

Dante Rosellini shrugged and lifted his hands. He pushed his chair back and walked around to lean back on his desk, watching Marcus astutely. "What are you up to, my young friend?" He grinned suddenly. "I cannot believe that this is a new form of conquest for you."

Marcus sighed. "No...not exactly." He sighed. "I wish she would leave Italy, but she is not going to do that."

"*Mia bellisima?* My pretty little patient? You are worried. What is it that you suspect?"

"I don't know. I don't know where the truth lies anymore."

Dante Rosellini walked around his desk again and sat in his chair. "You blame her for your father's death—"

Marcus interrupted him with a grunt of impatience. "I never blamed a child—"

"But you do—in a way. From what you say, you are refusing to trust her. Open your eyes to the things around you. You came to me to tell me about the staircase. You do not even trust your family. I suggest you find your answers quickly."

"I plan to," Marcus said quietly. He shook the little bottle of pills. "I just want to keep her alive while I do so and discover what it is she really wants."

"I just wish I knew exactly what you were doing," Dante said seriously.

Marcus paused, then sighed, and fully explained himself. Dante stared at him, not sure whether to smile, or protest emphatically.

"It's a rash plan and very dramatic. And I'm going to pretend that you never told me about it."

"Do you see another, if she refuses to leave?"

The doctor sighed. "No. I hope it will be enough. Perhaps you should be making a few demands on your family."

Marcus laughed with little humor. "I can hardly see anyone admitting to blackmail or murder. Can you?"

"Perhaps not, perhaps not. Ah, well. Best wishes—and *salute!*"

"Thanks," Marcus said dryly. *"Arrivederci,* and oh, *per favore,* tell her that I will come at about five o'clock."

"Si," Dante murmured unhappily.

Marcus left the hospital and returned to the palazzo in the launch. As soon as he arrived he went to check the staircase. It had been fixed and completely checked for faults. It was now in excellent condition. The carpenter had told him that the only way the wood might have fallen in was if it had been purposely weakened.

The palazzo was quiet. It seemed as if it slept, along with its inhabitants. Marcus walked slowly up to his room, but he didn't turn on the light. Instead he slipped out onto the terrace and into Christina's room.

He sat on the bed, smiling sadly as he smoothed a hand over the cover. *"Amore mio,"* he murmured. "You came, and you changed everything. You changed me."

Changed him, yes. In many ways. He had never known fear like this before, because he was afraid for her. He had held her, kissed her, felt her sleek body grow fevered next to his. He knew the light scent of her French perfume in his sleep; it haunted his dreams. Her shape, supple, rhythmic, alive and lovely. Her eyes, as rich as honey, as tawny as those of the lioness. She was a challenge, a fighter—and a temptress, and he could all too easily be tempted. A touch, a glance, and he had wanted her. He had known that she would be a glimmering fire. Warm and sweet, a tempest. He could still feel the wonder of her breasts, filling his hands, taunting his senses along with the taste of her lips, her throat.

She hated him. She was drawn to him. If only they had met on a beach in France, or on a ski vacation in Switzerland.

But they hadn't. She was James Tarleton's daughter returned. And she had stirred up embers of the past that were setting a slow fuse to the present.

He stood abruptly, walking back out to the terrace. She was really going to hate him by tomorrow night, he thought dismally. But he really had no choice. He could prove nothing; he didn't even know what to suspect. And the only thing he could do until he trapped the attempted killer was protect her with all he had to give.

And somehow get her to keep her damn nose out of things. And find out what she knew—and what she had really come for.

The money? It was possible. Revenge? That was possible, too, if she believed her father had been horribly wronged.

And it was also possible that she was everything she seemed, everything that was haunting him, teasing him, taunting him....

She was trapping him in her silent web of beauty; he was falling more and more deeply in love with the daughter of a man who it still appeared to him could have been the only one to murder his father....

He sighed. Tomorrow night...

At four o'clock the next afternoon Marcus phoned the hospital. The nurse came on the line, and then the doctor.

"Marcus, she's gone," Dante told him unhappily.

"Gone! I told you to keep her there. Dear God, Dante, didn't you understand—"

"*Si, si!* But I wasn't here. She twisted the day staff around her finger. She planned to surprise everyone by getting back home by herself and all. She—she hasn't come home yet?"

"No, she's not at the palazzo," Marcus murmured uneasily. He found out that she had left several hours earlier, then hung up the phone.

For a long moment he stared down at the receiver, completely tense. He needed help. Right now he needed help badly. But it had come to a point where he didn't trust anyone. At least, he had warned himself not to trust anyone. Not even those who were his blood, people he loved.

Not even his brother.

But that, he decided firmly, was foolish. He knew Tony almost as well as he knew himself. He had to trust someone.

Suddenly he was furious with himself. How had he let his own mind become so narrow that he couldn't see the obvious? Tony *was* his brother. Marcus turned, shaking his head a little at his own foolishness. He was in trouble now, and his brother was the one to call on for help.

"Tony! Tony!"

His brother came running from the courtyard when he heard Marcus's call. "Tony, Chris left the hospital. Hours ago," Marcus told him.

Tony gazed at him worriedly. "Where do you think she went?"

"I don't know. Take the launch, please, and see if you can't find her on the canals or the streets. I'm going to the galleries."

Chris had had no problem whatsoever wheedling her way out of the hospital. She was, after all, she had reminded them sweetly, an adult and an American. Responsible for herself and her own welfare. And, of course, she was very, very sweet.

Neither did she have any problems getting to the galleries—or inside them. They were open today. There seemed to be tourists all around; Chris joined them for a while, wondering just what it was that she was looking for.

She eventually made her way over to the historical exhibit. She didn't see Joe, Fredo or anyone else that she knew. It was easy to be anonymous.

She walked around the figures, smiling as they went into action. They really were excellent. Lucrezia Borgia was the best; she had a voice and face that implied determination. She might have been a murderess, but she had also been a woman out to get what she wanted. Chris shrugged and walked on past her. Someone called out something in Italian, but Chris wasn't paying any attention. She kept following the circle, pausing as she saw that a costume had been laid out on a glass case, probably for the Catherine di Medici figure that was still missing.

Chris started as the lights suddenly went out. She realized then that the galleries were closing for the day. She must have heard the announcement earlier and simply not understood it.

She should hurry up and get out.

But should she? Apparently the guards hadn't seen her, or they wouldn't have turned out the lights. Now was the perfect time to do a little exploring, and she wouldn't even have to break in.

But how was she going to get out? Chris wondered. The alarm system would probably go off if she tried to get out through the door.

She shrugged, certain there would be a way. She could even go down the trapdoor if she had to, then ignore the tombs and race along the subterranean tunnel to the palazzo. Or, much easier, she could get on the phone and call Tony or Marcus to come get her.

Chris moved to the door and looked outside. Beyond the balcony she could see the last two guards in their medieval uniforms, chatting as they set the switch by the entry doors, looked around the place one last time—and exited.

She glanced back at the silent figures in the robotronics room. She shivered a bit, then slipped along the long hallway toward the gem salon. Marcus hadn't found the note or her earring, but she knew that they had been there. But then, she thought miserably, did she really know yet that she could trust Marcus?

Or did she just *want* to trust Marcus?

Chris went straight to the case with the di Medici jewels and carefully got down on the floor—avoiding the trap-door, just in case someone was beneath her!—then searched studiously in the moonlight. Frustrated, she sat back. Marcus was right: there was no earring, and there was no note. She sighed. Someone had found them. Or else Marcus had found them himself and wasn't admitting it to her.

Chris started suddenly as she heard a door open below. She stood quickly, frowning, and walked silently back to the door. She couldn't see anyone—and there were no more sounds.

Quietly she walked to the balcony to look down to the courtyard. A soft gasp escaped her, and her heart began pounding wildly.

There was a figure in the courtyard, a tall figure clad in a long dark all-encompassing cloak.

Chris started to back away from the balcony just as the figure looked up. Its features were so shadowed that she couldn't see them at all. She sensed that the figure had seen her, though.

And she knew it when she saw the figure starting for the stairway. Chris emitted a little cry and started running down the hall. She slipped through a door, barely aware that she had reentered the robotronics exhibit. She dared a quick peek through the door, but could no longer see the cloaked figure. But then she heard a noise: the sound of a secretive footstep. It was coming from the gem salon, right next door. This room would be next. And it was almost certain that the cloaked form was carrying the knife that had glinted so lethally in the moonlight on the night Alfred had died.

Chris spun around desperately. She saw all the figures, silent in their poses. And then she saw the Catherine di Medici costume, lying on the case.

She ran to it, throwing the full old-fashioned skirts over her head and pulling them down quickly. Her own skirt and blouse were completely hidden. There was a headdress, too. Like horns with a veil. Chris threw it on, praying it was straight. She swept the veil across her cheek and over a shoulder. She pitched her purse far beneath the pedestal and jumped onto the circular stage with the other figures, finding a pose in a deep curtsy before a courtly gentleman with bloused trousers who was bowing deeply himself.

Her heart began to thunder again. She had been just in time. The door to the room opened, and the hooded figure entered.

Chris longed to look up, but she didn't dare. She listened as the figure walked around the room, coming closer to her, closer. Footsteps, slow, one after another. Coming closer still. Pausing, until she could feel her heart thunder and her blood run cold, the hair seeming to rise at her nape. . . .

And then the footsteps passed her by. Chris began to breathe more easily in relief, then froze once again in horror. At the doorway the cloaked figure was playing with the switches.

The lights came on. The figures began to move. All at once. Saying hello, introducing themselves.

The courtly fellow in the bloused trousers moved, slapping her in the face as he extended an arm.

Chris didn't allow herself to react. She prayed that her light Italian would be up to par for a few words. She allowed herself to blink once, remembering all the times she and Georgianne had posed as robots in Parisian boutiques to make extra money. It was just like mime: separated mechanical movements. A tilt here, a bend there, nothing smooth or flowing, a little slower than real life.

"Io sono Catherine di Medici," she murmured, deepening her curtsy to the "friend" who had slapped her with his own mechanical movement. It was all she could think of to say, and it didn't really matter, because all the other figures were talking, and the conversations were blending in the

night. *"Io sono Catherine di Medici,"* she repeated. *"Mi piace Venezia."* Softly, softly. Just enough that her lips moved, so she looked real . . .

The hooded figure flipped the switch, and the figures were still. Chris caught herself, posing in a deep curtsy once again. She wanted to look up so badly that she thought she would explode, but if she did, she could all too easily die. She waited, barely breathing.

And then she heard the figure turn away and pull the door shut.

Still Chris waited. Waited and waited. Finally, when she could bear her stance no longer, when her limbs were about to break, she moved. Carefully, very carefully. She stepped from the circular stage and silently crept to the door, wincing as the costume skirts rustled around her. She opened the door a crack, but could see nothing. She waited for a few more minutes, leaning against the wall, trying to breathe slowly. Then she peeked out the door again. No one. Silently she stepped out into the hallway and moved to the balcony. She could see nothing on the ground floor. She kept looking, hugging the balcony as she moved closer and closer to the stairway.

And then she heard a movement on the stairs. She looked quickly to her right, and the cloaked figure suddenly pointed a blinding flashlight into her face.

Chris screamed and spun around. The door to the gem salon was right behind her. She ran into the room, closing the door and leaning against it. She glanced around a little desperately, saw one of the jewel cases and ran to it, then dragged it back hurriedly and braced it against the door. Then she hurried to the di Medici case, crawled to the floor and searched for the hinge to the trapdoor. For several seconds, in which she began to pray fervently, the spring eluded her. Then at last it gave. Closing her eyes and praying again, she pitched her body downward.

She hit the hard stone and met total darkness, as she had known she would. And she tried very hard not to panic at knowing that everything she touched was part of the tombs—including the spiders that lived among the dead.

For several minutes she just sat, breathing hard and trying to muster her courage and sense of reason. Then she stood, silently apologizing to the long-dead di Medicis for crawling over them. She ducked her head, aware of the archways. If she could only find her way through the tombs and locate the hallway, she would begin to see light, the light from the chapel at the end of the tunnel.

It seemed to take forever to make her way around the first set of stone monuments. Then she began to pray that she was going in the right direction, and that she wouldn't panic and start running like an idiot until she killed herself by crashing headfirst into marble or stone.

In the end she did panic. At first she hadn't heard it: the soft sound of a footstep against stone. But finally she did. Footsteps, footsteps in the tombs, coming toward her.

Suddenly a flashlight sent a golden ray into the darkness, and Chris screamed, long, shrill and terrified.

"Good God! What are you doing down here again?"

Chris brought a hand to her eyes to shield them from the glare. "Marcus?" she whispered.

The light danced, and then he was next to her, holding her before she could fall.

"What are you doing?" he demanded. "Another lost earring? And just for kicks you decided to dress up like Catherine di Medici to find it this time?"

He was alive and real, warm and strong, and she was so glad to see him. But he was furious, and she was still terrified—and she wanted to tear his heart out.

"Damn it, Marcus! Someone was up there! Coming after me."

"And what the hell were you doing up there? You were supposed to be at the hospital, waiting for me!"

"Marcus! There was someone after me—"

"Yes! Probably the guards. People aren't supposed to be prowling around after the galleries have closed."

"Marcus, the guards don't wear dark cloaks."

Chris broke off. His arms were around her, and she was clinging tightly to him, glad of the strength of warm living muscle beneath her fingers. But then a chill touched her. Where had he come from? He could have been the figure; he would have known that she was down here.

No, no, no! Because he could kill her as easily here as he could have in the galleries. But suddenly she didn't want to say any more. Her heart was sure of Marcus's innocence, but her head told her to trust no one. If it had been Marcus...

She had to be charming and sweet. Had to convince him that she hadn't seen anything, didn't know anything...

"Uh... maybe it was one of the guards. Maybe I panicked."

Chris threw herself against his chest, her heart pounding. She pleaded in a muffled whisper, "Marcus, help me, get me out of here. *Per favore*, Marcus!"

His fingers wound into the hair at her nape, his touch almost rough as he tilted her head back, staring into her eyes. His were cynical and angry. Then his mouth ground down on hers, consuming her with a brutal kiss that softened almost instantly. Did he hate her? Or care for her? Was it possible that he had been a murderer—or was he her "winged lion" of justice, her only salvation?

None of it mattered when he kissed her, when his lips moved against hers with persuasion and hunger. His lips left hers to find her cheeks and throat, and then returned to consume her mouth once again, his tongue parrying deeply, as if desire could be assuaged in that single assault.

Chris went limp, weary and lost as she leaned against him, dismayed to know that she cared for him beyond all reason. Could she manipulate him with honeyed words? Could she seduce where her anger failed...? If she did, she would only be giving in to the demands of her heart.

"Please... Marcus," she whispered, clinging to his shoulders, allowing her fingers to roam over them.

"I don't think you should make an appearance upstairs as Catherine," he warned, and she felt his hands on her body as he helped her strip away the awkward headdress and costume. He started to toss them aside. Chris suddenly gasped, seeing something in the beam of the flashlight.

"What is—"

"Marcus!" It was barely a whisper. "Look! The cloak!"

He frowned and bent down next to a sculpted angel that stood sentinel over a tomb. He picked up a large swath of dark material.

"It is a cloak," he said curiously. "How did it get there?"

She wanted to scream and back away from him. Only two people were there: she and Marcus. But illogical as it was, she still couldn't believe that Marcus would harm her. She didn't want to believe it.

"I—I told you, the figure wore a cloak."

He held the material for several seconds, then dropped it. "Leave it and leave Catherine's gown. Let's see if we can get out of here without being seen."

His fingers were tight around hers as he led her quickly through the tunnels. Chris was glad to follow him blindly. But when they neared the other side and she could see the light from the chapel and the stairs to the palazzo, she hung back suddenly, swallowing fiercely and forcing herself to speak.

"Marcus, what were you doing down there?"

"Looking for you," he said bluntly. He pulled her into the light, staring at her critically, trying to brush away the few spiderwebs that still clung to her hair.

"But . . . why?"

"Why? Because you just got out of the hospital!" he said impatiently.

"What made you think of the galleries?"

"Instinct. Or maybe I'm coming to know you. I don't really know. What difference does it make?"

She evaded that question and asked another one. "Marcus, who has keys to the galleries?"

"Tony and myself. Alfred had one, but I don't know what became of it. Why?"

"It's obvious. Oh, never mind. Let's go up."

"Yes, let's go up. And you can go straight to your room and get dressed."

"Dressed? For what?"

He smiled suddenly. It was a little grim, his teeth very white against the copper of his features. "For something nice. We're going to go to dinner and spend the evening out. Away from the palazzo. As you wanted—away from everything."

Chris stared up at him. Slowly she nodded. She had to get him to talk to her. They would order wine; she would be as sweet and charming as possible. She would force him to admit that Alfred had been blackmailed because someone other than her father had murdered Mario di Medici.

"That would be wonderful," she said softly, smiling at him, then walking past him to the steps. Suddenly she turned back, watching him as he followed her. "Will you give me an hour? I really would like to dress up tonight."

"An hour is fine." He squeezed her hand, and they continued up the stairs.

"You found her!"

Tony was standing at the top of the stairs, smiling with relief. "Christina, I combed half of Venice."

Marcus's hand tightened around hers. "She was in the chapel. I told her one of us would wring her neck if she ever pulled such a disappearing act again."

Tony shrugged, trying to give Chris a glance that was reassuring, as if to say, "His bark is much worse than his bite."

But she couldn't be reassured. Not when Marcus wasn't telling Tony the truth.

Not Marcus, not Tony. It just couldn't be one of them. But Tony was right there at the top of the stairs, and it seemed that they didn't even trust each other. . . .

"We're going to go out, Tony. Would you mind letting Sophia or Genovese know that we won't be here for dinner?"

"Not at all," Tony murmured. He touched Chris's cheek with his open palm. "I'm glad to see you safe and sound, *bella* Christi." He smiled at his brother. "I'll find the gorgon."

As Tony started down the hall, Chris turned to Marcus. "My purse!" she whispered. "It's back in the robotronics room—"

He caught both her hands. "I'll get it. And I'll be waiting for you in the entryway. One hour."

Chris nodded and headed away from him. She felt him following her. At her door she paused, staring at him.

He smiled. "I just wanted to see you get to your room." She smiled and hurried inside.

"Use your lock," he told her curtly, and then he was gone.

Chris showered, shampooed and dried her hair, then dressed in the new black cocktail gown she'd purchased. She was nervous, excited, apprehensive and exhilarated. She was going to get away from the palazzo with Marcus. And somehow...somehow she would force him to get to the bottom of things.

Unless he was there himself...

No!

Chris gave herself a critical gaze in the mirror. The gown was dazzling, low-cut, sheer, with a V at her back. The skirt was fluted; it swirled with her every movement. Her hair was clean and swept around her shoulders in shining waves. She closed her eyes; she could and would be charming. She would disarm the man....

She would have to, she realized. Because the hooded figure would really be after her now.

Chris glanced at the old German clock on her dresser. Her hour was up. She exited her room and came to the balcony. Marcus was at the entryway; he looked up, saw her and smiled, a devilish fire in his eyes. He whistled softly, a low sound that warmed her from head to toe. She smiled dazzlingly in return and started down to him.

He was in black, too. Black tux, black vest. A stark-white shirt emphasized his dark looks, the indigo intrigue of his eyes, the hard lean strength of his frame. She had never seen him more handsome or compelling. More like a black panther than ever, sleek and cunning and at home with the night.

Chris took a deep breath as she reached him, and offered him another smile. He took her hand and slowly kissed it, his eyes touching hers. She would be all right, she promised herself. She was quite certain she knew the nature of her prey.

Chapter 8

He had a hired gondola waiting for them by the steps. She raised her eyes in inquiry, aware that he usually preferred to use the family's own means of transportation.

He smiled and took her hand to help her into the boat. "It's our grand night out, remember?" he whispered softly, and she shot him a seductive look in return. His breath caught momentarily in his throat; she was stunning, all the more so in beautiful motion. In the arresting black gown she moved like the waves of the sea, like a soft cloud floating across the sky, lulling, beguiling. When she smiled at him, he felt as if strings inside him tautened, as if, should she beckon, he would follow her anywhere, through all the fires of hell and back again....

Ah, but I am the puppeteer, and she the dancer on the strings tonight, he reminded himself.

He kept smiling as he seated himself beside her. The scent of her perfume was subtle; it wafted around him like a woven chain of golden angel's hair.

The gondolier pushed away from the Palazzo di Medici.

Marcus reached beneath the seat and produced a chilled bottle and two frosted glasses. She laughed lazily, easily; her eyes were a brilliant burst of gold and green beneath the sensual heavy-lidded crescents of her deep-honey lashes.

"Wine, on a gondola?" she inquired.

"Asti spumante," he returned, handing her a glass and adding lightly, "It's the only way to see Venice, you know."

"Is it?"

"Of course." He entwined his elbow with hers, careful not to spill the sparkling liquid. He took a sip, watching her do the same. The gondola was cushioned, and he leaned back on one elbow, inviting her to follow suit. Her lashes lowered briefly; a small secretive smile curled her lips. When her lashes rose again her eyes were bright, like topaz in the night, and he knew that they were playing a game of cat and mouse, circling warily, and that there was a very dubious distinction between the role of cat and the role of mouse. She was out for something; she intended to play things her way and win. That was why she was with him. But tonight the round was going to go to him.

Still, there was no reason for her to realize that yet.

He leaned over and brushed her lips with a light kiss. She seemed perfectly relaxed, ready to purr at his touch. He kissed her again, dumping his champagne overboard as he did so.

"You're not drinking up," he told her softly. "We're out to forget everything, to watch the moon, to see Venezia as lovers might."

She allowed him to refill her glass, as he did his own. She cast her left elbow over a cushion, stretching her body luxuriously near his, idly playing with the lapel of his jacket. "Marcus, it would be much easier to enjoy the night if you would admit a few things."

"Such as?" He caught the fingers that teased his chest, uncurled them slowly and kissed her palm.

"Your glass is empty again," she told him, taking over the role of hostess.

"And so is yours."

"So it is . . ."

She poured more asti spumante for them both, stretching one arm over the side of the boat. He pretended not to notice as she dumped hers overboard.

"Marcus," she murmured, resting her head against his shoulder.

"Hmmm?"

"You know that Alfred was being blackmailed. Admit it."

"We're not here to talk about Alfred."

He ran his fingers through her hair, smoothing it from her face as the breeze lightly tossed it about. Her cheek felt as soft as a rose petal.

Another gondola passed. The young couple in it laughed and called out to them in Italian, and threw flowers on board. Chris laughed as she clutched the flowers. The moon played on the water; the lights on the palaces they passed added hues of sparkling crimson to the deepest blue. They passed St. Mark's Church, and she smiled up at the winged lion.

Her head still lay against his shoulder. "Marcus, you think someone in your family is involved in something, don't you?"

He ran his finger slowly over her lower lip. "I think you're involved in something."

"Me?"

"You do keep turning up in the strangest places. And you did say that you were after Alfred's money. *And* it seems that you managed to obtain it."

"Don't be absurd," she began, and then she laughed. "I told you why I was in the galleries—"

"Yes, you told me what you chose to."

"And you have told me nothing."

"But perhaps," he whispered softly, nuzzling her ear, "you will persuade me to do so. Ah, here's the restaurant."

Inside, they were led to a secluded booth, with the water before them. He sat beside her, slipping an arm around her shoulders. He explained all the items on the menu. When the antipasto came he teased her into feeding him olives, and his teeth lingered over her fingers, his tongue playing across their tips. In the black gown, her shoulders bared, her hair a cascade of tawny silk about them, she was very beautiful and very exotic. He had to remind himself that he didn't really trust her in the least, that she had airily proclaimed herself a huntress....

And that he knew damned well she was on the hunt right now.

He smiled. "More wine?"

"You've hardly touched yours."

"Oh, on the contrary! I've finished it."

"Let me pour you more."

"Ah, not without you!"

Her smile was a little weak, but she accepted more of the sparkling wine. How much had she consumed?

Quite a nice amount, he calculated, smiling as he watched her drain her glass along with him.

The rest should be very, very easy.

He teased her again, telling her that he divulged his deepest secrets when the vintage was right. She kept drinking to keep him drinking.

And he kept smiling, subtly amused. She was forgetting that he was an Italian—raised on wine.

Between the pasta and the scungilli he led her to the dance floor. She moved like a ripple of water, graceful, sensual. He allowed himself to inhale the fragrance of her hair and flesh, to savor the brush of her body against his.

By the time they finished dinner she was giggling delightedly at his stories. She leaned against him as they walked out and tripped over the dock, still laughing when he swept her into his arms to carry her onto the gondola. Her head was tilted back; her eyes met his. They were cat's eyes, topaz, sizzling with laughter, sensual as a purr, as the soft touch of her fingers against his cheek. He waved a hand at the gondolier and sank to the cushions, holding her, smiling as she trustingly curled her arms around his neck. He kissed her, long and deeply, his hands molding over her shoulders, enjoying the satiny feel of her arms, finding her breast in the shielding darkness, curving over it, loving the way it filled his hand.

And then he held her against him, shuddering, forcing himself to become remote. They were almost there.

The gondola rocked against the dock. "Come on," he whispered to her.

"Where are we?"

"An old church."

"Oh, you're going to buy it?"

He grunted, helping her from the gondola. She tripped again, laughing, smiling up at him. A twinge of guilt touched him; he was taking a very drastic measure. As she stared up at him, smiling with her wide topaz eyes, he reminded himself that though she might be as sweet as a kitten now, she had the claws of a tigress when she chose.

"Oh, Marcus! These steps . . . they're moving!"

"Don't worry, I'll help you."

"*Will* you help me, Marcus?"

"Of course."

They walked into the nave of the old building. She stared up, fascinated by the frescoes on the wall. He tugged at her arm. "Come on, the priest is waiting for us."

"Oh, we're going to get a tour!"

"Something like that."

He held her tightly as they walked up the aisle. The priest was there, along with his clerk and a cleaning lady.

"Oh, they're on the tour, too!"

"Yes. Listen to what he's saying."

Marcus glanced at the priest and nodded. The man began a monotonous chant in Latin.

"I don't understand him!" Chris whispered, and then she giggled.

"Just nod and say *si* when I tell you."

She did so. Then the priest served Mass. Chris tried to suppress a giggle when he came out with the chalice.

"Oh, Marcus! More wine! I really can't."

"Just a sip."

And then it was over. Done. The priest blessed them. All she had to do was sign a certificate.

"What is it?" Chris queried.

"Just a register. It says that . . . you've been a guest."

"Oh." She signed her name with a lovely flourish. "And now?"

"Now we're going home."

"Yes, I really think that I should. I'm so tired all of a sudden. . . ."

She practically collapsed in his arms. Marcus picked her up easily and paid the priest a very hefty sum for his evening's work.

He carried Christina out to the gondola and told the gondolier to return to the palazzo as quickly as possible.

At the steps he also paid that man very well. Then, hoisting her in his arms, he entered the main entry hall, where he heard voices from the courtyard. He hurried up the stairs.

In his room, he laid her on the bed. She was light and limber, floppy as he set her down. "Marcus . . ." she murmured, and she tried to sit up, throwing her arms over his shoulders.

"Shhh, you can sleep now, Christina."

She opened her eyes and smiled in a daze. "Hold me, Marcus. The boat is rocking."

He held her for a moment, then pressed her back to the bed. She brought her palm gently to his cheek. "You really are a nice guy, Marcus."

"Yes, I'm just charming," he muttered dryly. "Hold on. I'll be right back."

He slipped onto the terrace and into her bedroom, where he found one of her gowns. When he returned her eyes were closed, and she was curled up with a pillow. He tried to pull it away from her. She smiled and murmured something, pulling it closer. He sighed, then pulled off her shoes and stockings. She laughed and wiggled her toes. "Marcus, you're tickling me."

I'm tickling you! he thought, dismayed at the hot rush of desire that ravaged his body as his fingers touched the bare flesh of her thighs. "Sit up, Chris," he told her harshly. "You can't sleep in that thing."

He pulled her up, and she fell limply over his shoulders. He fumbled with the hooks at her back, then managed to pull the dress over her head. She fell back against him, her bare breasts crushed to his chest. He pushed her gently away and felt that fullness again, flesh that was soft, breasts that were firm and beautiful and shapely, rose peaked, and so tempting that he groaned. In the morning, she would hate him. If only she were screaming and yelling now...

"Marcus..." she whimpered softly.

He laid her back on the bed, closing his eyes and shuddering fiercely. He reached for her nightgown and opened his eyes. For a second he paused, breath drawn. She was stunning. Tanned and slim, with haunting dips and shadows; long, long limbs, sinewed, firm; a curving waist; a rounded bottom hidden by the thinnest wisp of lace.

He raised her again, fumbling with the white gown. Her breast brushed against his arm, and he muttered several soft curses in Italian. Finally he got the gown over her head and pulled over her torso.

But his nerves were shot. He quickly smoothed the gown down and pulled the covers over her. Then he walked to the terrace to allow the breeze to cool his burning flesh and painful desire.

At length he meticulously stripped off his own clothing and crawled into the bed beside her, keeping his distance. It was difficult. Her back was to him, but she kept inching over. Her derriere became a soft battering ram against his hips.

"Ummm...Marcus," she muttered. He gritted his teeth together, then turned to hold her, fitting his arm around her, his hand at the curve of her breast. He cursed himself a thousand times over. She was pliable. As soft and pliable as a kitten purring beside him. He need only encourage her and she would turn to him....

Strange, he reflected in haunting agony, it didn't really bother him a bit that he had conned and coerced and deceitfully tricked her into marriage. It was the only way that he could stay beside her and protect her. But no matter what she did, he couldn't allow himself to take sexual advantage of her. No matter how much he wanted her. One day he would have her. But she would know all about it. Her heart and soul would be as willing as her supple sensual body.

Lying there seething, fuming, aching—screaming inside—he forced himself to plan for the morning. She was going to be in a rage, so it would be most effective for him to take the offense.

When she awoke he would be ready. Waiting, watching, poised for attack and as hard as rock.

And when morning came he *was* ready. He saw her awaken; he saw her confusion and her horror. And when her eyes met his with topaz fury and accusation, he smiled....

"Buongiorno. Buongiorno, amore mio," he drawled softly. Then he stalked slowly toward the bed and sat down beside her. His eyes were hard, his body tense, his voice taunting and implacable.

It was time to tell her—if she didn't remember—that the game had been played for real. The laughter was over, along with the cautious circling; she had to be made aware that his actions were in deadly earnest and that she couldn't fight him. Whatever he said or did, she would have to support him and be the perfect blushing bride.

Whatever her feelings were—and she looked as if she'd gladly strangle him at the moment.

She would have to bend to his will. Her life might very well depend upon it.

But inwardly he flinched at the cold fury and hatred that seemed to gleam from her eyes. He braced himself and continued to keep his voice cool and mocking. "What? Can she be angry? Dismayed? How so, my love? You wanted a di Medici man. You said so often enough. Well, you've gotten one. I could resist the temptation no longer. But perhaps you feel that you brought the wrong di Medici to the altar?"

He saw her fury increase and her muscles tighten, and he caught her wrists right before she could slap him.

"Why?" she demanded in a whisper that was violent and heated and incredulous . . . and very, very hurt.

He could not apologize, but neither could he remain so hard. *"Cara . . ."* Tenderness softened his voice, but he had to play the game out. "Why? Because it was your wish, of course." He touched her cheek, and again he felt the misery of his betrayal. *"Cara . . ."*

She jerked away from his touch, lowering her eyes. Well, Marcus asked himself dryly, what had he been expecting? He stood up impatiently.

"We have both known that something had to happen between us. Did you take me for a saint? I have only given you what you wished."

She didn't believe a word of what he was saying . . . and why should she, when it was all lies?

"Or perhaps," he said mockingly, "it was truly Tony whom you wished to captivate. He is the more malleable, is he not? But, alas! As you Americans are so fond of saying, You have made your own bed. Now you shall lie in it."

Why was he goading her so? Marcus wondered as one of the silk pillows came hurtling at him.

Because he couldn't explain things to her yet. And because he couldn't bear her hating him.

And because he wanted her so badly, because he had come to care with such a terrible obsession, and was so terribly worried about her. . . .

He forced out a dry laugh. "Another cliché, but you're truly beautiful when you're angry!" She was ... So beautiful as she stared at him with such dismay, such fury—and such hatred.

"Why?" she raged again.

"Why? You were there, too, my love. Oh, I admit, we were neither of us completely lucid, but...that is the course of love, my sweet." He had to get out of there. Away from the reproach in her eyes.

And he had to announce their marriage.

He started to open the door. She was out of the bed, racing toward him. "Wait! What are you doing? We have to do something about this. Surely we can arrange an annulment—"

"An annulment?" He gripped her shoulders, his fingers tightening. "*Cara,* I am on my way downstairs to make the announcement to the family. If you have any sense, Christina, you will keep your mouth shut! You will give the appearance of a sheepish—embarrassed, perhaps—but very happy bride. For God's sake! Haven't you the sense to stay alive!"

Fleeting emotions passed through her eyes, but the strongest remained fury. Marcus tightened his jaw and bit his inner lip. He wanted to shake her. He wanted her to understand that he was trying with all his might to protect her.

But he couldn't explain.

Nor could he admit his own suspicions to her.

He closed his eyes quickly, then gave her a little shove and hurried from the room.

Chris felt as if she were drowning. Everything moved too quickly through her mind. Everything. Everything that had happened since she had come to Venice.

She couldn't move. She could barely reason.

She was in shock.

She was Marcus di Medici's wife.

Chapter 9

Chris stared at the door after Marcus had left, still stunned, still unable to believe what she had done. What *they* had done. And the one single question continued to ravage her pounding head: *why?*

Shivering, she sank back down to sit on the bed, trying to gather her wits about her. Marcus had married her, and she was quite convinced that though he was attracted to her, he certainly wasn't in love with her. So... why?

Because he was protecting her? Or someone else?

Marcus couldn't have murdered his own father. He had only been twelve at the time. But neither, Chris believed with all her heart, could her father have killed anyone. Marcus had tricked her into marriage without loving her; he had gone down to make a pointed announcement to the others about their marriage. Again, *why?*

Because he wanted someone in his family to believe that Alfred Contini's money and holdings would all stay in the di Medici family?

Oh, God! It was all so confusing. And it was getting worse and worse, and now she was really terrified. . . .

No, Marcus hadn't murdered his own father. But there was a blackmailer as well as a murderer running around. There had to be, because Contini must have been blackmailed into keeping quiet about the murder. And that blackmailer must have been the one to cause Alfred's death. A blackmailer capable of murder, too.

Chris had seen a cloaked figure on the night Contini died; that same cloaked figure had appeared in the galleries, hot in pursuit, only yesterday. And both times when she had seen the figure, she had seen Marcus immediately afterward. They had even found the cloak together. . . .

At first she had assumed that the di Medicis were as wealthy as Contini. But from all the talk—including their own words—they were not. Marcus and Tony both claimed not to need Contini's money, yet both of them were always spending money as if it were water.

Oh, God! Chris thought again, the pain in her head and the tumult in her heart making her dizzy. She lay back on the bed, conflict raging inside her. If she could only remember more of the night! What had happened after they had come back to the palazzo? He had too much power over her, way too much power. And she didn't know if she could trust him or not. . . .

There was a knock at the door. Chris started and bolted up quickly, so quickly that her head began to pound all over again. "Who is it?" she called out. Dear Lord! This was his room; she was in it, ostensibly living in it. . . now. . . with him. It was crazy. She felt like panicking, running. . . disappearing. Maybe she had pushed her luck too far; maybe she should just get away while she still could. She was being a fool, seduced into belief in a man who had just proved himself more dangerous than she had ever imagined.

"Christina! It is Sophia. Marcus said you wanted coffee. Let me in, please."

She needed coffee! Nice time for him to think so! When all the damage was done...

She took a deep breath and opened the door.

Sophia swept into the room, setting down a tray with a silver pot and a china cup and saucer. Without glancing at Chris she poured out black coffee and handed her the cup, then stared at her critically.

"So, he married you."

Chris raised the cup a little helplessly. What had he told her to be? A happy, if sheepish, bride?

"I had expected something between you," Sophia muttered. "It was most obvious... but this!" She shook her head as if disgusted, then murmured, "Well, *salute*, Christina. You've done quite well here, haven't you?"

"I thought I was doing quite well before I came here," Chris murmured dryly, but then she remembered that she was supposed to be a happy blushing bride and she stepped past Sophia to stare out the terrace door, wincing slightly as the sunlight seemed to rip into her eyes. "But, of course, nothing in my life has ever been like Marcus." That was true. Nothing and no one had ever touched her life as Marcus had.

"Hmmph!" Sophia muttered. "Yes, they are something, aren't they, the di Medici men? But don't count your blessings too soon, Christina. They are temperamental. They would be the kings of their castles. And they are as attractive to all women as they are to you. You must ask your mother-in-law one day. Life with a di Medici will not be all one glorious romp between the sheets."

Chris took a sip of her coffee; it was so hot it burned her throat. She choked, but was careful not to look at Sophia, not to give anything away.

"Mario and Gina di Medici had marital problems?" she asked innocently.

"Of course. Who would not?" Sophia supplied maliciously.

Chris tensed, suddenly determined to draw Sophia out. "Sophia, do you mean that they fought . . . frequently?"

"Constantly. But you will see for yourself. It will be worse for you. You're an American. And Marcus is an Italian man. Gina at least was Italian, too. But . . . it has been your choice."

"I don't believe you!" Chris charged. "Gina di Medici was very much in love with her husband from all that I hear!"

"Yes, yes, she loved him!" Sophia said impatiently. "That's half the problem, yes? To love so much . . . and feel so little in return! And so the fights. Row upon terrible row. Why, even on the day that your father murdered Mario—"

Sophia broke off suddenly, and Chris tried not to pounce on her. "My father did not murder Mario," she said flatly, then quickly added, "But you were about to tell me, Sophia—weren't you?—that even on the day that Mario died, he and Gina were involved in a marital battle."

"It is none of your concern!" Sophia snapped.

Chris smiled with what she hoped was naïveté. "It *is* my concern; I've just married Mario's son! And I must learn to keep him. Poor Gina! It must have been all the worse for her to lose her husband when they had been engaged in a marital spat! It must have made the pain all the worse."

"I'm sure it did," Sophia murmured, watching Chris curiously. Then it seemed she lost all patience with the conversation. She shrugged. "I am amazed that Marcus married you, yet he has, and so I wish you both luck. You will excuse me, please? Gina is going to church, and I wish to get her key to the galleries."

Chris frowned. "Gina's key?"

"I've told Marcus that I shall go in today and defer his appointments."

"I, uh, I thought only Tony and Marcus had keys to the galleries."

"No, no. Gina has one, too. Why?"

"Nothing, nothing," Chris murmured. Sophia swept her with another critical gaze, murmured that she looked like hell, and told her that she needed some rest if she intended to keep her husband for a week. Chris smiled and thanked her icily for the advice.

As soon as Sophia left Chris walked weakly back to the bed and sank down. She braced herself and swallowed her coffee, praying it would help.

Despite its heat, her teeth were chattering. Gina di Medici had a key to the galleries. Marcus had purposely lied to her about his mother. Gina and Mario had been fighting on the boat. Did Marcus think his mother had killed his father? Did he believe that this charade of a marriage would hold his mother at bay without incriminating her? Did he believe that, if Gina was behind things, she would no longer attempt to harm Chris if Chris were his wife? Or perhaps it was the money! If they all believed that the money was still in the family—through marriage—did Marcus think that she would be safe?

Oh, dear God, she had to get away from them all!

There was another tap on the door. Chris was as jumpy as a bruised boxer about to receive another right punch to the jaw. "Who—who is it?" she called.

There was no answer, only a scraping sound against the door. She jumped up to swing the door open. There was no one there, only a note lying on the floor. She picked it up.

Someone had worked very quickly. In large block letters were the English words: "A di Medici bride has a place awaiting her in the di Medici crypt."

Chris dropped the note, inhaling deeply. The night had been insane; the morning was becoming sheer lunacy. She had to get away and sort things out, had to find some way to make her head stop pounding. And dear God, she didn't want to see Marcus again....

Chris set the note on his dresser and nervously hurried from his room along the terrace to her own. She was shaking so badly that she could barely dress, and as she dressed she started wondering how she had gotten into the white gown, and when she started thinking along that line she started shaking all over again.

Somehow she managed to pull on a corduroy skirt and knit blouse, and then she remembered that her purse must be back in Marcus's room. She slipped quickly back along the terrace, and nearly screamed with tension when the phone beside the bed, French Provincial like the clock on the dresser, started to ring.

She froze, certain that someone would catch it on an extension downstairs. But the shrill ringing continued until her nerves were at the breaking point. Chris grabbed the phone and practically screamed, "Hello!"

There was a long silence. And then a very soft, heavily accented voice spoke. "Christina . . ."

Her name was drawn out. Shivers, like icy rivulets, raced from her nape along her spine.

"Who is this?" she demanded. "What do you want?"

"I have what you want," the voice told her. "Information."

"Tell me what you're talking about!"

There was silence again, and then, "Can you pay? My price will be high, but my information will be worth it. I know who killed Mario di Medici."

"What?" Chris gasped. She realized with a sick feeling that she had the blackmailer on the phone. But he had information to sell to her, and at this point she was very willing to pay.

"Yes, yes! I'll pay," she promised. "Tell me—"

"Not on the phone. Go to St. Mark's. To the Basilica. Sit in a pew and I will find you."

"Wait—"

The phone went dead. Chris stared at it, hung up the receiver, then picked it up again hurriedly, wondering if there were any way she could get an Italian operator to know that she wanted to trace a call.

She shivered again. Had the call come from outside the palazzo? Or was it possible that it had come from within the palazzo itself?

She sighed with frustration. She would never be able to make an Italian operator understand what she wanted. If she tried, she could end up with the operator calling back several times and possibly wind up with someone else on the phone.

Chris hesitated for a second, wondering if she shouldn't tell Marcus about the call. In turmoil she reminded herself that she couldn't trust Marcus any more than anyone else at the palazzo.

Indeed, she could trust him far less! she thought bitterly. Her life was a legal tangle because of him; he had taken her out and married her....

No! She definitely couldn't trust him, and only moments ago she'd been desperately wanting to get away from him. She saw her purse on his dresser and grabbed it, then quietly opened the door and stepped out onto the balcony.

From the courtyard she could hear voices. She couldn't go that way. She hurried down to the landing, then out the main entryway, practically racing down the steps.

She could see a vaporetto coming, but it wouldn't stop for her, not on the di Medici steps. Anxiously she started looking for a gondola. It seemed forever before she saw one; she hailed it quickly. And for once in Venice she didn't see or appreciate a thing. All she could think about was reaching the Basilica. The gondolier spoke a smattering of English; he tried to point out the impressive palaces. He told her how those condemned to death had walked the Bridge of Sighs, but she barely heard him.

When they reached St. Mark's Square Chris shoved a wad of lire into his hands and stared up at the Basilica, then started hurrying across the Square. Pigeons soared and scattered all around her, but she ignored them, impatiently weaving her way through a crowd of tourists to walk up the steps into the church and enter the nave.

She didn't see the artwork or the tombs, or any of the soaring beauty of the Basilica. She stared straight ahead at the altar, then looked around nervously, searching for someone who might be looking for her. She slipped into one of the pews, knelt—and waited.

No one came. Tourists flocked around the artwork and the smaller altars that lined the sides. They lit candles; they knelt and prayed. Chris grew restless. She stood up herself and walked around. She lit a candle, unable to pray, or even think. Eventually she wound her way back to the pew where she had been seated.

Her heart began to pound. There was a note on the pew exactly where she had been sitting. She picked it up. "You were followed. Same time. Same place. Next week."

A bright flash of red at the rear of the Basilica suddenly caught her attention. Glancing up, Chris felt a chill settle over her. She saw a figure in a bright-red hooded cloak leaving the Basilica.

"Wait!" she called.

Priests and tourists turned to stare at her in shocked disapproval. Chris ignored them and started to run.

Outside the sunshine blinded her. She blinked furiously. The figure in red was gone.

Feeling sick and disappointed, Chris started down the steps. The Square seemed to be filled with dozens of tourists and hundreds of pigeons. Her headache returned a thousandfold.

She emitted a sharp expletive and started slowly across the Square, trying to scan the crowd for traces of red. Someone gripped her elbow and she spun around, a startled gasp escaping her. "Marcus!"

His fingers felt like talons, rough around her arm. His eyes were dark and churning, like the sea, and a pulse was beating in his throat at a furious rate.

"What in God's name are you doing?" he demanded harshly. "I go up after announcing my newly acquired state of marital bliss, only to discover that my blushing bride has disappeared! Just what do you think you're doing?''

She could feel his anger rushing over her like hot simmering waves. Instinctively she tried to shake free of his hold; he didn't even appear to notice.

"I, uh, I felt the need to go to church!" she retorted, forcing her chin up in a show of bravado. "Quite frankly, I was praying for a way to get away from you—oh!"

He gave her a shake that wrenched her arm roughly, and she paused quickly, wondering what would happen if she started to scream insanely in the Square. He smiled as if reading her mind.

"This is Italy, Christina. And I am an Italian. Don't expect much help against your legal husband here. I asked you: what are you doing?"

"How did you find me?"

"Quite simply. I asked among the gondoliers. Talk to me, Christina."

"Talk to you! Why?" she asked him a little hysterically. "You've already tricked me and put us both in a totally untenable position. What more can you do?"

He raised a brow politely. "Would you like to find out?"

No, she thought, swallowing nervously and lowering her lashes very quickly to hide her eyes. She knew damned well that she'd never win in a one-on-one confrontation. She had to change her approach with no qualms. Not after what he had done.

"No," she murmured out loud, wondering again how she could get away from him. She was going to have to trick him somehow. She would have to make him believe that she had entirely accepted the situation, then get to the police and the American embassy.

She raised her eyes to his, trying to appear very hurt, very lost and a little helpless. "Oh, Marcus! I'm just so confused and...miserable. Marcus, you know that Contini was murdered. You know that things are going on.... Marcus, we need the police."

He released her arm, but entwined her fingers tightly with his own and started walking back through the Square toward the boats in the canal. "Marcus!" Chris snapped.

He stopped, staring at her. "What?"

"Damn it, Marcus! Why did you...why did you pull last night? Why did you marry me?"

He blinked. A shield as effective as a cloud fell over his eyes. "Because I couldn't bear life without you one more second, *cara mia*," he said with a humorless smile. He started walking again.

"You're a liar, Marcus!" Chris snapped. His fingers tightened around hers; she felt the heat of his tension enveloping her like something tangible. Sensation rippled all along her body in a massive shudder, making her hot, making her weak. Where was he dragging her now? What was he going to expect of her? For a moment she hated herself. Hated her absolute weakness. No matter what happened, no matter how intelligent her thoughts, how aware her reason, he could touch her and he would have all the power. She would sizzle, she would tremble, unable to discern fear from the engulfing excitement that ravaged her when he was near.

She had to get away....

"Where are we going?" she asked him.

"Back to the palazzo—to act like newlyweds," he told her curtly.

Chris lowered her head, not trying to escape his hold. She had to make him trust her again....

He waved down a motor launch and rather roughly helped her aboard. When they were seated Chris slipped her fingers around his arm and rested her head against his chest, not daring to check his eyes for his reaction. He tensed for a moment, then eased, running his fingers lightly through her hair with a tenderness she had not expected. "Marcus," she murmured, "I'm so frightened."

"Don't be," he told her a little huskily. "I mean to protect you."

Protect her. Protect her. She had been called to St. Mark's. He had appeared. He was always appearing....

She shivered. Not Marcus, not Marcus...

Too soon, the launch reached the di Medici palazzo. Marcus helped her out and she continued to cling to him. "I don't understand what we're doing," she whispered to him, trustingly, she hoped.

He smiled down at her. Again she felt that there was tenderness in his eyes, in his touch.

"Is it truly so horrible to find yourself married to me, *cara*?"

Chris pressed her cheek against his chest. "No, Marcus." God help her, it was the truth.

His fingers moved gently over the top of her head. "Let's get back upstairs. Perhaps no one will realize that we've been gone."

Chris smiled. What was she going to do? Charm him? Disarm him? But they were slipping quietly back into the palazzo, quietly back up the stairs....

Quietly back into his room.

Marcus closed the door and leaned against it, staring at her. His eyes fell over her, touched hers. He grinned slowly, then started walking toward her. Chris tried not to tremble when he took her into his arms. The sensation of fire lapping all along her flesh washed over her. There was a roaring in her ears, and she felt a sweet, sweet dizziness. An ache inside her...

His lips touched hers gently, moist and warm. His tongue probed her teeth, delved beyond them. Chris held on to him, feeling engulfed. She closed her eyes and fought for strength.

She teased his nape with her fingers, returning his kiss. And then she drew away, smiling shyly.

"Marcus, will you give me a few minutes? I—I'd like to slip back to my room, to shower and change... and come back to you," she added huskily.

He watched her, neither smiling nor frowning. She couldn't read a thing in his indigo eyes, in his tense stance or rigid features.

"I'll wait for you," he said simply.

Chris nodded and turned to the terrace. Not until she was certain she was past his vision did she hurry.

And then she did so on tiptoe, rushing to the French doors from her room to the terrace, waiting as her heart pounded away and then biting down hard on her lower lip as she tried to silently open her door.

She slipped off her shoes and padded onto the balcony. His door was still closed. She tiptoed down the stairs, praying that no one would make an appearance in the entryway. Again she opened the main door slowly, barely breathing.

When she had closed it behind her she raced down the steps to the canal, waving frantically for a boat. One came to her, and as soon as she was seated she told the gondolier, "Pronto! Polizia, per favore!"

The gondolier looked at her as if she were a crazy foreigner, then shrugged and started down the canal. Way too slowly, Chris thought nervously. She should have held out for a motor launch. At this rate she was never going to reach police station.

Finally the gondola pulled up to a square. Chris realized with dismay that she didn't even know where she was. She paid the man, asking him, "Dove polizia, per favore?"

He pointed around a corner. Chris thanked him, then started up the square to a narrow via, staring at the buildings carefully. She saw a sign and sighed. The man really had brought her to a police station.

Chris opened the door and walked in. The outside of the building had appeared ancient. Inside there were modern desks with typewriters, glass partitions and shrilling telephones. There was a man at the front desk in a uniform, and he went up to him.

"Per favore, parla inglese?"

The man set down his pencil and looked at her. He shook his head, smiled and asked her in Italian to wait a minute.

Chris nodded gratefully. She walked nervously around the small outer chamber. A second later a door opened and another man in uniform, an older man with a kindly smile started out. Chris smiled with even greater relief and started hurrying toward him. But then she gasped, stopping dead in her tracks as Marcus stepped out from behind him.

"No!" she cried, stunned.

Marcus smiled. *"Cara!"* he cried in apparent relief. She didn't know exactly what he said to the fatherly police officer, except that it had to do with how horribly worried he had been and how relieved he was to see her, especially since her mind was still so fogged after the accident on the staircase, which had seemed to steal away all her reason.

The middle-aged policeman clucked in sympathy.

"No, no! You don't understand at all," Chris began backing away from the pair. Marcus was still smiling, still calling her his beloved and sounding truly like a grieved husband; Chris could see his eyes, and there was an expression that she was coming to recognize all too easily.

He was furious with her. He also knew that he had her cornered, and he was very much enjoying the situation.

"Wait, sir, listen to me!" Chris pleaded to the officer; he shook his head blankly, and she realized that he didn't speak any English. She tried desperately to come up with some Italian; instead, she started babbling in interspersed French and English, convincing the officer if Marcus hadn't already, that she was definitely suffering from delusions.

Chris stared at them both in growing frustration, fury and fear. "Oh, never mind!" she cried, backing toward the door, then turning blindly to run. She reached for the door then gasped as firm fingers grabbed her arm, jerking her back. She spun and found herself encircled by Marcus's arms, crushed tightly to him. He was still smiling, his touch upon her gentle; his voice was soft, the tone very solicitous

But his words—spoken in English—quite bluntly belied his tone. "You've had it, Chris. You're caught, tied, cornered. I've given him our marriage certificate and the doctor's report on your concussion. Now, shape up, *amore mio*. Smile at me sweetly, or by all the saints, you will be able to charge me with abuse before the night is over."

He was serious. But she did feel cornered—too cornered to behave rationally.

She kicked him as hard as she could in the shin. He grunted slightly; she heard his teeth grate. His eyes narrowed to glittering ice but he didn't relax his hold one iota.

He turned to the police officer and said something in Italian. The man shook his head, then waved, glad that she was the di Medicis' business and not his. Marcus gripped her arm with no mercy, and half pushed, half dragged her back out into the waning sunshine and along the via.

He was walking so quickly and so angrily that she could barely keep up. To her dismay, she felt herself shivering. She had no idea where he was leading her or just how far his fury would take him.

And it was getting dark.

Chris tripped over a break in the tile of the walkway. "Marcus!" she gasped breathlessly. He didn't hesitate in his stride at all; he just gripped her more tightly, dragging her along.

"Marcus..." There was a plea in her voice. He stopped, but not out of courtesy. His features were so tightly drawn that she would gladly have sunk into the ground.

"Sorry, Christina," he snapped coldly. "No more tricks. If you have any sense whatsoever you'll just shut up."

He started walking again. She had no choice but to follow him, her anxiety growing by the minute. Her heart kept insisting that he could never hurt her, but her head kept saying that he was ready to wind powerful fingers around her throat and strangle her.

They soon reached the square. She saw that he had brought the motor launch. Seconds later she was being rather roughly lifted down to the rear seat. She started to rise, but he pressed her back. "I'm warning you, Christina. Don't push me."

The motor roared to life. Marcus obeyed the speed and traffic restrictions, but just barely. He didn't touch her; he kept his hand on the tiller, his profile implacable as he stared straight ahead.

Chris swallowed uneasily as she noted they weren't following canals that were even remotely familiar to her. She was even more horrified to realize after several speedy swerves and turns that they were on some kind of an open waterway.

"We're not going back to the palazzo," she observed moistening her lips.

"No, we're not," he replied bluntly.

He increased his speed. They were slicing through the water, and the color of the sky was beginning to match that of the water. Chris felt a little ill, suddenly seized by panic

"Marcus . . . ?" she murmured.

He faced her again, his countenance as dark as the water by night. "Don't even talk to me right now, Chris. I mean it. Do us both a favor and *don't talk to me!*"

She closed her eyes and miserably shut up. She opened her eyes again when she realized that the wretched speed of the launch was slowing.

They were coming to a dock, a regular boat dock. Chris realized that they had left Venice and reached the mainland. The motor idled while Marcus steered the boat into berth. Then he jumped to the wood planking and reached a hand down to her. Chris hesitated, until he snapped out her name. She took his hand and allowed herself to be pulled up. He kept her hand and started walking, his strides uncomfortably long as he started down the dock to a parking lot. He knew where he was going; he led her straight to bright-red Ferrari, pulled a set of keys from his pocket opened the passenger door and practically shoved her in.

Chris considered bolting as he walked around the car, but he was too quick. She saw his face as he opened the driver's door and reconsidered immediately. If there was any sense of mercy left in him at all, any further aggravation from her would strip it away entirely.

The Ferrari roared into action with a fury that seemed to match that of its driver.

Chris buckled her seat belt, leaned back and closed her eyes again. They were on the road for several minutes before she found the nerve to open them. They had traveled at high speed for at least fifteen minutes before she dared to ask him where they were going.

"Adazzi," he answered briefly. He glanced her way, but his eyes were in shadow, and she didn't know if his temper was beginning to ease or not. "To the villa."

To the villa...Chris couldn't see anything at all. They had gone through one town, but now all she could see in the darkness was shadowed landscape.

Then Marcus cut his speed, and they took a sharp turn to the right. They were on a rutted road that ran past scattered buildings. They took a sharp left then, and the car began to climb. She saw light suddenly, and the car jerked to a stop before a walled whitewashed villa.

Marcus got out of the car. There was a wrought-iron gate in front, up a short pathway from the car. He opened the gate with a key, then turned back to Chris. "This is it, Chris. And there isn't anywhere to go. Believe me, this isn't a tourist town. You won't find a soul who speaks English. Get out!" he finished.

Chris took a deep breath and crossed her arms over her chest. "You must think I'm insane if you expect me to go anywhere with you when you treat me the way you do."

"I'm going to think that you're insane if you don't get out of that car now and quit making my life an absolute misery within the next few seconds," he snapped, his words carefully enunciated.

Her voice, to her absolute horror, was barely a whisper. "Marcus, I'm afraid."

"At the moment you have no reason to be. But if you're not out of that car..."

She slammed the door and walked with a rigid spine to the gate.

She followed him through a small but beautifully flowering garden to a porch, where he unlocked the front door of the small two-story building.

Taking a breath and hoping that her show of bravado was real, Chris followed him.

She was startled by the up-to-date flavor of the villa: modular sofas and chairs were grouped before a contemporary fireplace in a sunken pit. She could see that past a small dining room area, only a counter separated a bright white-and-yellow kitchen from the main room.

There was also a staircase leading to darkness above.

Chris stayed near the door, her back to it. Marcus strode into the room, throwing his keys down on the nearest sofa. He stripped off his tweed jacket, tossed it on top of the keys, pulled off his tie, threw it down, too, then walked around to sink down, leaning his head back and closing his eyes—totally ignoring Chris.

Chris stayed where she was. After a minute he rubbed his temple, then opened his eyes, turning around to stare at her with an uplifted brow.

Chris shook her head in exasperation. "All right, I give up. What are we doing here? Come to think of it, I give up entirely on the past twenty-four hours. What the hell are you doing?"

"What am I doing?" he repeated. He shook his head. "Damned if I know," he muttered, as if it were all her fault. Then she saw his lashes lower, his eyes narrowing once again, as if her question had rekindled his anger. "There's one thing I can tell you, Chris, and that's that we're going to be here until you choose to tell me what the hell is going on!"

"*Me!* You're the one who—"

"Sneaks around galleries with rope and grappling hooks? Disappears the morning after her marriage, then runs to the police station after very sweetly declaring that she needs a shower?" he taunted. Then he smiled. "There's a shower upstairs."

"I don't want a shower anymore."

"Oh, yes, you do."

"No, I—"

He stood up, still smiling. Chris moved away from the door, circling him to reach the stairs. "I haven't got anything with me," she muttered. "You chose to take off like this without warning—"

"You'll find everything you could need."

"Whose everything?" Chris heard herself query, feeling an absurd tug of jealousy. To her horror, he noted it.

"I'm thirty-three years old, Christina. And not a monk."

"If you think I'm going to—"

"Yes, I think you are." He smiled again. "My shin is still killing me."

"It should have been more than your shin," Chris muttered. Then she was suddenly furious. "You bastard! What you've done is totally illegal! You purposely fed me wine, you coerced me . . . you're crazy!"

"Yes, and tired and hungry. So—"

"Don't think you're going to touch me, Marcus," she said, praying it would come out as a warning, not a desperate plea.

"Quite frankly, I believe I've lost the desire," he stated disinterestedly. "But you are going to tell me exactly what you've been up to!"

The argument could go in circles forever. Chris realized that she felt gritty, exhausted and famished. Marcus had obviously sent someone up to the villa to prepare it for occupation; the light had been on. Hopefully there would be food here. And if she meekly melted into the woodwork, he might just leave her alone for the night, and by morning she could think of something.

Chris straightened her shoulders and started up the stairs.

"Light's to your right on the wall," he drawled to her.

"Thank you," she said briskly.

Chris found the hall light, then the bathroom. It was very modern, with a huge shower and sunken tub, and a wall-length closet. She opened the closet door and found soap, towels, toothbrushes, toothpaste and a feminine floor-length, terry-cloth robe.

"And I wonder who the hell it belongs to!" she muttered angrily, throwing it to the floor. She stepped into the shower and turned the water on hard—and started shivering again.

She still wasn't sure that she wasn't in the clutches of a maniac, and here she was worrying about his previous companions!

She closed her eyes, allowing the water to run over her face. She was in love with the maniac. No matter what he had done to her, she had to cling to the belief that it was because he cared. . . .

Fool, she berated herself in silence. Then she hurried to scrub herself and get out of the shower, worried suddenly that he was going to burst through the door and either strangle her—or seduce her.

She was forgetting something very important. However ludicrous it seemed, she was legally married to him. He would never have staged such an elaborate scenario if he hadn't been certain of what he was doing.

Chris turned off the shower. She stepped out and dried herself, then picked up the robe that she had tossed on the floor. It wasn't a bad fit, but there were no buttons, only a sash. She hugged the robe around herself tightly, then belted it, took a long breath and walked back downstairs.

Marcus was in the kitchen. He didn't look up as she approached the counter, compelled to do so by the aroma of something cooking. There was a frying pan on the stove; oil was simmering there, with a touch of garlic and herbs. Then was a bottle of unlabeled wine on the counter; Chris poured herself a glass, noticing a little uneasily that Marcus was chopping chicken pieces with a massive cleaver.

"Want to tell me what you were doing at the church?" he asked without looking up.

"Why? You won't believe me. Or you'll pretend not to."

He glanced up at her. "Humor me," he suggested. "And while you're at it, get a pan under the sink for the spinach."

Chris walked around the counter to get the pan. She didn't like being as close to him as she was. The kitchen was modern and convenient; it was also very small.

"Start talking, Chris. And now that you've got the pan, you might want to wash the spinach."

She turned on the water, thinking that if he hadn't been doing the majority of the cooking, and if she hadn't been starving from not having eaten all day, she would definitely have resented his tone.

"I was called," she said.

"Called?"

"Yes, I was called. I assume it was by the same person who was blackmailing Alfred. He told me to come to the church, that my father didn't murder yours, but that he knew who did."

"So why the hell didn't you tell me?" Marcus demanded in a low growl.

Chris hesitated. Maybe her evidence was slim, but it seemed sound to her. Gina and Mario had been fighting on the boat. According to Sophia, they'd always had marital problems. Crimes of passion were well-known throughout Italian history. And Gina had a key to the galleries, which Marcus had lied about. Why, if not to protect his mother?

There seemed to be only one thing to do: accuse Gina before Marcus and see what his reaction was.

"Because it's obvious," she murmured. "You think your mother killed your father. That's why you staged this—Marcus, no!" Chris screamed.

She had wanted a reaction. Had she drawn too much of one?

He had turned around in fury, the cleaver in his hand. Suddenly all she could see was the knife that had flashed in the galleries on the night Alfred Contini had died, and she panicked.

She instinctively jerked around, pulling the spinach pan with her. It flew up in the air, catching Marcus's temple. Not all that hard, but hard enough for him to know he'd been hit! And, of course, just as the pan grazed him, she realized that he hadn't been about to stab her. All he had been doing was holding the cleaver.

"Marcus, I didn't mean to..." Her voice trailed away.

But it was too late. He was staring at her with anger, as if he certainly didn't believe her.

"I am going to strangle you," he muttered, a little bewildered. And then she saw his lips compress until they were nothing but a grim line and he took a step toward her, reaching for her.

"Oh, no!" Chris said, gasping, and tried to barge past him. She felt his hand grasping for her arm. He missed, but his fingers caught the terry-cloth robe. She tried to keep running. The robe stayed in his hand, and her impetus sent her crashing to the floor half naked, the rest of her tangled in the robe.

"No!" she shrieked again as he straddled her, grabbing her wrists and pulling them over her head to keep her from wildly pummeling him. Chris closed her eyes and started babbling desperately. "Please, Marcus, I didn't mean to! I don't care what happened in the past. I don't care if you were blackmailing Alfred. I don't care what you're guilty of. I don't care who's guilty of anything. I don't care about any of it. I don't—"

She broke off. He hadn't moved; he hadn't said a word. She opened her eyes to see that he was staring at her with a curious light in his eyes and a bemused smile on his lips. She moistened her lips, then realized that she really was naked.

His thighs were around her bare hips; her breasts were completely uncovered and heaving as she gasped for breath. The pressure he used on her wrists wasn't painful, nor did he seem furious anymore. He was a little amused, but not completely; there was an indigo glitter in his eyes, yet his features were very, very taut. "Chris, I didn't blackmail Alfred. Why would I?"

She hesitated. "Because he was sheltering the real murderer?" she whispered.

He laughed. "First you accuse my mother. But if I'm protecting my mother, why would I blackmail Alfred for doing the exact same thing?"

"I don't know," Chris murmured miserably. "I'm sorry...."

"Nor, Chris," he said quietly, "did I murder anyone. I'm not guilty of anything... except coercing you." He fell silent for a second, then took a long breath. "But, Chris, I do know that Alfred was being blackmailed."

"You do?" she whispered uneasily.

"Yes." He paused. "Large sums were going out of the company account for years. I never realized it before, because all of us were free to use that account when we needed it."

"You knew..." was all that Chris could think to whisper.

"I suspected, and then I knew."

She felt her flesh burn because his eyes were raking over her, and she felt as if they touched her with a slow unquenchable blaze.

"Did you really think I meant to attack you with a cleaver?" he demanded huskily.

"I—I panicked...."

"Perhaps," he murmured, smiling, "you should panic." He released her wrists and shifted his weight from hers, but she was still pinned to the floor. His hand coursed lightly down her arm where it was still caught in terry cloth, and then his palm was against her bare flesh, cradling her breast, teasing the nipple to a peak with slow sensual circles. She felt herself redden, and she closed her eyes with a shudder, willing her body not to arch to his touch. Yet her body ignored her will. His fingers moved over her ribs, caressed her hip, trailed down the little angle between her belly and her hip, and moved erotically over her inner thigh.

"I want you now, Chris," he murmured to her, a fever that defied denial in the husky timbre of his voice. She opened her eyes to see his above hers, probing, demanding. And then she closed her eyes again with a little sigh that caught in her throat as he kissed her, slowly, sensually, then commandingly. Chris rolled against him, glad of the hand that continued to sweetly torment her body, to touch her like a fire that promised to build and build and build....

His lips moved to the pulse at her throat, and then his dark head dipped low. He cupped one of her breasts in his hand and savored it with his mouth, taking the nipple between his teeth and raking it again and again with his tongue. Chris cried out softly, stunned by the shattering depth of the sensation. Yet while his mouth continued to lavish attention on her breast, his hand moved again, following the curve of her hip and moving along her thigh. His knee remained between hers, giving him the freedom to taunt and explore her flesh, and bring a rush of pleasure rippling through her as he sought her most intimate places with bold audacity.

Christina unknowingly raked her nails across his back, gasping out his name. He buried his head in the shadowed valley between her breasts, then brought his lips to hers once again. Finally his eyes met hers and she saw the question in them. Didn't he know he was assured of an answer? She couldn't give him one, not in words. She wrapped her arms around him, pressing her face against his shoulder, almost afraid of the depth of her need for him. "The ... oil ... is burning," she murmured.

"So am I," he chuckled hoarsely, but he unwound her arms from around his neck and rose. Chris closed her eyes.

She heard his footsteps and the sound of a click as he turned off the stove. Then she felt his arms around her as he drew her to her feet, smiling at her as he lifted her. "I'll be damned if I'll take you for the first time on the floor when there's a wonderful bed upstairs," he told her.

She closed her eyes again, loving the feel of his body, the ripple of muscles, as he carried her up the stairs. He knew the way; he didn't turn on a light. There was a waning moon outside, and it cast enough of a glow so that they could see one another.

He didn't set her on the bed, though, but placed her on her feet, slipping his hands beneath the robe that still clung precariously to her shoulders so that it fell away from her, like an unveiling. She felt his eyes, hungry as they moved over her, and again she burned and shivered at the simple delight of his gaze. She wanted to touch him, but she didn't seem to be able to move. She stood with her eyes locked with his as he unbuttoned his cuffs and then the front of his shirt. He slipped off his shoes, kicking them aside, then tugged at his belt buckle. With the lithe movements she had come to expect from him, he shed his pants and briefs. Chris closed her eyes, shaking with her desire for him as he stepped forward and took her in his arms again. His body was flush against hers: hard thighs, muscled chest, throbbing arousal. And still he kissed her lingeringly, backing her toward the bed until she fell against it, welcoming him with a fever as he followed her down.

Now she was able to touch him. Her hands moved in a frenzy, stroking his face, kneading his shoulders, trailing down the long line of his back, her nails scraping over his buttocks, her fingers fascinated at his tight muscles. He whispered husky encouragement to her, Italian words that made no sense, yet made all the sense in the world. He nipped at her earlobe and at her neck, and again he moved to taste her flesh, her breasts and her belly, and all the while his hands soothed and ignited her, roaming where they would, eliciting sharp cries from her.

She was amazed and stunned and almost frighteningly aroused by his touch. He made love to her with no hesitation, giving no quarter, and she quickly lost control of all thought, consumed by the wonder of sensation, completely pliant to his will. She felt his fingers beneath her bottom, lifting her, and she felt a new burning between her thighs, deep and sensual, moist, as his intimate probing stroked her to a total frenzy where she heedlessly cried out his name, her head tossing, her hips arching with an urgency all their own. She begged him, and she didn't know what she was begging for. All she knew was that she wanted him, all of him, so badly that she was almost in tears.

He moved beside her, clutching her hand, bringing it to him. She swallowed, clutching him, caressing him, moaning softly, barely aware and yet thrilled that she had created the throbbing ardency of his passion, a little frightened and awed again at the ferocity of her feelings, at the absolute fever that controlled her. And yet his whisper was with her, the beautiful, encouraging cadence of his words.

He moved over her, spreading her thighs with the powerful force of his knees and his body. She saw his eyes, indigo in the night, laced with desire, and she clutched his shoulders before he could lower himself.

"Marcus . . . I . . ."

"*Cara?*" he whispered.

"I don't . . . know what I'm doing."

"Christina," he murmured, "you certainly do."

"No, I . . ."

He seemed to start. "The first time?" he queried with a ragged breath.

"I've spent a lot of time in school," she whispered lamely. "I've been involved . . . but never this involved."

The sound of his soft chuckle enveloped her all over again with warmth; he touched her face with a tenderness all the more gratifying because she could feel the leashed ferocity of his passion. He kissed her, and as his lips savored her, he thrust carefully, slowly into her, holding her body tightly to his own, absorbing the initial shock and immediately soothing her from it. There was pain, like the flash of a knife, but his strokes were slow and deep, and she was arching to receive them while her body still shuddered with both the shock and the growing wonder. The blaze began to build again, soaring like an indigo fire, and she gave herself up to its flames, kissing him, pressing against him, biting him lightly on his shoulders, grazing her hands again and again over his back, drawing delighted words from him when her fingers curved over his buttocks, inviting the total unleashing of his passion.

She had known since she had first seen him that he had promised this abandoned wonder, this absolute flaring passion. And now, as she writhed and cried and moaned, craving something ultimate, she knew the true extent of his promise. He lifted himself, thrusting deep...deep... deep...and it burst upon her, like shimmering light, totally shocking and magnificent, and she shuddered again and again in the aftermath, stunned by the shattering delight of complete sexual sensation.

For a long while she lay without moving, loath to allow the satisfied and drifting sensation to fade. A summer breeze swept through the windows, cooling them. Chris could feel his flesh, damp beside hers; in the pale light she could see his arm stretched across her midriff. She had never felt so close to a person before in her life; she had never been so content, and yet even as she tried hard to hold on tight to all that had been so wonderful, something within her began to withdraw. She'd always believed instinctively that she could trust him; now she believed so more than ever. But he was a di Medici; if he talked to her, he would still conceal his real feelings and his real thoughts. He had gone through quite a charade to keep her safe, and yet she still wasn't certain whether it had been done to protect her—or his family.

Lying in bed, feeling him, touching him, she realized very clearly that they were at opposite ends of the spectrum. She was a Tarleton. No charade could really turn her into a di

Medici, not when James Tarleton was still considered to have been a murderer. And not when she had become a di Medici by dark and secretive means. She shivered suddenly, remembering Sophia's warnings about her future happiness . . . or lack thereof.

Well, it didn't really matter, Chris thought dismally. Sophia didn't know that Marcus had taken drastic measures merely because he didn't want another corpse on his hands.

He must have been thinking, too. He traced a finger idly between her breasts to her navel. Chris swallowed, not willing to deny him, but aware that she had to withdraw to salvage her emotions. She was glad that the room was dark.

Marcus sighed, as if sensing that he had lost her. He made no comment on their being together; he swung his feet over the side of the bed and found his pants. "Let's go downstairs and get something to eat," he said, and the suggestion sounded like an order. "And get everything straightened out that's happened from the very beginning." He picked up her robe and brought it to the bed, bending with a little smile on his lips before he kissed her briefly. "Belt it tightly, please. You're not going to get away with distracting me this time."

"Me!" Chris protested. She was glad of the robe, though, and quickly slipped back into it.

"Umm," he murmured, walking barefoot and bare chested to the door. He paused, looking back at her. Chris tied the robe, flushing beneath his scrutiny, even in the dim light.

"What?" she demanded at last, unnerved.

He shook his head. "You're a bit of an anachronism these days. For an American, that is."

"Oh?"

She saw the flash of his teeth in the moonlight. "Isn't it unusual for an American woman to actually come to her husband's bed untouched?"

Chris felt new color flood her features; he sounded mocking. She forced herself to walk smoothly across the room and past him on the way to the small hall and stair-case. "I don't remember saying that I was actually 'un-touched,'" she murmured coolly. "Nor, for that matter, are we really married."

He laughed, but she sensed no humor in the dry sound. "Oh, it was quite real. Trust me."

"But not intentional," Chris retorted, her face averted from his as she preceded him down the stairs. "It's another problem that's going to have to be worked out. Something you got us into and you're going to have to get us out of."

"Let's take things as they come, shall we?" he said impatiently, moving her out of his way so he could step into the kitchen and light the burner beneath the frying pan again.

She didn't respond, but just stared at him, wondering how they could be so close—and yet so distant.

He picked up the cleaver and started on the chicken again. When she still didn't move, he looked up at her impatiently.

"*Mi scusi*, darling, but for the moment you are my wife, Christina di Medici, and though I like to think we Italians have come a long way, it's not customary for the husband to be doing all the cooking. Especially after his wife just struck him with the spinach pan. Even if she did make amends rather nicely. Want to help?" The last was rather pointed.

Annoyed, flushing again, Chris lowered her head and moved into the kitchen.

Fifteen minutes ago she had forgotten that anything in the world except the power of his pulsing body and her own. Yet he could talk to her as if he had barely as much as kissed her.

But he did intend to get to the bottom of things. To talk, to thrash it out. Wasn't that exactly what she wanted?

Yes, but...

She had wanted more. Some wild proclamation of love and devotion. Sweet words of adoration. A humble admission that, yes, he had tricked her into marriage, not only to protect her but because he had loved and needed her....

Chris sighed and bent to pick up the spinach pan, think ing a little guiltily that she should ask him if he was okay But then his hand smacked her derriere and she straight ened instead to give him a nasty glance of outrage.

He laughed. "Come on. Let's get this show on the road I'm starving. And," he added softly, pausing for a secon to draw her body against his and span his hands around he waist as he whispered against her earlobe, "I'd very muc! like to get business out of the way for the evening. This op portunity is just too wonderful to waste."

For a minute Chris felt like hitting him over the head wit the pan again, but she held dead still, closing her eyes an fighting for serenity instead.

She had no intention of denying her fascination for hir or his desire for her.

Only of denying her love.

Chapter 10

They ate at the kitchen counter, across from one another. Chris was glad, because as he listened to her, she had the feeling that he still doubted something about her, and the sensation was very irritating.

"So," he said, watching her as he sipped his wine, "you came to Venice only because the mime troupe came to Venice. You'd never called, written or sent a Christmas card because your family had shied away from the past. But you met Alfred and came right home with him."

Chris set down her fork, pushed her plate away and folded her arms on the counter with exasperation. "I knew a little about Alfred Contini, the di Medicis and the galleries. I was curious. Wouldn't you have been?"

He shrugged. "And right after you came to the palazzo, Alfred started hinting that he knew your father hadn't killed mine."

"Yes."

"He told you to meet him at the galleries. You went. You saw this figure in a cloak arguing with him. Then the figure pulls out a knife. Alfred starts running . . . and has his fatal heart attack.''

''Yes.''

''But you didn't bother to tell anyone about this cloaked figure at the time.''

''I tried to talk to you!'' Chris flared. ''You didn't want to listen!''

He ignored her. ''Anyway, in the gem salon, you saw what you thought to be a blackmail note. So you went through extravagant preparations and broke into the galleries.''

''It wasn't at all extravagant or difficult,'' Chris retorted cuttingly, then she hesitated. ''Until you hit the trapdoor.''

''If you *were* being chased the second time, be damned glad that you knew about the trapdoor. Especially,'' he murmured softly, ''after you'd crashed through the stair case.''

''You don't think the staircase was an accident, do you?'' Chris demanded.

''No,'' he admitted.

''And that's why you pulled the whole marriage thing?''

He shrugged. ''It had crossed my mind before. It didn't seem that you would leave Venice—until after the wedding,'' he added dryly.

''I was . . . frightened.''

''You idiot. You should have been frightened a long time ago,'' he snapped at her.

''Then you're admitting that my father didn't kill yours!'' Chris exclaimed triumphantly.

''I'm not admitting anything except that Alfred was being blackmailed. And maybe that he was driven to his death by your cloaked figure. But tell me, what made you believe I might be a part of it all?''

Chris hesitated. ''It seemed as if you were continually showing up exactly where things were happening! And also seemed as if you needed money.''

"I see," he murmured. "But apparently you think that Alfred was being blackmailed because of my father's death. was twelve at the time. And if I had known something about my father's death, I would have shouted it down every street in Italy."

"Marcus, let's assume that my father didn't kill your father. But Alfred knew who did."

"You're not making any sense. Alfred was the one being blackmailed. Don't you think that could mean that Alfred was the one who killed him?"

Chris shook her head. "No, I think that Alfred was protecting someone else. Marcus, that has to be it. Because if the blackmailer has turned to me, and someone is trying to kill me, then it must be because the blackmailer has something to say about someone who isn't dead."

"All right, so we go over everyone on the boat that day," Marcus murmured. "Your father, my father. Our mothers. Alfred and Sophia. Genovese, Joe and Fredo. We've decided to leave ourselves out, right?" he queried a little sarastically. "And Tony...he was too small to have killed my father."

"We probably need a motive," Chris murmured uneasily, looking down at her hands, then straight into his eyes. "Marcus, I know that your parents were fighting that day. And you lied to me about something. You told me that only you and Tony have keys to the galleries. Your mother has one, too."

He emitted an impatient oath that made her cringe a little. "I didn't tell you because you're dying to condemn my mother. And you're forgetting something."

"What?"

"My mother adored my father."

"Yes, but crimes of passion—"

"Get off it, Chris!"

"Fine!" she snapped angrily. "Let's hang my father, but God forbid we touch *your* precious noble family!"

He pushed back his chair and stood, taking his wineglass with him as he strode into the living room and sat on one of the modular sofas. "Why don't you quit with the attack and take a wider look at things?" he demanded coolly.

Chris began to pick up their dishes, scraping them distractedly and almost throwing them into the sink. "I am looking at things in a broad sense. You're not. And I don't believe a word you're saying, because you obviously think it's someone in your family or else you wouldn't have pulled this marriage bit."

"Leave the damn dishes alone!" Marcus muttered. "And come over here so we can get on with this."

"You walked away from me!"

He leaned back, closing his eyes and rubbing his temples. "Chris, we're not going to get anywhere arguing about this. Bring your wine over here."

She compressed her lips and stiffly complied with his suggestion, sitting primly on the edge of the sofa. He smiled and stretched out a hand, running his fingers over the tense muscles in her back. Chris despised her instant reaction to him; she remained straight, but longed to curl up against his bare shoulder.

"Ease up," he warned her softly.

"I saw the person in the cloak again today," Chris told him.

"Where? When?"

"Right before you grabbed me at St. Mark's Square. And whoever it was that called me left a note telling me that I had been followed." She hesitated briefly. "That's why I was so frightened today, Marcus. I had seen the figure—and then there you were. And then that night when I went through the trapdoor... you were there, too, and so was the cloak."

His hand paused on her back. "Chris," he murmured, "there's another chute into the crypt."

"There is?" she demanded, startled. "Where?"

"Into the section where we really keep the family skeletons."

"But I thought that was completely walled off."

"So did I—until that night."

Chris shivered and took a long sip of her wine. "I got nother note today, Marcus. One telling me that di Medici rides belong in the di Medici crypt."

"Damn it, Chris!" he exploded. "If you had told me bout all of this I would have been in a much better posion to trace what was going on! Have you still got all these otes?"

"The two from today," she murmured. "I never found e blackmail note."

"Well, give them to me in the morning. I want to get them the police."

Chris nodded.

"What are we going to do now?"

He didn't answer right away. She sensed that he was niling, and she turned to look at him. He *was* smiling, but e appeared tense, wired, and his eyes had a heavy-lidded ittering sizzle to them.

"Go to bed," he drawled softly in reply, causing her to ush and lower her lashes.

"Together?" she heard herself murmur stupidly.

He laughed. "It's what I had in mind." He reached up d plucked her wineglass from her fingers, drawing her to his arms. "Unless," he demanded a little tersely, "our onversation has given you an aversion to the idea."

She met his eyes, her own wide. "No," she said simply. was enough; it satisfied him.

He stood, then walked around to check the door and turn f the lights. Chris rose herself, walking to the stairs ahead him and pelting up them.

Tonight... tonight she was glad of the darkness. He was ill new to her; the shattering excitement was still new to r. So new that she felt she needed the gentle cover of the ght.

A little breathlessly she shed her robe and slipped naked neath the covers, pulling them to her chin.

A few minutes later she saw his silhouette as he silently entered the room on his bare feet. She heard the rasp of his zipper and a soft thud as his pants fell to the floor.

She felt his naked flesh as he crawled in beside her. Her nerves seemed to dance with that simple pleasure, with anticipation.

But he didn't reach out for her right away. He propped himself on one elbow, and in the soft moonglow she could see his eyes and the small smile curving his lips. He did touch her then, placing his palm between her breasts, feeling the wild and erratic beat of her heart.

"It thunders like a frightened rabbit," he murmured lightly, and then his fingers curled and his palm closed over her breast, stroking. She moaned softly and moved against him, touching his chest, then running her hand down the length of his body, over his hips and toward his thigh. He leaned to kiss her lips, to trace them with his tongue, and then to brush light kisses over her cheek until he reached her ear, where he murmured softly, "If you wish something, *cara*, you must learn to reach out for it."

She hesitated just a second, feeling her heart skip a beat, then thunder again. Then she did reach for him, feeling hot flashes invade her body with sweeping delight at the passion she discovered. He moaned deeply, clutching her shoulders, caressing her breasts, brushing her knees apart to stroke her thighs and play between them.

"Oh," Chris whispered, burying her face against his neck, feeling on fire.

Suddenly his hands were raking through her hair, holding her head still, and his lips were on hers with a ravaging hunger. Chris shuddered with delight, then started at the smooth but shattering thrust of his body as he entered her. She welcomed him with a burning heat, crying out in wordless delight at his abrupt invasion, amazed at the pleasure of just feeling him inside her. She wrapped her legs tight about him, absorbing the deep thrust, shuddering again and again as he filled her with wild rhythms and an exotic heat

This time she realized that, as sweetly primal as it was with him, it was more than sex. Her delight was in holding him, in feeling totally that he was hers. Perhaps that was also a primal feeling: holding, cherishing, nurturing the man that she loved. Being the woman that he needed. Feeling his hands and his lips as he moved, the moist heat of his kisses and his body. Wanting not only the glorious sensation of total release, but the gratitude of knowing that she, her breasts, her thighs, her hips, her flesh, her movements, were his and he was hers. She was his need, his desire, as much a part of him as he was of her. It was, for these moments, being totally possessed, while losing nothing. The reward was in being his woman . . . his wife.

She realized then, too, that it would always be different with him. Sudden hot passion at times, slow building delight at others. He was as unpredictable as a black panther. As sleek and wild as that cat of the night.

"Cara," he murmured again, and he whispered things to her in Italian, things that urged and encouraged and abetted the running quicksilver in her blood, sending her thoughts spinning away on clouds, causing her body to tremble with fever and urgency. She was shuddering, writhing...exploding above the clouds, and shivering again with the wonderful possessive feelings and the warmth of him inside her. His warmth was with her still, even as he left her to roll to his side and pull her close.

Chris inhaled deeply and sighed with a contented little catch. His fingers moved idly, gently against her hair. She rested her head against the damp strength of his chest, wrinkling her nose slightly as the dark hair there tickled it. She wrapped her arm about his waist, happy as she felt his light kiss upon the top of her head.

She yawned and drifted quickly into a pleasant totally contented sleep.

Morning had broken when she opened her eyes again. The sun was streaming through the windows, and a variety of birds were carrying on a trilling cacophony.

Chris knew she was alone in the bed. The sheets beside he
were cold. She gazed toward the window, and as she ex
pected, Marcus was there leaning against the frame, starin
out at the day as he sipped coffee. He was in a robe, the su
touching the gold medallion on his chest.

Today he didn't know that she had awakened; he wasn'
waiting for her to open her eyes. She was able to study hir
for several seconds without facing the too-knowing indig
depths of his eyes.

A little chill crept through her at the sight of him. Th
sunlight seemed to make his reflections evident. His posi
tion was relaxed and thoughtful; his eyes were intense. Chri
knew that he was thinking about the situation . . . or pe
haps not thinking, but worrying. And Chris thought at tha
moment that his preoccupation stemmed from his ow
fears.

Because it was very probable that his mother or hi
brother was involved.

She closed her eyes quickly. Tony di Medici certainl
hadn't killed his own father. But wasn't it possible that h
could have been capable of blackmail? How, why? Becaus
the di Medicis had expensive tastes. Because it might be ver
easy to stumble upon information that someone else woul
be willing to pay to have kept silent . . .

Not Tony, Chris thought painfully. Tony . . . who had bee
fun and caring. Tony, who had really welcomed her . . .

If not Tony, there was Gina di Medici. Had Gina bee
angry enough to kill her husband? Would Alfred Conti
have paid a blackmailer to protect Gina?

"What are you thinking?"

Chris opened her eyes. She hadn't heard Marcus move
but he was standing beside the bed, smiling down at her wit
amusement easing some of the intensity in his eyes.

She blinked, hugging her pillow and smiling ruefully i
return. "I was thinking about . . . our mystery," she told hir

He sat down, tracing a finger over her shoulder, offerin
her his coffee cup. Chris accepted, warmed by the intimac

of his action, watching his dark lashes shield his eyes and his thoughts.

"That wasn't the answer I was expecting," he teased her when he met her eyes again. "As a loving bride, you should have been thinking about our night together. You should have been wondering where I was...and longing to have me beside you again."

Chris smiled, lowering her gaze, a little flush coloring her cheeks. She took a sip of the hot coffee, keeping her eyes averted from his. Yes, I was thinking about you, too, she thought. But I've thought of you since I first saw you. I lay awake often wondering what it would be like....

And now I know, and I'm more hopelessly tangled within your web than ever. Body and soul, I need you and I want you, and God forbid you ever know how much, because it would be terrible to be so sadly pathetically vulnerable to a di Medici man.

"I, uh, can't help but worry..." she murmured as she sipped the coffee again.

He took the cup from her and set it down, then tugged at the pillow she was clutching to her breasts. Chris released it, meeting his eyes.

"We'll worry together...soon," he told her, and a hot vibrant shuddering took hold of her body as he swept his arms around her, rolling her against him. She felt the sleek hardness of his body, the implacable power and desire, and with a little sigh she gladly left all thought until later. Marcus would have it no other way.

Di Medici. At that moment she was Christina di Medici. His wife, lying in his arms, thrilling to his touch. She was madly in love with him, beneath his spell as she had never thought she could be. It didn't matter that her life might hang by a dangerous thread. When he touched her, when she turned and trembled and he moved like an all-consuming and demanding flame, she wanted nothing more than to give herself to that spiraling blue heat.

It was afternoon before they went downstairs.

Chris followed Marcus into the kitchen, where they prowled around the refrigerator and cabinets until they came up with a large stick of pepperoni, an assortment of cheeses and a thick loaf of Italian bread. They carried it all out to the sofa, placing the food between them. The inevitable bottle of wine was between them, too, and Chris stared at i warily as if it were a snake. She believed now that Marcus would never really hurt her, but she had learned that he could be manipulative when he so chose, and she didn't want to be manipulated again. He wasn't being entirely honest with her; he didn't intend to tell her his thoughts o: his feelings—and she wasn't about to be his puppet again whether she was in love with him or not.

Marcus broke the bread and handed her a piece. "The first thing we have to realize here is that there are two peo ple involved. The blackmailer and whoever the blackmailer is afraid of. Possibly the one who killed my father, assum ing that your father didn't.''

"The figure in the cloak," Chris murmured, taking a bite of her bread. She was famished again. Being with Marcu was like touching the moon. It was also pleasantly exhaust ing, and had a tremendous effect on her appetite.

He gazed at her briefly, his eyes opaque as they traveled over her. "Yes, the figure in the cloak. It seems to me tha Alfred must have had the note from the blackmailer. He wa showing it to our mystery figure and saying that he didn' feel like paying up anymore. If he wasn't going to pay up the figure apparently decided that he should die. Am making sense so far?''

"Perfectly," Chris agreed. "So, if we catch the black mailer, we can catch the murderer. And both of them ha to be on the boat the day that your father died. That mean your mother, Sophia, Genovese, Joe or Fredo.''

"Or one of us.''

"The children?''

"Tony, you or I.''

"I'd thought we'd decided that we were innocent."

He shrugged. "I think it's a fair decision. We have to let your mother out, too, because she isn't in Italy."

"That's big of you," Chris muttered dryly.

Her comment drew a sharp look, cold as the moon's blue gaze. "Your father still isn't exactly in the clear," he told her.

"But my father is dead," Chris replied coolly. "He isn't running around Italy, either. Unless you think his ghost is dressing up in a cloak to haunt me. Which seems unlikely, since he's my father."

"You're not amusing, Christina."

"And you don't want to face facts."

"Oh, stop it, Christina! We have no facts to face! You were so determined that you were the angel of righteousness that you didn't tell me anything when something could have been done. We have nothing—*nothing*—Christina."

"How could I tell you anything? You appeared everywhere there was trouble, and you didn't want to listen to a word I had to say! Then you seduced me into marriage. How far would you trust a man like that?" Chris demanded angrily.

He tossed one of the cheeses into her lap, rising with a swift movement to step behind her and catch her shoulders beneath his hands. He whispered heatedly in her ear.

"You are the cat burglar who breaks into galleries. Who makes sudden appearances to con old dying men out of their money. Perhaps you want the palazzo, too. You've gotten everything you wanted, haven't you?"

"No," Chris lied, wrenching herself from his touch. She met his dark gaze with a tawny fury glittering in her eyes. "I wanted Tony, remember?" she taunted.

"Ah, yes, sorry," he murmured, moving back around the sofa to pour wine into their glasses. "But you got me," he added softly.

"I don't have anything, and I don't want any wine."

"You've got me, *amore mio*—for the time being—and don't get any other ideas," he warned her lightly. "You might as well enjoy some wine, since it improves your disposition, and you're not going anywhere."

"I don't want my disposition improved!" Chris declared passionately. "Every time my disposition is good around you, I wind up in trouble. You have no sense of decency."

"What? I have a hell of a sense of decency! It's a pity you don't remember more about the night of our marriage."

"Oh . . . God!" Chris exploded in frustration. Then she threw the cheese back at him, taking him completely by surprise.

Somehow he caught the cheese. He looked at it for a second, then flew into a stream of colorful Italian curses. Chris froze for a second, certain he was going to tear her hair out, but then, as she watched him, she burst into nervous laughter instead.

He paused, looking at her as if nothing but violence was on his mind. Then he lowered his head, and when he looked up an almost imperceptible grin was tugging at the corners of his mouth.

"You should speak nothing but kindness to your husband, *cara*," he advised with a level edge. "Especially to the Italian husband you brutalized last evening."

"Brutalized?" Chris demanded.

He tossed the cheese to the floor and caught her face between his palms, sliding his fingers into her hair.

"Absolutely."

Now she saw that he was smiling. But as he pulled her into his arms, hard against his chest, she knew his smile would always hold a hint of danger. "Would you want a brutal husband, *mia moglie*?" he queried softly.

She shook her head, lowering her eyes. His palm moved gently over her cheek, then shifted to caress her breast. "Nor do I care to feel the steel of your knives," he murmured.

She wasn't quite sure what he meant, only that for once she could sense some deep emotion simmering beneath his words. That touched her heart and reawoke all the feelings she had for him. Not for anything would she have reminded him that he had married her only to protect her, because he had known she faced a danger he had not wanted to admit.

When she looked up at him, he smiled, laughed and pulled her into his lap.

"These arguments are ridiculous," he said briskly.

"Yes, they are," Chris agreed, leaning against him and fingering the medallion on his chest. "So what are we going to do?" she asked a little breathlessly.

"Do?"

"Marcus . . . we've got to do something. We can't just let this go on and on."

He sighed. "No, we must find our blackmailer and our murderer before . . . before something else happens."

"So?"

He laughed. She heard the sound from his throat, from his chest. It touched her cheek and made her shiver.

"First," he told her, lifting her chin, "we complete our honeymoon. Just a few days, but that is something at least. No healthy Italian male would not do so. We'll go tomorrow to the Italian Riviera, to Portofino." He shrugged. "Maybe we'll go on into France, to Nice, or to Monte Carlo."

"And then?" Chris murmured.

"Then . . . we go back. In time we meet your blackmailer at St. Mark's."

She shivered slightly again. "Marcus . . ." she murmured, and then swallowed, not willing to create distance between them again. "Marcus, who do you think might have killed your father?"

She immediately felt the tension in his arms. "Not my mother . . . she was in love with him. Alfred, your father, Genovese . . . Joe, perhaps, or Fredo."

"Wouldn't it make more sense for Joe or Fredo to have blackmailed Alfred? Marcus, the di Medicis and Alfred had the money. Why blackmail someone with no money?"

"Yes, why blackmail someone with no money?" Marcus repeated. She felt his gaze on her and lifted her head, noticing something in his eyes.

"You're onto something!" Chris exclaimed.

He shook his head. "No, Christina. I was just thinking that you have the money now. Which is why, of course, the call came to you. You want the information. You desperately wish to clear your father." His arms tightened around her. "Christina, when we return to the palazzo, you must listen to me, do you understand? Blackmailers go to those they believe to be...vulnerable. Which means weak. You do nothing without me, do you understand? Unless you do wish to be brutalized?"

The soft threat in his voice caused her heart to take an erratic leap. "Marcus, we need to go to the police."

"I will go to the police. But I cannot prove that Alfred was murdered—or driven to his death—because he did die of a heart attack. The notes may help. I will take them to the police as soon as we return to Venice."

Would he? Chris wondered. Or was he still determined to catch someone himself? Someone he loved. Someone he could perhaps . . . dissuade from any further violence.

Chris didn't know. But she did believe with all her heart that he intended to let no harm come to her; she believed he would protect her with his own life.

But she wasn't sure of any of his motives.

Did it matter, as long as he cared for her and meant to shield her from all harm?

It might—if the murderer was more talented, more devious than Marcus thought.

"Do you know," he murmured to her suddenly, smoothing her hair from her forehead, "that your hands are always moving?"

She gazed at him a little suspiciously. He laughed. "No, I'm serious. It's your fingers, I think. I've noticed that when you're thinking about something or talking, your hands move. Like waves."

Chris started, then laughed. She placed her hand in the air, pulled her knuckles back taut, then straightened her fingers. "Is that what you mean?"

"Yes. Not so obviously, but that's the motion."

She smiled. "It's practice. Mime practice." she added softly, wondering a bit at the dark expression that touched his features. "It's a basic lesson," she continued. "Here." She sat up, smiling as she tugged his hand and brought it to the small coffee table before them. "Put your hand down, the palm flat. Now bend your fingers without allowing your palm to rise."

"I can't."

"Yes, you can! It just takes practice. That's how we 'build a wall.' See?" Chris proceeded to show him how the exercise helped to create the illusion of a flat surface. She smiled, but her smile faded quickly at his brooding disinterest.

"You are very good at what you do," he murmured.

Chris shrugged a little uneasily. "I hope I'm decent. I've studied under some of the very best."

"And you love it, too, don't you?"

"Yes." She smiled dryly. "It requires a very rigid physical discipline to keep your body in shape for the things it must do. You have to love mime to accept the discipline. But it's like anything else, really. Once you accustom yourself to the regime it becomes a little like breathing. As you noticed, I work my hands frequently without even realizing it."

He nodded, but again he seemed very distant. He had asked the questions as if he wanted answers, but it didn't seem as if he wanted to hear what she was saying.

Chris turned away from him, picking up her wine and sipping it quickly. She wondered if she would ever understand him, or feel that she knew him at all. Or that she could

possess any part of him besides his sinewed body when she
held him in a tight embrace. So many intimacies, and yet she
didn't really know him at all. He was his own person. . . .

A di Medici. And Sophia had warned her that di Medici
men could bring a heartache to match all the ecstasy that
could be found in their arms.

She felt his fingers trailing through her hair, and she
turned to watch him. His expression was a curious one. He
touched her as if she were something very special and
unique; his fingers were gentle. And yet that wariness was
there, as if he didn't understand much about her, either.

"Marcus?" she murmured.

"Yes?"

"Did I say something wrong?"

"No, Christina. What could you have said?"

"I don't know." She tried to grin. "Don't you like
mimes?"

He shook his head evasively. "What would I dislike about
a mime?"

"Then . . . it's me."

He shook his head again, smiling. "There is nothing
dislike about you at all." He laughed suddenly. "Except that
you are stubborn and seem to have a passion for dangerous
stunts. But at the moment—" he shrugged, and his gaze
held a cobalt glitter "—you are perfect."

He pulled her back against him. Chris was content when
he rested his chin against her hair and mentioned that they
needed to shop for some clothing, since they couldn't wear
robes to Monte Carlo.

Perfect, he thought again later as he lay in bed and waited
for her. In so many ways. She had been born with her tawny
beauty; her craft had perfected her movements and poise.
She moved like a shimmering silver wave, her limbs long and
sleek and graceful.

She appeared in the doorway, naked, hesitating. Now, in
the semidarkness, her hair cascaded over her bare shoul

ders, rich tendrils of reflected copper and gold, enticing his touch. Her flesh was bathed by a soft glow; the moon cast its rays over the curves of her body and awoke his fantasies.

His heart pounded in his chest, and for a moment he was afraid, though not so much of the danger that awaited them because he was determined to solve things—and end them. That sheer determination and his simmering fury at the things that had been done made him confident that he could keep her safe and solve the riddles that had reached out to haunt them from the past.

But when the skein of mystery and confusion was unwound . . . what then?

He would never be able to hold her. Like an elusive nymph, she would escape his grasp. She was an American, proud and independent. He loved her for what she was but their cultures were different. The things, many of them intangible, that were an ingrained part of his life were worlds away from hers. The palazzo, art, the canals, religion...even language. He could speak hers fluently, but he thought in his own. And her profession . . .

She was an artist. A visual artist. Her graceful form was her canvas. The graceful, vibrant, sensual form that was totally wild and untamed in his arms. Her face, her smile, her wide, beguiling, topaz eyes. Onstage she entranced and delighted; only when he held her was she his completely.

He wouldn't want to change her, to hurt her, to take anything away from her. He did not want to claim the artist, only the woman. And though he could command and manipulate and hold her by strength alone, it would not be right, and it would not be enough. He didn't even understand what made her so uniquely special to him, only that she was.

And when she left the doorway, coming to him, naked, her steps as sensually slow as the supple ripple of her hips, he felt a shiver of need—and the fear of loss.

For a moment he felt something like paralysis constrict his throat and stop his breath. He couldn't reach out. Like the breeze, she could too easily elude his grasp.

Touch her, he commanded himself. Reach out; touch her. Feel the fullness of her breasts, the warmth of her skin. Touch her; hold her. Savor her caress.

Make her yours...

She came to him, sleek and slow. She slid between the sheets, and his hands moved to her hips, pulling her to him. He felt all the softness of her flesh, and the infinite warmth.

Fiercely, tenderly, he made her his.

Chapter 11

They took a small charter airline into Nice, and the two days that followed were the happiest Chris could remember. She lived on a passionate cloud, entranced by all the little things done by lovers, eager to forget everything but the moment.

They spent long hours on the beach, sipping tall cool drinks, playing in the water, returning to the sand. Chris would be ready to purr with contentment when he ran his fingers idly down her back beneath the sun, and she would know that he would suggest shortly they return to their room.

They had spent the first afternoon shopping. Chris had been a little bit staggered by the amount he had been willing to spend to supply them with a wardrobe for just a few days, and she had laughingly demanded to know if he was spending her inheritance or his own. He had shrugged and replied, "Both."

And then he had reminded her that they had agreed that there would be no future or no past for them during these days. They had agreed to forget everything and enjoy themselves.

It was ideal. Chris was a little glad to be back in France, and gratified to be the one who was totally comfortable with the language. Marcus was willing to sit back politely and watch her as she did the ordering in restaurants and the bartering in shops.

And for two days they didn't find a single thing to argue about. They combed the streets and shops, and drank espresso and wine at little cafés. They savored the sun and the delight of returning to their room whenever the urge struck, of bathing together, ordering up champagne and little trays filled with cheeses, meats and fruits, among them grapes, which, Chris laughingly learned, were a great deal of fun to feed to one another.

She was never quite sure what happened to stop their idyllic vacation so abruptly, only that it did end on their last night—at the casino in Monte Carlo.

The evening had started out the same as any other. He was in black tails that emphasized all the intrigue and darkness of his startling good looks. Chris had allowed him to splurge on a forest-green silk gown for her. It had jet beading at the shoulders and a low-cut neckline. She had decided that between them, they were beautiful, and the night was filled with easy laughter. He was close beside her as they gambled recklessly and successfully at the roulette wheel.

Then Chris felt a touch on her arm, and she heard her name called with surprise and enthusiasm. She turned to see that Georgianne was beside her, and that Tomas stood behind Georgianne.

"Christina!" Georgianne broke into a long and excited monologue in French, asking Chris what she was doing, and telling her what a wonderful time she and Tomas were having. Chris vaguely realized that Marcus was pulling in their chips and waiting behind her for an introduction and explanation.

Chris didn't know why, but there was already a stiff tension about him. Even when he wasn't touching her, she could feel it.

After she had greeted the tolerantly smiling Tomas, Chris turned back to Marcus. "Marcus, Georgianne and Tomas. We work together. We are all from the school in Paris, and went on tour together this summer. Georgianne, Tomas . . . Marcus di Medici."

He was very polite and courteous, and apparently very interested in the other two. When Tomas suggested that they leave the casino for somewhere quieter where they could talk, Marcus was ready to accept the suggestion.

While they waited for a taxi in front of the grand and glittering entrance to the casino, Georgianne demanded to know what Chris was up to. But as she spoke her eyes were on Marcus with open fascination and speculation; Georgianne was, above all things, a Parisienne. A soft lovely kitten—open and honest.

"I leave you in Venice with an old man; I find you in Monte Carlo with a young one!" Georgianne teased. "Is this a last fling before you return to Paris, or what?"

"It's a little vacation—" Chris began, but Marcus interrupted her smoothly, blandly.

"It's a honeymoon," he said, smiling.

Georgianne gasped and clapped her hands with pleasure. Tomas quietly congratulated them both.

Chris wanted to stamp on Marcus's foot, but his hands were on her shoulders, his fingers warningly tight. She gritted her teeth and smiled instead.

A taxi came, and they all climbed in. Georgianne kept switching from French to English as she asked Chris what she intended to do, had she informed Jacques yet of her marriage . . . and what of the school? Chris stared hard at Marcus and replied that as yet, she had made no decisions.

They came to a small bar overlooking the Riviera and drinks were ordered all around. Tomas and Marcus began a conversation about the roads and sights between the Ital-

ian and French cities along the coast. Georgianne turned to
Chris suddenly, switching instantly into hushed French.

"Christina! *Il est magnifique!*" She went on to comment
on his striking eyes, his wonderful physique, his dark, intriguing, spellbinding looks. Her eyes sparkled as she congratulated Chris again, telling her in typical blunt good-
natured fashion that it was somewhat amazing to see Chris
up and walking, since it was most obvious that the man
would be a demon in bed.

Chris listened with a flush warming her cheeks, and she
urgently tried to shush Georgianne. Georgianne merely
waved a hand in the air. "He is Italian, no? He does not
understand me! Tell me, Christina! How romantic. A few
weeks and voilà! You are married. He is wonderful, yes? A
man. And what a man!" She laughed. "But Italian! How
is that working with your American soul? Or does passion
overwhelm all your American feminism and independence?"

"Georgianne—"

"Ah! Admit to me that he is wonderful and that at last
you know the meaning of losing your heart."

"*Oui*, Georgianne! *S'il vous plaît*, sshhh!"

Marcus was across the table, ostensibly listening to Tomas's comments in English. But Chris kept catching his eyes
on her. Along with the tension, she noticed a dry curve to his
mouth, and she didn't know what he was thinking or feeling at all.

"You will not return to Paris," Georgianne said in
French.

"Yes, I will," Chris retorted.

"And leave such a man behind? I wouldn't. He is too attractive to other women, and not a saint at all, I would assume."

"I have my life, too," Chris murmured unhappily. There
was no way to explain the circumstances of her marriage.
She glanced uneasily at Marcus again. She felt his eyes on

er, burning her. Again she didn't know what he was thinking or feeling.

Except that this chance meeting—for all that he was being courteous and welcoming—had made him angry.

They spent several hours together, conversing in English. Tomas was fascinated by the galleries; Georgianne was knowledgeable about the art field, and discussed numerous painters with Marcus.

Both Tomas and Georgianne knew of The di Medici Galleries, and that they had opened a branch in Paris. Tomas gave Chris a wry grin and turned to his wife. "C'est la vie, n? We are the Europeans, Chris the American. But here is our Christina . . . Contessa di Medici!"

Georgianne laughed, but Chris thought she would scream. She had felt as if she were on the edge of her chair all night.

Finally, the couples broke up for the evening, with Chris promising to get in touch with Georgianne soon and tell her what she had decided about work.

Marcus was silent when they entered a cab to take them back to their hotel in Nice. Withdrawn, brooding.

But when his eyes touched her, she felt their fire. Cold, icy fire from out of the shadows.

Chris kept silent, determined to show him that his unwarranted moods didn't affect her in the least.

But alone in their room, facing the shore, it was difficult. Marcus silently removed his jacket, cuff links and shirt. She felt his eyes on her all the while. Chris disappeared into the bathroom, donned a gown and then ignored him as she crawled into bed, now miserably tense herself, ready to jump at the slightest sound. But he didn't speak. He neatly hung up his clothes. She yawned and closed her eyes, pretending exhaustion. Then she was sorry she had closed her eyes because she couldn't hear him anymore, and she felt as if her nerves were screaming.

She felt his weight as he crawled in beside her, and his hand on her waist as he pulled her around. She opened her

eyes. His were burning jet in the moonlight. A shiver (
dismay streaked through her as he taunted in perfect French
"So, you have your life to lead and you're returning
Paris?"

What had she and Georgianne said? Chris wondered wi
growing alarm. He seemed so angry. . . .

"You speak French," was all she could think to murmu
uneasily.

"Mais oui," he murmured, a sharp edge to his low ton
"Venezia is in the north of Italy, contessa. And busine
often takes us to France, as well as Switzerland and Au
tria. If you choose to discuss me again, may I suggest th
you don't do so in German? Perhaps I should also warn yo
that most Europeans study languages with far greater fe
vor than Americans. We share a continent, you see, wi
many neighbors."

He released her, smiled dryly and turned his back on he
"We'll return to the palazzo in the morning. We must sol
the problems in your life—yes?—so that it may be returne
to you."

Chris lay there, swallowing in pained and aching silenc
She didn't understand quite what had happened, only th
he had apparently tired of his own game. He had seduce
her into his life; now he wanted her out of it.

She didn't sleep for a long while. She felt his weight b
side her, his heat . . . but not his touch. She wanted to rea
out to him, but hurt and confusion kept her still. And it fe
so strange. She had grown so accustomed to being loved a
held. . . .

She stared miserably out at the moon and listened to t
waves pound lullingly against the sand. She felt like cryin
but she couldn't. He might hear her.

She should never have come, she thought. Never have
lowed him to seduce her into these days of drifting a
never-ending pleasure. For Marcus it was a casual affa
just like any number with which he had probably ente
tained himself over the years. True, he had married her, b

nly to protect her. Their lovemaking was a fringe benefit, 'ell deserved after such a sacrifice, she thought bitterly.

But neither bitterness nor anger could shake the pain. She ad fallen in love with him.

It was probably natural that when she finally slept that ight, she dreamed.

She was in the crypt again, running along the tunnel. omeone was behind her. Marcus? She didn't know. She nly knew that she was frightened. She watched the arch-ays, wondering if the shadow that pursued her would be-omc a panther, black in the night, threatening to claw her) shreds.

But when she looked back she didn't see Marcus or a anther. And certainly not a winged lion of justice.

She was being pursued by a figure in a bright-red cloak.

And tonight she was carrying something. There was ›mething in her hand. Something she knew she had to hide. ecause if the figure in the cloak discovered what she had, ie would be beaten and punished....

Chris ducked behind a tomb. She reached a hand over the 'figy of a long-dead di Medici and peeked over the edge. A ›ider crawled over her hand, and she inadvertently :reamed. The figure in the cloak heard her, and she :reamed again and again....

"Christina! Christina, shhh, shhhh, *amore mio....*"

Chris awoke to feel Marcus's arms around her, holding ›r, soothing her. She had broken into a cold sweat. Her ›wn clung to her damp flesh; her hair felt plastered to her :ow. For several seconds her heart continued to pound.

"Christina... what is it?"

Her eyes at last focused on his. His features were tense ad concerned. She swallowed nervously, remembering how : had rejected her. But the dream had frightened her badly, ad she closed her eyes and rolled against his chest, bury-g her face against the dark mat of hair there.

"I dreamed that . . . the figure was after me in the tomb
That I had something that the figure wanted. Oh, Ma
cus . . ."

"Shhh, *amore mio*. It was only a dream. You will not l
alone. Never alone. And there will be no reason for you
be in the catacombs." He held her close, soothing her un
the trembling left her body and she began to cool off in t
air-conditioning. Until she left behind the shadowy nigh
mare, and the fear drained from her body.

"Better?" he asked her.

She nodded.

"There is nothing to fear, Christina. I will be with you

"I know."

He held her in silence for a while, and then she smile
because she felt his palms moving over her body. He tugg
at her gown impatiently. "Why have you worn this? Did yo
seek a barrier against me?" he teased.

She shook her head, meeting his eyes. "I don't think th
a barrier could be erected against you," she whispered.

"You are right," he promised softly in return, and the
she felt the touch of his lips against her bare flesh. Famili
heat and the sweet aphrodisiac of anticipation claimed h
body, as did he. She could only be glad of the dream the
glad of the night hours that it gave them.

Because they did return to Venice, to the palazzo, in t
morning.

Perhaps she could create no barriers against him, b
Marcus was quite adept at building them against her.

He was remote during the entire trip back. Not until th
entered the palazzo did he touch her again with more th
absent consideration. And as they came into the entryw
with its magnificent chandelier and Roman columns, s
knew that his apparent affection for her was only for t
benefit of others.

Genovese took their luggage. Sophia announced th
there was coffee in the courtyard. Tony embraced Chris w

is usual fervor. "You did take a di Medici husband after ll!" he teased her. "Pity it wasn't me!" But he smiled at his rother, and Chris was convinced that the two cared deeply bout one another.

She braced herself for her greeting from Gina di Medici, ut to her uneasy surprise, Gina seemed to have quite ac-epted the situation. She smiled at Chris a little shyly, and en embraced her warmly. "I feared for a long time that my oung tigers would never make me a grandmama. This was our home, and now it is your home again. Make it so fully, *ia figlia*."

My daughter. Did Gina mean it? Chris didn't know. She miled, feeling a little ill.

"Alfred would have been pleased," Sophia murmured, id then they all moved to the courtyard. Joe and Fredo ere going to stop by for coffee and to offer their congrat-lations, Gina told them.

The two men did come by. Marcus and Chris were toasted ver and over again. Chris tried very hard to talk and laugh ith enthusiasm about their honeymoon, but now that they ere back at the palazzo life had become sinister again, and ie distance Marcus had created between them seemed to ive left her entirely alone in a pit of vipers.

Chris was glad when the discussion turned to business and pe Conseli apologetically announced to Marcus that his esence at the galleries was urgently needed. Tony com-ented that she looked tired, and Chris was grateful that she puld sheepishly admit that she was exhausted and retire.

Marcus glanced her way sharply. He told Joe, Fredo and ony that he would be right with them as soon as he had en his wife to their room.

When the door had closed behind them, he gripped her oulders tightly. "Keep the door locked and go nowhere ithout me, do you understand?" She felt like an errant iild with a schoolmaster, and heartily resented him.

"I'm not going anywhere," she murmured, slipping from s hold to wander across the room to where their luggage sat at the foot of the bed. But suddenly she was angry as we as frightened, and she wanted to hurt him, just as h brusque distance hurt her.

"If you want me, though, I'll be in my own room." Sl turned around, facing him blandly. "I think that playtin must be over, Marcus. We've come back to find a blac mailer and a murderer. Serious business," she said with dry smile.

"What are you saying, Christina?" he demanded, his ey narrowing tensely.

She shrugged negligently, but her lashes fell over her eye "I'm saying that the relationship ends here. Your moth said something that gave me quite a start. I, uh, wasn't e actly prepared for...the physical aspects of things." Sl moved around the bed, uneasily straightening the sheet "Marcus, a divorce is going to be sticky enough. The could be other complications, which I...stupidly, I a mit...didn't think about. But I'm afraid there's not mu work around for pregnant mimes."

At that moment Chris didn't think there could be greater danger in the world than Marcus di Medici. She fe his anger radiating from him like steamy heat waves off hot sidewalk. She felt herself shivering inside, waiting, e pecting a terrible explosion.

None came.

"Suit yourself," he said curtly.

Then he turned abruptly on his heel, exiting the roo without another word. Chris let out a long ragged sigh ar sank to the bed. And then she started to cry.

She didn't know how long she had been in the room wh the phone started to ring. She waited, certain that someo would get it elsewhere in the house. But it continued to rin and even before she picked it up, she was certain that it w the blackmailer.

"Hello?" she said breathlessly.

"Contessa di Medici, you must come now."

"Now... I can't come now."

"You must. You must come to St. Mark's. Now. There will not be another chance. I will be there. I will give you thirty minutes. If you do not come, you will never know. For all time, your father will be the murderer."

The line went dead.

She hung up the phone, then anxiously, feverishly, paced the room. Marcus had warned her not to leave, yet she didn't dare miss this opportunity. She gritted her teeth together, then hurried to the phone and called the galleries. She went through an operator, then a woman who didn't understand English or her attempts at Italian. Chris kept repeating that she was the Contessa di Medici and that she needed Marcus.

Finally Joe Conseli came on the phone. He asked her to wait a minute. When he returned to the line, he sounded very uncomfortable.

"Christina, I'm sorry. Marcus is on another line, long-distance to New York. It's very important. He can get back to you, but he asked me to say—"

"To say what?"

He cleared his throat. "That if you are calling merely because you have more complaints, you must simply wait until he can come home. Christina, I must go. He will see you later, yes?"

"Tell him..." Chris began furiously, then she paused. "Tell him not to bother!"

She slammed down the phone, then stared at it, swearing vehemently. Damn Marcus! And damn herself, she thought fleetingly, for creating the rift between them.

She gazed at the French Provincial clock on the dresser. She had already wasted ten minutes.

Still muttering out epithets about what Marcus could do with himself—and fighting the tears that stung her eyes—Chris grabbed her purse and made certain that she was leaving with an ample supply of lire. She stared at the phone one last time. "If you can't bother to speak to me, Marcus

di Medici, don't you dare get angry over missing the gran
finale!''

Chris was able to flag down a motor launch. The
skimmed quickly over the canals to St. Mark's Square. Sl
paid the driver and jumped anxiously to the ground, sca
ning the crowd even as she hurried through it. Tourists we
everywhere. And so were the pigeons. They squawked an
flapped their wings in frenzied flight as she ran anxious
through the flock.

She raced up the steps to the entrance of the church. Fe
a moment the darkness blinded her; she allowed her eyes
adjust to the muted light. As always, people were ever
where, studying the statues, the graceful altars, the fas
nating tombs. Chris kept studying the people around he
There was a tour group of Japanese gentlemen who smile
at her scrutiny, and bowed politely. Chris smiled absently
return. A number of old Italian women were praying
black widows' weeds; there was an American tour grou
near the main altar.

Chris sighed and walked to one of the pews. She sa
staring at the altar, waiting. No one came. She saw nothir
out of the ordinary. Still she waited. And waited, ar
waited.

A full hour must have passed before she finally gave u
No one was going to approach her. She had come on a
other wild-goose chase.

Despondent and frustrated, Chris rose at last. She didr
see any of the magnificence of the Basilica as she walke
back out to the Square, to the sunlight. She was so preo
cupied with her own depression that she didn't even noti
the activity on the Square at first. Only when she neared t
dock, where she planned to catch a vaporetto, did she lo
up and notice the police cordons and the men in unifor
running around, holding back the crowd, soothing a d
traught woman.

There was a body on the Square, dripping wet, havi
been pulled from the canal. Chris made her way through t

crowd. Police photographers were there; a coroner was bending over the body. Chris looked over the shoulder of a short woman in front of her, and she gasped sharply, almost screaming out loud at the terror that ripped through her.

The body on the ground was Genovese.

He was slightly blue, and there was a gaping red slit in his throat.

She did scream then, hysterically. A policeman came to her, gripping her. She tried to tell him that she was Christina di Medici, that Genovese was from her household. He tried to calm her down. Someone brought a flask of something; someone else started shouting orders.

And a blanket was drawn over the body.

Chris was seated by a pillar in the Square. The kindly officer placed another blanket over her shoulders while she sipped at some calming liquor. People were talking and talking and quizzing her; the only words she could understand were "di Medici." And all she could think was that Genovese had been killed. It was so obvious: Genovese had been the blackmailer. She had found the blackmailer.

But not the murderer. The murderer had managed to strike again.

At last, from her web of fear and horror, she heard a voice she knew. Deep, resonant, a little harsh and strained. He was talking to one of the officers, answering questions, then demanding impatiently, *"Dové la mia moglie?"*

Chris looked up to see Marcus, his features tense, coming toward her. He slipped an arm around her, then continued to speak to the officer in quick Italian. The officer nodded, very courteous to Conte di Medici. Marcus led her away from the cordons, away from the police, away from the body. In minutes she was seated in the family launch and he was steering them away from the Square.

She wanted sympathy. Instead, he burst out with a furious spate of Italian that matched the roar of the launch's engine. Chris put up a hand and pleaded softly, "*Per favore*, Marcus..."

He stopped speaking. She felt his tension, his anger. "Marcus, I tried to call you—"

"It could have been you!" he thundered, and she went silent again, staring at the wooden floor of the boat. Seconds later they reached the palazzo. An anxious Tony met them in the entryway. Marcus spoke to him quickly, and Tony nodded. Marcus took Chris up the stairs, shutting the door abruptly behind him once they had entered his room. Chris walked to the bed, where she lay on her back, pressing her temples between her hands while she waited for his words.

"I am sending you away from Venice tomorrow," he told her coldly. "Until then, Christina, you will not leave this room. For your life, you will listen to me."

She didn't answer him.

"Christina!"

He was next to her, standing over her, and then he was sitting, shaking her shoulders.

"Yes! Yes, I understand!" she cried, and despite the dark fury in his eyes, she threw her arms around him. "Marcus," she whispered, "I tried to get you.... I tried...."

For a moment he was stiff; she barely noticed. Then his arms wound tightly around her. "Don't you think I know that it was my fault?" he demanded gruffly. He unwound her arms from his neck and eased her back to the bed. He stared at her, and she couldn't understand the raging turmoil in his eyes.

He rose, securely locking the doors to the terrace. "I've got to go to the police station. You will lock yourself in, and you will not leave."

"Yes," Chris replied in a whisper. She forced herself to rise. He was still staring at her, a furious warning in his eyes again. "I'm locking it, I'm locking it," she promised.

"I'll make your travel arrangements," he said. "I'll be back as soon as I can."

Chris locked the door in his wake. She returned to the bed and lay there, terrified. She couldn't forget the color of Genovese's flesh, nor the red at his throat.

She remained in a daze on the bed until darkness fell and the shadows became too deep. Then she rose to turn on the lights. She showered, continually placing her face beneath the cool water. She dressed in one of her white gowns again and paced the room, longing for Marcus to return.

Genovese hadn't been the murderer. That left Gina, Fredo, Joe, Sophia—or Tony. People she lived with, ate with, laughed with...

There was a knock at the door. She froze, catching her breath. She inhaled again with shaky relief as she heard Marcus's voice, telling her that it was all right to open the door.

He brought a tray of wine and bread and steaming pasta. She hadn't realized how hungry she was; yet she couldn't eat because she kept feeling ill. Marcus told her that Genovese's throat had been slit, that the police had no real clues but that he had given them the notes she had received and told them everything.

Everyone in the house and at the galleries would be questioned. It was out of their hands.

Chris nodded. She kept drinking wine; it soothed away the raw edges of fear and pain. It stopped her from shaking.

At length Marcus told her irritably to go to bed and try to sleep. She crawled in, certain that she would never sleep. She didn't really want to, because she didn't want to dream about the catacombs again. And she didn't like closing her eyes anymore; when she closed her eyes, she saw Genovese's body on the Square.

Marcus didn't slide in beside her. She heard the shower running; she heard it stop. She saw him come out of the bathroom in his robe; she watched him as he walked to the French doors to stare out into the night. Time crept by. The numbness of the wine left her, and tension wound like a coil inside her. She slipped out of bed and walked to him, disregarding the ice in his eyes as he watched her. But when she reached him, she could go no farther. She stood before him, her lashes lowered, her heart sick.

"Marcus, my God," she whispered at last. "How can you do this to me? How can you remain so distant when . . ."

He lifted her chin with his forefinger, meeting her eyes. "When you are frightened?" he asked softly. "*Mia moglie*, there has been a murder. But between us, nothing has changed since this morning. I cannot allay your fears. It has been an eventful day. I have not had time to seek out a pharmacy nor would I have. You seemed rather adamant."

She tried to wrest her chin from his touch, but he would not release her. She lowered her lashes against him, almost closing her eyes. "I . . . don't care," she whispered at last. Still, he stood like a rock. "Marcus!" she cried, flinging herself against him. "Please, Marcus, for God's sake, hold me!"

His arms came around her at last. She felt his whisper against her cheek. "Christina, I cannot simply hold you. If I hold you, something else will follow."

"That's . . . what I want," she admitted, her voice muffled against his chest. With her head lowered she tugged at the buttons of her gown; then she shimmied the material from her shoulders and forced it to fall to the ground. Naked, she stepped into his arms, slipping her hands beneath the V of his robe, running the tip of her tongue over his chest. She felt the fierce pounding of his heart, the sharp intake of his breath.

His fingers tore into her hair, tilting her head back. "*Cara,*" he said bitterly, "are you aware that we might already have to face the consequences of our actions?"

"Yes," Chris whispered painfully.

"If so," he warned her heatedly, "you will not leave me. This is Italy, not the States. You will not take my child."

She couldn't tell him that she never wanted to leave him, that her greatest fear next to death was accepting the fact that he might not want her anymore.

"No," she said simply.

"It rests with you, *amore mio*," he told her.

"Yes."

At last he clasped her body to his. She felt the hardness of his desire, the force of his arms and his hips. She shuddered, sinking in sweetness to be held by him, to feel his power and need as he swept her into his arms.

And when he carried her to the bed he made love to her with a shattering ferocity, making her forget everything.

She wasn't afraid. Not at all. Not when he held her.

Chapter 12

Chris woke very slowly... puzzled. She had been dreaming, but not really dreaming.

It had been more like remembering, and the Chris she kept seeing was not an adult, but a child.

A child, running along the subterranean tunnels of the catacombs, clutching something in her hand—terrified that she might be caught with it. It was something pretty she had seen, something she had taken. And if anyone found out that she had taken it, her father would be angry. Furious. Everyone would be furious. And she kept running, because she was certain that someone was after her.

The dream—or the memory—faded. Chris blinked, then realized that her eyes had been open; the image had been so strong that it had been as clear as day in her mind.

She rolled over quickly to wake Marcus and tell him about the memory or dream, or whatever it had been. Maybe it would make sense to him.

But Marcus wasn't there. Her heart quickened a little as she remembered the night and her total surrender. But then, hadn't it been his surrender, too? Hadn't she had at least proved to herself that he could no more deny her than she could him? But what of the words she had whispered in desperation? What had he really been asking of her and what had she promised? What did he really want from her...?

Her musings came to an abrupt end as she idly ran her fingers over the indigo silk where his body had been and came upon a sheet of notepaper with the di Medici crest at the top. It was brief and quite to the point.

Christina,
 Had to go to the galleries. Closed for the day—police order—but had to give them names and addresses.
 Don't leave the room. *Don't.* Teresa has been told to bring you coffee at eleven; lock the door after her. *Don't leave the room, capisce?* Unless you wish to learn all about temperamental and brutal Italians.

Marcus

Chris stared at the note resentfully. She was surprised he hadn't signed it Conte di Medici... or Marcus Rex.

She sighed, chewed nervously at her lower lip, then decided that he was right. She was safer behind locked doors.

But, she realized shortly, being safe was not quite the same as feeling sane. She showered and dressed, then nervously started pacing the room. Something was going to happen; she could feel it in the air. Or maybe that was just her imagination. Maybe she was certain that something was going to happen because the police were involved now. Knowing that the police were involved gave her a feeling of relief; it also allowed her mind to wander to her personal position.

Apparently Marcus no longer intended her to leave today. What did he intend? She started gnawing at a fingernail. She knew that he cared about her, but caring wasn't love. And to live with a di Medici, one would have to be loved by him. She couldn't endure to stay, wondering what he felt, certain that he sought out other women. He had married her to protect her; being Italian, or perhaps just being male, he was possessive. He wasn't about to let her leave with anything that was his, especially a child.

Chris picked up a pillow and slammed it across the room. She'd been so stupid! She should have thought of all this before ever becoming involved with him....

But really, it had all been so sudden....

And she didn't know if she had anything to worry about or not. It would take time to find out. But what should she do in the meantime? Keep going...like last night? Then she'd definitely have something to worry about.

She reminded herself that none of this would matter much until the mystery at the palazzo had been solved. Thank God her mother was safely playing ranch wife out in the American West. She'd be crazy if she knew that her daughter had married a di Medici—and fallen in love with him.

There was a tap at the door. Chris glanced at her watch. It was exactly eleven o'clock. Teresa called out that she had a tray; Chris opened the door, accepted the tray with a *"grazie,"* and locked the door once again. She took the tray to the bed and leaned against a pillow to gulp down her first cup of coffee, then slowly sip a second while inspecting the bowl of minestrone and the crescent sandwich she had been brought. Last night she had felt too sick to eat. This morning she was starving. She was also tense and bored. Eating proved to be a wonderful diversion.

But when she had eaten everything and finished the last of the coffee, she lay back, trying to analyze her dreams and memories about the catacombs. She really had remembered something. Something that she had apparently stolen as a child. Something pretty and fascinating. But what?

Hours passed. Chris worried about Marcus, about the police. About her personal commitment. Or had she made one? She didn't understand. She didn't understand him, or what he wanted, at all. He had been so angry after they had met Georgianne and Tomas, but she had been certain that he liked the couple.

She started as the phone began ringing. She almost answered it—but then remembered that yesterday Genovese had probably been murdered because she had answered a phone and agreed to meet him to pay for his information.

Finally it stopped.

Chris breathed a sigh of relief and went back to trying to untangle her dreams and the past again.

There was a tap at her door. Her stomach knotted. She didn't answer the door, and she didn't call out.

"Christina!"

It was Sophia, calling to her in annoyance. "Christina! Will you get the phone, please? It is Marcus."

"Oh!" she cried out, picking up the phone. but the line was dead; she had hesitated too long. She tried to get the galleries back, but the line was busy.

Cursing herself, Chris ran to her door and opened it. Sophia was halfway down the staircase.

"Sophia, excuse me. Marcus wasn't there anymore. Did he say what he wanted?"

"Yes," Sophia replied impatiently. "He wanted you to go to the galleries. To talk to the police or something, I believe." She shook her head uneasily. "Poor Genovese . . . all the years that he was with us . . ."

"Yes, poor Genovese," Chris murmured. Apparently Marcus had chosen not to tell the rest of the household what was going on. It appeared that Sophia considered Genovese the victim of a madman. "Sophia, I'm going to go to the galleries. If Marcus should call back, tell him I'm on my way."

Sophia nodded and started down the stairs again. She paused, looking back. "You'd better take a key. If they're in the offices, they won't hear you."

"Oh," Chris murmured. "I don't have one."

Sophia waved a hand in the air. "I'll find Gina and ge[t] hers for you."

Chris thanked her and hurried into her room to find he[r] purse. Sophia was in the entryway when she got down[stairs, ready to hand Chris a set of keys. "You will nee[d] both. The top turns off the security, and the bottom re[?] moves the bolt, yes?"

"I understand. Thank you. By the way," Chris sai[d] "where's Tony?"

"At the galleries with Marcus, I believe."

"Thanks again," Chris murmured. "And please, don'[t] forget. If Marcus calls tell him I'm on my way."

Chris left the palazzo by way of the rear courtyard. Sh[e] felt a little uneasy and didn't understand why. The sun wa[s] shining with a frenzy. The water in the canals danced wit[h] its brilliance. People were walking along, smiling, laug[h]ing, hurrying. But then, Genovese had been killed in brigh[t] daylight. And, she thought a little uneasily, the dayligh[t] wasn't going to last much longer. In another thirty minute[s] the sun would start to set. In another hour it would be dar[k.]

She reached the square and looked up at the gallerie[s.] Black crepe still draped the columns. Up on the roof, th[e] gargoyles seemed to stare back at her.

Chris ignored them and hurried up the steps to the door[s.] She banged on them for a minute, but got no response. S[o]phia, she decided wryly, had done her a favor by remindin[g] her about the keys. Chris fooled with the alarm key firs[t,] hoping that she wouldn't set the sirens shrilling. Sh[e] frowned as she played with the key to the dead bolt, wo[n]dering why something about Sophia's words had bothere[d] her. She shrugged, unable to think of what it was that elude[d] her. Probably nothing important.

Chris allowed the doors to close behind her. Inside, aw[ay] from the sunlight, it was already dark. Dark, and plea[s]antly cool. The galleries were air-conditioned, of course, b[ut] the marble and tiles were also cool, and it was a relief fro[m] the warmth outside.

"Marcus!" Chris called. Her voice echoed in the cavern-ous courtyard. Grimacing, she decided that she wouldn't call out again; she would just find him.

Where? she wondered with exasperation. She didn't know where his office was. She should probably have waited for him to call her back.

Chris started for the stairway to the second-level bal-cony. She was fairly certain there were no offices on the first floor; everything there was decorative, or set up for the convenience of the tourists and buyers.

She thought she heard something coming from the ro-botronics room. She started to call out, then remembered how her voice had echoed.

Chris hurried up the rest of the stairs, uneasily noting that it was growing darker and darker. She was anxious to get to Marcus and the police.

She burst into the historical room with his name on her lips. "Marcus?"

He wasn't there. No one was there. The figures all stared at her, frowning, smiling, their arms lifted in silent wel-come, their faces macabre in the growing shadows of night. It almost seemed that their grins were evil.

They were just robotronics, Chris reminded herself. Ma-terial objects, run by computers manned by men. She started to turn around; it was obvious that Marcus wasn't there. But something caught her eye; a movement. Chris felt a rising terror as she turned back to the figures. Something was moving. One of the figures wasn't an inanimate object at all. It was a person, draped in a dark hooded cloak, a person who sliced the air with a touch of chilling laughter and jumped from the stage to the ground. Something glittered in the pale light that remained to fight the shadows of night. Something long and wickedly sharp. The blade of a razor-edged knife, raised high in the cloaked figure's hand.

"Christina."

She heard her name whispered; again the throaty laughter followed. It was too late to realize that she'd been an idiot.

She spun around to run.

Marcus waited impatiently, drumming his fingers on the front desk at the *stazione polizia*. How long had the damn phone been ringing at the palazzo? Five times, ten times? He kept waiting, trying to still a growing alarm. Where was everyone?

At last, at long last, there was an answer. *"Pronto."*

Madre?" Marcus queried.

"Si, si," Gina murmured.

"What took you so long to answer the phone? Where is everyone?"

"I don't know. I was out, Marcus. This is Tuesday, my day at church. And since Genovese will have his... service there, I wished to put in more time. Where are you?"

"I'm still at the police station. It's taking much longer than I thought it would." He hesitated for a moment. "Listen, Mama, I know this will hurt you, but they think that Genovese's death—and even Alfred's—stem from the time of Papa's death. You're going to have to answer some questions down here, too."

"What?" Gina inquired with a little gasp.

"I can't explain it all now. I will soon, I promise. I need you to do something for me, please. I can't understand why Christina did not answer the extension in the bedroom. Will you go and tell her I'm on the line?"

"Un momento."

Marcus waited impatiently again. It seemed that he sat at the desk forever, and the longer he waited, the greater his unease. At last he heard the line being picked up, and he started to breathe a sigh of relief. But then he heard his mother's voice again, and it felt as if a blaze of tension and fear raged down the length of his spine and beyond.

"Marcus, she isn't there. I can't find her."

"What?"

"I'm sorry, Marcus. I can't find her anywhere. Perhaps she decided to go shopping. Marcus, really, I did not approve of your marriage, but of course it was not my business. But you cannot treat a wife like a prisoner—"

"*Madre!* I've no wish to make her a prisoner, I wish to keep her alive! I've got to go. I've got to find her. If you do see her, *stay with her*!"

He dropped the phone, not even hanging it up properly. He was shouting to the police and to Tony, and rushing out the door. Suddenly, clearly, he knew who had murdered his father, driven Alfred to his death and slit Genovese's throat. The answer had been there all along. He simply hadn't seen it.

Dear God in heaven, if only he wasn't too late.

Chris burst from the historical room and raced along the balcony. She knew that she needed to reach the square and people. But when she reached the top of the stairway, she looked down to see Fredo Talio entering the double doors, dapper as a hit man in a pin-striped suit. He looked up at her; she saw his sallow features, his dark and somber eyes.

Fear washed through her heart in fresh waves. Fredo Talio . . . he was in league with the cloaked figure.

"Contessa di Medici . . ." he said, looking at her.

Chris screamed and tore away from the stairs.

"Christina, Christina . . ."

He kept calling to her, but she hardly heard him because she was facing the figure with the cloak. Her only escape would be through the trapdoor in the gem salon.

She flew for the door to the salon and ripped it open. The cloaked figure was right behind her. Chris raced for the case containing the di Medici jewels, followed by laughter. She chanced a glance back. The figure was by the door, a gloved hand on a rusted lever near the floor. Chris frowned, then gasped. The floor gave way beneath her—and she wasn't at the trapdoor.

Not the trapdoor she knew of, at any rate. Yet even as the floor gave way, she remembered that Marcus had mentioned another trapdoor, another chute. . . .

Her body was plummeting downward, sliding, falling along a dark passageway. She slammed against the ground and was met by a fierce cold—and a musty scent of salt and decay. Desperately she tried to get her bearings in the darkness. She had to be in the catacombs. Somewhere in the subterranean tunnels.

Chris rolled, reaching up carefully to assure herself that she wouldn't crack her head against an arch. The cold here was startling, the stench of decay almost nauseating. Where was she? She had to find out; the catacombs could be like a maze, like a trap from which there was no escape. . . .

She stuck her hand out, bracing herself to find a tomb or an effigy. She touched a ledge. Marble, and very, very cold. She tried to rise to follow the ledge.

She was startled by a fierce thud from behind her, from where she had lain just a second ago. And then every nerve within her seemed to scream in silent agonized panic as she heard the laughter again. Soft throaty laughter. A light blazed in her face; she threw her hands up to her eyes, but she was blinded. Instinctively she backed away from the light. She bumped into another ledge; she reached behind her to steady herself, and she touched something dry and brittle and wispy. She glanced down—and started to scream.

It was a centuries-old corpse. The hair remained about the skeletal head; the toothless jaw of the skull seemed to mock her scream. The bones were dressed in decaying silk.

For aeons it seemed that she screamed; only the sound of that cruel laughter brought her horror to a halt. She was desperate to survive; some inner sense told her that the skeleton belonged to the world of the dead. The skeleton could not hurt her.

The danger to her life came from the living figure who wielded the flashlight.

Chris vaulted over the marble ledge that held the corpse. The cavern was filled with ledges, and bejeweled and bedecked skeletons. She had to use them, to stay behind them, until she could discover the way out....

Poised to spring, Chris stared at the hooded figure, which was rising now. The figure, too, had taken the secret way down, knowing full well where it would lead.

Chris narrowed her eyes, trying to see beyond the blinding light. But it seemed that the game of disguise was over. As Chris watched warily, ready to vault again at a second's notice, the figure pulled back the hood and allowed the cloak to drop to the floor.

"Sophia!" Chris said. She should have known. The *key*. It was Tuesday. Tuesday—when Gina di Medici was *always* out.

"*Si, bella* Christi. Sophia," she said nonchalantly. She laughed again. "You are stunned, yes? But then, you were so anxious to blame poor Gina. Poor, long-suffering Gina! Twenty-one years ago I did her a favor...and she never had the sense to appreciate it."

"I don't understand," Chris said slowly. She didn't understand, and at the moment she wasn't sure that she cared. But she had to play for time. Time to find a way out. As terrified as she was in the dank and macabre tomb, she still refused to believe that this could be the end. Perhaps no one believed that they could die...until the moment came.

She had to believe! She had to believe and fight. Marcus! He would come home; he would find her gone. He would search for her—relentlessly—until he found her. Dear God! He had to. He had to search for her. She loved him; he had to love her....

Sophia shrugged pleasantly, as if they had met at a sidewalk café. "Perhaps I'm doing you a favor, too. Life, *cara*, is not sweet with the di Medici men. I warned you about that. But you are a little fool, hopelessly in love with Marcus. He's so much like Mario. And you see, I knew Mario very well."

"You . . . knew Mario . . . very well?" Chris breathed.

"Yes, but of course," Sophia murmured. "They all thought it was over the stupid statuette! We were on the ketch that day because they were trying to decide what to do about its disappearance, but the arguments . . . they had nothing to do with it." She smiled like a friend, like one woman expecting understanding from another. "You know how Marcus is . . . the attraction. I had been with Alfred for several years, but then, by chance, Mario and I were thrown together at the strangest times."

"You had an affair with him," Chris said.

"Yes. An affair. Wild and chaotic and as passionate as heaven! But Mario was in love with his little mouse of a wife. And I liked my life with Alfred. I never had money . . . cherished his." She paused. "Mario wanted to tell them both about the affair. Gina would have forgiven him. Alfred would have thrown me out. Your father and Mario did get into a fight that day, over the statuette. I was on deck when it happened. They struck each other several times, then made up like little boys. When James went back into the cabin I determined to talk to Mario again." Sophia smiled again, very nicely. "You were out on deck . . . you don't remember?"

Chris shook her head. She didn't remember any of it; she couldn't believe that she had been there and had erased it all from her mind. She also wanted Sophia to keep talking.

Sophia sighed. "I thought that you had seen it all, that someday you would remember. I believe James thought you knew something too, something dangerous. That is why he left Venice."

"I don't remember anything," Chris whispered, moistening her dry lips. "What happened?"

Sophia leaned against one of the ledges, heedless of the corpse lying on it. The flashlight hung easily from one hand, her knife from the other.

"Ah, yes! You should get to die at peace, shouldn't you? All mysteries solved here, among a host of di Medici brides.

very dramatic, don't you think? I'm getting ahead of myself. I tried to reason with Mario, but he was set upon confession. We began to struggle. Alfred came out then. Poor Alfred! He thought that Mario was trying to hurt me. He came into it and pulled Mario from me, throwing him against the mast. He just struck it . . . wrong. His neck was broken, you see.''

Sophia ran a hand along the marble slab of an open tomb, pausing. "Poor, poor Alfred! Such a good man. He was horrified. I had to convince him that he might lose his life for murder if he did not toss Mario overboard.''

Chris tried to speak as conversationally as Sophia while hiding her desperation as she looked for a way out. She could see nothing, just stone walls, shadows and corpses covered with spiderwebs and decay. But there had to be a way out! Sophia had taken it on another night, the night Chris and Marcus had found the cloak in the tunnels. . . .

"What about Genovese?" Chris asked. "Did he . . . see what happened?''

"Yes, yes he did. And he did quite well for a number of years because of it. But then he became too greedy. When it seemed that you would have money, he was willing to sell the truth.''

"But why did you kill Alfred?" Chris demanded.

"Alfred no longer wished to pay. He wanted to confess the whole thing. He spent his lifetime worrying about your father and you. Then you reappeared, and he was an old fool. I knew he was meeting you to tell you the truth. I couldn't let him do that. But. . . I did not have to kill Alfred. He very conveniently dropped dead for me.''

Chris began to breathe very quickly. She had seen something. A crack in the wall, an uneven place where it appeared that the stone might move. If she could keep Sophia talking just a minute longer . . .

"You know the palazzo very well," she murmured.

"Yes. When I started working for Mario di Medici— Conte di Medici!—I was very young, and very beautiful. I

had dreams. . . . I loved the palazzo. I dreamed of being a d
Medici bride, you see. I hated Mario for being a fool. He
denied me everything. But he died . . . and I remained in his
palazzo. I learned it all. The history, the architecture. But
Christina, you became the di Medici bride. You are the one
with the right to remain here forever and ever.''

"Sophia . . ."

"I'm sorry, Christina. Your time has run out. It has been
drifting away since you came. You see, I was always terri
fied that you would remember. You should have left i
alone.''

She started walking toward Chris, very smoothly, as if she
knew every slab and every skeleton so well that she didn'
even need to look around. Chris leaped over another slab
putting distance between them. She was younger, she re
minded herself. Far more agile. She had a chance. Perhap
she was even the stronger of the two of them.

But Sophia had the knife.

"Fredo! Fredo Talio!" Chris exclaimed, causing Sophi
to halt. "He was downstairs at the galleries. Is he in this wit
you?"

Sophia frowned. "No, of course not. He was at the gal
leries?"

"Yes, yes he was. He saw both of us. He heard m
screaming."

"So?" Sophia queried, quite pleased with herself. "H
will have seen you . . . and a mysterious figure in a cloak
Nothing more."

"Sophia! How long do you think you can keep this up
Death after death . . . you will be caught."

"No, *cara* Christi, there is no proof. Genovese is gone
Alfred is gone. And you . . . you will stay. Here with thos
lucky wives who came before you!"

Was Sophia insane, or just deadly? Chris didn't know
nor did it matter. Chris knew that she would have to pa
Sophia to reach the break in the wall. But Sophia was com
ing toward her again. Chris instinctively set her hands upc

slab, ready to move, seeking a weapon, any weapon, to use .gainst the other woman. Her fingers grasped bone and otting silk; she couldn't even let herself think about what he was doing. She threw her skeletal club at Sophia, catch-ng the older woman off guard. As Sophia gasped and tumbled back, stunned, the flashlight fell to the floor; hadows careened and danced. Chris leaped over the slab nd raced for the break in the wall, her only hope.

She could barely see the wall. The dank mustiness of the ges clung to her like a shroud. She passed slab after slab of ranite and marble, veering from the blank grins of skele-ons, half sobbing, half listening for the woman who would urely pursue her again.

Then the shadowed wall before her seemed to move. It *did* 1ove. It was as if the skeletons had come to life, as if a host f di Medicis had risen to embrace and restrain her.

They were reaching for her; shadows were reaching for er. She started to scream.

"Christina!"

The arms that wound around her were living and real, not 1st bone, but flesh and blood and muscle and warmth. The i Medici who held her was not a remnant of a forgotten ast, but vital and strong and secure.

"Marcus!"

"Are you all right?"

"Yes."

"Tony, take Chris..."

"Chris, come on." A second set of arms swept around er. She saw Tony's smile, reassuring against the shadows nd darkness and death. But Marcus was gone.

"Tony, wait. Sophia is there. She's got a knife."

"Marcus will be all right," Tony assured her. "The po-ce are right behind us."

They were; the wall was moving again. Several men—alive nd well and purposeful—were moving in. Lights were ooding the tomb. Chris shivered, not so much frightened as she was sad, touched by all those bygone lives, frayed silks, rotted furs, the mockery of elegance.

"I don't see Marcus!" she said with sudden alarm.

"There must be another exit," Tony muttered. "Come on, I'm supposed to get you out."

"Marcus—"

"Will be careful. He's a grown man."

"She killed Genovese."

"Marcus will be wary. Chris, come on."

She couldn't fight him; he had a lot of his brother's tenacity. And she did want very, very badly to leave the subterranean caverns of darkness and death behind.

There was another exit; Marcus knew there had to be when he could find no trace of Sophia. There was a marble slab on the floor, slightly askew, and as he moved it, he marveled at the woman's strength. It was heavy, but once it was shifted he saw a flight of slippery well-worn steps leading downward.

They led to a narrow walkway, one beneath the water level, but where the walkway ended another flight of steps began, leading upward. They, too, were well-worn. In days of political upheaval they would have been a wonderful escape route.

Just as they were now. Dank and slimy and worn smooth, they still provided an escape.

When he reached the top he was on a small via facing a bridge.

On the bridge he saw her, her hooded cloak on again. She stared back and saw him, then started to run.

Marcus started over the bridge. She rounded an alley. For a moment he lost her, and then he saw her again, on the next bridge. "Sophia!"

He heard a shrill whistle; the police were behind him now. Sophia heard the whistle, too, and saw that men were coming from either end of the bridge. She hopped up to the wide carved stone railing and jumped.

Marcus hurried to the bridge and vaulted over. The water was cool as his body sliced through it, as he kicked his
way cleanly to the surface. There was no sign of her. He
dived again. It was dark, very dark. The lights of the city
glittered on the surface, but did not come into the canal.

He jackknifed his way downward again, reaching out. His
hand found fabric, and he tugged at it. He managed to grasp
her chin, to raise them both to the surface. He hauled her to
the nearest dock; an officer was there to pull her out, to help
him.

She lay there, swaddled in her cloak. Marcus, panting and
gasping, dragged himself over to her. Her eyes opened, and
he smiled. He saw that she still had her knife, and he wondered why she hadn't used it on him.

She reached out to touch his chin. "Never you, Marcus.
Never you," she said gently in Italian. "You are...his son."

She smiled again, a little weakly. Her hand fell to her side.
She shuddered a little, and then her eyes closed. Stunned,
Marcus tugged the cloak away, certain that she couldn't
have drowned.

He paused, lifting his hand away. A crimson splotch was
running quickly over her side. Sticky. She had either taken
her own life with her knife as a final escape, or else she had
inadvertently stabbed herself when she hit the water. He
would never know.

He rose, dripping wet, weighted down with the sorrow
and anger of it all. So many people whom he had loved so
dearly had been broken and destroyed because of warped
passions he wasn't sure he would ever understand. His father, dead. James Tarleton's life ruined in a haze of suspicion. Alfred...Genovese...and Sophia.

But his mother was innocent. And Christina was alive. He
took himself furiously. He would never allow the past to
darken the present again.

The officer began to speak to him, telling him that it
would all have to be sorted out for the official reports.

Marcus already knew that, but tonight he wanted to g home and try to salvage the present.

He needed to hold Christina, to cherish her—and con vince her that they could start anew, with all skeleton cleared from the closet, the specters of their youth laid t rest.

Gina di Medici, appearing very lost, stunned—and anx ious with worry about Marcus—was still trying to under stand the whole story.

But she wasn't alone. Chris met Umberto that night. H was a middle-aged banker, quiet, reassuring, supportive an as confused as Gina.

They were gathered at the courtyard table, as they had s often been before.

Neither Tony nor Chris was helping much. They bot broke into explanations at different times.

"You see, Gina," Chris tried again, taking a huge sip c espresso laced with sambuca, "I knew my father couldn have murdered Mario. He was too gentle and honest."

"And your father," Tony reminded her. He grimaced her his mother. "So she suspected us."

"Oh!" Gina cried out, hurt and incredulous as her eye found Chris. "You thought that I would have killed my ow husband!"

Chris wanted to crawl beneath the table. "Not really," sh lied. "I—I didn't know who to suspect . . . or who to trust.

Gina looked blankly at Tony. "I still don't understand Why would Sophia have done this? She and Mario wer friends, and Alfred and Mario were the best of friends."

"It was really an accident," Chris said. "A fight that g out of hand." She wasn't going to tell Gina now that th husband she had adored had been having an affair. N when Mario had been so determined to straighten things o with his wife that he had lost his life because of it.

Gina shook her head. She held tightly to Umberto's han "For twenty-one years I lived with the people who had kill

Mario. They stayed in his house. . . . They were my family.
Christina, I did you a great wrong. And I did a greater
wrong to your father and your mother.''

"You couldn't have known, Gina," Chris said.

"Of course not," Tony assured his mother, rumpling
Chris's hair. "Only a daughter could be so completely
guided by blind faith."

"Daughters, wives, brothers . . . and lovers."

The assertion came from the rear of the courtyard. They
all started, turning around. Marcus was standing there, his
hair wet and as dark as jet, plastered against his forehead.
Little pools of water were forming at his feet; his face appeared strained and weary.

"Marcus!" Chris knew that her glad cry was repeated
round the table. She didn't think; she jumped up, knock-
ing over her chair to run into his arms. He was soaked
through and through, but she didn't care; she barely noticed. All she needed or wanted was the way that he held her
in return, his hand slipping about her waist, his kiss touching the top of her head, his chin nuzzling a little absently
over her forehead.

Tony was on his feet behind Chris.

"Sophia . . . ?" he asked his brother.

"Is dead," Marcus said briefly. He squeezed Chris's
hand, then walked past her to kneel by his mother and take
her hand. "Are you all right?" he asked her quietly.

She smiled at him. "Now that I see you, yes. I'm not sure
that I understand completely, nor that I want to. It hurts to
have it all come to the surface again, but not so badly. I am
sorry for them all. Get off your knees. It is a humble position, one in which I am not accustomed to finding you. You
need dry clothing."

Marcus grimaced and rose. Umberto handed him a drink,
which Marcus accepted gratefully.

"I have a bit of a surprise for you all," Gina murmured,
smiling at Marcus, then at Umberto. "Perhaps this is not the

night for such news, but since we are all making confessions ... Umberto and I are going to be married.''

"What?" Tony gasped, then laughed. *"Mamma mia. Salute!"*

Umberto was flushing. "You are pleased?" he asked Gina's sons.

"Enormously," Marcus informed him, grinning broadly at last as he gave the older man a handshake. He kissed his mother, then Tony kissed her, too. Chris hung back a little awkwardly. Gina noticed her over Tony's shoulder, smiled and stretched out her arms.

"Figlia mia, come here!" she commanded. Chris stepped forward, and Gina rose, giving her a warm hug. "You are my daughter now, yes? With no bitterness of suspicion between us."

Chris hugged her and wished her congratulations, but could say nothing else. Gina drew back suspiciously. She gazed from Marcus to Chris. "This marriage between you it was real, yes?"

Chris couldn't see Marcus; she knew only that he was behind her. And he wasn't answering.

Neither could Chris.

Tony stepped in cheerfully to save them both for the moment. "Of course, Mama. Has Marcus ever done anything by half measures?"

"No, that's true," Gina admitted. She began bustling about the table, collecting the glasses. "Then we must have another drink—to a new future!"

"To the future!" Tony declared. The drinks were passed around. Chris downed hers quickly, wincing at the strong taste of the sambuca.

Marcus set his glass down with a little click against the table. "If you will excuse me, I am soaked. Mama, couldn't be happier. Christina ..." He reached out a hand to her. She took it. He glanced at his brother. "In the morning ..."

"Yes," Tony agreed. "In the morning."

His mother was frowning in confusion. "We see the po-lice and really end it all," Tony told her. He shook off his seriousness and grinned at Marcus and Chris. *"Buona notte."*

Chris found that she was shivering again as Marcus led the way silently, pulling her along with distance-eating footsteps. The night had been a violent one, weakening, shattering.

But it wasn't going to end. It was showdown time on a different level. She could feel it in the heat and power of his grasp on her hand.

He closed and locked the door behind him when they reached his room. Chris stepped ahead of him and stood silently, waiting, staring out the French doors into the star-speckled night.

She heard him behind her, stripping off his sodden cloth-ing. "You're a mess," he told her. "Spiderwebs and all."

She didn't respond; she walked a little closer to the win-dow. "What happened, Marcus?"

"I don't care to discuss what happened," he said, but he wasn't curt. "Tomorrow there will be time to talk again. Come here, Christina."

She started. His wet jacket, shirt, shoes and socks were on the floor in a heap. He was standing in his damp pants only; his bare chest was glistening copper. She had never seen his eyes appear so deeply blue, so penetrating. His hands were on his hips. She knew again that there would be no way out; tonight all things between them would be said.

She was terribly nervous, but she walked over to face him. He smiled, brushing at her hair. "I'm wet, but you're filthy."

He started undoing the buttons of her blouse. She felt herself tremble beneath his touch.

"What are you doing?" she asked, ignoring the obvious in her state of agitation.

"Taking your clothes off, so we can take a shower."

"We . . ." she murmured.

"Yes, we. You and I. The two of us," he said with an amused grin.

He kept at it, sliding the blouse from her shoulders. Chris reached out and touched his cheek, drawing his eyes to hers. "Marcus...?"

He sighed, catching her hand and holding it between his own. "I had wanted to seduce you again before getting to this..." he whispered. He dropped her hand, and pulled her against him, crushing her into his embrace. His left arm was around her; his right hand coursed over her chin and her throat. "I am in love with you, Christina," he told her, almost harshly. "I tricked you, seduced you, kidnapped you...because I thought I had to. Chris, I can't ever tell her, but until today I couldn't, in my heart, clear my own mother. I am very aware that you are an American. I am aware of your work, and I know that I cannot take that away from you."

Chris smiled, incredulous, awed, beautifully delightfully dizzy. "Tell me again, please," she whispered.

"I understand about your work, but—"

"No, no, no. Say I love you. In English and in Italian. And in any other way you know how."

He pulled her closer, whispering against her ear. "I love you. *Ti voglio bene. Je t'aime. Ti amo.* I love you, *Te quiero.*"

She caught his face between her palms and pressed her lips to his hungrily, adoringly, savoring the warmth, the heated dampness, the surging strength of his desire.

He broke away. "You have to listen to me, Christina."

"Yes," she murmured, her topaz eyes huge. She would listen to him, but nothing that he could say could matter much at this moment. The stars had invaded the room; nothing could mar this moment, because he loved her.

Loved her. Loved...her.

"I could not tolerate your being gone," he was saying. "I am trying very hard.... I had thought that if you wished to keep your position we could move to Paris, for the time east. We need to be away from the palazzo. I cannot give it up, though. It is my heritage. Still, we are opening galleries in the States, and perhaps we will both discover that is where we will wish to live. Christina, it will not always be easy. But I can swear that I respect—and adore—you for all that you do. You will maintain your profession. We will—"

"Compromise?" she supplied breathlessly.

"Yes."

"Yes, oh yes!" she cried, flinging herself against him again, half laughing, half sobbing. "Oh, Marcus! I didn't come here with the intention of trapping a di Medici husband, truly I didn't. But I've got one now, and Marcus, I'd fight heaven or hell to keep him."

"Tell me that you love me," he commanded her.

"I love you."

"In Italian . . . and any other way you know."

"Ti voglio bene . . . mio marito," Chris whispered. *"Je t'aime, je t'adore. . . ."*

She caught at his belt buckle, and shuddered at the heated ripple of his muscles in response. "I'll tell you in 'mime,'" she promised him, "in the very best language of all. I'm very, very good with my hands. . . ."

"The best . . ." he agreed.

Moments later they had stripped one another, and moments after that they were in the shower. Water, hot and delicious, skimmed over their naked bodies, and they joined again and again, expert lovers, yet tonight given something new, something very precious. Spoken love, given, received, tenderly cherished.

Shadows receded; brilliance touched their lives.

Beneath a cascade of tumbling water he took her into his arms. His kiss deepened, heated and wet. Her body slid along his, her kisses savoring his flesh, finding him, taking him, loving him, until he pulled her from the shower, forgetting all about towels, and laid her on the bed, tender and fierce, fevered, demanding and delighting. He ravaged her length with his palms, with the taunting dampness of his tongue. His intimate kisses sent her soaring to the stars, which seemed in easy reach, showering them with ecstasy. When he entered her, she embraced him, adoring his body with her own, shuddering with the force of his passion.

And she knew that nothing in life would ever be so sweet as loving him, and being loved by him.

It was late when they slept that night, having shared all the details of the past—and their dreams for the future. Very late, almost dawn. And some mechanism in Chris's mind warned her that she shouldn't be dreaming; it was all over.

But she *was* dreaming. Dreaming about the catacombs. There was something in her hand, and she was running because she had to hide the treasure she carried. Someone meant to take it from her; she would be severely punished if they knew she had it.

There was an angel near the wall, an elaborate angel that overlooked a carved marble tomb. Behind the angel was a little niche where a treasure could be secreted.

In her dream Chris saw the child reaching up and slipping her treasure into the little niche.... She could hear a voice, a woman's voice. Irate. Calling her...

She awoke with a start, bolting up in bed.

Beside her Marcus was instantly alert. *"Cara..."* His arms came around her, and she was deeply touched, because she knew that he thought she was frightened, that she could not forget the night among the dead.

Chris turned to him excitedly. "Marcus! The statuette! I know where it is. It's down in the catacombs behind an angel. Oh, Marcus! I'm certain of it!"

He frowned, and she knew then that he was worrying about her mind.

"Christina..."

"Please, Marcus! Please, I have to see if it's there!"

He sighed and threw his legs over the side of the bed. "All right, we'll go."

Chris threw herself joyfully after him, hugging him
iercely in her excitement, giving him a quick wet kiss.

"Mind putting on a robe?" he suggested dryly.

"Marcus!" she retorted, but her enthusiasm was too great
) be contained. She hurriedly slipped into her gown and
obe, and was at the door while he was still tying his belt.
he started down the stairs.

"Wait, I'll get Tony and a flashlight," he called.

Chris impatiently tapped her toes against the floor. Mar-
us reemerged on the landing with Tony and two huge
ashlights.

Tony was rubbing his eyes. He smiled at Chris. "Are you
oing to make a habit of such emergencies?" he asked her.

"No!" She laughed. "Just tonight. Please, come on!"

She led the way; the catacombs held no more fear for her.
hey trailed behind, continually warning her to wait. Chris
ouldn't. She burst through the gates and wound her way
eedlessly through the tombs.

The angel was right beneath the trapdoor. Chris winced
little as she stuck her hand into the niche; she didn't know
hat else might be there. But her fingers met marble, beau-
ful pink-streaked marble. She lifted out the statuette.

It was labeled at the base in Italian, but she knew the
ords. "Daylight—tomb relief for Dante di Medici."

Chris handed the statuette to Marcus. He looked at it,
en he looked at Tony.

"They were right," Tony murmured, fingering the mar-
e.

"Yes," Marcus agreed.

"About what?" Chris demanded.

Marcus shrugged. "I believe it was very definitely done
Michelangelo. He had a style that could not be copied,
t even by his students. We will find out."

"What does it mean?" Chris asked anxiously.

Tony laughed. "It means that if we weren't all filthy rich
eady, we'd be filthy rich all over again." He sobered,

touching her hair, smiling. "It means, Chris, that a reall
marvelous piece of art will be given back to the people."

Chris gazed at Marcus. He smiled, too, slipping an arr
around her. "It will go on display, Chris. We will probabl
give it to the government. Which means, of course, that w
won't be 'filthy rich' all over again, but then, we don't re
ally need to be, you know. What do you say?"

"I say that I'd like to give it to the government," she tol
him. "I...couldn't really remember, not until tonight. Bu
Marcus, I didn't steal it. Not at first. I saw it . . . in Sophia
room. I went in to touch it, and she came back. I hid wit
it, and then, of course, when she knew it was missing,
couldn't put it back. Everyone was so furious . . ."

"That you ran," Marcus finished matter-of-factl
"Chris, the statuette did not cause what happened. Sophi:
Alfred—even my father—caused their own problems."

"I know," she told him.

She looked around them, then pulled her robe clos
about her. "I think I'm ready to leave the tombs for a lon;
long time," she told them.

Marcus and Tony exchanged wry glances. They starte
back down the tunnel.

"Marcus?" Chris asked.

"Yes?"

"If I'm really going to be the Contessa di Medici, do yc
think I might do a few things with this place?"

"Oh, no! She's going to start changing furniture!" To
moaned good-naturedly.

"Such as?" Marcus asked.

"Tony, take a pill," Chris remonstrated before replyi
to Marcus. "I'd really like to give those relatives of yours
the other section a *decent* burial. Like seal them all in, yc
know?"

Marcus and Tony both started laughing.

"I think we could manage that," Marcus promised h
They reached the stairway leading to the ground floor. I
turned around to kiss her.

Tony turned to say something, then paused, closing his outh with a shrug. He continued up the stairs.

They were man and wife, he thought. Had been for a hile now. He hoped they had sense enough to go to their om before getting too carried away.

But this was Venice.

And that was love.

Amore.

Epilogue

Ummm...she knew exactly where she was.

At the Palazzo di Medici in Venice. Her home. Marcus's home.

Marcus...

She opened her eyes slowly.

The first thing she saw was her own hand, lying beside her face on the silk-covered pillow. Her long fingers appeared very delicate there. Her nails, with their polish of soft bronze, seemed fragile against the deep indigo of the sheets.

Indigo...

Christina opened her eyes wider. Without twisting her head, she further surveyed the room. Soft Oriental rugs lay pleasingly against a polished cream Venetian tile floor. The walls were papered in a subdued gold that lightened the effect of the deep indigo draperies and mahogany furniture. Across a breezy distance, highlighted by the morning dazzle of the sun streaming through French doors, was a large Queen Anne dresser, its only ornament a French Provincial clock.

A year had passed since she had first awakened in this room. A year of learning, of laughter, of love. There had been any number of fights. Marcus was a temperamental man, passionate, intense. She hadn't expected every minute to be congenial bliss.

But never once in that time, through laughter, anger or tears, had she doubted his love. Nor his honesty, nor his never ending belief in her. They'd spent the year in Paris so that she could teach; he'd accompanied the troupe on their summer tour. In a few days' time they would leave for New York. Marcus would be opening the new gallery; she would be taking a position at a college for the performing arts.

And next summer they would come back to the palazzo. When, she wasn't sure. Chris felt rather strongly that their child should be born on American soil; Marcus was quick to remind her that *she* herself had been born in Venice.

She smiled. She would convince him. And if not, well she *had* been born in Venice....

A shiver suddenly ran along the length of her spine. He was in the room. She knew it. She always knew when he was near. When she opened her eyes once more and turned, she would find him leisurely leaning against the frame of the French doors. But there would be nothing truly leisurely about him. He would be watching, waiting, a little impatient, perhaps. He tended to be the earlier riser.

She knew that he tried to be patient, but he was fond of waking her. Chris smiled. She didn't mind. He had a nice way of doing it. Fingers caressing her back, slowly, sensually. A whisper against her ear. A kiss...

But today... today she had known he would be at the doors. It was an anniversary. Their first. And there was a touch of the romantic about Marcus. He was, after all, a Venetian. And a di Medici.

There was a slight movement in the room. A whisper of sound in the air. He *was* watching her, Christina knew. Watching her, and waiting.

She smiled. *She* could suddenly bear the waiting no longer. He was there, and the force of his presence caused her to open her eyes and turn... and meet his smoldering indigo stare.

He was leaning against the doors, as she had suspected, dressed in a caramel velour robe. The V neck of the haphazardly belted garment bared the breadth of his chest with its profusion of crisp dark hair. A gold St. Christopher's medallion seemed to emphasize the masculinity of copper flesh and muscle.

His legs, too, were bare beneath the knee-length hem of the robe. Long sinewy calves, covered seductively with short black hair, gave way to bare feet.

"Buongiorno. Buongiorno, amore mio."

Chris stretched luxuriously and smiled, reaching out her arms to him. *"Buongiorno, mio marito, amore mio."*

He stalked slowly toward the bed. She met the striking sizzle of his eyes and embraced him with a sudden fever.

Over his shoulder she could see the brilliance of the Venetian sun flooding in. She closed her eyes, smiling with contentment. She still wasn't sure if she had married a great lion of justice, or a panther, as dark and intriguing as the night.

But she knew him very well now; she knew he would always be there for her, and that he had *always* been there for her. Willing to do anything for her, face anything for her. Fierce or tender, lion or panther...

It didn't really matter; he was, perhaps, a bit of both. And she loved him for that.

"Happy anniversary, Chris," he told her softly. "I love you."

She laughed delightedly, slipping her arms around his shoulders. *"Salute,* Marcus. *Ti voglio molto bene."*

He caught her hands, laughing in turn. "I like your silent language best. Tell me all about it in mime."

"Ummmm . . ." she murmured, and gladly complied.

* * * * *

Take 4 bestselling love stories FREE

Plus get a FREE surprise gift!

Special Limited-time Offer

Mail to Silhouette Reader Service™

3010 Walden Avenue
P.O. Box 1867
Buffalo, N.Y. 14269-1867

YES! Please send me 4 free Silhouette Romance™ novels and my free surprise gift. Then send me 6 brand-new novels every month, which I will receive months before they appear in bookstores. Bill me at the low price of $1.99* each plus 25¢ delivery and applicable sales tax, if any.* That's the complete price and—compared to the cover prices of $2.75 each—quite a bargain! I understand that accepting the books and gift places me under no obligation ever to buy any books. I can always return a shipment and cancel at any time. Even if I never buy another book from Silhouette, the 4 free books and the surprise gift are mine to keep forever.

215 BPA AJH5

Name	(PLEASE PRINT)	
Address	Apt. No.	
City	State	Zip

This offer is limited to one order per household and not valid to present Silhouette Romance™ subscribers. *Terms and prices are subject to change without notice. Sales tax applicable in N.Y.

USROM-93R   ©1990 Harlequin Enterprises Limited

Silhouette Books
is proud to present
our best authors,
their best books...
and the best in
your reading pleasure!

Throughout 1993, look for exciting
books by these top names in
contemporary romance:

DIANA PALMER—
The Australian in October

FERN MICHAELS—
Sea Gypsy in October

ELIZABETH LOWELL—
Chain Lightning in November

CATHERINE COULTER—
The Aristocrat in December

JOAN HOHL—
Texas Gold in December

LINDA HOWARD—
Tears of the Renegade in January '94

When it comes to passion,
we wrote the book.

BOBT3

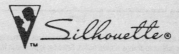

When the only time you have for yourself is...

STOLEN *moments* ™

Christmas is such a busy time—with shopping, decorating, writing cards, trimming trees, wrapping gifts....

When you do have a few *stolen moments* to call your own, treat yourself to a brand-new *short* novel. Relax with one of our Stocking Stuffers— or with all six!

Each STOLEN MOMENTS title is a complete and original contemporary romance that's the perfect length for the busy woman of the nineties! Especially at Christmas...

And they make perfect **stocking stuffers**, too! (For your mother, grandmother, daughters, friends, co-workers, neighbors, aunts, cousins—all the other women in your life!)

Look for the STOLEN MOMENTS display in December

 **WORLDWIDE LIBRARY** ®